D0959785

the Distant Dead

ALSO BY HEATHER YOUNG

The Lost Girls

WILLIAM MORROW
An Imprint of HarperCollins*Publishers*

the Distant Dead

a novel

Heather Young

This is a work of fiction. Names, characters, places, and incidents are products of the author's imagination or are used fictitiously and are not to be construed as real. Any resemblance to actual events, locales, organizations, or persons, living or dead, is entirely coincidental.

HarperCollins books may be purchased for educational, business, or sales promotional use. For information, please email the Special Markets Department at SPsales@harpercollins.com.

FIRST EDITION

Designed by Elina Cohen
Title page photograph by francis.framethewild / Shutterstock
Illustration by Kudryashka / Shutterstock

Library of Congress Cataloging-in-Publication Data has been applied for.

ISBN 978-0-06-269081-4

20 21 22 23 24 LSC 10 9 8 7 6 5 4 3 2 1

For my brother, Matthew Lewis Young

1971–2002

Our dead are never dead to us until we have forgotten them.

—George Eliot

the Distant Dead

LONG AGO

The boy shouldn't have been in the cave. He knew this. He was a good boy, the sort of boy who cared about *should*s and *shouldn't*s, but the thrill of this particular *shouldn't* made him feel like a different sort of boy, the sort of boy he wished he were. It was why he was there. The air outside the cave was wavy with late-summer heat, but the air inside was cool, and on his tongue it tasted of dust and daring. He was twelve years old, and he was alone for the first time in his life.

The cave was some distance from where his people made their camp by the great lake, but they could see it, a black eye in a cliff that surveyed the wide, flat basin. They came to this shore every few seasons, following rabbits and other small game through the wetlands. In their stories the cave was a place that drove men so mad that they returned from it unable to speak, even the seers, who lived mostly in dreams. There was a seer among them now, a bent old man who had visited the cave the summer the boy was born. The boy kept his distance from him, as all the boys did, but he watched as the old man spent long, wordless hours drawing circles in the dirt. Sometimes the seer looked up from his tracings, and in his bottomless black eyes the boy thought he saw not madness or terror but something like awe.

As he stood at the mouth of the cave, the boy marveled at the earth stretched wide below him. The grasses close to the lake gave way to low brush at the feet of the rocky bluffs that rose above the basin floor like blisters. The lake itself was vast, a blue sheet vanishing into the shimmering sky to the north and east. His people called it Allelu, which in their language meant "water of life." Ten thousand years later a different people, half the world away, would make *allelu* a song of praise. By then the great lake would be gone, leaving a flattened desert in its wake. Above the boy's head an eagle soared, black against the sky, a beautiful, wild thing that would be dead before the season was done.

The boy was beautiful, too, with a face as delicate as a girl's, and long-lashed brown eyes. He was his mother's only child to live past the suckling years. Like her other babies he had been sickly and small, and even now he was slight, but unlike his brothers and sisters he had latched his translucent lips fast to her breast and would not let go. Now he was a singer of songs and a teller of stories, with a voice even the elders hushed to hear around the fire.

Tonight the elders would anoint the boy a man, together with two other boys born in the same season, but the boy didn't feel like a man. He saw the arcing muscles of the other boys' arms and the proud bones hardening in their faces, and believed himself to be a child. He heard them talk about the hunts they would join and knew himself to be afraid of the wild boar and the charging mastodon. He didn't see how the elders listened when he read the stars, or how the other boys looked at him when they spoke, to see what he thought. He saw only how far short of the other boys' his stone fell when he threw it in the lake, and how far behind them he ran.

He had come to the cave because, in the last hours of his boyhood, he wanted to do something brave. So in the lazy part of the afternoon, while his mother slept on the dirt floor of their shelter, he ran through the grass to the foot of the cliff and climbed until the eye in the rocks became a mouth. Now he took one last look at the bright curve of the world and walked inside.

The air was suddenly cold. The ceiling was low, the walls barely visible in the dark. A fine dust, bat guano mixed with sand the wind blew in, sifted over the boy's rough tule sandals. He moved slowly, braced for the visitation that had struck the old seer dumb, but found only silence. After twenty halting steps he had reached the back of the cave. Still nothing disturbed the cool, dead air. He put his hands on the stone and waited for it to speak to him, but it said nothing.

Then, in the ghost-edge of daylight, the boy saw a narrow opening, the width of his arm and half as high, where the wall met the floor. He looked back to the cave's mouth and the bright blue disk of sky. He knew he should leave now. His mother would be awake soon and calling for him. But the cave, after the trouble he'd taken to get here, was a disappointment. He turned from the sky and crawled into the crevice.

It was narrow, but there was enough room for him. He shimmied forward on his elbows, the rock cold and sharp against his skin, his nerves tingling with the thrill of exploration. He'd gone the length of his body when the thrill gave way to panic. The dull weight of the cliff pressed down and the tunnel felt like a noose about to tighten. He was a child of open space and unbroken sky, and his mind screamed at him to go back to the air and the light. He closed his eyes and breathed slowly, in and out. Then he forced himself to push on, a few inches at a time. At last, after he'd crawled three times his length, he felt the tunnel expand around him. He opened his eyes and rose to his feet, his arms outstretched, feeling for purchase and finding none. Then he froze, stunned into stillness.

The darkness was absolute, and the silence was deeper still.

The boy had never experienced such an utter absence of light and sound. He could not see his hand in front of him, and he could not hear his own heart beating.

Without warning, he lost his body. His mind flooded beyond his skull, his spirit came untethered from his bones, and he was floating among eons he'd never imagined, ages beyond number. The lives of men and women winked past by the billions, bright sparks flaring and gone. The seasons of his own life vanished, unremembered. He saw the entire chasm of time: the births of planets and suns, the surging of mountains and seas, and the rise and fall of civilizations like heartbeats in a darkness that was the beginning and ending of everything, the womb and crypt of the world. His terror was beyond measure.

He reached out his hands, grasping at the dark, and invisible, sharp-edged crystals scraped his palms. The pain snapped him back into his body. He was a twelve-year-old boy again, breathing ragged breaths in the dry air of a cave. He touched his face, his trembling fingers tracing the bones of his nose, the soft skin of his cheeks. He thought of the old seer, and the circles he drew in the dirt. Had he, too, stood here, in the cave within the cave, while his spirit rose up to meet the universe? The eternity the boy had glimpsed brushed his arm with fingers of cold gossamer, and he shivered.

He drew in a long, slow breath and called his voice forth. It came in a whimper, but it came, and it brought with it a hot surge of triumph. He, alone of all the seers who had come before him, would return to his people to tell them the secrets of the cave. He imagined himself at the campfire that night, the blood of the eagle still wet on his forehead, describing the vastness of time while the other boys watched in awe and the old seer squatted on his haunches, the memory of it lighting his eyes.

He shouted, a crow of joy. The sound echoed through a dozen

unseen caverns as though hundreds of boys were calling to one another. This made him laugh, and the laughter, too, bounced back to him a hundredfold. When the reverberations faded he turned toward the tunnel. It was time to return to his mother; to the hearth and the cooked rabbit that awaited him, and the ceremony that would mark him a man.

He heard a stirring in the dark.

Restless. Gathering. Alive.

The boy listened, one hand on the wall above the tunnel. The stirring became a mutter, then a high whine, rising from somewhere deep in the cave. The smell of cold stone yielded to the stench of something else, something ancient and feral. The boy groped for the tunnel, but it was too late. A swarm erupted around him. Thousands of small, dense bodies beat against his upraised arms, pummeling him with hair and teeth and leathery wings as they circled the tunnel. The boy screamed for his mother, but his voice vanished in the shrilling. He stumbled backward, one blind step, then another, until the earth disappeared beneath him.

The bats took no notice of him. They poured through the tunnel, out of the cave, and into the day, their eyes stabbed by light and their brains aflame with fear. In the harrowing radiance of afternoon they crashed into one another, as unmoored by light as the boy had been by darkness. From the shore of the lake their terror was invisible; they seemed to float upon the sky, as graceful as birds.

That night, by the lake Allelu, two boys became men. Before the ceremony, the old seer spoke for the first time in twelve summers. The missing boy had been taken by the bird gods, he said. It was a great honor. The people rejoiced, but the boy's mother wept.

In the autumn the boy's people moved on, tracking their prey south. Years passed. The boy's mother died. The boys who became men died. Within a dozen generations the boy's people were replaced by another people, born of the same distant land but with different gods and other names for the places the boy had known. More years passed, and another people replaced them, then another, and another. Allelu, *allelu*. Through it all the cave's round, blank eye watched from the bluff, its darkness clenched like a fist around the boy who once sang songs and told stories and read the stars and who, one afternoon while his mother slept, climbed a cliff and touched the fabric of time.

His name meant nothing in the language of his people. But to his mother, it meant "beloved."

YESTERDAY

There was no moon, only stars. Below them lay the flat land. Lights shone there, too, in scattered handfuls: streetlamps and headlights and the small square windows of houses. High above them, in the hills that once rimmed the lake, a fire burned. It leaped and played among the acacias, golden, laced with orange, and black at its heart. It danced for a long time, this fire did, singing its fevered song to the night.

It takes longer than you might think, for a man to burn.

NORA

The day they found the math teacher's body, Nora was late to work. It was her father's fault.

The morning started like any other. After she ate breakfast she carried her father's tray across the backyard to his camper, stepping around the sandbox he'd built for her brother when Jeremy was five. After thirty-two years in the desert sun the sandbox's wooden frame was rotten and the sand where Jeremy once drove his Tonka trucks was crusted with bird shit. Nora knew she should take it out, but she also knew she wouldn't. Most days she didn't even see it.

Her father's camper was a 1990 Fleetwood Prowler, white with faded teal-and-brown trim, that he'd bought used when Nora was ten and Jeremy was thirteen. He'd been proud of it in the good-humored way he'd been proud of everything then, from his barbecue grill to his athletic son to his pretty auburn-haired wife. He'd never been farther from home than Elko, where his brother lived, but now that he had the camper he was going to drive his family all over the country, maybe as far as Florida. Nora's mother's smile was as dreamy as a child's. Florida, she'd said. Just imagine.

That summer he drove them to Yellowstone. The park itself was a blur of neon-colored pools, but Nora never forgot how it felt to leave Nevada for the first time. Idaho hadn't looked any different—scrubby desert, rolling hills—but when she saw the WELCOME TO IDAHO sign something inside her opened. She loved that they would go somewhere else the next summer, and the summer after that, every trip widening the world a little bit more.

But that fall Nora's mother was diagnosed with cancer, and they never took the camper anywhere again. After she died, during Nora's freshman year of high school, Nora assumed her father would sell it, but he didn't, and while Nora was away at college it had migrated here, to the back fence. Since the accident it was where he lived, even though he still had his bedroom in the house. Nora had never questioned this arrangement, figuring it was part of some complicated penance only he understood.

She walked up the makeshift plywood ramp and opened the camper door to find him sitting at the banquette table in his undershirt and pajama bottoms. He hadn't shaved, and when Nora saw this a thin band tightened around her forehead. The days he didn't get dressed were bad. The ones he didn't shave were worse.

She set the tray on the table—Wheaties, toast, and coffee—and put her hands on her hips. She had a tall, angular body, with long limbs and sharp elbows. She'd been a frilly girl, all tutus and spangles, then a teenaged beauty in Daisy Dukes and halter tops, but now she was a woman who didn't make a fuss: crisp khaki pants and a plain blouse, hair in a ponytail, no makeup.

Her father stared at his breakfast, and Nora knew he wouldn't eat it. She told herself she didn't care. She had to be at the school in fifteen minutes; she didn't have time for this. But when she reached the door she stopped. Through the worn screen she saw the back of their small ranch house, its white siding gone a ruddy gray. Her father's rusted Weber and the empty planters where her mother used to grow tomatoes sat on the cracked cement patio, and the fenced yard was bald except for clutches of weeds in the corners. It all looked the same as it had yesterday, and the day before that, but for a moment Nora saw it the way it had been when she was a girl, with pansies along the fence, tomatoes in the boxes, the siding a crisp white. Even a few years ago there had been grass. She couldn't think when the last blade had died.

Her father coughed a sodden, weepy cough. Nora took a steadying breath, then turned around. In the light from the window his blue eyes were watery. She sat on the vinyl seat and put her arm around him. "How about I come home for lunch today?"

"You don't have to," he said, but of course he wanted her to. Nora didn't know what had set him off. A dream, maybe, or a memory. What was the date? March 14. It sounded familiar. It wasn't the anniversary of anything she could think of, but that didn't mean it wasn't the anniversary of something.

"It's no trouble. I'll heat up the pot roast."

Usually Nora's father defrosted a Stouffer's in the camper's microwave for lunch. He brightened at the thought of the pot roast, and she promised to be home at twelve fifteen. Then she had to reheat his coffee, because it had gotten cold, promise twice more to come home for lunch, and take the pot roast out of the freezer. When she grabbed her car keys it was five to eight. She drove too fast down Franklin, but it was still four minutes past the bell when she ran through the double doors of the middle school, feeling like her seventh grade self, dashing late into this same building, her face hot with the same shame she'd felt then.

When the math teacher didn't show up, nobody thought much about it at first. Dee Pratzer, the office secretary and emergency substitute teacher, covered his first period class with her usual aggrieved competence. Between first and second period

Mary Barnes, the science teacher, stopped by Nora's social studies classroom and said, with a hint of malice, "Adam's late. I wouldn't want to be him when Dee gets hold of him."

Adam Merkel had never been late before, but he'd only been teaching at the middle school for seven months, the replacement for old Jim Pfeiffer, who'd finally retired. He was new to the town, too, which was unusual in itself. Lovelock was a sand-blasted hamlet of ranch houses, prefabs, and mobile homes strung along a mile of Interstate 80 a hundred miles east of Reno and seventy-five miles west of Winnemucca, surrounded by a desert so vast it ran into three neighboring states. Nobody moved there except divorced second cousins from Sparks with no place else to go and the occasional mine supervisor doing hard time on his way up the corporate ladder. When Adam applied for the job it had created a buzz: a professor from the University of Nevada wants to teach here! Think what that will do for the school's test scores! But when he turned out to be a curled-up middle-aged man whom the students promptly named Merkel the Turtle, the buzz died away.

"Has anyone called him?" Nora asked. She didn't like Mary. Mary was a divorced, faded beauty who, thirty years and thirty pounds past her prom queen heyday, still acted like a bitchy high school girl. She'd circled around Adam when he first arrived, but Adam had been unmoved by her pushup bras and red-glossed lips no matter how many times she brought him coffee from the staff room. Now she lifted her shoulder in a who-cares shrug.

"I imagine. Isn't he throwing that party today?"

That was when Nora started to worry about Adam, because that was when she remembered March 14 was Pi Day. 3.14, Adam had explained at last week's staff meeting, was a national math holiday, and he was going to bring pies for all thirty-six eighth graders. The other teachers were surprised. They didn't expect parties from Mr. Merkel. Or pie baking. *Good for you,* Nora had thought. In the hallway afterward, she told him it was a great idea.

"In Reno," he said, "everyone in the math department brought a pie on Pi Day." He smiled, but the sadness that had drawn Nora to him was still there. She'd gone to the University of Nevada in Reno herself, graduating with a major in anthropology. She'd planned to go to Africa to hunt the earliest traces of humanity. Or to Europe, to dig for Neanderthal bones in the caves of Spain. Anywhere, really, that was on another continent and promised a bunch of ancient mysteries that had nothing to do with Lovelock. Other people went to college and came back, as her best friend Britta never tired of reminding her, but Nora hadn't wanted to come back, and she suspected that Adam hadn't wanted to come here, either. Something in the way he carried himself, as if he were heavier than his bones, made her think his reason might even be as tragic as hers.

"I can help you bake," she'd offered. She made a good rhubarb pie, her mother's recipe.

"No, thank you. I can manage." His eyes were normally a light gray behind his silver glasses, but that day they had a darkness in them. That darkness had almost been enough to make Nora insist, and more than enough to make her wish, later, that she had. Now, as she looked at Mary Barnes in her frilly pink blouse, she knew Adam wouldn't miss Pi Day if he could possibly help it.

Dee was erasing the whiteboard when Nora walked into Adam's classroom after second period. "Adam's still not here?"

"No. He hasn't called, either." Dee snapped the eraser down on Adam's desk with her long, organist's fingers. The desk was so neat that even Dee, with her prim skirt and shellacked hair, looked disheveled beside it. An in-box, desk blotter, stapler, and tape dispenser were arranged with linear precision beside the district-issued

Dell computer. The only thing that wasn't utilitarian was a single chess piece, an ivory rook, that sat next to the stapler.

"He's supposed to have that party after lunch," Nora said.

"He'd better get here quick, then, hadn't he?" Dee saw Nora's frown and sighed. "Talk to Bettina if you're worried. I'm too busy covering his behind."

Bettina was the principal, a no-nonsense, white-haired woman who reminded Nora of Barbara Bush. Bettina would care more that Adam hadn't arranged a substitute than about where he might be, so Nora went reluctantly back to her classroom. As it filled with seventh graders she tried to convince herself there was nothing to worry about. It was strange that Adam hadn't called, but surely he would be here soon, and all would be forgiven in the glow of watching thirty-six eighth graders eat homemade pie.

Near the end of third period Bettina came on the loudspeaker and called everyone to the gym for an assembly that wasn't on the schedule. Nora was in the middle of a lesson on Lovelock's glory days, when covered wagons filled the Big Meadow, the last stop on the California Trail before the Forty Mile Desert. Every year she dutifully presented this piece of history as an exercise in civic pride, as it had been presented to her, even though she thought it merely highlighted the shabby ruin Lovelock had become in the 150 years since. Her students were grateful for the reprieve, but one look at Bettina in the doorway fanned Nora's misgivings about Adam into full-blown anxiety. The principal was as pale as her white linen skirt, and as each teacher arrived she sent him or her to the staff room. Behind her, in the gym, Dee snapped orders at 130 confused and excited middle schoolers. Nora headed down the hallway with leaden feet.

In the small staff room the school's seven other teachers and two counselors crowded together, buzzing about what was so urgent it couldn't wait fifteen minutes until lunch. Nora wrapped her arms around her ribs and leaned against the counter beside the P.E. teacher, Josie Wilson, a bubbly girl who'd played soccer at the high school five years before and looked young enough to play there still. Then Bettina walked in with the sheriff, and everyone else stopped talking. Dee had let the students onto the playground, and in the silence they heard them: the shrieks of the sixth and seventh graders playing, and the lower tones of the eighth graders, gossiping, probing, posing.

The sheriff closed the door. Bill Watterly was the same age as Nora's father, with a jowly face and the soft body of an ex-football player. His shoulders carried his weight with the ease that only a big man's shoulders can, but they didn't carry bad news well at all. He'd only been to the school once since Nora started teaching, when Chris Mitchell, a junior at the high school, shot himself with his father's Colt and Bill needed to pull his sister out of class to tell her. His shoulders hadn't been up to the task then, and they weren't bearing up well now, either. Nora braced herself against the counter.

"We've found a body up by Marzen." Bill looked at Bettina, and she nodded at him to continue. "We think it might be your new math teacher."

The room erupted in shocked exclamations, but Nora barely heard them through the sudden chaos in her head. Adam Merkel was dead. Of course he was. That was why he wasn't here. But he couldn't be dead. He was having a party after lunch. He definitely couldn't be dead up by Marzen. Marzen was a crummy little town in the hills where nobody from Lovelock went if they could help it. Adam probably didn't even know where it was. Yet here was Bill Watterly, stocky and grim in his tan uniform, saying they'd found Adam's body. Up by Marzen.

"How did he die?" she asked. Everyone looked at her, then looked back at Bill Watterly.

The sheriff puffed out his chest. "I'm not at liberty to say." His belly hung over the black belt of his uniform and his crossed arms were smug against it. She'd misjudged him, Nora realized. He was enjoying this. She felt the slow tightening in her mind, like small screws winding shut, that meant she was about to lose her temper.

"Everyone in town is going to be talking about this by dinnertime," she said. "If you don't want speculation and rumors messing up your investigation, you should tell us what happened."

A tide of pink crept up the sheriff's thick neck, but a look from Bettina made him swallow whatever he was about to say. He drew himself up and looked around the room. When he felt he'd regained his authority he said, "You all might as well know what happened. We received a call this morning from the Marzen fire department. When we responded we found one male, deceased, about a mile from the town. The body was burned." He paused for dramatic effect. "We're treating it as a homicide."

"Oh my God," said Josie.

Nora imagined Adam burning, his arms pinwheeling in flame, and her stomach slipped sideways. She made herself think instead of the last time she'd seen him: in the staff room yesterday morning, putting three creamers and four sugars into his coffee. Kevin Keegan, the language arts teacher, told him he was killing himself with condiments, and Adam had laughed in his uncertain way, not knowing if he was being insulted or teased. He'd had only a few hours left to live, but he'd shuffled out of the staff room with his coffee in one hand and his briefcase in the other as if it were any other day.

Your new math teacher, Bill had called him. He hadn't even said Adam's name. But why would he? To the sheriff and his fat, inadequate shoulders, that's all Adam Merkel was. Seven months hadn't been enough for him to become anything else. Even seven years might not have been. Back in Reno, Nora was sure, Adam Merkel wouldn't have been just a dead math teacher. He would have been a dead friend. He might have been a dead brother, or a dead son.

Shit. Her body jerked backward. She couldn't believe she'd forgotten. March 14 wasn't just Pi Day. It was also the day, twenty years ago, when Lovelock's high school basketball team played in the state championship for the first and only time, and Nora's brother, Jeremy, senior point guard and team captain, scored 43 points in a win that was still the biggest thing to happen in this town since the last covered wagon pulled out of the Big Meadow. Nora's father was never more proud of anything than he was of his son that night. He sealed Jeremy's jersey in Lucite and hung it in the living room. He hung a brass plaque beside it with the date, the score, and the words: 43 POINTS. For the next seven years he bragged about that game to anyone who would listen, and many who would not, right up until the night he drove his truck into the guardrail on the Highway 95 bridge and killed his son instantly.

Fucking March 14. Her father was alone right now, in the camper. He was probably already drunk.

JAKE

To get to Marzen from Lovelock, you took Interstate 80 thirteen miles east to the Lovelock-Unionville Road. Then you drove south through three miles of sage and sand, climbed into the foothills of the Humboldt Range, and took a nameless dirt road that forked to the right halfway up Limerick Canyon. This road rose through more hills furred with sagebrush until it ended in a small, square valley where a few dozen buildings huddled together. Only when you were upon them would you see that they sketched a town: a smattering of houses and trailers, a general store and a bar, a small school, a fire station, and a church the size and shape of three shipping containers welded together with MARZEN BAPTIST painted in red letters on one side.

Two hundred and seven people lived there. Eighty-four men, seventy-six women, and forty-seven children. Most of the men, and some of the women, worked at the open pit silver mine farther up in the hills. Their fathers had been miners, too, and their grandfathers, but they knew the ore would be gone before their children could punch the clock. They didn't talk about this, though. In Marzen, you took your problems one day at a time.

The town had no police force—its citizens managed the occasional drunken fight just fine on their own—so the fire station was where you had to go if you wanted to report a dead body. Jake

Sanchez was the volunteer on duty the morning of March 14, which for him meant watching *The Price Is Right* on the black-and-white television with his feet on the desk. He didn't notice the boy in the doorway until the boy said, "Jake?"

Jake put his booted feet on the floor and turned the swivel chair to face him. He knew him, of course. His name was Absalom, though no one called him that, not even his mother. One night, after last call at the bar she ran, she'd told Jake she picked it because she sang in the Baptist church's small choir and loved the anthem "When David Heard." *O Absalom, my son, my son,* it went. *Would God I had died for thee!* Her own son had no father to weep for him, so she'd decided to name him after King David's favorite son, whose father beat his breast upon the walls of Jerusalem when he heard Absalom had fallen in battle. Of course she'd known her boy couldn't really be Absalom, not in a town like Marzen, so she called him Sal. She'd died nine months ago, and sometimes Jake wondered if he was the only one left, other than Sal and the uncles he'd been sent to live with, who knew her son's secret, unspoken name.

"What are you doing here, Sal? Did you miss the bus?" When Marzen kids finished fifth grade the Pershing County school district sent a bus to take them to Lovelock for middle and high school. Sal had started sixth grade in the fall. Jake looked at his watch. It was just after seven thirty; the bus had left fifteen minutes ago.

Sal didn't answer right away, and Jake peered at him more closely. He hadn't liked it when Sal was sent to live with his uncles. Gideon and Ezra Prentiss lived three miles outside town on land that had belonged to their family since the Gold Rush. They were pariahs of long standing, thanks to family history, a reputation for violence, and rumored criminal enterprises that, depending on who was talking and how imaginative they were, included cattle theft, meth cooking, drug running, and money laundering for the Russian mafia. Since Sal had moved up there he'd grown thinner and he always looked tired, but this morning he looked even worse than usual. He was pale beneath the tawny skin that was the only clue to his father's identity and his shaggy dark bangs flopped into eyes that were sunken with exhaustion.

"I found a dead person," he said.

Jake rocked forward. "What?"

Sal's shoulders twitched, as though he thought Jake was going to grab him. "I found a dead body. Up the hill a ways."

"Holy shit." Jake stopped and got himself in hand. He was wearing the uniform of the Marzen Volunteer Fire Department, and despite the game shows he took that responsibility seriously. He turned off the television. "Is it a skeleton?" No one in Marzen was missing that he knew of, and every once in a while somebody turned up the bones of a miner or a settler who'd taken a wrong turn on the way to California.

Sal hesitated. "No."

"Do you know who it is?"

The boy's dark eyes slid sideways, to the station's narrow refrigerator. There was a sign taped to the door that warned of terrible consequences if food was left in there too long, or if anybody took food that wasn't theirs. "I think it might be my math teacher."

"Your math teacher?"

"There's a car. I think it's his."

Jake didn't know what to do. He looked around the small station for help, but of course there was none. Leon Petrelli wouldn't relieve him until two. Maybe he should treat this as a medical call, he thought. Marzen was small enough that its fire department volunteers doubled as paramedics, and Jake was even more proud of his EMT license than he was of his fire department uniform. He could take the ambulance up there, see what Sal had found. He wiped his palms on his pants. "Okay, why don't you show me."

They drove up the dirt fire road that led from the town to the Prentiss place. Jake figured Sal had found the body on his way to the school bus, and sure enough, about a mile along they came upon an old brown Corolla parked just off the road, and Sal told him to stop. Jake walked over to the car. He knew better than to touch it, but he looked inside. It was empty.

He walked back to where Sal waited beside the ambulance. All around them the foothills of the Humboldt Range rose in bristly mounds, treeless and dry. To the right the land sloped up toward a rocky cliff that threw man and boy into shadow. The wind pushed Sal's Denver Broncos sweatshirt against his thin chest. It was cold in this high desert country in March; the tops of the mountains were still white with snow.

Sal turned and led Jake up the slope. They climbed in silence, through sagebrush that snatched at their pant legs. When they reached the top the ground dropped into a seasonal wash that ran along the base of the bluff. A cluster of acacia trees stood there, their canopies lifted to the sky like open palms. They were the only trees Jake had seen since they left Marzen, and the dense little grove spoke of shelter, of safety. Of a place to hide.

Sal stopped. The wind whipped in the sagebrush and the gray-green leaves of the acacias, and moaned as it curled among the hills. There was a smell, too, faint but insistent. Tangy, ripe, burnt. Far above, two chicken hawks floated in lazy circles, their wings tipping in, then out, then in again.

Jake looked at the boy. His eyes were closed, his shoulders drawn in tight.

"Is it down there?"

Sal nodded without opening his eyes.

"Wait here." Jake pressed one hand against his belly, tucked in his shirt, and walked into the wash.

When he reached the grove of trees, he didn't see the math

teacher right away. He saw the careful ring of stones that made the fire pit, and the ashes piled in the center. Around it lay trees that had grown and died and fallen, their corpses blackened in the long, quiet decay of desert things. At first, Jake took the math teacher's body for one of these. Only when he saw the empty vodka bottle and the children's jump rope did he see what was left of the man. Then Jake, too, closed his eyes.

The Pershing County sheriff and his chief deputy drove up from Lovelock and met them at the fire station forty-five minutes later. Jake knew Sheriff Watterly by sight, and he'd gone to high school with the chief deputy, Mason Greer. Mason didn't seem to recognize him, but Jake wasn't surprised. Lovelock kids had never had much to say to Marzen kids.

After Jake told them how Sal had led him to the body, the sheriff turned to Sal. "How'd you find it?"

"I was on my way to the bus." Sal spoke so quietly the sheriff had to lean forward to hear.

"Well, it wasn't lying in the road, was it? Jake here says it's a ways off."

Jake gave the sheriff a sharp look. The boy wasn't a suspect, for Christ's sake. Sal looked at the floor. "I saw the car. And there were birds. Flying around like something was dead." A small breath, in and out. "I was early for the bus. I went to see."

The sheriff wrote something in his notepad, then snapped the pad shut. "Okay, let's have a look."

In the grove, the two policemen surveyed the corpse curled beside the firepit. Jake stood to one side as they made notes about the empty three-liter bottle of Smirnoff and the charred nylon jump rope, which was tied around the body's ankles. He tried not to look at the body, with its blackened arms bent at the elbows like a boxer about to jab, its howling mouth, and its burnt-out eyes. In his ten years on Marzen's volunteer fire force he'd never seen first-hand what fire did to human flesh.

Mason squatted behind a rock about six feet from the firepit and called to the sheriff. Neither officer had told Jake to keep his distance, so he came over to see what Mason had found.

It was a soft leather briefcase, black, with worn handles. Mason used his pen to open the flap, and the tips of his fingers to pull out a wallet. He flipped it open and a Nevada driver's license faced the sky, with a photo of a pale, balding man in his fifties. *Adam H. Merkel,* read the name. Jake looked back at the body. At the face, tar black and screaming.

"That's the new math teacher over at the middle school," Mason said. His voice was shaky, and he was as pale as Jake felt.

"Call Phil," the sheriff said. "Tell him to bring an evidence kit and call the coroner. I'll go to the middle school, see if the math teacher showed up."

"What about Sal?" Jake asked. Sal was in the police cruiser, back on the fire road.

The sheriff and Mason looked at each other, and Jake had the feeling they'd forgotten about their young witness. "Chief Deputy Greer will get his contact information," the sheriff said. "Then he can go home. We'll call his parents later about getting a statement."

"He doesn't have parents. He lives with his uncles." Jake couldn't bear to think of Sal walking back to the Prentiss place alone. "Maybe we could drop him off."

The sheriff hesitated, and now Jake saw how far out of his depth he was pretending not to be. Jake figured the only dead bodies Bill Watterly and Mason Greer had seen were overdoses, suicides, accidents, and old people who died alone and weren't discovered until the mail piled up. He couldn't remember the last time anyone in Pershing County had been murdered, and this murder—

the burning, the jump rope, the empty vodka bottle—was steeped in a calculated, horrifying malice that chilled him. He didn't envy the sheriff the task of solving it.

"You could talk to his uncles about the statement," he suggested. The sheriff nodded, and Jake fell in behind the officers as they headed back to the cruiser.

When they started up the dirt track toward the Prentiss place Sal went rigid. "Where are we going?"

"We're giving you a ride home," Jake said.

"No, thank you. I can walk."

"It's no trouble." Jake glanced at the sheriff and Mason in the front seats. He lowered his voice. "Relax."

The boy picked at his jeans with a dirty fingernail. The jeans were too small for him. They were probably the last pair his mother had bought him before she died, Jake thought. The sweatshirt, too, was short in the sleeves. The only things that fit were his sneakers, a new pair of white basketball shoes. At least his uncles had managed to buy him those.

The track was riven with troughs carved by the rare but violent storms that scoured the land in the winter, and the cruiser jounced and slid. After two slow miles they rounded a curve and came upon a few shabby buildings in a small valley. A sign at the top of the dirt driveway said PRENTISS RANCH NO TRESPASSING. Mason drove past it and onto the property.

Jake had never seen the Prentiss place, though he'd heard stories about the Prentisses all his life. The first Prentiss was a con man and itinerant preacher who'd landed in Lovelock when it was still a busy stop on the California Trail. He'd married a Paiute girl from a local whorehouse and tried to make an honest living as a rancher, but eventually he and his sons devolved into rustling, herding stolen cattle from Idaho and Montana south to Denver. Their descendants ran a bootlegging operation during Prohibition, then a numbers racket, and were ear-deep in the Vegas mob in the 1980s. Or so people said. Jake didn't know what was truth and what was myth, but he did know the current Prentisses were a surly pair of recluses who only came to town to buy supplies at the general store and drink at the Nickel, where their sister, Grace—Sal's mother—had been the bartender.

Still, even knowing the Prentisses' reputation, Jake was taken aback by the ranch. At the end of the driveway was a ruined two-story farmhouse, its white paint peeling, all its windows shattered, its porch smothered by a clot of sagebrush that was trying to drag it into the earth. A dense ring of garbage surrounded the house: furniture, rusted appliances, mattresses with their stuffing shredded by mice. A hundred feet to the house's left was a beige double-wide on a concrete slab, and scattered around both buildings were a half dozen crumbling wooden sheds, a chicken run, a listing barn, an old well with a rusted winch, a water tank, a propane tank, a small set of solar panels, and a generator. There were no cars or people in sight.

Jake looked at Sal again. The family court in Lovelock had sent him here because these men were his uncles. Open and shut case. They probably hadn't even checked to see whether it was a fit place for a boy to grow up.

A yellow dog was chained to an upended wheelbarrow in front of the double-wide, and it walked stiff-legged toward them, its teeth bared. In the sand were a thousand prints that marked the boundaries of its range, paces upon paces upon paces, and its eyes held not just hostility but a dull, perplexed misery.

Beside Jake, Sal took a deep, quiet breath, held it, then let it go.

"Are your uncles home?" Sheriff Watterly asked.

Sal shook his head. "No."

Mason turned around in the driver's seat. He had his notepad out. "What are their names?"

Sal opened his mouth but didn't speak. His palms were pressed flat against the vinyl car seat. Jake answered for him. "Gideon and Ezra Prentiss."

"What's their phone number?" Mason asked.

Sal glanced over his shoulder at the road. "I don't know."

"Look around, Mason," Sheriff Watterly said with disgust. "You think these folks are on the grid?"

Mason ignored him. "Listen, buddy," he said to Sal. "I know it's tough, finding something like this. But we're going to need to talk to you about it some more, at the police station. Have your uncles get in touch with us, okay? As soon as they can."

"Okay." Sal was trembling, but Mason didn't seem to notice.

"Get on out, then," Sheriff Watterly said. Sal slid out and Mason backed the car up the driveway. The boy stood beside the dog and watched them go. It wasn't until they reached the curve in the road that Jake saw him turn toward the double-wide, and it wasn't until he disappeared from view that he realized Sal wasn't wearing a school backpack.

SAL

Sal met the math teacher six and a half months before the math teacher died. It was the first day of sixth grade, a beautiful morning under a cloudless sky, and Mr. Merkel saved him from humiliation with a touch of his hand.

The school bus stopped outside the Marzen General Store at seven fifteen, and Sal got up at five thirty to make sure he wouldn't miss it. His uncles were still asleep, so he moved quietly, making a bologna sandwich for lunch and checking his backpack to make sure the notebooks and pencils from fifth grade were in order. When he set out the sun hadn't risen above the hills, but the sky was a faint blue, and he could see Samson under the wheelbarrow. The dog lifted his square head as Sal walked by, then laid it down again.

The only sound as Sal walked the fire road to Marzen was the crunch of sand under his worn sneakers. He felt grown up and brave, walking alone to the bus that would take him to a new school in another town, but he couldn't help thinking about how this day would have gone if his mother were alive. She would have made him scrambled eggs for breakfast, packed him a peanut butter sandwich and Fritos for lunch, and walked him the two blocks from their house to the bus stop. Though it was also possible she would have slept too late to do any of these things, and this thought made Sal's head feel bigger on the inside than it was on the outside. To distract himself he made up a story.

Sal was a quiet boy, but his stories were loud, filled with angels and demons and epic battles between good and evil. Today the armies of Heaven and Hell flooded the hills with blood until Angelus, the greatest archangel of them all, slew Hell's minions with a scythe Death himself had given him. Angelus had been Sal's champion since Sal was five, sick with a fever so high it painted monsters in the corners of his room until the archangel strode in and killed them all. As Marzen came into view he knelt on his mighty knee in the fire road, victorious as always, while the heavenly host sang his praises to the sky.

Sal was thirty minutes early for the bus, so he sat on the curb in front of the general store and watched Angelus and the host dissolve in the newly risen sun. Then he took a sketchbook and a pencil from his backpack and drew Angelus with stars for eyes and his scythe raised high, battling a demon. He would color it that night, with the colored pencils his mother had given him for Christmas two years before.

Ten minutes before the bus came the seventeen other middle and high school students straggled up in ones and twos. None of them spoke to Sal; none were in his grade. It was dumb luck, his mom always said, that nobody else had a baby the year he was born. They barely spoke to each other, either—they were slurry and tired, yanked from their summer slumber and shoved into the morning. When the bus came they took seats as close to the back as they could. Sal sat by himself behind Mr. Curtis, the bus driver.

Thirty-five minutes later the bus pulled up to Pershing Middle School in Lovelock, and Sal stood on the sidewalk amid a swirl of students and parents. The confidence that had carried him from his uncles' house had evaporated as the bus lumbered down the interstate, and now he felt the first stirrings of panic. The school stretched low and flat to his left and right, and it was so much bigger than the three-room Marzen elementary school that it made him dizzy.

Gretchen Suarez, a seventh grader from Marzen, studied a piece of paper before setting off, her pink flip-flops smacking the cement. A group of Lovelock kids walked by, and they had those papers, too. Everybody had them. Everybody knew where to go except Sal, because he didn't have the paper. His mom would have given it to him, like all the other kids' moms had done, but she hadn't woken up that one morning, and now Sal was going to cry, and this made him angry—at himself for being such a baby, and at his mother for leaving him all alone without the paper that would tell him where to go. He couldn't be the kid who cried on the first day of school. It wouldn't matter that he was wearing basketball shorts like all the other boys', or that his backpack was the same dull blue as everyone else's; he would always be the kid who cried on the first day, and that would ruin everything left that could still be ruined.

Then Sal felt a hand on his shoulder. He looked up to see a man in his fifties, with kind gray eyes behind silver glasses. "You seem a little lost."

Sal couldn't speak, so he nodded.

"Let's see if we can figure out where you belong." The man led Sal through the blue front doors and into a small office. A woman with plastic-looking blond hair sat at a desk, typing on a keyboard with the longest, skinniest fingers Sal had ever seen. He couldn't stop looking at them, even when she raised them from the keyboard and folded them together like a spider bunching up its legs. She looked over his head at the man.

"Can I help you?"

"This young fellow doesn't know where to go." The man's voice was whispery, but a thin wire of sound ran through it that settled Sal's anxiety from a boil to a simmer.

"Didn't you get the email with his schedule?" The woman sounded annoyed.

The man coughed an apology cough. "I'm not his father. I'm Adam Merkel, your new math teacher."

At this, the woman's whole face changed. She pushed back her chair and reached out one of those skinny hands. She'd painted her fingernails the same color as her skin, and it made her fingers look even longer. "Dr. Merkel! How wonderful to meet you! I'm Dee Pratzer."

"Mr. Merkel is fine," the man said as he shook her hand.

Sal was very good at telling what people were thinking. His mother used to say that as a baby, he'd touch her face when she was sad, and he'd have a look of knowing, as if he were older than the oldest man. Now he watched Dee Pratzer flutter her eyelashes, and he knew she was flirting, but not in the sexy-sexy way his mom used to flirt with her customers at the bar. Dee Pratzer was impressed by this man, and wanted him to like her. Sal gave the man—Mr. Merkel—a good look for the first time. He was short, with thinning gray hair combed over his head. Even though the temperature would be over ninety by noon, he wore a brown tweed jacket over a crisp white dress shirt. He wasn't wearing a tie, but he looked as though he wished he were. As though, that morning, he'd started to put on a tie, then decided against it.

Dee Pratzer turned back to Sal. She was still annoyed with him but didn't want Mr. Merkel to see. "Didn't your mother give you your schedule, sweetie?"

"My mom's dead," Sal said, and waited to see what she did. People's reactions to this statement said a lot about them, he'd found. Some people didn't know what to say, so they stammered and looked away. These people Sal liked. The ones who popped right out with their pity didn't mean a word of it, and they weren't to be trusted. He had a good idea which type Dee Pratzer would be.

She puckered her lips and said, "You poor dear." Sal looked down so she wouldn't see his satisfaction.

"Do you have a copy of his schedule?" Mr. Merkel asked, and Sal realized he hadn't checked to see what he thought of his mom being dead.

Dee Pratzer printed out a sheet of paper like the ones the other kids had and handed it to Mr. Merkel. He turned to Sal and smiled a twinkly, generous smile. "You're in my class for first period. How about I show you where it is?"

Mr. Merkel's first-period class had twenty-three sixth graders, and the other twenty-two were there when Sal and Mr. Merkel arrived. In fact, Sal and Mr. Merkel were late, and the students were chasing one another around, swinging their backpacks, and rummaging through the boxes of rulers lined up on the air conditioner. The noise they made was joyful and animalistic and loud, and Sal found it harrowing.

Mr. Merkel, too, seemed taken aback. He stood in the doorway, his black leather briefcase hanging from one hand. Then he stepped inside and pulled the door shut. This small gesture had the effect of reducing the decibel level by half. A dozen of the children looked stricken, as though caught in very bad behavior, while the remainder merely looked disappointed.

"Take your seats, please," Mr. Merkel said in his soft voice, but that filament of sound thrummed just enough to nudge twenty-two summer children into fall. Sal watched them sort themselves according to a hierarchy they must have established in elementary school. Six pretty, white girls sat at one table. They'd glued sparkly beads on their sneakers, so their feet glittered as they bounced their thin legs on the plastic seats. Eight brown kids crowded around another table, Paiute and Latino, their handed-down backpacks faded and frayed. Three kids with the hangdog look of misfits took a third table. Five boys sat at a table in the back, the ones whose shoulders had begun to spread just a little and who wore their athleticism like invisible capes. Sal sighed. The Marzen elementary school had been the same, only smaller.

When everyone was seated one chair was left, with the boys at the back table. Sal sidled along the wall and sat in it, trying to look as though he belonged there. He might not have athletic shoulders or the crisp, white, back-to-school Nikes they wore, but at least he was wearing basketball shorts like theirs. The five boys looked him over, first with curiosity and then, when they'd scanned him from his unruly hair to his ragged sneakers, dismissal. Sal's face warmed. He wouldn't be sitting there tomorrow, he knew. His chair would mysteriously migrate to the misfits' table, as it had in Marzen.

Mr. Merkel pulled a sheaf of paper from his briefcase and stood beside his desk. He smiled, but it wasn't the twinkly smile he'd given Sal in the office. This smile was thin and didn't reach his eyes, and it made Sal uneasy. Mr. Merkel looked a little like Sal had felt when he got off the bus.

"I thought I'd start by telling you about myself," he said. "My name is Dr.—Mr. Merkel. I moved from Reno to teach here." He set the papers on his desk. He drummed his index fingers together, then picked up the papers again. "I was a professor at the University of Nevada, in the mathematics department. Number theory, mostly. Though I taught calculus, too, and statistics." He ruffled the edges of the papers with his thumb. "You're probably wondering why I'd leave that job to come here."

Sal didn't think anybody was wondering this except for him,

but the frenzy of the early minutes had been smothered by the hum of the fluorescent lights, so they were listening, at least.

"I wanted to get back to the beginning," Mr. Merkel said. "Back to when kids first get excited about math. When they start to see it's more than multiplication tables and long division and realize it explains everything. Why the sky is blue. Why your chair holds you up. Why the wind blows from the west. It explains these things whether you speak English, Chinese, or Spanish. Two plus two is four no matter where you live, and the circumference of a circle is its diameter times pi no matter your religion. Our ability to understand these things is what separates us from the rest of the animals, and binds us together as a species." He had an energy about him now, sparking and electric. "Math," he said, "is the one true language of humanity."

One of the pretty girls smacked her gum, but the girl next to her watched Mr. Merkel without blinking. Sal glanced around at the boys at his table. Two were bewildered. Another two were intrigued, but Sal could tell that the flush on Mr. Merkel's cheeks made them uncomfortable. The fifth, a lanky boy with straight dark hair, watched Mr. Merkel with curiosity, spinning a pencil between his thumb and forefinger. Sal looked back to Mr. Merkel, waiting for the next verse of the poetry that had sprung so unexpectedly from this unassuming man.

But Mr. Merkel had lost his way. He cleared his throat and looked at his papers. In the silence he seemed to shrivel. The air in the room deflated as students shifted in their seats, some in disappointment, others in relief that the odd little speech was over.

Mr. Merkel handed the papers to the nearest student, a girl with black hair in a high ponytail. "Take one and pass them around."

When the papers made their way to Sal he read the title: "Sixth Grade Math Topics and Expectations of Students." A single-spaced outline filled both sides of the page, with headings like

"Ratios and Proportional Relationships," "Number Systems and Fractional Equations," and "Prime Numbers and Prime Factorization." Nowhere did it mention the color of the sky or the direction of the wind.

"We will start with ratios and proportional relationships." Mr. Merkel turned to the whiteboard. His back in his brown tweed jacket was rounded like a shell.

The lanky boy at Sal's table leaned forward, a smirk lifting one side of his mouth. "He looks like a turtle," he said, and the other boys laughed.

NORA

Nora didn't make it home for lunch with her father. The sheriff questioned them in the staff room right through recess. Other than the make of Adam's car and the address Bettina pulled up on her computer, nobody had anything helpful to say, but that didn't stop Bill Watterly from asking how long they'd known Adam and whether they'd seen any strangers lurking around the school while Nora watched the clock, thought about her father drinking in the camper, and seethed with frustration.

After the sheriff left the day trudged by. Nora's afternoon classes didn't know what had happened—Bill had asked them not to tell the students yet—but they knew it was something big, and their excitement made them antsy. Nora clung to her patience with difficulty. Her mother had taught language arts here for fifteen years, and she'd been beloved by students and teachers alike. When Nora told Bettina she was getting her teaching certificate, the principal had embraced her. "We'd be honored to have your mother's daughter teaching here," she said, but in this, as in many things, Nora knew she wasn't her mother's daughter.

But by the time the last bell rang, the anxiety of lunchtime had given way to a familiar resentment, and Nora no longer wanted to rush home to the camper. It would just be the same mess it always was, and by now there'd be nothing to do but clean it up. After her classroom emptied she sat at her desk and rubbed her eyes, feeling the scratch of sand under the lids. Sand was everywhere, always—in her pores, her hair, even in the grinding space where her molars met. She was sure that when her flesh rotted away there would be a pile of sand in her coffin, inside the cage of her bones.

A quick knock made her look up to see Mary Barnes in the doorway. Mary's perfume, flowery and cloying, flooded the room.

"Can you believe it? That poor man." Her eyes were wide with ghoulish excitement.

"It's terrible," Nora said, neutrally.

"It's shocking! A murder, right here in Lovelock!" Mary smacked her bright red lips. "Why would anyone kill Adam, of all people? He was—well, you knew him. He didn't seem worth the trouble."

Nora kept her temper with an effort. "The sheriff asked us not to talk about it."

"How can we not? He was our colleague." Mary pressed her hand to her breast, as she had in the staff room. "Our *friend*." Her blouse was open one button too far, showing the wrinkled skin of her cleavage. Her hair was dyed blond and teased into curls that fell past her shoulders, just as they doubtless had in her 1988 Homecoming Queen portrait. Nora, who'd been one of the two most popular girls in her own class, prided herself on little these days, but she would never be like Mary Barnes, clinging desperately to bygone glory. That was something, at least.

"I'm sorry, Mary. But I'm not going to talk about it," she said, and Mary's mouth shut with a snap.

Once Mary was gone Nora leaned back in her chair. She still couldn't bring herself to leave, so she watched students board the Marzen bus outside her window. There were eight middle schoolers from Marzen this year, which was more or less how many there were every year. They looked like all the other kids, with their basketball shorts and pink leggings and secondhand Old Navy tee shirts, but Nora knew they were a clan apart. It couldn't be easy trying to fit in with the Lovelock kids, who'd known one another since kindergarten, but there was also something insular and wary about Marzen itself, crouching in its little valley in the hills. In high school Nora had ridden that bus many times with a Marzen girl. Lily DeSanto, with her fragile face and thin blond hair, wasn't in the popular crowd Nora ran with by then, but Nora liked the delicate horses Lily drew in her notebooks during class. She liked Lily's mother's tapioca pudding, too, and the spongy mattress of Lily's twin bed, where they slept head to toe. But no matter how often Nora rode that bus to Lily's house she'd remained as much an outsider as the first time. That's how Marzen was.

Sheriff Watterly had asked the staff why Adam might have gone there. Nobody had any idea, including Nora, but now she remembered the Marzen boy in the sixth grade, a small, quiet boy who sat in the back of her classroom with the misfits. An outsider even among outsiders, this boy—Sal Prentiss was his name—had eaten lunch with Adam almost every day. Nora had seen them on Thursdays after school, too, the only members of Adam's chess club. If she worked late enough on Thursdays she'd see them getting into Adam's car afterwards, and she'd thought it was nice of Adam to give the boy a ride home. So that explained how Adam knew where Marzen was. But yesterday was Wednesday, so it didn't explain why he'd gone there the day he was killed.

Nora tilted her head back and stared at the asbestos ceiling tiles. All year she'd wondered why Adam had come to Lovelock. He'd been running from something, that much she knew. Everyone who moved to Lovelock was running from something, even the supervisors sent by the mining company, whether they knew it or not. But what could it have been? Nora was good at getting people to talk when she put her mind to it, so she'd assumed she could get Adam to tell her why he'd left a university professorship to teach middle school in a small desert town, but he'd gently deflected all her questions and politely ducked out of conversations the moment they turned personal.

"Why Lovelock?" she'd asked him once, trying the direct approach.

"Suffice it to say," he'd said, in that stilted way of his, "that I am where I need to be."

Eventually she'd stopped probing and relaxed into what became a warm, though not close, friendship. She had liked him. He was awkward, but he had that sadness about him, and an unaffected kindness that was refreshing. When her brief marriage to Mason ended, ten years ago, Nora had dropped all of her old high school crowd except Britta. That made Adam her only other friend, even though she'd never seen him outside of school and they'd never talked about anything that mattered.

Ironically, Nora thought she'd come closest to making an honest connection with him just this past Monday. She'd stopped by in the morning to say hello, and his appearance had startled her. His skin was the color of paper, his hair was uncombed, and his dress shirt, normally as starched as a shirt in a 1950s magazine ad, was wrinkled.

"Are you okay?" she'd asked.

He'd stared at her with wide eyes, and she thought this was it: he was finally going to say something real. Then he looked away. "Just a bit under the weather," he said, and she let it go.

Now guilt rose about her like water, familiar and cold. She should have pressed him. What if whatever was bothering him on Monday had something to do with his murder two days later? Had he seen it coming? Did it have something to do with the past he'd never talked about? Nora couldn't imagine Adam having a secret so dark it had gotten him killed, but if his murderer hadn't been someone from his past, then it was someone from here, and who in this dry, lifeless town had it in them to set a man they barely knew on fire? She couldn't imagine that, either.

She shook her head, feeling her ponytail brush her shoulders. Her father was waiting, and she wasn't going to figure out who killed Adam. That was Bill Watterly's job. And Mason's.

But when she got to Fourteenth Street Nora turned right instead of going straight. Two blocks, then a left, past small houses on cramped, sun-blasted lots to the address Bettina had given the sheriff. She just wanted to see if Adam's car was there; that was what she told herself. Her father could wait another five minutes.

The house was a one-story bungalow like scores of others in Lovelock, and Nora had been in enough of them to know it would have a living room and a dated kitchen on one side and two bedrooms on the other. A low chain-link fence surrounded the yard, as if a prior tenant had kept a dog. Through the front window she saw the outline of a lamp. The lights were off, and Adam's Corolla was nowhere to be seen.

There was, however, a white pickup parked in front of the house, and as Nora stopped her Civic across the street a man came out Adam's front door and got in it. He was about Nora's age, with straight, dark, shoulder-length hair, and he carried a blue backpack that he put on the passenger seat. As he turned the ignition he saw Nora and froze. Nora looked quickly away, and he drove off. When he turned onto Fourteenth she let go of the steering wheel, feeling in her knuckles how tightly she'd been clutching it.

She tried to think why anyone would be in Adam's house—and what they might take from it—the day after he was murdered. Maybe the man knew Adam from Reno, though Adam had only been confirmed dead four hours ago, when Sheriff Watterly came to the school; surely it was too soon for anyone from Reno to show up. Maybe he worked for Adam's landlord. But Nora hadn't recognized him, and she knew all eighteen hundred and twelve people who lived in this town. She hadn't liked the way he looked at her, either, as though he were memorizing her face.

The neighborhood was quiet and empty, so she walked to Adam's front door. Through the narrow windows she saw a small foyer with a table that had a few pieces of mail on it. Nothing seemed disturbed. She examined the doorknob. There were no obvious signs of a break-in. She went to the back of the house, where sliding glass doors faced a concrete patio. When she looked through the doors, she saw the pies. Six of them, their tinfoil covers glinting in the late afternoon light, in a neat row on the white kitchen counter. Beside them was a piece of paper with something written on it. A recipe, perhaps. The kitchen was immaculate, all traces of the baking cleaned and put away.

Nora rested her forehead against the glass. She imagined Adam baking in there, slightly stooped in that way he had of taking up less space than his body demanded. It must have taken him hours to make all those pies. Whatever had happened to him had to have happened late at night, and it had to have caught him by surprise, because he'd clearly been planning to come to school the next morning for his Pi Day party.

The sun slipped behind the hills and the air turned purple. From the street came the slam of a car door and the shriek of a child. A dog barked. In the house next door, a kitchen light came on. The neighborhood was coming back to life, the cozy, tired heartbeat of evening. Nora pushed herself away from the glass, watching her fingerprints flare then dissolve. She took a last look at the neat kitchen and the pies, shadowed now in darkness, then drove home to her father.

SAL

On the second day of sixth grade, as Sal expected, there was no chair for him with the boys at the back table, so he sat with the misfits: Sylvana Eggers, who sang to herself under her breath; Ronnie Triplett, who picked his nose and wiped the dirt on his jeans; and Seventeen Jones, whose real name nobody had used since Rudy Gonzalez shoved his face into the sandbox seventeen times in first grade. None of them looked at Sal when he sat down.

By the end of the first week it was obvious the boys at the back table didn't like Mr. Merkel. They didn't like any of the teachers except Miss Wilson, the pretty P.E. teacher, but Mr. Merkel's halting first-day speech seemed to have earned him a special disdain. Whenever he turned to the whiteboard they hunched their backs in mockery while the rest of the class, even the misfits, stifled their laughter in their hands.

Mr. Merkel must have known what they were doing, but he didn't turn around fast to try to catch them. He just kept talking about ratios and proportions while the snickers ran through the room like mice. Sal could hardly bear to watch him, but being the only kid who didn't laugh at him was a duty he felt honor-bound to perform.

After math, Sal had social studies with Ms. Wheaton, a square-shouldered, sternly pretty woman who talked about the settlement of Nevada as though she were reading a grocery list. Then he had science with Ms. Barnes, a busty blond lady who wore too much perfume. After science came lunch. Lunch was the hardest part of Sal's day. He didn't have anyone to sit with, so he sat by a window in the library and drew pictures of Angelus fighting demons on the cracked blacktop where the boys from the back table played basketball in their Nikes. When recess ended he crept to the trash bin beside the picnic tables, fished out a half-eaten sandwich or an unwanted banana, and ate it on the way to fourth period. The bologna sandwich was never quite enough.

It was during the third week that he first had lunch with Mr. Merkel. Kip Masters, the lanky leader of the boys at the back table, had been so flagrant in his mockery that morning that Mr. Merkel actually stopped writing ratios on the whiteboard, standing stiff-backed in front of them. The class waited in a thrill of anticipation. Even Kip and his gang were still. But when Mr. Merkel turned around, he just talked about proportional relationships in the same soft voice he always used. Sal was the only one who heard the metallic fiber at its heart tighten and sing. Sal, and maybe Sylvana, who stopped her tuneless humming for a moment.

That moment, brief and perilous, was why Sal went to the math classroom instead of the library at lunch that day. A group of eighth grade girls walked out as he approached, and he pressed himself against the wall, away from their shimmering hair and their shorts that rode so high you could see the curve of their butts. They didn't even glance at him as they passed by.

Mr. Merkel was at his desk. As Sal watched, he reached into a drawer and pulled out a sandwich on white bread. Hunched over, with his nose poking down at his lunch, he looked like nothing so much as a turtle. Sal sighed in a misery of pity.

Mr. Merkel looked up. "Sal," he said, and his mournful face lightened. "What can I do for you?"

Sal fidgeted with his basketball shorts. Behind Mr. Merkel the whiteboard was covered in algebra for the eighth graders, who'd also begun to call him Merkel the Turtle. Sal imagined the girls from the hallway sitting at a table, their eyes rolled to the ceiling or glued to the phones they held in their laps, the *x*'s and *y*'s of Mr. Merkel's equations flattened against their foreheads.

"Why is the sky blue?" he asked.

"I'm sorry?" Mr. Merkel said.

"The first day. You said math explained why the sky is blue."

"It does."

"When are you going to teach us that?"

"First we have to cover ratios. And fractions." Mr. Merkel touched his glasses. "But we will get to it."

Sal hadn't thought about the color of the sky since the first day of school, yet he had also, he realized, thought about it constantly. "I want to know now. Please."

"Well." Mr. Merkel stopped, seemingly at a loss. Then he put his sandwich on his desk. "Light from the sun is made up of all the colors of the rainbow. When you see them from space, they all blend together into white."

"What does that have to do with the sky? Or math?"

Sal's mother would have told him he was being rude, but Mr. Merkel only blinked. Then his shoulders straightened. "Sit down," he said.

Sal pulled a chair over and sat facing Mr. Merkel across the desk. Mr. Merkel stood and brushed off his dress shirt, even though it wasn't dirty. Then he erased the algebra on the whiteboard. "Every color of light moves in waves," he said. "But the waves are different lengths." He drew a series of wavy lines, and next to them wrote *red, orange, yellow, green,* and *blue*. "Math lets us measure the waves." He looked at Sal, and there it was again, the electricity that had charged the classroom that first day. Sal caught his breath.

Next to the wavy lines Mr. Merkel drew a bunch of small circles. "The atmosphere is made up of molecules of oxygen and nitrogen. Math tells us how close together they are, and how big they are." He extended the wavy lines to meet the circles. "The biggest light waves are much bigger than the molecules, so they pass through without touching most of them." He ran the big, swooping lines for red, orange, yellow, and green through the field of circles and out the other side. "But the smallest waves, the blue ones, hit them." He drew the squiggly line for blue into one of the circles. "Whenever a light wave hits a molecule, its light gets scattered, like a tiny, blue firework exploding." He drew arrows shooting from the circle in all directions. "Imagine that happening trillions of times every second, all over the sky." He drew more tiny explosions, then a stick figure beneath the waves and arrows, looking up. "To us, it looks like the whole sky is glowing with steady, blue light."

He looked out the window, and Sal did, too. Above the rusted basketball hoops on the playground the sky was the searing sapphire of a desert autumn day. Sal imagined Angelus running his fingers through it, scattering light like luminescence in water.

Mr. Merkel sat. He tapped the marker against his palm. Sal thought of all those molecules, shining like billions of tiny blue suns, and said, "You need to stop those boys from making fun of you."

Mr. Merkel stopped tapping the marker. "Oh, that's all right, Sal. I don't mind. Boys will be boys. Believe it or not, I was a boy once, too."

He was lying. Sal knew it. And he knew, too, that Mr. Merkel had never been a boy like these boys. "Nobody will listen to you if you don't make them stop."

Mr. Merkel lined up the marker parallel to the edge of his desk blotter. "We'll see about that." But he sounded tentative, that mysterious energy banked once more. He glanced at his sandwich, then at Sal, and cleared his throat. "Would you like to get your lunch and eat with me?"

Sal looked at the open classroom door. He knew he shouldn't be the boy who ate lunch with Merkel the Turtle, but he didn't want to eat in the library, either, where Mrs. Simmons, the librarian, ate her salad with loud, crunching noises. He closed the door, then pulled his bologna sandwich from his backpack. It was thin and limp compared to Mr. Merkel's, which was packed thick with turkey, cheese, tomato, and lettuce. Mr. Merkel looked at it, then, with gentle dexterity, tore his own in half. He held out one of the halves to Sal.

"Please," he said. "I can never eat the whole thing."

Sal wiped his hands on his shorts. His hands were dirty, and the bread was so white.

"When I taught at the university," Mr. Merkel said as Sal took a bite, "one of my students had lunch with me often. It's nice to have company when you eat, I think."

After that Sal went to Mr. Merkel's classroom for lunch every day, and every day Mr. Merkel brought him a whole turkey sandwich. In class Mr. Merkel still droned on about ratios while Kip Masters and his friends mocked him behind his back, but at lunch he told Sal how math measured the age of rocks, predicted the changing of the seasons, and explained the interdependence of predators and prey, all with a passion that was so at odds with his dull classroom lectures that he seemed to be a different person entirely. After the first few days Sal didn't even bother to close the door.

NORA

The mess in the camper was just as Nora had expected. Her father was passed out on the banquette, his breath a wet rattle, and an empty bottle of Jim Beam sat on the table. She supposed she should be glad there was only the one. She tried to keep alcohol out of the camper, but he had his friends still: buddies from the mine, high school teammates, and fathers whose sons he'd coached who felt sorry for the man who'd lost his own. They didn't come often, but they always brought something, and there were hiding places in this tin can Nora would never find. The bottle made a satisfying smash in the trash can by the back door.

She cooked spaghetti and ate it at the kitchen table where she'd eaten as a girl, the three empty chairs as invisible as old friends. Afterward she took a plate and a *National Geographic* magazine to the camper. It was dark now, and the glow from the camper's window cast a rectangle of light on the bare ground and the rotting sandbox. The generator Nora had bought with her father's disability payments chugged in the corner.

Her father was sitting at the table, smoking a cigarette. He still wore his pajama bottoms, but he'd put a Giants sweatshirt on over his stained undershirt, and his eyes, though bloodshot, were sober. Nora was relieved, then annoyed. "You could have come in for dinner."

"I wasn't hungry." He stubbed out the cigarette in a plastic ashtray with YELLOWSTONE NATIONAL PARK stamped on one side. He coughed a hacking smoker's cough as Nora set down the plate and the magazine. "What's this?"

"Something cool."

On the magazine's cover was a drawing of a girl with long black hair and the words "The First Americans." When her father opened it Nora sat opposite him and folded her hands.

They'd found the girl in an underwater cave in Mexico. She'd died thirteen thousand years ago, in the last days of the Pleistocene, when the great ice sheets peeled away from the bones of the world. In the forensic reconstruction her eyes were Asian, but her cheeks were wider and her jawline narrower than in any race alive today. The effect was haunting in its individuality and unsettling in its otherness. Nora's father touched the image with a gentle, reverent finger.

American prehistory was an odd fascination for a man with a high school education who otherwise talked of nothing but sports, but when Nora was a girl it had offered a back door into her father's heart. She would read his *National Geographic* and *Archaeology* magazines, then bring up an article about Kennewick Man or the Anzick Boy and watch him become a different father altogether. Jeremy mocked their obsession with "old bones," but Nora reveled in the rare frustration of the favorite child, shut out by a passion he couldn't understand.

She was ten when her father started taking her into the hills to look for spearpoints. As they walked he told her about the people who came over the Bering land bridge and down the Pacific coast fifteen thousand years ago, then went inland to the shores of a vast, prehistoric lake that once had covered the Great Basin from Oregon to California. How brave they must have been, he said. Or how desperate, Nora thought. No one knew whether they were exploring or fleeing, only that they'd come.

Even now, her best times with her father came when some new discovery splashed its way into *National Geographic*. As he did with his liquor, she hoarded them for the mourning days. But today it wouldn't be enough.

Her father closed the magazine, and the spell cast by the dead girl dissipated into the cigarette-stained air. His eyes, bruised with memory, found the darkness outside the window. "Do you know what today is?"

Nora laced her fingers together. "It's the day Jeremy won the championship."

His sigh rattled with phlegm. "Best game he ever played."

He said this every year, and every year it made Nora's pulse pound. She couldn't think of Jeremy without picturing him bloody and broken by the side of Highway 95. Meanwhile her father, who'd been the one to break him, could still remember him perfect and whole. In her worst moments—and this was definitely one—she thought it was a mercy he didn't deserve.

"Come kiss me," her mother had said to Jeremy the night of the championship, "for luck." She was lying on the couch while Nora sat in the La-Z-Boy and waited for her father to come home and drive them to Reno. Jeremy, tall and handsome in his blue and white uniform, stopped tossing his basketball.

"You're not coming?"

Nora's mother's hand fluttered over the yellow afghan that covered her. "I don't think I'm up to it," she said, and the room spun in on Nora in the La-Z-Boy. Her mother had never missed one of Jeremy's games. Five days after her mastectomy she'd watched him rush for 120 yards against Battle Mountain. Despite rounds of chemo that made her vomit in the Porta Potti, she'd never missed a baseball game. Now she was looking at her son in helpless apology, her skin so tight against her cheekbones that it shone, and telling him she was going to miss the biggest game of his life.

Nora's mother had been sick for three and a half years by then. It was the sort of sick that made her pass the meat loaf without taking any, but never kept her from making the meat loaf. It didn't stop her from doing the laundry, either, or running the rummage sale at the community center, or tutoring kids from the Indian Colony. Her long, sunset-colored hair fell out, grew back, then fell out again, and it had seemed she would go on being sick forever. Nora's fingernails gouged semicircles in the leather armrests of the La-Z-Boy and Jeremy dropped to his knees beside the couch. Nora couldn't hear him crying, but she watched her mother stroke his back from somewhere so quiet and far away it was outside time itself.

At the game that night, Jeremy was unstoppable. He drove through the lane, shaking opposing players off like water. He knifed shots from the perimeter, his face bright with savagery. At every basket Nora's father leaped to his feet, but Jeremy didn't see him. He seemed to see nothing but the ball, the basket, and something dark and terrible in between. At the buzzer he collapsed and his teammates dove on him, a pile of jubilant young bodies gleaming with sweat, and Nora's father disappeared in a throng of men who pounded his back. Nora sat in the seat where her mother should have been and waited until it was time to go.

When they got back to Lovelock Nora's father took Jeremy to the Whiskey. Never mind that Jeremy was only seventeen—he was a town hero, and Fred, the bartender, would pour him a man's drink. Nora's father didn't ask if there was a high school party Jeremy might rather go to, where his friends would douse him in beer and glory, or if he'd rather go home to his mother. After they dropped Nora off she stood on the porch and watched the taillights disappear down Sixteenth Street. The neighborhood was quiet under a carpet of stars.

Inside, her mother lay so still that Nora was for a moment

rooted to the floor. When she saw the yellow afghan rise she had to press her hands together to stop them from shaking.

Her mother opened her eyes. "Did we win?"

"Yes."

"Where is he?"

"Dad took him to the Whiskey."

Nora's mother looked up at the ceiling. Then she patted the couch. "Come here."

Nora perched on the edge of the cushion. She felt the strangeness of their solitude and realized she couldn't remember the last time they'd been alone together. Once upon a time her mother had taught her to knit, make a pie crust, and set a table. They'd spent hundreds of nights on this couch watching *The Cosby Show* and *Murder, She Wrote*. Then her mother got sick, and Nora became a teenager. They might have survived one of these, but against both they were lost.

"You'll have to walk down and get them," her mother said. "Give them an hour."

Nora wanted to crawl into bed and pull the covers over her head. "Jeremy can drive home."

"If you don't go, they'll stay until closing, and he won't be able to."

Nora knew she was right. Every Saturday Nora's parents used to go to The Oasis in Imlay. Nora's mother drank a little, her father drank a lot, and her mother always drove them back. After she got sick he started going to the Whiskey as often as he could, with whichever buddy he could pry from the filaments of home, and Nora's mother picked him up at closing time. Once Nora asked why she didn't let him drive himself. It was only one mile, through empty nighttime streets. Her mother said it was nice to be able to take care of him, despite everything. Meanwhile Nora had watched her brother party his way through high school and knew he would drink as many of the "man's drinks" Fred would pour him.

Nora's mother took her hand. "Those boys." A faint whistle came from deep inside her chest. "They're going to need taking care of."

Nora was crying, and she didn't know when she'd started. For three and a half years, while her mother fought for her life amid piles of laundry, Nora had been at Britta's, in the park, at the library—anywhere but here, with the prescription bottles and the smell of Bengay that for the rest of her life would be the smell of futile hope. Now her mother's skin was translucent, her eyes were as bright as emeralds, and Nora knew that she was done. That all the quiet battles had ended. Nora wanted to tell her no. She wanted to tell her to keep fighting. She wanted those three and a half years back so she could watch stupid television shows with her. But it didn't matter what she wanted, and it didn't matter what her mother wanted, because her mother's wedding ring was so loose on her finger it would slide off if she let it. So Nora said yes, and when she did a light bloomed beneath her mother's papery skin and made her beautiful again.

She died two days later.

At first Nora kept the promise she made that night. She did the laundry, cooked dinner, and made pulled pork for her father's Sunday football parties. When Jeremy got the job at the prison nine miles up the interstate she made him scrambled eggs for breakfast. She knew it was hard for him to watch the high school games from the stands, and her father missed his wife, so Nora said nothing when they went to the Whiskey three, four, even five nights a week. She drove them there and back even though she was too young to drive, and Sheriff Watterly, who'd played football with her father in high school, looked the other way. When she walked through the family room she ran her fingers along the yellow afghan, folded on the back of the couch.

But she was a long-legged child becoming beautiful, and as the blemishes of puberty faded she learned what it meant to have every man's eye follow her down the street. In her sophomore year the pulled pork gave way to pizza deliveries and grilled cheese sandwiches, and the laundry began to pile up in the hamper. By her junior year she was partying in the alfalfa fields that lined the Humboldt River, smoking pot in Britta's backyard, and making love to Mason up on Lightning Ridge, the sparse lights of Lovelock dusted below, while Jeremy and her father parked the truck diagonally in the driveway. When she walked through the family room she didn't look at the yellow afghan.

Still, she wasn't planning to leave. As poorly as she'd kept her promise, she did consider it a promise. Besides, if Lovelock was good enough for Britta and Mason and everyone else she knew, who was she to think it was grubby and small and limiting? She would marry Mason and they would raise their children here just as her parents had done, and she would be happy. But when the high school counselor told her she had the grades for a full scholarship to the University of Nevada, the inside of her chest fluttered as it had when she was ten and the camper lumbered into Idaho.

The day the acceptance letter came she drove to the Big Meadow cemetery, five acres of hard-packed sand wedged between the interstate and the railroad tracks a mile west of town. She walked past Wilsons, Finneys, and Menendezes until she reached the row of dead Wheatons, their markers like jagged teeth. Like many Lovelock families, the Wheatons protected their dead from the harsh land by paving their plot like a cheap backyard patio, and Nora sat cross-legged on the cement. She took the letter from her pocket and laid it in front of her mother's headstone.

"Do you remember when we went to Yellowstone?" she asked.

The marker looked back at her. BELOVED WIFE AND MOTHER, it said, but Nora remembered her mother standing before Old Faithful, the camera she'd bought for the trip pressed to her eye and her hair whipping like a flame in the breeze. Married at eighteen, a mother a nineteen, she'd been thrilled by the RV and all it promised. She'd wanted to see Florida.

Nora had wept for her mother many times by then. On birthdays; on Christmas; at her first high school dance, when her mother wasn't there to curl her hair and do her makeup. That day in the cemetery, for the first time, she wept not for the mother she'd lost but for the woman her mother had been. The mother she'd lost had asked Nora to live the life she'd led, in service to the people she had loved. Nora hoped the woman her mother had been would understand why she couldn't.

Now her father sat in the camper and talked about Jeremy's championship game as he always did. *He came through when his team needed him most.* It was how he remembered his son: the brave captain carrying his team on his back. Nora looked at the girl on the magazine cover, with her winged cheekbones and high, smooth brow. She'd been sixteen when her people threw her body in a pit with the carcasses of the animals they hunted. Thirteen thousand years later, she was their sole ambassador.

"He didn't win that game for his team. And he didn't win it for you." Nora's tongue tasted like the tears she'd shed at her mother's grave. Her father was looking at her with dull, confused hurt. He was ruined by grief, and the one thing that brought him any joy was remembering the warrior son he'd killed. He couldn't imagine why she would try to take that from him.

"He won it for Mom," Nora said. She took the magazine and left him there alone.

JAKE

Two days after Sal found the math teacher's body, Jake drove to the Prentiss place with a bag of clothes from the Lovelock Family Dollar store. As he drove past the cliff that overlooked the little copse of trees he sped up, and his truck lifted a plume of dust that hung in the air.

Jake had lived in Marzen all his life. He'd never been on a plane, never seen the ocean, and never eaten Chinese food, but he didn't care if he ever did those things. He loved his life in this small, hill-bound town where everyone knew his name. He loved working three twelve-hour shifts a week driving a haul truck at the mine and volunteering for the fire department. At thirty-five he still lived with his mother, Rosita, and he loved that, too. The only thing he didn't love was that he wasn't married yet. It wasn't that women didn't like him. He was good-looking in a sturdy way and he had a steady job, so he'd dated his share. But the only woman he'd ever loved was Grace Prentiss, the bartender at the Nickel, whose singing in the Baptist church pulled his soul right out of his body and who told him, the one time he asked her to dinner, that he was "sweet."

They'd been friends in elementary school. They shared a desk and at recess they played make-believe games that Grace invented and Jake didn't understand, but in which he obeyed her every command. Then they went to Lovelock for middle school, first Jake, then Grace the year after, and when Grace got there she didn't want to be Jake's friend anymore. At sixteen she moved in with a man who lived in the Indian Colony, a rough collection of trailers and crumbling houses on Lovelock's western edge. He was a big Paiute man, well into his twenties, and while Jake hadn't had the imagination for Grace's games in second grade, he'd had no trouble imagining this man undressing her, touching her small, round breasts, and straddling her with his broad thighs.

When she moved back to Marzen a few years after high school, Jake had hoped she was finally ready to settle down. Then he saw the men who hung around the Nickel waiting for her to close up. They were tight and edgy, with guarded eyes that slid sideways when you looked at them, and they took her down the hill to God knew where. Still, when she was behind the bar she treated Jake like an old friend, teasing him for liking imported beer but giving him a Stella on the house when he finished his EMT training, so three nights a week Jake sat on a barstool and nursed his hopes.

She never talked about the pregnancy. Even as she got bigger she didn't mention it, and none of the regulars mentioned it either, as though they'd all decided to pretend it didn't exist. But as Jake watched her press her hand to the small of her back his heart swelled with anguish. The father wasn't around; she was on her own. To think a man had made a baby with Grace Prentiss, then decided she wasn't worth his time. Jake raged about this into his beer, quietly, so no one would see.

After Sal was born the edgy men never returned, and Grace's brothers, Gideon and Ezra, started coming to the bar every Friday, keeping a baleful eye on anyone who flirted with their sister too much. That was when Jake finally asked her out. When she said no he was mortified, but afterward she treated him with the same easy familiarity, as if he hadn't offered her his heart, tender and open, in the palm of his hand. This only made him love her more.

She started bringing Sal to the bar when he was around six. He sat at a table in the corner, ate bar food for dinner, and read lurid graphic novels about angels and demons until nine, when he walked home by himself. He was quiet and well-behaved, and he watched Grace serve drinks with the deep, uncomplicated love boys that age have for their mothers. He had Grace's mouth, full lipped yet delicate. A beautiful boy, Jake thought, though he knew not everybody would agree.

One Saturday night in June Grace closed the bar at eleven, went home, and lay down on her couch. In the morning Jake heard the call on his scanner and went right over, getting there before Hank Fullman, the other EMT, arrived in the ambulance. Heart failure, everyone said, though Jake knew different. At her funeral Jenny White, a pimply girl with a wobbly voice, sang Grace's favorite hymn, "Abide with Me," and a hundred people mourned the unfairness of it all. As Jake helped her brothers and three other regulars from the Nickel carry her casket from the church he thought of all the times he'd imagined walking down that very aisle with her arm in his, and his head swam with misery and regret. He hadn't seen her death coming. He hadn't seen one single sign.

Now he rolled his truck onto the Prentiss property, parked by the rusted remains of a box spring, and waited to see if anyone appeared. When no one did he was relieved. The thought of meeting the Prentiss brothers without the sheriff and Mason Greer had rattled him more than he realized. He decided to leave the clothes on the front steps of the double-wide, then find Sal at the school bus stop on Monday and tell him they were from him.

As soon as he got out of the truck the yellow cur emerged, growling, from behind the wheelbarrow. Jake veered away, into the ring of trash, to approach the double-wide from the side. As he weaved his way through the debris it sharpened into forlorn particularity: a broken plastic dollhouse that must have been Grace's beside a walnut wall clock, a beautiful old thing, ruined now. A tufted ottoman, its springs poking through the fabric. A couch, upside down on the sand; a rusted sewing machine; a metal bread box; a pile of school textbooks soaked by years of rain and rotted by the sun.

Jake looked up at the farmhouse. Its sturdy siding spoke of a modest prosperity, once upon a time, but the last twenty years had been a different story, written in a landscape of garbage and poverty and not giving a damn. Imagine raising three children in a low-slung double-wide while an ancestral home slides into decay a hundred feet away. It made no sense to Jake, who was the fourth generation of Sanchezes to live in the tidy wooden house his great-grandfather had built on Second Street.

Beside the double-wide, just beyond the ring of trash, was a wooden shed that, unlike the rest of the outbuildings, looked new and well maintained. Curious, Jake opened the door, and the industrial smell of glue and varnish swam out to meet him. He looked around. The road was empty and the hills were quiet save for the low murmur of the wind. The dog watched him with thuggish malice, but it had stopped growling. Jake stepped inside.

It was a workshop. Dozens of tools covered metal shelves on the walls. Chunks of wood lay on the counters, not scrap lumber but pieces of old and broken furniture, oak and walnut and golden heart of pine. In the middle of the room were metal shapes—wheels, arcs, fans. Jake ran his hand along a piece of wrought iron from an old gate. It was soldered to part of an antique plow and attached to a wooden seat. Other, half-finished pieces of furniture made of shattered things filled the rest of the floor. Which of the Prentiss brothers had made these? he wondered. They didn't look utilitarian, let alone comfortable. He couldn't think of a single person who would want them.

Jake closed the door and continued toward the house. His mind was so busy with the surprise of the shed that he forgot about the dog until it lunged to within an inch of his leg. Jake jumped back, the bag of clothes bouncing against his thigh.

"Samson, down!"

The dog lay down, rested its head between its front paws, and rolled its eyes toward the boy in the doorway of the double-wide. Sal walked over and scratched its ears, sending its tail into a frenzied thwapping. He ran his hand around its collar, paused, then unhooked the chain. The dog leaped up and licked the boy's face.

"He's not really mean," Sal said. "Mostly he's bored."

The dog still looked mean, wagging tail or no, but it forgot about Jake and took off sniffing the ground. Jake held out the bag. "I brought some things I thought you could use."

Sal was wearing the jeans and the Broncos sweatshirt he'd worn when he came to the fire station two days before, and he looked, if anything, more tired. But when he opened the bag, his eyebrows jumped in surprise. "Thanks."

Jake fiddled with the zipper on his jacket. Since Grace died he'd put himself in Sal's way half a dozen times to ask how he was doing. Sal always said he was fine. Jake never believed him, but he hadn't pushed it. Now a rush of wind whipped through the canyon, Sal shivered, and Jake said, "Can we talk?"

"Gideon will be back soon."

"Just for a minute."

Sal sat on the cinder block steps that led to the double-wide's front door, making room for Jake beside him. Jake wondered what the inside of the double-wide looked like, and felt the same quiet rage he'd felt when he thought about Sal's absent father. How could two brothers fail to do right by their sister's son? At the funeral Gideon and Ezra had been gray and quiet, their grief so palpable that no one but the minister dared speak to them. Jake remembered a middle school scene: Gideon, skinny and fierce, beating the crap out of a much bigger boy, his fists lunging and biting with grown-up violence. Later Jake heard the whispers: don't mess with Gideon's sister, or that's what you'll get. Apparently that protective fervor hadn't transferred to Grace's son.

The dog came over and lay in the sand beside Sal. Jake eyed it nervously, but it ignored him. "Listen," he said. "About that guy you found. You can talk to me about it if you want."

Sal pulled a small ivory amulet that looked like a chess pawn from beneath his sweatshirt. Above them the sky was covered in a white scrim that bleached the sunlight to the color of bone. He rolled the amulet between his fingers and said nothing.

Jake waited nearly a minute, then put his hands on his thighs. He wasn't getting anywhere with Sal, so he might as well leave. But before he could get up the dog got to its feet and pointed its snout at the road. The rumble of an engine began in the middle distance, and with a crunch of gravel, a pickup sped over the rise and into the rutted driveway. Jake and Sal stood. Sal tucked the chess piece inside his sweatshirt and held the bag of clothes behind his back.

Gideon Prentiss got out of the truck. He wasn't a big man, but he was lean in a way that seemed predatory, and his eyes were a shade of gray so light they were almost white. Prentiss eyes, people called them. Neither Grace nor Ezra had them, but their father had, and his father before him, all the way back to the original outlaw. Or so it was said.

Gideon stared at Jake, then closed the door in a way that made Jake think of the NO TRESPASSING sign at the top of the driveway. Jake was a head taller and thirty pounds heavier, but neither fact gave him much comfort. He unzipped his jacket so Gideon could see the Marzen Volunteer Fire Department badge.

Gideon seemed unimpressed by this display of civic authority. "What do you want, Jake?" They'd gone to school together for years and seen each other dozens of times at the Nickel, but this was the first time Gideon had ever said Jake's name. It didn't sound friendly in his mouth.

"I was at the fire station when Sal reported the body," Jake said. "It's a tough thing for a kid, seeing something like that. I wanted to check on him."

Gideon didn't look much like Grace, but Jake caught an echo of her in the quick tilt of his head, down and to the right. "He's fine. Thanks for checking."

"It's no trouble. But the police want to talk to him again. They want you to contact them." He wondered how Gideon would manage that. Sheriff Watterly was probably right: this place was off the grid. Gideon might not even have a cell phone. But that wasn't Jake's problem. "I brought him some clothes, too," he said as he headed for his truck.

"He doesn't need clothes."

Gideon's sharp tone made Jake turn around. Gideon's weight was back on his heels, his chin raised. He didn't care enough to buy his nephew clothes that fit, but he sure as hell cared about being called out on it. "It's just a couple things from the Family Dollar," Jake said. "I was in there anyway, and they seemed like they would fit him."

Sal held the bag in front of him as though he expected Gideon to walk over and rip it away. Both men looked at Sal, at the jeans that were too short and the Broncos sweatshirt whose sleeves didn't reach his wrists.

"We don't need any handouts," Gideon said, but a muscle jumped in his cheek, and he didn't move to take the bag, or tell Sal to give it back.

Jake swung into the front seat of his truck and closed the door. "You take care, Sal," he said through the open window. Then he left them there, the man and the boy and the dog.

SAL

Before Sal moved to his uncles' place, he lived with his mother in a little blue house on Third Street in Marzen. It had two bedrooms, one small, the other smaller, and a front porch just wide enough for a rocking chair. In front the road was hard-packed sand, and in back the yard ran up against a hill. Sometimes rabbits came down the hill, and foxes. Sal's mother wanted to get chickens, but she worried about the foxes, so she never did.

When Sal asked the social worker if he could stay in the little blue house after his mother died, she told him children couldn't live without adults. He'd known that, of course, just as he'd known the house really belonged to Mr. Simpson, the retired army man who lived on the corner. He'd only asked because he needed her to know how badly he wished he could stay there, where he could smell his mother's soap and sit in her favorite chair. She hadn't seemed to understand him, though.

The social worker's name was Mrs. McDonald. She was a big woman with long blond hair, and her chin sat atop the flesh of her fat neck like a little knob. She meant well, but she was very busy. When she found out Sal had two uncles, relief made her wide bosom heave. "It's always best when there's family," she said. The day before the funeral she met Gideon and Ezra in the living room of the little blue house while Sal crouched by the heating vent in his bedroom and listened.

"Are you employed?" Mrs. McDonald's voice was high and tinny.

"Self-employed," Gideon said.

"What do you do?"

"Make furniture."

"How much do you earn in a year?"

"Fifteen thousand. Maybe twenty."

"And you live on—" She shuffled some papers. "Prentiss Ranch Road? Where is that?"

"Three miles south."

"Do you own the property?"

"Free and clear."

"What about you? Do you work?"

Ezra: "I'm looking."

Papers shuffled again. "Your sister named no guardian for Absalom in the event of her death. The family court will decide where he goes, but my recommendation will carry a lot of weight. Are you willing to take him?"

When Sal heard Gideon say, "We take care of our own," he rested his head on the oak floor in relief. He pictured Mrs. McDonald nodding, her fat neck swelling in and out like a bellows. She would be back in Lovelock before supper.

Sal was glad his uncles wanted him not because he wanted to live with them—he only ever saw them at his mother's bar, where they rarely spoke to him—but because he was afraid of where he'd go if they didn't. Since the day his mom didn't wake up, three ladies from the church had taken turns sleeping in her bed and serving him enormous helpings of casseroles he couldn't eat, but none of them had talked about where he'd go once the funeral was over. He was afraid it might be foster care. He knew a kid in foster care:

Billy Redmond. Billy's mother went to rehab when Billy was in second grade, and Billy went to live with a family in Imlay. When he came back he said the family's son took him to the garden shed every day after school and beat him with a bicycle inner tube. Six months later Billy's mom was back in rehab, Billy was back in foster care, and no one had seen him since.

Also, while Sal didn't know his uncles well, he did know the most important thing about them. Every Friday night they sat at the end of his mother's bar, watched her flirt with the regulars, and glared at anyone who seemed too friendly. When they left, Gideon in the lead and Ezra behind, relief rippled through the room. They never did anything but drink their whiskey and watch, but they had a tension in them, especially Gideon, that Sal imagined could explode into the sort of violence that gets a man a reputation. That was okay by him. From his corner table he could see they loved his mother with a fierce and capable protectiveness, and surely they would protect her son now that she was gone.

A week later the church ladies had him packed and ready. The last of them, Mrs. Amity, sat with him on the porch beside his school backpack, a secondhand suitcase, and a cardboard box. In the box were his graphic novels, his colored pencils, a sketchbook, a framed photograph of him and his mother, and a scrapbook of Sunday church programs with his mother's name as the soloist. When Mr. Brand, the bent old choir director, gave him the scrapbook Sal had felt the wooden pews of the Marzen Baptist Church against his back and smelled the perfume and sweat of the small congregation as his mother sang, her dark hair tumbling down the front of her red choir robe. "Nearer My God to Thee." "Amazing Grace." "Carry Me over Jordan." She wasn't religious. She just loved to sing. That was a secret they kept between the two of them.

It was early July, and hot. The sun made waves that rippled above the sandy road, and in the yard across the way the Finnegans' big boxer panted in the shade of their house. Gideon was due at two, and it was ten past. Mrs. Amity wiped her forehead. She was very young; too young to be married, Sal's mother had said, but sometimes things happened. She hadn't explained what those things were, but Mrs. Amity had a baby, so Sal could guess.

At two fifteen Gideon drove up in a pickup truck. Sal and Mrs. Amity stood, and she put her arm around Sal. "Here he comes, now," she said, almost to herself.

Gideon stopped at the bottom of the porch steps, his thumbs hooked in the pockets of his jeans, his white tee shirt bright in the sun. His dark hair was slicked back and scored with lines from a comb. His odd, light eyes tracked Mrs. Amity from the top of her blond head to her pink-painted toenails in their white patent leather sandals, and Sal felt her weight shift from one leg to the other.

"This all his stuff?" Gideon said.

Mrs. Amity rested her hand between Sal's shoulder blades, then took a step back. "He don't have much."

This wasn't true. There were many things that were Sal's. Things like the chipped blue bowl his mother used when she made chocolate chip cookies, the still life she'd painted in high school that hung in the living room, and the Bob the Builder bedspread that had embarrassed Sal with its childishness until she died and took his childhood with her. No, no, the church ladies said. Your uncles don't want that stuff cluttering up their place. We'll have a tag sale and put the money in a savings account for you. You'd much rather have the money. But Sal stood beside his box and his backpack and his suitcase and wanted all of it. Just thinking about everything he was leaving on the other side of the screen door made his eyes swim with tears.

Gideon picked up the box. Sal followed with his backpack and the battered Samsonite. As his uncle loaded the truck Sal turned to look at Mrs. Amity, who stood on the porch with her fingers plucking the skirt of her pink sundress. If you didn't know better, you'd think it was her porch and her little blue house, with her husband waiting inside and her baby sleeping in the smaller bedroom. She waved, and Sal didn't think she knew whether she was waving to him or to Gideon.

Sal had been to the Prentiss place just once, the summer before when his grandmother was dying, and he'd been careful not to remember what it had looked like then. Now, as Gideon's truck rounded the final curve and the crumbling farmhouse in its circle of trash came into view, his stomach dipped in a slow, rolling arc. *It's better than what Billy Redmond got,* he reminded himself.

Gideon glanced over at him. "It doesn't look like much. But it's where our people have been for a hundred and seventy years."

His words were steeped in an accusatory sort of pride. Sal's mother used to say her family was "off the grid," and Sal had thought she meant it literally: she and Sal lived in town and got their electricity from NV Energy, while her mother and brothers lived in the hills where there were no power lines. Now, looking at his uncle's lean, hard face, Sal began to suspect there was more to it than that.

Gideon parked the truck at the bottom of the driveway. A yellow dog came from behind an upended wheelbarrow, dragging a chain. Sal headed toward it.

"Don't," Gideon said. "That's Ezra's dog. Mean as hell."

Sal backed away. He knew a mean dog or two: Mr. Simpson's Doberman, for instance, would take your hand off if you reached over his fence and tried to pet it. This dog's eyes were sadder than the Doberman's, but they were just as mean.

As he followed Gideon to the double-wide, memories of his

visit the summer before pressed against the inside of Sal's skull. The smell of cigarettes and cat piss. The rattle of an old woman's cough. The dark closeness of the air, like the inside of a closet. He braced himself as he walked in, but while the blotched and sagging sofa was the same, and the stained carpet, the smell of cat piss was mostly gone, and he smelled disinfectant beneath the cigarettes. Ezra, sitting on the sofa, put down his beer and stood.

"Hey, nephew." He had the same wiry frame as Gideon, though he carried his with the tautness of a scavenger. Otherwise he looked like Sal's mother, with her wide smile, dark hair, and brown, thick-lashed eyes. He put out a hand, and Sal shook it. It was sweaty; the air in the double-wide was as hot as the inside of a slow cooker.

"Get his things from the truck," Gideon said.

"Yes sir, brother sir." Ezra gave a mocking salute and walked out. Gideon picked up Ezra's half-empty beer with his thumb and index finger and set it in the metal sink in the kitchen. He motioned down a narrow hallway.

"We've got you set up back here."

At the end of the hall was a small, dark bedroom that smelled, despite the recent cleaning, of mildew and cats. The only piece of furniture was a twin bed, and Sal startled when he saw it: the headboard was five feet tall and made of what looked like scrap metal and animal bones twisted together. Gideon saw his reaction. "I didn't have much time. If you don't like it, I can make a different one."

Sal didn't know what to say. He couldn't imagine why anyone would want to sleep in such a bed, or why Gideon would think he might like it. He set his backpack on the thin bedspread, which was covered with faded pictures of footballs, baseballs, soccer balls, and basketballs. A fluorescent bulb hung from a socket in the ceiling, and there was one narrow window above the bed. If he looked out, Sal knew he would see the field of garbage that circled the farmhouse and the barren hills beyond. A vise clutched his windpipe, making every breath hard and painful.

Ezra barged in with his suitcase. "Here you go, nephew." He set the suitcase on the floor and left to get the box. Gideon and Sal looked at the Samsonite, which seemed to fill the room.

"We'll get you a dresser," Gideon said. Sal hoped that didn't mean he would make it.

His uncles left him to unpack his things. It didn't take long. He stored the Samsonite under the bed, his clothes still inside. He put the picture of his mother and him on the windowsill and shoved the cardboard box into the corner. Then he sat on the bed. He tried not to look at the headboard. He tried not to think about what he would do out here, in the middle of nowhere, without his mother. He tried not to cry.

After a while he walked down the hall to find Ezra back on the sofa with his beer. Gideon was gone. "He's out working," Ezra said. "Making more of that crazy-ass furniture. How do you like your bed?"

"I like it fine."

"Bullshit," Ezra laughed. "It's fucked-up, am I right?"

Sal blanched at the profanity. "A little."

"I'd have nightmares sleeping in that thing," Ezra said. "But Gideon's got folks that like that shit. Folks in Vegas with no fucking taste. And it keeps him busy. Dude gets crazy when he ain't busy." He pointed his beer at a stuffed reclining chair covered in mottled plaid fabric. "Have a seat, nephew."

Sal sat. It was the chair where his grandmother had sat, her oxygen tank beside it with tubes running up her nose. Sal had never seen her before that visit, so his only memory of her was of a sack of brittle bones with her hair almost gone and her flat breasts sagging, staring at him with mean, sad eyes like the eyes of the dog outside. She'd died a week later. Sal and his mother hadn't gone to the funeral.

"I've got my own thing going, of course," Ezra said. "We got separate enterprises, Gideon and me. Separate clients. Separate money." He drank his beer, looking at Sal sideways. "We got some Cokes in the fridge."

Sal didn't want a Coke, but he got up. A six-pack of cans sat next to a half-empty six-pack of Budweiser on the top shelf of the refrigerator. On the shelf below was a bottle of ketchup, a jar of peanut butter, a loaf of Wonder Bread, and a package of bologna. He pulled out a Coke and returned to the chair. Ezra reached his arm along the back of the sofa, the beer dangling from his fingers. He smiled an easy smile, the sort that drew you in, like Sal's mother's. Sal took a sip of the soda. It was deliciously cold.

"Basically, I sell medicine," Ezra said. "Lots of people around here, they don't have doctors. They can't afford 'em, and they got no insurance. Even if they do got a doctor, a lot of them are no good. If you get a sore back they tell you to get physical therapy, when all you really need is something for the pain. And there's medicine for that. Percocet, OxyContin, Norco. All FDA approved, totally legit. But folks can't get it, or they can't get enough of it. It's a failure of the medical system, to be honest." He took another sip of his beer. "So I get it for them."

Sal ran a finger around the thin metal lip of the Coke can. OxyContin. That's what they were called, the pills that had appeared on the bathroom counter in the little blue house about eight months ago. He'd seen Ezra's hand sliding across the bar, changing the little bottles for cash when nobody but Sal was looking. "You got it for my mom."

Ezra raised his eyebrows. "That's right. She had that back pain, ever since she was pregnant with you. Made it hard for her to stand behind the bar. So you know what I'm talking about."

Sal's mother did say the pills made her back pain go away. But Sal hadn't liked what they did to her. It wasn't just that they sometimes made her sleep too late to make him breakfast. They made her eyes look empty in a way that scared him. Four months before she died Sal flushed them down the toilet. It was the only time she ever struck him, once, hard, across his cheek, and afterward they both stared at each other in horror, feeling the jagged edges of something broken that would never be repaired. That night, at the bar, she ran her finger under his bangs and said she was sorry. He asked how much longer she was going to take the pills, and she said he didn't understand what it was like to live with pain all the time. A little sleepiness was a small price to pay to be rid of it. Sal thought she was paying a steeper price than that, but his cheek burned with the memory of the slap, so he kept quiet.

"The weak link in my operation is distribution," Ezra said. "Lovelock's where my people are, and Gideon's an asshole about lending me his truck. That's where you come in, I'm thinking." He waited for Sal to say something, but Sal sat with his teeth clenched tight. "You're going to school in Lovelock this fall, right? I'm thinking you can take it with you, meet my people somewhere close." He winked. "I'll even cut you in for ten percent."

Condensation from the Coke can dripped onto Sal's leg, but Sal didn't feel it. Ezra leaned forward, his eyes warm with understanding. "You're scared. I get it. And it's not exactly legal, I'm not gonna lie. But it's not like it's meth or dope. It's medicine. It don't hurt nobody, it helps them. So we get to help folks out and make some cash at the same time. It's perfect." He patted Sal's knee. "So what do you say? You wanna be my partner?"

Sal had to swallow twice before he could get the words out. "No, thank you."

Ezra's grin didn't waver, but a flash of anger singed the air around him. He walked to the kitchen, set his empty Budweiser in the sink, and pulled another from the refrigerator. "I'll tell you what, nephew. Why don't you take some time to think it over. School don't start for a couple months." He leaned against the counter and popped the cap. "Keep in mind, though, everybody has to pull their weight around here. Or this arrangement might not work out."

The air was suddenly so dense Sal could barely breathe. Ezra raised the beer in a toast, as though they'd reached an agreement.

That night Sal lay under the thin bedspread on sheets that smelled of dust no washing could ever pry loose. Above him he felt, but could not see, the fevered scrawl of metal and bone his uncle had made. He tried to conjure Angelus for a story, but his mind was too agitated for angels and demons. He looked out the window at the stars, bright in the moonless sky, and remembered Mrs. Amity's palm pressed between his shoulders, warm and soft. He tried to think of his mother instead, but all he saw was her hand hanging from the couch, the fingers that held the syringe purple with quiet blood.

NORA

As Jake drove back down the dirt road from the Prentiss place, Nora and her father drove to Comforts Café in Lovelock. Comforts was at the corner of Main and Cornell, at Lovelock's only traffic light. That light had mattered once, back when Cornell was part of the old Route 40 and you could drive it all the way to Atlantic City, but now all people saw of Lovelock was the billboard near the interstate. LOCK YOUR LOVE IN LOVELOCK it said, next to a fading photo of a padlock on a chain, while the traffic light on the dead highway cycled patiently from red to green and back again. Nora waited until it gave her permission to park in front of the café.

Nora's friend Britta was behind the counter, short and curvy in her blue apron, making espressos, counting change, and serving croissants as if she had six hands. In high school she'd been class president, cocaptain of the cheer squad, and Homecoming Queen twice, even though Nora was prettier. Now she ran Lovelock's Memorial Day parade, the Frontier Days festival, and the Fourth of July barbecue from her coffee shop. The rest of Main Street looked like a dying strip mall, with faded FOR RENT signs in every third window, but in Comforts a group of mothers and toddlers sat at a bistro table, five old men ate pastries in the corner, and there was a line at the register. To Nora it seemed like a coffee shop in a town that mattered, like Reno or Portland.

Britta wasted no time once Nora and her father sat at the counter. "The math teacher! Oh, my God!" Her blue eyes were wide. Comforts was the epicenter of Lovelock gossip, and Nora was sure Britta's customers had talked about nothing else for the past two days.

"What math teacher?" Nora's father asked. Nora hadn't told him.

"The middle school math teacher," Britta said. "Somebody murdered him. He was set *on fire*." Her excitement dimmed, replaced by confusion and a hint of fear.

The front door chimed, and Mason walked in with Lily and their three children. Alex, the oldest, was wearing a baseball uniform smudged with dirt. He ran to the ice cream counter in the back, where Britta's daughter Cindy waited in an apron that matched her mother's. The two girls and Lily followed, and as Lily lifted the youngest girl to see inside the case she looked over at Nora.

Lily and Nora usually kept a cool distance, but today the memory of their high school sleepovers made Nora wave at her. Lily furrowed her pale brows. She might not wear her thin hair in braids anymore, but she was still the shy girl who'd sighed with envy when Nora told her Mason had kissed her behind the Safeway during sophomore year. Mason had finally noticed Lily after Nora left for college, but when Nora came home he'd dropped Lily like the consolation prize she'd always known she was. That he'd gone back to her three years later couldn't erase that. She didn't wave back.

Mason came to the counter, and Nora allowed herself an appreciative glance at his lean body in jeans and a gray sweatshirt. She might not want to be married to him anymore, but she'd never tire of looking at him. His dark blond hair had receded from his temples in a way that made him look like Matthew McConaughey, and he still had that lithe way of moving, like a panther, that had made center field his kingdom. He greeted her with a nod. Eleven years, one wife, and three children later they were comfortable with each other without being overly familiar, as old ex-lovers should be. Nora was glad of it. It was a small town, after all.

"I'm sorry about your math teacher," he said. "How's everybody doing over there?"

Nora wanted to ask him if they'd found out who the stranger at Adam's house was—she'd reported it the day before—but she knew better than to do that in the midst of Comforts' gossip-ready ears, so she said, "We're doing okay, thanks."

That was an understatement. The school had handled Adam's death with a bureaucratic efficiency Nora found chilling. The district posted the job vacancy the day after he died, while Dee Pratzer taught his classes with an air of martyrdom. After the police searched his desk—finding nothing important, Mary told Nora with a deprecating little shrug—someone put his personal items in a box, wrote MERKEL on it in black Sharpie, and stuck it in the staff room next to the coffee machine.

"Do you have any idea who did it?" Nora's father asked.

"Not yet." Mason gave Nora a glance that acknowledged her tip and told her they hadn't figured out who the man was. "We do have a witness, though. Sort of."

"Somebody saw it?" Britta asked.

"Not the death. But a Marzen kid found the body."

"Which kid?" Nora asked.

"Sal Prentiss," Mason said.

Nora let out a breath. She pictured the quiet sixth grade boy who sat in the back of her social studies class. How horrible it must have been for him, finding his teacher dead like that. And what a terrible coincidence it was that of all the places Adam could have been killed, in Lovelock or in Marzen, he'd been killed where his favorite student would find him.

On Monday Nora stood before her second period class, pretending to choose a student to change her bulletin board display during recess. Sixth graders still thought things like this were privileges, so she awarded them with a certain moral discretion. That little shit Kip Masters, for example, never got to change the board. Today, though, she had a different agenda in mind.

"Sal Prentiss," she said.

The other students sighed in collective disappointment. At the table where he sat with Sylvana Eggers, Ronnie Triplett, and the boy they called Seventeen, Sal watched her from beneath his unruly dark bangs, and instead of pleasure Nora saw wariness. When the bell rang he slipped out like a shadow ahead of his classmates, and she wondered if he would come.

But five minutes after recess started he stood in front of her desk in his basketball shorts and a faded blue hoodie. Nora crossed her arms and looked at him closely for the first time all year. She rarely looked closely at any of her students. Her mother's empathy had made her a great teacher, but Nora had hated how her moods rose and fell with the joys and tragedies of everyone around her, so when she became a teacher herself she'd been careful to keep her students at a safe emotional distance.

Sal Prentiss, though, pricked at that reserve. It wasn't just that he was thin, or that his hoodie was too small, or that his skin was sallow with fatigue. There were other children in Nora's classes who were underfed, poorly clothed, and tired. It was the look in his eyes: a brittle, secretive look that no sixth grader should have. She found she didn't know what to say to him. She knew what she wanted to know; she wanted to know how close he'd been to Adam, and whether he knew why Adam had gone to Marzen the night he died. She wanted to know what it had been like to find him, burned so badly the police hadn't been sure who he was. She couldn't ask this fragile boy those things, of course; not straightaway. But by now the whole school knew Sal had found their math teacher's charred body, so there was an opening, if she could find the delicacy to navigate it.

"How are you doing?" she asked. "I know last week must have been hard for you."

The knuckles on the hand gripping his backpack strap flared with white. "I'm fine."

"Did you talk to Mrs. Linney?" Mrs. Linney, the school's head counselor, had offered to talk to the students about Adam's death, but most of them seemed energized rather than traumatized by the brutal murder just offstage, and awestruck by Phil Burns and Smitty McGinnis in their police uniforms. The two deputies were in the conference room right now, interviewing staff members one at a time. Nora's own interview had been that morning, and she'd told them, again, about the man she'd seen at Adam's house. She understood from Phil's sour look that they still had no idea who he was.

"No," Sal said.

Nora wasn't surprised. Marzen kids weren't the type to ask for help, especially from someone who lived in Lovelock. "You were in Mr. Merkel's chess club, weren't you?"

She'd thought this was a simple question, but Sal's face went pale. She softened her tone. "Mr. Merkel was my friend. I'm very sad he died. Maybe you could have your mother call me, and we could talk about—"

"My mom's dead."

He watched her keenly as she groped for what to say. She remembered after her own mother died, all the choruses of *she was such a fighter* and *at least she's at peace now*. She'd wanted to slap every mouth as hard as she could. "My mother's dead, too," she said, finally. "She died when I wasn't much older than you."

The hand gripping the backpack relaxed a little. That was interesting. The death of his mother was safer ground than the death of his math teacher. Nora pressed her advantage. "What about your dad?"

"I never had one."

"Who takes care of you?"

"My uncle."

"In Marzen?"

"Yes."

"Mr. Merkel drove you home sometimes, right?"

Again she'd pushed too hard. Sal looked down, knuckles tight. Then he said, "Excuse me, Ms. Wheaton. Aren't we going to do the bulletin board?" There was an edge to his voice that belied his hunched and diffident posture. Nora abandoned the interrogation for now and handed him a staple remover.

"First we need to take down the California Trail."

Together they pulled off the tired posters of covered wagons in the Big Meadow and the maps of pioneer migration routes. When they were done the pink bulletin board looked like the skin of a hairless beast stung to death by bees. Nora heard the other students on the playground, and wondered who Sal ate lunch with, now that Adam was gone. She couldn't remember seeing him talk to any of his classmates, not even Sylvana, Ronnie, or Seventeen. He was more of a watcher than a talker.

She pointed to the materials for the next unit. This one, on the ancient people of the Great Basin, was the only one she liked. "You get to decide where they go."

Sal spread the posters out on a table, handling them with unusual care. He handed her a poster of Paleolithic stone tools and pointed to the top corner. She followed his directions: left, right, lower, higher. They filled the board in near silence, Sal handing and directing, the two of them hammering staples into the ragged corners of the posters. When they were done they stood back and looked at their work: a montage of illustrations and charts surrounding a map swooped with colored arrows running from Siberia through the vanished land of Beringia down to North and South America. Across the top were the red letters Nora had cut out of construction paper and laminated when the job was new: THE FIRST PEOPLE.

"Who were they?" Sal asked.

"They were from Asia originally. But they came here fifteen thousand years ago, maybe more."

"What happened to them?"

"They're still here." She smiled. "The DNA from those people is in the genes of the Paiutes, and all the other indigenous people in the Americas."

He turned to her with his sad, dark eyes. "No. They're gone."

Nora crossed her arms, reassessing him. She knew what he meant. The small tribe of people who had forged their way past the glaciers and down the Pacific coast might have millions of living descendants, but they were gone in every sense that mattered. Their traditions, their names, their language, their songs and stories, all had disappeared from the earth, erased by migration and dispersal and a thousand generations that had left them beyond the reach of even the most robust of oral histories. One of the posters on the board showed a group of brown-skinned people walking through marshy grass, carrying spears, woven baskets, and babies on backs. It was accurate enough as a general representation of a vanished way of life, but every face wore the same vacant expression and every eye was on the same distant horizon. As though they wouldn't be talking, laughing, arguing, and flirting as they walked. It was an empty portrayal, rendered hollow by time. That was what time did. Nora hadn't expected Sal to know that.

She straightened the pile of Big Meadow posters on her desk.

The bulletin board was done, recess was almost over, and she still hadn't gotten him to talk about Adam.

"I was thinking." She felt the awkwardness of what she was about to suggest but forged ahead anyway. "I like to play chess, too. Maybe you and I could play at lunch sometime."

Sal looked back at the board. He reached for something small and white that hung around his neck on a string. "No, thank you. I don't really like chess."

"You don't?"

"No. I just liked Mr. Merkel."

Nora thought of their heads bent over the chessboard week after week. She'd suggested that Adam start an afterschool club because he wanted to get to know his students better. He did his best teaching one-on-one, he'd said, and looking at this boy's quiet grief Nora saw he'd been right. She wondered what they'd talked about during all those lunches and chess club meetings and realized Sal might have known Adam better than anyone else in Lovelock. Including her.

She followed Sal's gaze to the poster of the tribe walking through the grass. He might not like chess, but he was interested in these vanished people. "My dad used to take me to look for spearpoints the First People made. They're hard to find, but we did find one. Would you like to see it?"

He turned to her. Interested, but assessing. "Okay."

"Do you think your uncle would mind if you came home a little late one day?"

"No."

"We'll do it tomorrow, then."

After the final bell Nora went to the staff room where the box of Adam's things sat next to the coffeemaker. She waited fifteen minutes for the school to empty. Then she opened the box.

Mary was right; there wasn't anything of significance. Three stacks of papers in black binder clips, homework sheets for classes he would never teach. A collection of identical Bic pens and the black plastic cup that had held them. A thick, white textbook titled *Number Theory*. The ivory chess piece lay on top of the textbook. Nora picked it up: it was a rook, and the crenellations around the top were worn almost smooth. The chess set itself was at the bottom of the box. It was a clever thing: the squares were made of light and dark wood, and the board was hinged in the middle so it closed to make a case. Nora opened its brass clasp to find the pieces, all but the ivory rook, arrayed in green felt slots. It looked handmade, and antique.

The only other thing in the box was a manila envelope looped shut with string. When Nora opened it two photographs slid into her hand. In one, Adam stood in front of a Christmas tree beside a dark-haired woman who held a little boy of about two. All three were smiling, and Adam looked so happy that Nora hardly recognized the gray-faced man who had taught math three doors down. The woman had a sturdy figure and an open, freckled face, and although she looked much younger than Adam they both were wearing wedding rings. The second photo was a school portrait of the boy, older now, in a blue collared shirt and black-framed glasses. Nora turned it over. In a feminine hand was written, "Benjamin, fourth grade."

Both photographs were wrinkled and bent, as though they'd been carried loose for some time. Nora fingered their ragged edges. They'd been precious. Too precious to be tucked away in an album; Adam had needed to have them close. But he hadn't wanted them framed on his desk.

Before Jeremy died, there were pictures of him all over the

house, in football, baseball, and basketball uniforms; in formal wear with various pretty girls; his senior portrait beside Nora's in the hallway. After Nora's father came home from the hospital, they all disappeared. He hadn't done that when her mother died, but Nora knew why it was different this time. Her father could look at pictures of his dead wife, but he couldn't look his dead son in the eye. And Nora was glad, because she couldn't look at Jeremy, either.

She slid the photographs back into the envelope. She wondered what Adam regretted that made it so hard to look at this woman and child. She wondered whether it would have helped him to know he wasn't the only one who'd condemned himself to this particular purgatory, nor was he the only one who couldn't look at pictures of people he loved unless no one was watching.

SAL

Ezra didn't mention his medicine business again after Sal's first day at the Prentiss ranch, and by summer's end Sal hoped he'd changed his mind. But the first Thursday after school started Ezra came to Sal's bedroom and explained how it would work. Every Friday, Sal was to sneak out of school during lunch, walk two blocks to the park behind the Lovelock courthouse, and sit on the concrete bench next to the pagoda for thirty minutes. Ezra's people would meet him there, and Sal would give them what they needed.

The cramped darkness of Sal's bedroom held no room for resistance, so Sal sat with his knees drawn up as Ezra zipped open his backpack and stuffed several small brown bags inside. Then he patted Sal on the shoulder. "Don't worry, nephew. It'll be fine." His smile was the same one Sal's mother used to give Sal when he was worried, but like his mother's smile it didn't keep Sal from worrying. He worried about how he would sneak out of school. He worried about people asking him what he was doing in the park in the middle of the day. He worried about what Ezra's "people" would be like. The next morning he rode the bus with all those worries leaden in his chest, and he was sure everyone could tell he had a terrible secret in his backpack.

Ezra was right, though: it was fine. There was an opening in the playground fence behind the Dumpsters that was just wide enough for Sal. Nobody noticed him on the bench, and eventually he would realize he looked enough like the Paiute and Latino boys who lived in the Indian Colony to be invisible. He would even think of an excuse for missing lunch with Mr. Merkel on Fridays: tutoring with Mrs. Linney, the school counselor. None of it would be hard, and that, it turned out, would be the worst thing about it.

But that first day, Sal sat on the bench with the iron taste of fear in his mouth. The concrete of the bench was hot on the backs of his legs. Across the park, in a small playground, two mothers sat in the shade of a cottonwood tree while their toddlers crouched beneath a slide. Beside him was the small pagoda and the Lovers Locks, a circle of green posts joined by chains that sagged with hundreds of cheap metal padlocks. LOCK YOUR LOVE IN LOVELOCK said the faded sign on the interstate, and on every lock was a love story. KP + JS 1974. MARY AND MITCH 4EVER! JOHNNY AND APRIL 25 YRS. All were as hot as the bench in the late summer sun.

Sal didn't have to wait long for Ezra's people. Within five minutes a balding man in a shirt and tie came from the courthouse. Then a young woman pushing a little boy in a stroller stopped on her way to the playground, and a heavyset woman parked her Honda across the street. The courthouse man crossed his legs, casual. The young mother sat stiffly, the stroller facing away from her. The Honda woman's stomach hung between her spread legs like a sack of flour. Each time Sal slipped a shaking hand into his backpack, pulled out a paper bag, and took their folded bills into his palm, just as Ezra had made him practice the night before.

The fourth buyer was an old man, taking slow steps with a cane, then sitting on the bench with a sigh. He was the only one to look at Sal as one person looks at another, and the only one to speak to him.

"Ezra said he'd be sending his nephew, but I didn't expect such a young fella."

Sal's nerves screwed into a knot. Ezra hadn't said anything about talking to the buyers. "I'm eleven," he said, carefully.

"Well, eleven's old enough, I suppose. I was working in my daddy's auto shop when I was younger than that." The old man had a kind face, solid boned and fleshy, and square hands callused from sixty years of turning wrenches and ratchets. He pulled out a thin leather wallet, but he didn't open it. The other buyers had been in a hurry, but he wasn't. He tapped his right knee with the wallet.

"Football. I was a varsity starter all four years. Defensive line." Memories glowed around him like fireflies. "I was forty pounds heavier then. Nobody could get past me."

A wispy blond girl in a Ramones tee shirt walked across the grass. She stopped thirty feet away, picking at her elbow.

"When you're young," the old linebacker said, "you don't feel pain. When you're old, your body remembers it all." He looked at his knee with fondness and pity, as though it were a small, injured animal that had collapsed on his doorstep. "My doctor is young. He still thinks ibuprofen can fix everything."

Sal wanted him to hurry because the blond girl was waiting and she was the last one, but the old man kept talking. "I wouldn't trade those four years for a good knee in my old age, though. And your uncle's a godsend. Before I met him I could hardly walk to my mailbox. Now I take three of these a day, and I get around fine."

At last he opened his wallet and counted two hundred dollars in crisp twenty-dollar bills into Sal's hand. Sal slid a brown bag across the bench, and the old linebacker put it in his pocket. "See you next week, son," he said as he struggled to his feet. Once he was gone the blond girl glided over, her thin rubber flip-flops barely skimming the grass. She didn't say a word as she handed Sal a wad of crumpled bills and took her medicine, and she left as quietly as she'd come.

Ezra had given Sal the barest descriptions of the buyers—a young guy, a mom, a fat lady, an old guy, and a hippie chick. Sal had pictured sleepy, colorless people, like his mom when she took her pills. Or desperate people, with needy, grasping fingers. But they weren't like that at all. They seemed ordinary. Normal. Right now the young mother was pushing her boy in a baby swing in the playground. She didn't look like she would be too tired to tuck him into bed later, or forget to put the cheese mix in his mac and cheese at dinnertime. The man from the courthouse had had a lively step as he headed back to work, and the old linebacker's eyes had sparkled as he talked about his football days. As Sal watched the blond girl walk away his muscles unwound a little.

It was as easy to slip back into school as it had been to slip out, and no one noticed he had been gone.

That night Ezra came to Sal's room to collect the money. He wore a camping headlamp because Gideon didn't let them use electricity after nine o'clock, and by its fierce, small light he counted a thousand dollars on Sal's faded bedspread. When he was done he sat on Sal's bed with his legs crossed like a boy at a sleepover. The thick pile of bills gave him a nervous energy that made him talkative.

He'd gotten started after his mother died, he said. She'd been on OxyContin because the cancer went to her bones, and when Ezra cleaned out the medicine cabinet he found twenty pills left over. He'd asked his weed guy if he could trade them for pot, and his weed guy said sure. Gideon hadn't bothered to tell the doctor their mom had died—in her chair, so quietly it took her sons two hours to notice—so when Ezra called for a refill they gave it to him. For three months he traded pills for pot until he found out his weed guy was selling the pills for ten dollars each.

"Ten dollars for one pill!" he said. "And he was trading me two dimes for ten!" That was when he decided to go into business for himself. He had to promise his weed guy he'd stay out of the Colony, but Ezra was sure there were people who would never do business with a six-foot Paiute with arms roped in tattoos, but would happily deal with a scrawny white guy who would meet them somewhere safe. He was right—it only took a whisper at the Whiskey, and his ancient Android started buzzing.

Then, two months later, catastrophe struck: the doctor said he wouldn't order any more refills unless Ezra's dead mother came in to be seen. Ezra figured his gig was over, but for once he caught a break—his weed guy introduced him to a guy in Reno who would front Ezra as much Oxy as he could handle. That meant he gave Ezra the pills and let him pay for them after he sold them, which was a big deal for someone getting started in the business who didn't have a lot of capital to invest. The Reno guy took a steep cut for fronting, though, so Ezra wanted to make enough to buy the drugs outright. With Sal's help he could do that, and then he'd be rolling in bank.

"Enough to get out of this shithole and live my own life," he said, "without Gideon telling me what to do all the fucking time." Gideon, he added, could never find out about any of this. He was a goddamned Puritan like their daddy, both of them an embarrassment to a proud legacy of con men, cattle rustlers, and bootleggers.

"Prentisses are outlaws," Ezra said. "Always have been."

After he finished counting and boasting and plotting, he peeled a bedraggled twenty from the stack, handed it to Sal, and said, "Good work, partner." Then he left, the light from his headlamp bobbing down the hall.

Sal sat for a long time with the soiled twenty-dollar bill in his hands. Twenty dollars wasn't close to the 10 percent Ezra had promised him, and he felt as dirty as the bill for minding this. Ezra's customers might be regular people, and the medicine didn't seem to be hurting them, but Ezra's story about how he'd gotten started made it clear how illegal his business was. Taking any money at all made Sal feel like a criminal instead of a kid forced to sell drugs to stay out of foster care. But if he was going to get paid anyway, a silky voice in his head whispered, he should at least get his fair share. As Sal turned the bill over in his hands his fingertips tingled with equal parts anger and shame. Finally he crept to the cardboard box in the corner, pulled out the scrapbook of church programs, and pressed the bill between the pages. Then he crawled into bed, turned toward the window, and pulled Angelus into the valley for a story.

But when the archangel came, he wasn't alone. To Sal's surprise another archangel sailed into the valley behind him. This was Angelus's brother, Sal decided in a burst of inspiration as they circled each other beside the barn. Angelus's brother and sworn enemy. In fact, it was Catellus who had released the demons upon the earth, and now he was their general. Angelus had sworn to kill him for this cosmic betrayal, but Catellus, golden eyed and black winged, was Angelus's match on the battlefield. Outside Sal's window Catellus's sword rang against Angelus's scythe until they retreated in a draw, snarling threats at one another.

Sal lay back on his pillow, exhilarated by this new twist on his old story. In the weeks to come the brothers would skirmish again and again, in the hills, on the bus, and even beside the Lovers Locks, spilling their red-black blood while children played unaware and Sal waited for three women and two men to buy little white pills in brown paper bags.

JAKE

The night before Grace Prentiss died the Nickel was quiet. By ten thirty it was just Jake and, in the far corner, Bill Johnson and Medic Gonzalez arguing about the best place to hunt coyotes. Grace was wiping the bar, and she said, "Last call, Jake."

Jake spent three nights a week at the Nickel, but he wasn't a big drinker. Two beers was his usual. He had half a beer left, so he said, "I'm good."

"Your momma waiting up for you?" Grace arched one slim, dark brow.

Jake flushed. His mother was, in fact, waiting up for him. Grace laughed, then loosened the screws. "Having a mother who waits up for you is a good thing."

Jake turned his glass on the bar, smudging the ring of condensation it had made. He knew everyone in Marzen. He knew who could be counted on and who would disappear when you needed help. He knew most everyone's secrets, and he knew who had secrets he'd never know. But he knew nothing about Grace's mother. "Is your mom still around?"

"She died last year." Grace gave the spigots a casual wipe. "But she was not the waiting-up type."

"Believe me, it's not as great as you think."

She frowned at the spigots. "Yes. It is. I'm going to wait up for

Sal every night, even when he's too old to have a mother who waits up for him." Then she winked at Jake and walked to the other end of the bar. "Bill! Medic! Last call!"

The next morning Jake was in her small house for the first and last time, his hand on her cool skin, feeling for the pulse that was gone. Sal hovered at the edge of his vision, and Jake's first thought amid his grief was that she hadn't waited up for him. She'd fallen asleep before he could go anywhere.

Now, nine months after that bright-hot morning, Jake couldn't stop thinking about Sal, huddled and afraid in the fire station the day he found the math teacher's body. Nor could he forget the feel of the boy's shoulder, brittle as a bird's, on the front porch of the little blue house, the day Grace didn't wake up.

Two Pershing County sheriff's deputies had been in Marzen all weekend, questioning everyone they could find. They wanted to know if anyone knew the Lovelock math teacher, which no one did, not even the parents of the middle schoolers. They wanted to know if anyone had seen Adam Merkel, or his car, the night he died. No one had seen anything the night he died, but a number of people had seen a brown Corolla, with Sal Prentiss in it, driving through town on its way to the Prentiss place after school. Once or twice, some said. A couple of times a week, said others. Every day, said Sully, who ran the general store. The body had been found up by the Prentiss place, more than one person pointed out. Maybe the police should talk to the Prentisses.

Jake heard all this talk about brown Corollas and Prentisses and Sal, and it worried him the same way Sal's missing backpack worried him. So late Tuesday afternoon, when his shift at the fire station ended, he drove up to the little grove of trees. He wanted to see the scene for himself, without the police.

It was empty, of course. The body, the vodka bottle, the briefcase, and the jump rope were gone. All that remained were a tattered piece of yellow caution tape tied to a tree and a scorched stain on the earth. The wind muttered as it wound between the hills, but here in the lee of the bluff the air was still. The branches of the acacias reached inward, and even amid the echoes of violent death Jake felt again that sense of shelter he'd felt when he first saw the grove from the top of the hill.

He scanned the ground, finding nothing. He didn't know what he was looking for, and the search made him feel foolish. As if he, Jake Sanchez, volunteer firefighter, could find something the police had missed. He squatted next to the pile of ash in the firepit and poked it idly with a stick. He caught a quick glint of metal, and sifted the ashes with his fingers until he turned up a hypodermic needle. The syringe was gone; melted, he assumed. He wrapped the needle carefully in an acacia leaf and put it in his jacket pocket. He didn't feel foolish anymore.

He took his time searching the rest of the grove, but found nothing else. When the sun fell behind the cliff and the grove sank into premature dusk he turned to go, but then he saw the narrow, nearly indistinct path that wound away from the campsite, across the drain, to the base of the bluff. Jake had assumed the math teacher's killer had come from the fire road, as he had, but there was another way.

Jake checked his watch: he still had an hour before his mother expected him for dinner. He followed the path, his boots crunching in the crusty sand. At the base of the bluff the path veered left. A hundred feet farther along, the bluff softened into a steep hill and the path turned up in a series of switchbacks. Jake climbed, breathing heavily. Fire department volunteers were supposed to keep themselves fit, but none bothered, and it had been years since Jake's heart rate topped 130. Twice he lost the trace among the boulders, but both times he found it again: fine-packed sand marked by just-discernable footprints.

He was halfway up when he heard a car coming from Marzen. He looked down to see a red Civic passing his truck with the care of someone driving a two-wheel drive train on a road meant for four-wheel drive. It was heading for the Prentiss place, which was interesting. Gideon and Ezra weren't the type to welcome visitors.

At the top of the hill Jake stopped to catch his breath. Ahead of him the trail sloped down again, and after thirty yards it passed a small graveyard surrounded by a low iron fence.

Jake approached the graveyard slowly, as though it were a mirage that might vanish. It was about forty feet square, on the last bit of level ground before the hill dropped more steeply. There were twelve headstones in it, and all bore the name Prentiss. The newest was dated a year ago: Grace's mother, presumably, who didn't wait up. Grace herself wasn't here; Jake had watched her casket sink into the ground in the cemetery behind the Marzen Baptist Church. But all her people were.

The wind blew hard and fast across the exposed hilltop, flattening the thick yellow grasses that lay like a pelt on the graves. It was a desolate spot, even for the Prentisses, and Jake wondered why they buried their dead so far from where they lived. Then he saw the valley four hundred feet below. At the end of the trail that led down from the graveyard was the old farmhouse, the double-wide, and the ring of scattered garbage. Also the red Civic, parked behind Gideon's truck.

Jake ran his hand across his face, the import of what he was seeing dawning. The Prentiss place was two miles from the copse of trees if you followed the winding fire road, but it was only half a mile if you followed the footpath that led over the bluff. It was a shortcut, and it would explain how Sal could have found the body on his way to the bus. Except the boy hadn't said that. He'd told the sheriff he'd been on the fire road. That he'd seen the car and the turkey vultures and gone to investigate.

Maybe that was true. Maybe Sal didn't know about the footpath over the bluff. But Jake didn't think so. He didn't think Sal had been on his way to school that morning, either. He couldn't explain it, but something about the needle in the ashes, combined with the way Sal's mother died, deepened the worry he'd nursed since Sal showed up at the fire station without his backpack. He knew he should tell the sheriff's office about the needle, and the path that led from the murder scene to the Prentiss place. But before he did, he was going to talk to Grace Prentiss's son again.

SAL

Sal really didn't like chess very much. He wasn't very good at it, either. He only signed up for the chess club on impulse, moved by the same complicated knot of pity, admiration, and gratitude that drew him to Mr. Merkel's classroom for lunch every day.

In late September the school had Club Day, for students to join the groups that met after school. Sal wouldn't have gone, except the school knew nobody would go if given a choice, so they held it during second period. Ms. Wheaton, Sal's social studies teacher, herded them to the gym, where there were a dozen card tables staffed by students with sign-up sheets for the yearbook, the 4-H Club, the robotics club, even a knitting circle. Sal and the other Marzen kids hung out by the door. None of this mattered to them. They couldn't stay after school; they had to catch the bus.

Then Sal saw Mr. Merkel at a table with a chessboard, the pieces facing off across squares the colors of caramel and honey. He was the only teacher out there, and Sal saw him looking at the other teachers chatting in the bleachers and knew he was thinking he'd made a mistake. That he was making a fool of himself. So Sal signed up for the chess club. He was the only one who did.

The next day he told Mr. Merkel he couldn't actually come to the chess club because he had to take the bus to Marzen. Mr. Merkel told him not to worry; he would drive him home. So every Thursday after school Mr. Merkel taught Sal chess, and Sal didn't like it, and he wasn't very good at it.

He did like the pieces, though. The haughty queen, trailing destruction in her wake. Bishops, elegant and thin, whispering in the ears of their sovereigns. Clever knights lunging with sideways surprise, and pawns, those brave little soldiers, charging into strategic death. Sal had little patience for the logic and forethought the game required, but he never tired of watching the pieces in their martial dance, every game a new story of sacrifice, bravery, hard-won victory, and bitter defeat. Sometimes the chessboard swam with blood so vividly in Sal's mind that he touched the polished squares to make sure they weren't sticky with it.

One day, after Mr. Merkel had captured Sal's king in short order, he said, "You aren't paying attention. I telegraphed that play four moves ago."

But Sal had been paying attention. He'd watched the story unfold: the white knight's cutting attack on Sal's bishop that opened the field to Mr. Merkel's queen, who killed Sal's king from an imperious distance with a nod of her ivory head. Sal's bishop fell beseeching his god for mercy while three pawns watched helplessly, unable to repel the rearguard assault. Sal hadn't seen Mr. Merkel's foreshadowing, but the story itself had been a grand drama, tragic and beautiful.

"If you could be any chess piece, what would you be?" Sal asked. He'd been thinking about this instead of defending his king, and he'd decided he would be a pawn. Pawns were insignificant compared to the mighty knights and bishops, and they fell in brutal, unmourned numbers, but they were also the ones for whom the best stories were possible. They could kill anyone if they got close enough, including the king himself, and if they persevered, and took their quiet chances, they could even become queens, the most powerful players of all.

"The rook," Mr. Merkel said.

Sal had seen the white rook that sat on Mr. Merkel's desk. It was the rook from this chess set, and Mr. Merkel always chose white when they played. "How come?"

Mr. Merkel picked it up and ran his thumb across the crenellations. "It's the protector. The one who keeps everyone safe."

His face was hollow with regret, and the crenellations on the rook were worn, as though he had rubbed them many times. Sal remembered the way his mother's arms would wrap around his ribs and how her soft embrace had made him feel safe, even though, as it turned out, he hadn't been safe at all. "Do you have any kids, Mr. Merkel?" he asked.

Mr. Merkel sat back in surprise. "I had a son. Benjamin. He died."

Sal nodded. "I'm sorry." This was the best thing to say, he knew.

"Thank you." Mr. Merkel took off his glasses and rubbed his eyes. When he put the glasses back on, his eyes were red-rimmed but dry. "Now, let me show you how you could have stopped my attack."

He replaced the dead pieces on the board, explaining how one pawn moved into the queen's line of fire would have forced the knight to take out the pawn instead of the bishop and buy Sal's king time to escape. Sal listened, playing the new story in his head: the bishop spared, the pawn slaughtered in its stead, the king retreating to craven safety. The bishop saluted the fallen infantryman, who died knowing the gratitude of his better. Sal wondered if Mr. Merkel had taught Benjamin to play chess. He decided he had.

As Mr. Merkel finished, the fire alarm went off, a blaring whine that ran up and down the hall and banged on all the doors. Sal jumped to his feet.

"I'm sure it's nothing," Mr. Merkel said, but his fingers fumbled as he closed the chess set and pulled a manila envelope from his desk. "But let's go out. Just in case."

There were fewer than a dozen people in the school: the principal, the janitor, Ms. Barnes the science teacher, Mr. Lewis the music teacher, and the four members of the jazz club. They filed out the front door as the alarm shouted overhead, jarring the late November afternoon.

"Who pulled the alarm?" Principal Woodward said. She looked annoyed. Then one of the jazz kids pointed to a column of smoke coming from the metal trash can that sat under Mr. Merkel's classroom window. The flames were small, just a red glow through the mesh, and everyone went to stare at them. Only Mr. Merkel remained behind. When Sal looked back, he was leaning against the wall of the school, his head bent almost to his knees. Sal started to go to him, but Ms. Barnes got there first. She put her arm around him, her head so close to his that her stiff yellow curls brushed his ashen face.

From the fire station four blocks away a siren began. The fire engine careened down Elmhurst, trailed by its matching red ambulance, and came to a hard stop in front of the school. Firefighters in yellow rubber pants and jackets leaped out, looking around for a disaster. When they found only a trash can fire, their disappointment was palpable.

By now Mr. Merkel's coloring had returned to normal. He stepped away from Ms. Barnes, whose hand hung in the air, disappointed, and walked over to Sal. Inside the school, the alarm still wailed.

"Let's end our lesson," he said. "I don't know when they'll turn that off." So while everybody else watched Lovelock's finest douse a trash can with water, Sal and Mr. Merkel crossed the parking lot to Mr. Merkel's car.

As Sal opened the door he felt someone watching him. He

assumed it was Ms. Barnes, but when he looked around he saw a bearded man in mirrored aviator sunglasses sitting in a dented blue sedan. He was parked by the curb where parents picked up their children, and Sal assumed he was a father waiting for one of the jazz students. When he saw Sal looking at him he raised his hand in a small wave.

Mr. Merkel made a slow turn onto Western, then Main, before stopping at Lovelock's one traffic light. This was the town's main intersection, with the library on one corner and Comforts Café on another, but the sidewalks were empty and theirs was the only car. A quarter of a mile ahead, Interstate 80 roared past on concrete pilings forty feet high.

On the interstate Mr. Merkel hugged the right lane, going ten miles under the speed limit as usual. An eighteen-wheeler appeared behind them, approached quickly, then swerved into the passing lane. Mr. Merkel huddled over the wheel as it drove by. The interstate always made him nervous, but he seemed especially tense today. Sal looked out the window to give him privacy while he recovered. The sky was a blue so deep it was almost purple, and beneath it the wide fields of sage were silver.

When they were safely on the Lovelock-Unionville Road Mr. Merkel said, "I used to teach Benjamin chess, too. He was ten when he died. About the same age as you."

"What happened to him?"

"A car accident. Almost two years ago."

"That's terrible," Sal said. Mr. Merkel seemed too old to have had a ten-year-old son who died two years ago. Sal wondered if Benjamin had minded having such an old man for a father, but he supposed it hadn't mattered. He supposed you loved the father you had, no matter what.

"What about your mother?" Mr. Merkel asked. "When did she die?"

Sal had forgotten Mr. Merkel knew his mother was dead. He looked out the window. "Last summer."

It was June 24. A Sunday. They were supposed to walk to church like they did every Sunday, but when Sal woke he knew, from the color of the sunlight on the Bob the Builder bedspread, that it was way past time. He assumed he'd find her in bed, sleeping with her mouth open the way the pills made her sleep, but she was on the couch, still wearing her black jeans and white shirt from the bar. Her mouth was open, but she wasn't sleeping.

"What happened?" Mr. Merkel asked.

When Jake came, five minutes after Sal called 911, he pressed two fingers to Sal's mother's throat and felt the stillness there. He bowed his head. Then he picked up the syringe, untied the shoelace drawn tight around her forearm, and rolled down her sleeve to cover the small bruise above her wrist. He wrapped the syringe and the string in a paper towel from the kitchen and put them carefully in his pocket. On the coffee table were a few scattered pieces of red rubber, a lighter, and a spoon. He put those in his other pocket. He opened the bathroom medicine cabinet and took the bottle of OxyContin, then went to Sal's mother's bedroom and took something from the drawer of her bedside table. Back in the living room he cupped Sal's mother's face in his palm as if she were a sleeping child and used a second paper towel to wipe away the cone of brownish-pink foam that had sprouted between her lips like a toadstool.

Then Jake walked Sal to the front porch. The sun was high and the air was warm and the siren wailed as the ambulance rounded the corner. He put his hand on Sal's shoulder, and in the weight of his hand was a promise. Everyone would think Grace Prentiss died of heart failure, because that's what Jake would tell Gideon and Ezra, the people from the church, and Hank Fullman, who drove the ambulance. It was an act of almost unbearable kindness, and

Sal would always be grateful for it, but Mr. Merkel's thumb had caressed the rook with the tenderness of regret and he drove too slowly on the interstate, so Sal looked out the window and gave away his mother's secret.

"She put a needle in her arm."

If he focused just right, the sagebrush blurred into a uniform gray that looked like water. He felt Mr. Merkel glance at him, then back to the road.

They drove the rest of the way in a silence laden with memory, but when Mr. Merkel stopped in the Prentiss driveway Sal didn't get out. He knew Mr. Merkel had something more to say. Beside the wheelbarrow Samson watched them with eyes like hard little marbles.

"Benjamin asked me which chess piece I would be, too," Mr. Merkel said. "I told him I would be the king. I thought, who wouldn't want to be the king? The ultimate prize. The one everyone wants to capture and protect."

Sal would never want to be the king. The king was even more of a pawn than the pawns were. "What did Benjamin want to be?"

"Can you guess?"

The question fell like a heavy blanket on Sal's shoulders. The only thing he knew about Benjamin was that Mr. Merkel had taught him chess and he'd asked his father which part he would play in the drama of the game. Maybe he, too, had seen stories in the march of ivory and black soldiers across a checkered battlefield. If he did, Sal knew which piece he would choose. "A pawn?"

Mr. Merkel's smile was wobbly. "That's right. I couldn't imagine why anyone would want to be a pawn, but he said pawns could do great things when no one was looking. They could even kill a king."

Samson circled twice and lay down with his head on his paws. Mr. Merkel reached over and took Sal's hand. "There's something special about you, isn't there, Sal? Sometimes you seem to know exactly what I'm thinking. You knew I had a son. You knew he was dead. And you knew his favorite chess piece. How do you do that?"

When Sal was younger, he'd thought his way of knowing what people were thinking was an actual superpower. Now he knew that only people in stories had superpowers, but he still thought, secretly, that it made him special. He flushed with pleasure. "I just watch people, I guess."

"Yes, you do," Mr. Merkel said, thoughtfully. "And what do you usually see when you watch me?"

"That you're sad, mostly." Right away Sal wished he hadn't said that, but then he changed his mind. It was the truth, after all.

Mr. Merkel gave a small smile. "You're right. I am sad." His fingers tightened around Sal's. "Mostly."

The double-wide door creaked open, and Gideon stood on the cinder block steps. Mr. Merkel had driven Sal home nine times, but this was the first time either of Sal's uncles had come outside to greet him. Mr. Merkel let go of Sal's hand, and they got out of the car. Mr. Merkel smoothed his hair over the crown of his head, a nervous gesture, but his voice was firm and polite when he said, "Hello. I'm Adam Merkel, Sal's math teacher."

Gideon came down the steps. He and Mr. Merkel were the same height, but where Mr. Merkel's body was soft and sloped, Gideon's was sinewy and straight. "You're the one teaching him chess."

"He's a remarkable boy," Mr. Merkel said. "As I'm sure you know."

Gideon turned his chilly eyes to Sal. They held no acknowledgment of Sal's remarkableness. He turned back to Mr. Merkel, and his already stern face darkened further. Mr. Merkel took a step back.

"It was a pleasure to meet you," Mr. Merkel said, before turning back to his car.

Gideon and Sal watched him drive away. Samson paced, dragging his chain in the sand. Behind the Corolla a cloud of dust hung in the air.

"That man's trouble," Gideon said, but Sal didn't believe him.

NORA

Sal looked around Nora's family room, his dark eyes cataloguing, and Nora wondered what he saw. The room still had the brown shag carpet and fake wood paneling it had when it was built in the 1970s, and the La-Z-Boy, with the gouges Nora's fingernails had carved in its arms the night of Jeremy's championship basketball game, still sat next to the sofa where her mother had died. A flat-screen TV, their one extravagance, hung beside Jeremy's framed championship jersey, and every night Nora's father sat in the La-Z-Boy and watched whatever sport was in season, nursing the one Michelob Nora let him have. Something about the way Sal looked at the room made her think he saw all this, but of course he couldn't.

She took the dusty display case from the bookshelf, then sat beside Sal on the sofa and placed the spearpoint in his hands. It was a thin piece of chert seven inches long and an inch and a half wide. Small divots folded into one another on its surface like wavelets in a pond, tapering to serrated edges that were still sharp enough to cut flesh. Though Nora had seen it many times, it still awed her to think of the hands that had made it, ten thousand years ago, chipping away flakes of stone with patient deliberation.

Sal examined it with grave attention, as if he were thinking the same thing. "Where did you find it?"

"It was in a seasonal wash. That's one of the best places to find them. The water flushes them out, and when the wash dries up, they're just lying there waiting to be found." Nora was exaggerating. Spearpoints weren't strewn all over Great Basin washes; they were rare enough that she suspected her father had believed they'd never find one. When she'd kicked it loose, one Saturday a year before her mother died, he'd whooped as loud as he did at Jeremy's touchdown runs.

"How old is it?" Sal asked.

"That's the problem with washes. They take things out of context, so you can't tell how old they are. But it's a Clovis point, so it's somewhere between ten thousand and thirteen thousand years old."

She watched him mull this over. Most middle schoolers weren't able to comprehend time spans this vast, but Nora suspected Sal did. He traced the edge with one finger, gently. "What did they hunt with it?"

She smiled. This was going to impress him. "Did you know there used to be leopards here? And giant sloths, ten feet long. There were mastodons twice as big as elephants, saber-toothed tigers, even camels."

"Really?" He looked up at her, his eyebrows raised. "What happened to them?"

"Well, they—" Nora stopped. She and Sal looked at the spearpoint. At the utilitarian, deadly beauty of it.

In the backyard the door to the camper banged open with a metallic crash. Through the sliding glass doors of the family room Nora saw her father limping down the plywood ramp with his walker.

"Oh no." She jumped up.

"Who's that?"

"My father. He heard the car. He's wondering why I haven't come to see him."

"Is he not allowed out of there?"

"Of course he is. He's just not used to company." That was a stupid thing to say. As if her father were a recluse. Well, he was a recluse, but it wasn't because he didn't like company. She just didn't want him coming in here while she was talking to Sal. It complicated things. She rushed to the sliding door and yanked it open. "Dad! I'm here! I'll be out in a minute!"

It was too late; he was down the ramp. Nora waited while he clomped across the dirt yard to the patio and over the threshold. When he saw Sal a grin spread across his face. "Who do we have here?"

Nora blew out a resigned breath. "This is Sal. He's one of my students. Sal, this is my father, Mr. Wheaton."

Sal, the point still in his hands, scanned Nora's father from his disheveled hair to his brown suede slippers. This time Nora had no trouble seeing what he saw: a man too old for his years, trying to decide how many years were too many. The tangle of tenderness and bitterness in her heart cinched a little tighter.

"You're showing him our spearpoint," her father said.

"He seemed interested," Nora said. "We're about to start the First People unit."

Her father navigated the walker to the La-Z-Boy. "We found that up at Windy Gap," he told Sal. "There was a storm coming, and we needed to get back to the truck in a hurry. It was so steep we had to slide down on our behinds. Remember, Nora? We were going as fast as we could, and she knocked it loose."

Nora forced herself to smile. It was hard to reconcile the man he'd been, so agile in his canvas pants and hiking boots, with the man whose hands shook on the arms of his recliner. But as he took the spearpoint from Sal his hands steadied. He pressed a finger into one of the twin indentations at the base.

"See these divots? They're a marvelous bit of technology. You could slip this point into a spear haft, and if you bound it with sinew the joint would be unbreakable." He held the spearpoint out, as though his arm were the haft. "The people who made this were big-game hunters. Mastodon, mammoth, bison, even leopards. It was dangerous work, so they sent their bravest, strongest young men to do it. They circled the beast, feinting and jabbing, until it tired. Then the bravest and strongest of them all delivered the killing blow, deep into the heart." He mimed it all: the lying in wait, the feinting, the fatal thrust. "Can you imagine the celebrations when they returned? The bonfire, the dancing, the sacrifices? These young hunters were heroes. Their people worshipped them almost as much as they worshipped their gods."

Nora managed not to roll her eyes. The Clovis people almost certainly hadn't walked up to mastodons and stabbed them with spears. They'd probably used atlatls, archaic spear throwers that launched from a safe distance, or they'd driven entire herds off cliffs to their deaths. Nobody knew what gods they worshipped, either. Unlike the ancient Europeans, whose cave paintings and elaborate burials testified to their vanished lives, the earliest Americans left almost no art, and their bones—the handful that had been found—were scattered across two continents and seven thousand years. Yet here was her father, spinning stories about mastodon hunts as though they were no different from high school basketball championships.

Sal pulled at the talisman he'd fondled before, something small and white that looked like a chess pawn. His eyes flickered with the shadows of his imaginings: the hunts, the brave young men, the spear seeking the breastbone of the mastodon. Nora's father saw it, too—the thrall of the young boy—and in it he surely saw all the boys he'd coached, and the boy he'd raised. On the wall Jeremy's jersey hung in its Lucite frame, and the late afternoon sun shone like a floodlight on its empty blue shoulders and the white mustang rearing on its chest.

Nora reached for the spearpoint. "I need to take Sal home."

Her father's face dimmed. His hand shook again as he gave her the weapon, and he smothered a cough. Then he clutched his walker, his knuckles like walnuts. "It was nice to meet you, Sal."

"Thank you for showing me your spearpoint, Mr. Wheaton."

My spearpoint, Nora thought, but did not say.

Marzen looked the same as it had when Nora last slept over at Lily's sixteen years ago, so small and shabby it made Lovelock look like a metropolis. Lily's parents' house was at the end of one of the dirt roads that crossed the main street. Nora wondered if they still lived there, then thought: of course they did. Where would they go?

She glanced at Sal. He hadn't said a word since they'd left the house. She blamed her father. First he'd taken up all of her time with him, and now his stories about the First People had Sal so distracted that she couldn't think how to bring up Adam.

"I'm a little hungry. How about you?" She wasn't hungry, but she wondered what his dinner might look like. He shrugged, which she took as a yes. She stopped at the wood-fronted general store where she used to lean on the counter so Sully the cashier could look down her tank top while Lily swiped a pack of Marlboro Lights. It still smelled like tar and wood chips, still stocked its refrigerators with twice as much alcohol as soft drinks, and the cashier was still Sully. Nora picked out a Heath bar and told Sal to get something. He took a package of peanuts from the three-for-ninety-nine-cent rack. "You can get two more," Nora told him, and after a moment he did.

Sully didn't seem to recognize Nora, tall and severe with her Oxford blouse buttoned to her collarbone, as the sixteen-year-old with strawberry-blond hair who'd asked him what flavor of Tic Tacs he liked. She was relieved. She didn't like to be reminded of how she'd wielded her beauty back then, and for what? Cigarettes, vodka, and pot. And Mason.

The rutted dirt road that rose out of town made Nora's Civic nervous, so she drove slowly through the mounded foothills and the occasional eruptions of limestone that shot up in sheer walls. She read these cliffs with a trained eye, noting the ledges that marked the waterlines of the great Pleistocene lake as it rose and fell in slow, thousand-year tides before disappearing into the sand. Lake Lahontan, once bigger than Lake Ontario, now a desert.

After a mile they passed a black pickup parked half on the road and half in the chaparral. As she inched the Civic around it Nora saw that Sal's eyes were screwed shut. "Do you know that truck?"

He opened his eyes but didn't look out the window. "It's Jake's."

"Who's Jake?"

"He's a fireman." Every line in Sal's body was rigid. Nora wanted to ask why Jake the fireman terrified him, but she knew he wouldn't tell her.

At the Prentiss place she took in the farmhouse, the double-wide, the crumbling outbuildings, and the ring of broken furniture and trash. She'd seen crushing poverty before, in the Indian Colony, where there were houses almost as ruined as the farmhouse and yards just as deeply buried in trash, but something about this lonely outpost was worse. Its decomposing poverty seemed deliberate. Chosen. She looked over at Sal. He was watching her defiantly, as though daring her to comment. She smiled at him, but he didn't smile back.

A white pickup was parked beside the double-wide, a bizarre set of chairs made of wood and twisted iron in its bed. A man walked out of a shed carrying a plastic tarp and a coil of rope, and Nora's fingers went cold on the steering wheel. It was the man she'd seen at Adam's house.

"Who's that?" she asked Sal.

"My uncle. Gideon."

The man set the tarp and rope on the ground and walked to Nora's car. She rolled down the window. Casual. Friendly. As if she hadn't made the connection. "You must be Mr. Prentiss. I'm Sal's social studies teacher. I asked him to stay after school, so I gave him a ride home. I hope that's okay."

Sal got out of the car, walked around the front, and stood with both hands on the straps of his backpack, watching them. Gideon remembered her from Adam's house, Nora had no doubt. But what he said was "You're Jeremy Wheaton's little sister."

"Yes." Nora tried to cover her surprise. Gideon had a remarkable face—sharp cheekbones and an angular, sloping jawline—and eyes that were an unsettling shade of gray. She was sure she would have remembered him if she'd ever met him before that day at Adam's house, yet he seemed to remember her from twenty years ago.

"Jeremy and me were in the same grade," he said. "Different crowds, though."

"I bet." It came out more caustically than Nora intended. She debated softening it, but let it lie.

Gideon's eyes narrowed. He put one hand on the roof of the Civic and bent down. "I bet you miss him."

Nora's flinch was small, but he saw it. His lip curled in a slight, mocking smile. He cocked his head at his nephew, and suddenly their resemblance was clear. Sal's skin was darker, but in the fine bones of his young face Nora saw the lean features of the man. They held their bodies the same way, too, with a tense, watchful stillness. Even the expression in their eyes was the same: flat and careful.

Gideon stepped back, dismissing her. Nora backed up the driveway and drove slowly until she was around the bend. Then adrenaline took over and she drove too fast, ignoring the shimmy of the rear tires. Gideon Prentiss had been at Adam's house the day after he died. Why? How did he know where Adam lived? What had he been carrying in his backpack? Dark possibilities raced through her mind, and her foot pressed harder on the accelerator.

She had to swerve into the brush to avoid crashing into Jake the fireman's pickup, which was still blocking half the narrow road. After she skidded to a stop she sat with her hands on the wheel. She needed to calm down. If she wrecked her car up here, she'd have only Marzen to turn to for help.

Something moved to her left, and Nora saw a man in a blue uniform walking down the low hill toward her. Jake the fireman, presumably. She got out of the car, and he waved. When he reached her he pointed at her front bumper, nose-deep in a clump of sage. "Need a hand?"

"No, thank you. Are you Jake?"

"Jake Sanchez. Yes." He squinted at her in the late-afternoon sun. He was big—not fat, but thick and tall—with a broad, handsome face beneath neat dark hair. "Have we met?"

"Do you know Sal Prentiss?" Jake's face clouded at the mention of Sal's name. "I'm his teacher," Nora told him. "I gave him a ride home. When we drove by, he said this was your truck."

Jake's face opened in a relieved smile. "Sure, I know Sal. His mom and I were friends." He blushed, and now Nora remembered him: a shy, chubby boy a year ahead of her in school. Not in her crowd, to use Gideon's phrase, but he'd seemed nice. She thought she remembered Sal's mother, too. There'd been a Grace Prentiss in her own class, a dark-haired girl, beautiful in a wild sort of way. People told stories about her, the sort of stories that kept other girls at a distance, though Nora couldn't remember what they were. They sure hadn't kept Jake away, judging by his blush.

"He told me she died."

"She had a heart attack. Last summer."

He said this with honest sorrow, and Nora couldn't help warming to him. She hesitated, then decided what the hell. The only other person she knew from Marzen was married to her ex-husband and wouldn't talk to her. "Did you know about his math teacher? He died somewhere up here a few days ago."

"Right up there." Jake pointed at the low hill he'd walked down, and now Nora understood why Sal had been so uncomfortable when they'd passed this spot. "I was doing a little follow-up investigation. For the fire department."

"Did you find anything?"

"The cops took it all away." His fingers brushed his jacket pocket. "I was just checking to see if they missed anything."

Nora looked up the hill. It looked like all the other hills, rounded and spiked with sage and saltbush. Above it a limestone bluff loomed like a sentinel, watching. "The man who died up there was a friend of mine."

The wind sighed in the sage. Nora felt Jake thinking, stolid and slow. Finally he said, "Do you want me to show you?"

She nodded, and he turned around. They walked over the hill and down to a small grove of acacias near a seasonal wash fifty feet from the base of the cliff. Wordlessly he led her into the shade of their canopy.

A piece of yellow caution tape fluttered from a tree. There was a small hearth in the middle of the grove that sent Nora's mind back thousands of years to other hearths, built like this one in a simple ring of stones. So much had changed in the world, yet still people who found themselves outside in the dark would hunker in the lee of a bluff and build a fire. It gave the grove a feeling of safety, like a home.

Then she saw the blackened spot burned into the sandy ground. It was crescent shaped, like the blurry shadow of a man curled on his side. She sensed Jake's eyes on her and forced herself to face him. "What do the police think happened?"

"They didn't tell me." Jake walked over to the fire pit. "But his ankles were tied with a jump rope, and there was an empty bottle of vodka. One end of the rope was in the ashes of the hearth. My guess is somebody used the vodka as an accelerant, then lit the rope on fire. Like a fuse."

Nora saw it again: Adam burning, the flames leaping, but this time she saw his feet bound and the fire racing up the rope to his pant legs. She closed her eyes, but he was still there, writhing on the ground, unable to escape the flames that swallowed him whole. She shoved the image away and opened her eyes. Jake was watching her with the same sympathy she'd felt when Sal closed his eyes in her car. She smoothed her hair with one hand. "The police said Sal found the body."

"He came to the fire station. I was on duty." Jake cleared his throat. "It was rough on him."

"It's still rough on him. He and Adam—the math teacher—were very close."

Jake nodded miserably, and Nora liked him even more. Whether Sal knew it or not, he had a friend in this man, and Nora was glad to know there was someone up here who cared about him. Someone other than Gideon.

They walked back to the road. Nora moved easily in her flats, comfortable with the give and take of hard-packed sand and loose scree, but she sensed the care Jake took with each step. He wasn't a man who hunted, or hiked, or rode ATVs in the hills, which made him unusual for Marzen. When she got to her car she turned around.

"I don't know if you remember me. I'm Nora Wheaton. I was in the class behind you in high school." She saw his surprise, but it didn't bother her. She knew how different she looked from the girl he'd known. "Thank you for showing me where my friend died."

"You're welcome," he said.

"I'd really like to know what happened to him. Will you call me if you find out anything else?"

He hesitated, then said, "Sure."

She wrote her cell number on a scrap of paper, and he put it in his jacket pocket. Then she left, driving the Civic with care once more. It wasn't long before Jake's truck caught up to her, but he kept a respectful distance as she crept down to Marzen.

SAL

Four months before Mr. Merkel died, something happened that to Sal seemed like a miracle: the middle school held a book fair. Ms. Wheaton took them on Monday, and the drab little library, with its tired copies of *Little House on the Prairie* and *Harry Potter,* bloomed with paperbacks on every table. A thin, business-suited lady stood beside Mrs. Simmons, the flustered librarian, and said, "The proceeds benefit your PTA. You can shop all week." Two mothers tried to look helpful, and a third sat next to a cash box by the ancient set of encyclopedias. Ms. Wheaton sat in a chair by the door and looked at her watch.

The sixth graders fanned out, sorting themselves into readers and nonreaders. The readers picked up books and flipped their pages. The nonreaders stood in the corners, talking and laughing. Kip Masters and his gang hung out behind the periodicals, posing in their Nikes and sneering at the readers.

By now Sal knew all about Kip Masters. His father was one of the richest men in Lovelock, which alone could have explained his popularity, but Kip also had his own charisma, rooted in fey, asymmetrical features and a wicked intelligence. Even Sal was half in love with him. He also hated him. He hated how easily he surfed the social seas of sixth grade. He hated his casual vanity, and the cruelty that went with it. Most of all he hated that Kip never looked at him. Sal didn't want to be like Ronnie and Seventeen, Kip's favorite playground targets, but he hated that he wasn't worth even a glance from Kip's keen, bright eyes.

Sal found the graphic novels by the windows. They didn't have the *Sandman* books, or *Constantine*—his mother had said those were for grown-ups, though she bought them for him anyway—and the middle-grade books were disappointing, with babyish titles like *Miss Peregrine's Home for Peculiar Children* and *Diary of a Wimpy Kid*. Sal ran his fingers over them until he reached one called *The Graveyard Book*. Its cover showed a boy surrounded by headstones and pale ghosts, standing beneath the outstretched arm of a cloaked man who looked half angel and half demon. Sal's pulse quickened.

"Do you like that one?" One of the mothers, frizzy and plump in a blouse that gapped between the buttons, leaned over the table and took it from him. She turned it over. "It's fifteen dollars and ninety-nine cents."

Twelve times, as summer cooled into fall, Sal had slipped through the chain-link fence, listened to the old linebacker's football stories, and traded medicine for money. He'd watched Ezra count it on his bedspread, and he'd put twelve twenties in the scrapbook. Two hundred and forty dollars was far more money than he'd ever seen at one time, and every week he ran his thumb along the edges of the bills, savoring their growing thickness. But he'd never once thought of spending them.

Until now. Now the silky voice in his head was telling him to use one of those twenties to buy *The Graveyard Book*. Sal tried to ignore it. Even if the medicine helped the linebacker's knee and the young mother's rheumatoid arthritis and the courthouse man's carpal tunnel syndrome, selling it was still illegal, and the money Sal got for doing it was still dirty.

But he'd earned it, the voice argued. Wasn't Sal the one who carried the pills in his backpack where any teacher could find them? Wasn't Sal the one who went to the bench where the police could arrest him at any moment? Ezra called him *partner,* but all Ezra did was drive to Reno once a month while Sal did every dangerous thing. What would it hurt to spend some of the money he'd earned on a book? If his mother were alive she'd have bought it for him, and it was only because she'd slept herself to death that he was delivering Ezra's medicine in the first place.

Sal resisted the voice for days, but in the predawn light of Thursday morning he took out the scrapbook. He hesitated one final time. Then his fingers, stealthy from dozens of exchanges of paper bags for paper bills, slipped a twenty into his palm.

He went to the book fair at the beginning of lunch. He held his breath as the mother at the cash box took his money, but she put the bill in the tray as if it were any other twenty-dollar bill and gave him back two dollars and ninety-five cents. Sal was giddy with relief and the thrill of transgression. He could taste the Mountain Dew he would buy from the vending machine next to the boys' bathroom. He would buy one today, another tomorrow, and he'd still have ninety-five cents left.

As Sal turned to go he saw Kip Masters browsing the tables. For the first time all year Kip was alone, without the boys who followed him like an honor guard. He was turning the pages of a book, his straight dark bangs falling forward. When he carried a half dozen books to the cash box Sal saw, with a jolt, that one of them was *The Graveyard Book*.

As Kip walked away, his books stowed in his backpack where none of his friends could see them, Sal's fingertips tingled with excitement. Soon Kip Masters—*Kip Masters!*—would open the same book Sal would open that night. He imagined them, in bedrooms twenty miles and an ocean of circumstance apart, turning its pages at the same time. Maybe they would talk about it someday. Kip's eyes would round with surprise when he found out the invisible boy at the misfits' table liked the same stories he did. Maybe they would become friends, defying the laws of middle school society together. As he walked to Mr. Merkel's classroom for lunch Sal's stride lengthened. He wondered if the Family Dollar sold white Nikes like Kip's, and how much they cost.

Mr. Merkel was relieved to see him. "I was afraid you had a tutoring appointment."

"No, I went to the book fair."

"Did you buy anything?" When Sal handed him *The Graveyard Book* Mr. Merkel said, "Ah, Neil Gaiman. I used to read his books to Benjamin. This was his favorite."

"Did you ever read him the *Sandman* books?" Sal dropped his backpack and sat in his chair. "They're cool."

Mr. Merkel was staring at the cover of *The Graveyard Book,* where the angel-demon stood with his arm outstretched beside the boy and the graves. "Benjamin used to tell us he could walk the boundary between the living and the dead, like Bod. That he could fade from sight whenever he wanted. We used to pretend it had worked, Renata and I. That he was like the dead, and we couldn't see him."

The air in the room felt brittle, as though the wrong words would shatter it. "Invisibility is a good superpower," Sal said, carefully.

"It's not invisibility," Mr. Merkel said. "It's fading. When you fade, people still see you, but afterward they don't remember you."

His eyes had gone dark. Sal took *The Graveyard Book* from his unresisting fingers and started to put it in his backpack, but in his haste his sketchbook fell out, splayed open to a drawing of Angelus and Catellus in all their vivid, colored-pencil glory. He stooped to pick it up, but he wasn't quick enough.

"What's that?" Mr. Merkel was leaning around his desk. "May I see?"

Sal had never shown his drawings to anyone but his mother, but Mr. Merkel's eyes had brightened at the sight of it, so he handed him the notebook.

The drawing was of the archangels facing off in the hills above Marzen. Like all Sal's drawings, it was muscular and energetic, with violence exploding from sword and scythe. It was one of his favorites, but now he saw all its flaws. The angels' arms were too long. He wasn't good at drawing feet. Or hands. The only things he got right were the faces. You could see the nobility in Angelus's proud nose, and the corruption in Catellus's haunted eyes.

"It's magnificent," Mr. Merkel said. "Who are they?"

Sal shifted on his feet. "The one with the silver wings is Angelus. He's the captain of the angels. The one with the black wings is Catellus. He's his brother, but he's fighting for Hell."

"Why is he fighting for Hell?"

Sal hadn't given Catellus's motivation much thought. He was simply Angelus's evil twin, the dark side of the archangel's brilliant coin. "I don't know. He used to be on Heaven's side, but then he went bad."

He expected Mr. Merkel to hand the notebook back, but he kept looking at it, so Sal pointed to the buildings in the lower corner. They were a rough approximation of Marzen. "See this town? There was a boy there who tried to call a djinn to grant him three wishes. But he did it wrong, and he summoned the demons instead." He touched a squadron of demons. "Catellus let them out a long time ago, and now they hide on Earth, waiting for chances to attack people." Mr. Merkel was still listening closely, so Sal went on. "There was a preacher in the town, and when the demons came he prayed for help. Angelus heard him, and came down to Earth with his army. He was too late to save them, though. The preacher and the little boy and everyone else, they were already dead."

"Everyone in the town died?" Mr. Merkel looked taken aback. Sal's mother wouldn't have liked that, either, but Sal wouldn't have written it that way if she were alive. When she was alive, Angelus saved everyone and defeated villains with ease, and he didn't have an evil brother out to destroy the world.

"That's more blood on Catellus's hands. That's why Angelus wants to kill him."

Mr. Merkel looked at Angelus's harsh face, with its bared teeth. "Does he do it?"

"No. They fight each other all the time, but they never kill each other. I don't think they want to as much as they think they do." Sal hadn't thought that before, but it felt true. They were brothers, after all.

Mr. Merkel tapped the upper corner, where a tiny boy in red shorts watched the carnage from a hilltop. "Is that you?"

"Yes." Sal drew himself in all his stories, always on the outside looking in. He'd been doing it for as long as he could remember.

"What are you doing?"

"I'm watching."

"Why?"

"All stories need watchers. Otherwise, it's like they never happened." Sal had never tried to explain this before—how, in his mind, a story without an audience was like a tree falling in a forest with no one to hear—and he didn't think he was doing it very well. But Mr. Merkel nodded.

"I suppose that's true. And you are, indeed, an excellent

watcher." He smiled over the tops of his glasses, and Sal felt a warm rush of pleasure, just as he had when Mr. Merkel told him his ability to know what people were thinking was remarkable.

Mr. Merkel paged backward, through battle after battle. "How do you come up with the stories?"

The stories were simply there, inside Sal's head, almost as though they'd been put there by Angelus and Catellus themselves, but Sal didn't know how to explain this, either, so he said, "I don't know."

"It's a wonderful gift," Mr. Merkel said, "to be able to create stories in your mind."

This compliment, too, made Sal's skin prickle, even though he thought it was harder to make true things sound interesting, the way Mr. Merkel did. "I can tell you another one, if you want."

Immediately he worried that he'd made a mistake. Mr. Merkel wasn't his mother. He didn't want to hear another of his stories; he was probably just being nice about them. Yet he couldn't stop his heart from leaning forward.

"I would love that," Mr. Merkel said, and in the sun that spilled through the classroom window his eyes had almost no shadow in them at all.

NORA

Nora called Mason as soon as she got back from dropping Sal off at the Prentiss place and asked him to meet her at the Whiskey. She had something to tell him, she said, and he agreed to meet her that night, after he ate dinner with his family.

She arrived at seven thirty and took a table in the back, away from the patrons who, from the looks of them, had been there since happy hour. She knew them all, of course: Harry Staunch and Pete Garrity, who used to drink with her father; Mary Barnes; and Mindy Lonnon the court reporter with her horsey laugh. Nora remembered that laugh from when she used to pick up her father and Jeremy in high school. Your taxi's here, Nora would say. Jeremy would say, come on, Dad, the meter's running, and Mindy Lonnon would laugh and laugh.

She wasn't laughing now, though. The four of them were talking about Adam's murder in awed, excited tones. Mary was holding court, milking her connection with the dead man. As Nora listened, Mary said, "You'd never think he would be mixed up in something like this. He seemed like such a gentle soul. But we all have our dark sides, don't we?"

Everyone nodded knowingly. Though Nora had wondered about Adam's mysterious past herself, she knew the four at the bar would have thought he had secrets that made him worth killing whether he had them or not. It was easier for them to think that Adam, the outsider, had brought his murder on himself. That Lovelock had nothing to do with it.

"But who killed him?" Mindy Lonnon asked. "That's what I want to know."

"I bet it was somebody from Reno. That's where he came from," Pete said. "Or Marzen. That's where they found him."

More nods at this. This would clearly be the best outcome for all concerned. "I hope you're right," Mindy said. "I can hardly sleep. I've got all the windows locked and my Ruger under my pillow."

This prompted a spirited debate over the best concealed carry, with Mindy's Ruger pitted against Mary's Beretta and Pete's Glock. Then Mason walked in, and the group swarmed him as he ordered his beer.

"We were just talking about our local murder," Pete said. "Any news?"

Mason smiled and retreated with his Bud Light. "As soon as we make an arrest, Pete, you'll hear."

He sat at Nora's table and tapped his bottle against hers. He was wearing jeans and a blue Henley that emphasized his broad shoulders. Mindy Lonnon watched them with beady-bright eyes, and Nora knew her "date" with her ex would be all over town by tomorrow. As if two people who'd been divorced for a decade couldn't have a beer together like mature adults. Even if this was the first time they'd done that since Mason had moved out. Nora took a long drink from her Coors.

"What's up?" Mason looked relaxed, as if they really were just two old friends meeting for a drink, and Nora knew he'd told Lily where he was going. She could imagine what Lily thought about it, but his telling her was a statement of fidelity, even if Lily didn't appreciate it. She got right to the point.

"I want to talk to you about Adam Merkel."

Mason looked surprised. "What about him?"

Nora had asked him here to tell him Gideon Prentiss was the man who'd been at Adam's house, but before she did she wanted to see what she could get out of him about the investigation. He might not talk about it to Pete Garrity, but she was hoping he would talk about it to her. Listening to him talk about his cases was one of the few ways she'd been able to be generous to him during their marriage, and they'd spent many nights in this bar talking about the violences, large and small, he saw every day. The thing she'd ended up loving best about him was how heavily the job weighed on him, the high school golden boy turned small town cop. Lily gave him the emotional support Nora couldn't in a thousand other ways, but Nora suspected she didn't like to hear about his work.

"How's the investigation going?" she asked.

Mason ran one hand through his hair, an old habit. "It's a bitch."

"I can imagine. What do you know so far?" It had been almost a week; they had to have some preliminary evidence, at least. But Mason shook his head.

"Come on, Nora. You know I can't talk about it."

Nora leaned closer, resting her elbows on the table. Beneath the cigarette smoke and stale hops she could smell him: Ivory soap and Old Spice. It was the smell of seventeen, minus the pot. "Come on, Mace, it's a vault in here." She tapped her head. "I never told anyone about the Town Hall Tagger, you know."

The Town Hall Tagger had been responsible for a run of absolutely filthy antipolice graffiti spray-painted on the town hall building ten years ago. He'd driven the police crazy until Mason caught him in the act one night: an eighty-two-year-old pensioner who'd found in his advanced dementia a flair for political venom and an artistic style that would rival that of any teenaged tagger in Reno. Mason and Nora had laughed themselves giddy over it, and then Mason had quietly reached out to the man's daughter. The Town Hall Tagger wound up in the senior living center, the tagging stopped, and Bill Watterly never learned the identity of his nemesis.

Mason smiled—at the memory or the nickname or both—and the air between them warmed. He relaxed into the wooden chair with a sigh. "There's not actually much to tell. We got nothing from forensics, not even footprints. Somebody went over the whole area and brushed them clean. No fingerprints, either. The medical examiner gave us the time of death, but we won't have toxicology back for a couple weeks."

"Can they even get toxicology from a body that's burned?" Nora asked.

"It's hard to imagine it, but yeah."

Nora tried not to imagine it. "And time of death, too?"

"The M.E. says it was between nine and eleven the night before."

"How did he die?" Please, Nora thought, let him have been shot, or stabbed, or strangled. Anything but burned alive.

"It was the fire."

Nora pulled her cardigan tight. "Shit."

"I know. We haven't had a murder in fifty years, and now we get this. At least it wasn't somebody local."

Adam had been in Lovelock for seven months, but Nora knew that didn't make him a local to Mason, whose family had been here since 1870. "Do you have any suspects?"

Mason hesitated, but he seemed to have decided telling Nora what they didn't know was within bounds. "Not yet. But it's got to be somebody he knew. Because the way he was killed? That's not random. Somebody had a serious grudge against the guy. Hopefully it won't be hard to find out who he pissed off."

Nora knew he was right. Setting someone on fire was so horrific that it had to be rooted in passionate, personal hatred. But the fuse? That was cold, calculating malice. It was hard to imagine both in the same person in the same moment. If that person was Gideon, it made him very dangerous, indeed.

Mason interrupted her thoughts. "What do you know about the kid that found him? Sal Prentiss."

Nora found herself reluctant to talk about Sal. "Not much. He's quiet. His mom's dead, so he lives with his uncle." She wondered if the police had interviewed Sal yet. The thought of Sal being grilled by loutish Bill Watterly made her stomach queasy.

Mason looked at the group at the bar. "How about Mary Barnes?"

The science teacher held a gin and tonic in one pink-nailed hand, and she was swaying a little in her black stiletto ankle boots. "Why?" Nora asked. "Do you think she knows something?"

"Did you ever see her with Merkel?"

There were only eight teachers at the middle school; of course Nora had seen them together. She fought to hide her irritation as she realized what Mason was doing in the guise of their supposedly friendly get-together: he was questioning her. First he'd tried to pump her for information about Sal, and now he was trying to get her to tell him how Mary had pursued Adam when he first arrived. Nora had no love for Mary, but she wasn't about to throw her to Bill Watterly. "They were colleagues, not friends. I doubt she knows who killed him."

Mason took a drink from his Bud Light. Then he said, in an offhand voice that didn't fool Nora for a moment, "Some of the other teachers thought she was interested in Merkel, but he turned her down."

Now Nora couldn't hide her annoyance. "So what? You think she set him on fire for it?"

Mason colored. "It was Bill's idea. And she might have a history."

"Of burning people to death?" Nora gave a derisive laugh. "Come on, Mason. You guys can do better than that."

Mason looked at the group at the bar again. "When she and Mitch split somebody set his truck on fire, remember? We've always thought it was her, but we couldn't prove it. And a few months ago, somebody set Merkel's trash can on fire. It was by the curb in front of his house, waiting for pickup. We don't know who did that, either."

Nora stopped laughing. She could believe Mary had set Mitch's truck on fire. In fact, like Mason, she'd thought it at the time. It was exactly the sort of melodramatic move Mary would make at the end of a twenty-year marriage fractured by infidelity. Still. "There's a big difference between your ex divorcing you for his receptionist and a guy you barely know not wanting to take you out to dinner."

"I know. But Merkel was really shaken when we took the report on his trash can fire. He said it was a message. He wouldn't say what it was or who it was from, but he looked terrified. A few days later there was a fire in the trash can outside his classroom window. It was after school let out, but Mary and Merkel were both there."

"It wasn't Mary," Nora said. "It's not her style. Even if she was angry enough to kill Adam, she'd just shoot him with the Beretta she keeps in her purse."

Mary Barnes was leaning back against the bar. Her breasts swelled above her low-cut angora sweater, and Pete Garrity, who was married, was trying not to stare at them. Nora had a sudden flash of empathy for her: an aging beauty, needy and alone, in a town where the only men her age were married or drunks or exes. She'd spend the rest of her life having affairs and waiting for other women to divorce their husbands or die, and she knew it. No wonder she'd leaped at Adam.

Nora turned back to Mason. It was time to tell him what she'd come to tell him. "I found out who the man was at Adam's house."

"You did? How?"

"I saw him again yesterday, when I drove Sal home from school. It was his uncle. Gideon Prentiss."

Mason whistled. "Gideon didn't mention that."

"You've talked to him?"

"We heard Merkel drove Sal home after school sometimes. So I went up there yesterday." Mason drummed the table with his fingers. "Gideon swears he only met Merkel once, back in the fall, one day when Merkel dropped Sal off. So far we've got nothing else that connects them."

"He came out of Adam's house with a backpack. Was anything missing?"

"Nothing that we could see. Merkel's laptop and his cell phone were both there. There was no sign of a break-in, either, but the door wasn't locked." Mason took another sip of his beer. "We did find a bunch of pies, with a note. It said, 'For the eighth graders at Pershing Middle School, with best wishes for a happy Pi Day.' It was signed 'Merkel the Turtle.' Is that some kind of nickname?"

Nora couldn't help smiling. Damn, Adam. He'd planned to neutralize his nickname by embracing it. She hadn't known he had it in him. "It was a pet name the students had for him."

"What's Pi Day?"

"March fourteenth," Nora said. "You remember the number pi? It starts with three point one four."

Mason smiled. Nora had helped him pass every math class he'd taken in high school. "Well, that explains that, anyway."

"What happened to the pies?"

His smile faded. He knew what she was asking. "We brought

them back to the station. Then somebody put them in the staff room."

It made sense that the police would eat the pies, but Nora hated that they hadn't been given to the eighth graders Adam had made them for, kids who now wouldn't remember him as the man who surprised them with homemade pies but only as Merkel the Turtle, the math teacher who'd been killed out by Marzen. She saw the apology in Mason's eyes and knew he hated it, too. She sat back. "So you'll bring Gideon in for questioning?"

"Absolutely. Thank you for the tip."

"Make sure you question him. Not Bill."

"I'll do my best, but you know Bill. He's peeing in his pants over this case. He thinks he's going to be on CNN any minute."

Nora couldn't help laughing at this, and Mason did, too, raising his eyebrows in an unguarded gesture that flashed back to nights spent brainstorming over car thefts and break-ins, and other nights, too, long before that. An awkward silence fell between them, and their hands, resting a foot apart on the small table, suddenly seemed too close. Nora put hers in her lap. "How are Lily and the kids?"

Mason leaned back in his chair. "Alex hit his first home run last weekend."

"That's great." Nora's smile felt forced, and she was annoyed with herself for letting this conversation get to her. She hadn't wanted Mason's children. Hadn't even wanted Mason, as it turned out. He'd asked her to marry him three months after Jeremy died, when remorse had driven her to her knees. The night before the wedding she drank tequila with Britta until four, and she was still buzzed when she walked down the aisle in her mother's dress. Part of her knew even then that the peace she'd made with her unintended life was too uneasy for the promise she was about to make. Twenty months later she asked him to move out, and his heartbreak was one more burden on her conscience. But he was happy now. So was Lily. Everyone had moved on, including Nora.

"How's your dad?" Mason asked.

Nora's father had coached Mason in Little League and Pop Warner. He'd liked him as Nora's boyfriend and loved him as his son-in-law, and their mutual affection had survived the divorce. "He's doing okay," Nora said, even though it was no more true now than it had been at any time since the accident. Mason's sympathetic nod told her he knew she was lying, and that he was sorry for both her and her father for all of the reasons only he truly understood, and now Nora needed this conversation to be over. She drained the rest of her beer.

Mason pointed at the empty bottle. "Want another?"

"No thanks. Dad'll be waiting." Nora put a five on the table and stood. Mason didn't move. He still had half his beer, after all. Mindy Lonnon's braying laugh followed Nora out the door, and Nora wondered what in the hell could be that funny.

SAL

The stranger sat on Sal's bench the second Friday in December, three months before Mr. Merkel died. The old linebacker had already come, telling Sal about a Homecoming game against Battle Mountain fifty years ago before limping off with his OxyContin, thirty pills now, for pain that was getting worse. The young mother and the courthouse man had stayed for a few minutes, too, their breaths tiny clouds in the cold air. The young mother's son was about to start preschool, and she was nervous about leaving him. The courthouse man complained about his doctor, who didn't believe he had carpal tunnel syndrome. As always, Sal listened with a sympathy that made them seem lighter when they stood up than when they sat down, and this made him lighter, too. Now he was waiting on the Honda woman, who bought the medicine for her sister who had multiple sclerosis and no insurance, and the blond girl with the rock band tee shirts, who never talked to him at all.

Sal was good at this now—the silent escape from the playground, the fading, the quick exchanges—and the nerves of the early days were gone. Soon Angelus and Catellus were battling beside the Lovers Locks, sword and scythe sparking fire. "I did it for you!" Catellus cried, but before Sal could invent a reason for this intriguing statement the stranger slipped out of a seam in the universe like one of Catellus's demons and sat beside him.

Sal jumped, then calmed himself with an effort. The stranger was just a man, sitting on a public bench in a public park. It meant the Honda woman and the blond girl would miss their deliveries, but it couldn't be helped. Sal threw his backpack over his shoulder.

"Don't let me run you off," the man said. He was in his late twenties, lanky, with a reddish-brown beard. He was wearing threadbare khaki pants and dirty brown socks under weather-beaten leather sandals, and he smelled like grease and hamburger meat.

"It's okay," Sal said. "I have to get back to school anyway."

"You've got fifteen minutes." The man crossed his legs. "And you've got two more, don't you? The big lady and the girl."

The air cracked like a sheet of glass. Sal leaped to his feet. The man's right hand lashed like a snake and pulled him back down.

"Relax. I'm not the cops." His voice was light and even, but he held Sal's wrist in a viselike grip. "I'm just wondering what you're selling."

"I'm not selling anything." Sal's heart was beating so hard he was sure the man could see it through his coat. From the corner of his eye he saw the blond girl winding her way across the grass. When she saw Sal and the man she stopped. Her right fingers went to her left elbow and picked at it like the teeth of a tiny animal.

"You come here every Friday at twenty past twelve. You stay for thirty minutes. You meet the same people." The man smiled, showing narrow teeth. "I know a dope boy when I see one. You've got quick hands, though, I'll give you that."

Beneath Sal's panic his conscience raised a weak flag. He wasn't a dope boy, whatever that was. He was delivering medicine. Medicine that helped people. The old linebacker, the young mother, the courthouse man—he'd heard their stories, he knew how much they were hurting, and he'd seen how their eyes dilated with relief as they slid Sal's brown bags into purses and pockets.

The blond girl leaned against a cottonwood tree. A breeze lifted a lock of her milkweed hair, then let it fall.

The man reached his free hand into Sal's backpack and pulled out a brown bag. He turned it over and the bottle fell into his lap. "Oxy. That's what I figured."

Sal grabbed for the bottle. The man held it out of his reach and clicked his tongue like a disapproving parent. "Isn't there anyone who loves you enough to tell you this is a terrible line of work? It only ends one of two ways. You end up in prison, or you end up dead."

On Elmhurst a red Honda slowed to a stop, and the big woman watched Sal through her window. Sal shook his head at her, and she scowled and drove away. Her sister would have to wait a week.

"Tell your boss I want thirty," the man said.

Sal whipped back to him. "What?"

"You heard me. How much does he charge?"

Sal's muscles flooded with an acidic wash of relief. The man wasn't a cop; he was a customer. Sal didn't like that he'd been watching him, but maybe he was making sure it was safe before he approached. He ducked his head. "Ten dollars each."

"Bring them next week." The man's smile was thin. "And tell Adam Merkel Lucas says hello."

Sal tensed again. Carefully, not sure he'd heard right, he said, "Tell who?"

"Adam Merkel. You know, the guy who drives you home every Thursday." The man waited while Sal put it all together. The fire in the trash can, the man in the blue car, the lazy, two-fingered wave as Sal walked across the parking lot with Mr. Merkel. The man holding Sal's wrist wasn't wearing aviator sunglasses, but Sal knew that somewhere nearby, a dented blue sedan was parked.

"You were watching us. That day at the school." Sal gave his arm a yank, but the man tightened his grip. He smirked at Sal with amusement and a distant pity.

"You want to protect him, don't you? Of course you do. He seems so dull, but when he talks about the way math moves the world, he's a poet. And poets are fragile." He leaned close and whispered in Sal's ear. "You want to be careful, though, Sal. What he needs, you can't give him."

The breath that carried Sal's name was warm and foul, and it extinguished Sal's resistance like a child blowing out a candle. "Please," he said. "I have to get back to school."

"Yes, I suppose you do," the man said. "Tell Adam I'll be here Monday at four, if he wants to talk."

He let go of Sal's arm and tossed him the pills. Sal jumped up, darted around the Lovers Locks, and sprinted up the sidewalk, the worn soles of his sneakers slipping on the concrete. The blond girl took two quick steps toward him, but he didn't stop. As he flew past the playground she sank to her knees beside the tree, her elbows cupped in her hands, and watched him go.

Death comes in the dark, in Lovelock. It comes quietly, wrapped in soft gray wool. One pill, then another, and another, and another. First comes the melting of your muscles, and a sense of soaring. Then come the memories. Ah, the memories! Your body, ecstatic with violence. The crashing of shoulder on shoulder, titan against titan. The ripe smell of broken grass and the shouting of the crowd. Later, the wetness of her underwear and the taste of her tongue, like butter-rum candy. Do you remember the ripeness of your blood? The lightness of your limbs? The easy silence of your heart? That is what yesterday felt like, when it was yesterday. That is what youth felt like, when it was yours. And this is what dying feels like, in Lovelock, on a faded chenille couch in an empty house, in the middle of the night with the television on.

NORA

The day after she met Mason at the Whiskey Nora graded the quizzes the sixth grade had taken on the First People. She read Sal's first. His handwriting was blocky and neat, and it reminded her of the careful way he'd hung the posters on her bulletin board. The first question was *What was the First People's diet?* His answer: "Saber-toothed tigers. Sloths. Mastodon. Camels. Until they killed them all." Nora laughed at the brutal accuracy of it. The rest of his answers were almost as blunt, except the last one. *What happened to the First People?* she'd asked. The correct answer was what she'd told him: their descendants were today's Paiutes and the other modern tribes of the Americas. His answer ran to the bottom of the page:

> *Their gods were killed by new gods. The new gods told them they couldn't tell any of the stories they used to tell. After a while they forgot the old stories and the old gods. Later the new gods got killed by newer gods, and the newer gods made them change their stories again. Then those gods got killed, too. The Payutes don't remember the first stories or the first gods. Nobody does.*

She gave him an A. As she entered it in the grade book she saw it was the first A he'd gotten all year. Most of his other grades were C's.

On the top of his quiz, next to the A, she wrote, "See me at lunch."

When he appeared she told him to sit with her at one of the tables. He hung his backpack on the chair and slid into the seat. "I want to talk about your quiz," she said. He frowned, and she added, "Don't worry, you're still getting an A. I'm curious about what you said happened to the First People. Where did you come up with it?"

Sal started to say something, then changed his mind. "I don't know."

"Well, it's interesting, but it's not quite right. Just because the First People lived a long time ago, that doesn't mean all their stories are gone." Sal frowned again, and Nora said, "When I went to college, I learned about people who lived in Africa millions of years ago, long before the First People. Even they still have stories. There are people called anthropologists who look for them."

Sal's eyebrows twitched upward. "How?"

"They find the people. Their bones, I mean. And the things they made, like that spearpoint. When they find them, they can figure out lots of things. Like how long ago they lived, how old they were, what they wore, what they ate. Sometimes they can even figure out how they died."

Sal looked over at the bulletin board, where the First People marched in eternal lockstep through the grass. "They do that for the First People, too?"

"Yes, though they haven't found many of their bones. We think they probably cremated their dead."

Too late, Nora realized what she'd said. Sal looked down. His lashes were dark crescents on his golden skin. "Fire is matter at play," he said, softly.

Nora felt the nape of her neck tighten. The fire that killed Adam had not been playing. It had been greedy and hungry and savage. Still, maybe it helped Sal to think of it as just a jolly little chemical reaction. She tried to ease them past the awkward moment. "The First People probably believed it helped them get to the afterlife."

Sal brightened a little. "The Vikings thought that. They burned their swords with them, too. So they could have them in heaven."

"That's strange, don't you think?" Nora asked. "That you would need a sword in heaven?"

"Not if you have to fight," Sal said.

"Why would you need to fight in heaven?"

"To help the angels."

"Who do the angels need to fight?"

"The demons."

Nora was impressed by his imagination but disinclined to follow it. "I don't think I'd like the kind of heaven where I'd have to fight. I'd rather go someplace peaceful."

Sal dropped his eyes again, and the energy that had briefly animated him guttered out. "I think that's what my mom wanted, too."

Nora caught herself. She'd forgotten Sal's mother was dead. Of course he would think about what came after. Nora had done the same after her own mother died, and come up with her own, less imaginative, answer. She offered it now. "Maybe everybody gets what they want. Maybe that's what heaven is."

Sal's smile was wistful. "That would be cool."

"What kind of heaven would you want?" Nora asked. "Would you want a sword?"

"No." Sal looked at the bulletin board again. "I'd rather be a watcher."

"What's a watcher?"

"Watchers see everything and keep the stories." He picked up a pencil from the table. "Even the ones people forget."

Nora thought about how Sal moved through the school, almost invisible and always alert, and how he'd looked at her living room as though he saw the stories the furniture told. "Do watchers have to tell the truth? Or can they make stories up?"

"They have to tell the truth," Sal said. "That's their job."

"Do they have to tell all the stories they see?"

He stiffened a little. "No."

"How will people know those stories, then?"

"Sometimes people shouldn't know them."

"Why not?"

"Because they—" Sal stopped. He was gripping the pencil tightly. Nora pretended not to notice.

"Who decides whether they should know? The watchers?"

"They—yes."

Nora leaned back, studying him. "I guess I'd rather be a watcher, too, then."

Sal didn't answer, but the corner of his mouth twitched in what Nora hoped was a smile. Then the bell rang, and he fled so quickly he seemed to disappear even before he left the room.

Nora was still thinking about their conversation when school ended, so she almost missed the muffled sobbing from the classroom next door. Even then her inclination was to leave Mary alone, but as she passed her closed door she saw the science teacher through the window, hunched over her desk with her face buried in a tissue, and some hidden vestige of Nora's mother reared its head and made Nora open the door.

"Mary, what's the matter?"

"Oh, it's nothing." Mary tried with limited success to pull herself together. "I've got to go to the police station today. I'm a bit upset about it, is all."

Nora closed the door behind her. "Why do you have to go to the police station?"

Mary's shrug didn't look as casual as she hoped. "They want to know where I was the night Adam was killed. They said I have to give a statement."

Nora couldn't believe this. It had to be Bill Watterly's doing. "That's ridiculous."

"I know. But somebody told them I wanted to go out with him, and he rejected me. So now I guess they think I killed him for it." Mary tried a laugh but it came out as an angry sob.

Nora pulled over a chair. Mary's desk was covered with papers, half-empty bottles of Diet Pepsi, and a collection of rocks painted with words like LOVE, HOPE, and KINDNESS. There were three terrariums by the windows, home to a lizard, a guinea pig, and a pair of white rats. The bulletin board display was a riot of color that made photosynthesis look like a Mardi Gras party, and paper chains hung from the ceiling like the vines of a tropical forest. Mary clearly loved her job, and Nora envied her that.

"Just tell them where you were that night," she said. "That's all they need."

Mary scoffed. "Where do you think I was, Nora? I was in my house. Alone. Binge-watching *Jane the Virgin*. But I can't prove it, unless they want to interview my cat."

"It doesn't matter," Nora assured her. "They can't seriously believe you killed Adam."

"Can't they?" The bitter lines that bracketed Mary's mouth deepened. "I know what everybody thinks of me. Poor, divorced Mary Barnes. Couldn't have kids. Can't keep a man. Throws herself at the new teacher, but he doesn't want her, either. Then, just because Mitch's truck caught fire ten years ago, I'm that lady in *Fatal Attraction*." She wadded up the tissue, and in that tight, ferocious gesture Nora saw all the repressed rage this woman felt. How deeply she believed she'd been cheated out of the life she deserved. The life she'd thought was hers by right the day she stood before her classmates wearing her Homecoming crown. Nora leaned forward, over the painted stones.

"Mary, why are you still here? Go somewhere else. Somewhere with more people. Different people."

Mary blinked, and Nora knew she'd never considered leaving the town where, decades before, she'd been envied and admired. "My mother's in the nursing home," she stammered. "She doesn't know who I am anymore, but I couldn't leave her."

"I understand that. I'm only here because of my father. He might live another ten years, or even twenty, but I promise you, the minute he dies I'm leaving." Nora resisted the urge to pick up the stone with KINDNESS on it. "You should do the same. You're a good teacher, Mary. Any school in the state would be lucky to have you."

Mary's eyes welled with tears again, and she reached for another tissue from the pink flowered box on her desk. "Thank you, Nora."

Nora stood to go. When she reached the door she said, "And get a lawyer. Don't talk to the police without one."

She was almost to her car when she realized she was being followed. She turned to see Gideon Prentiss four paces behind her. He stopped, a lean figure in jeans and a camo jacket. His fingers twitched with that coiled energy she'd sensed in him at his property.

Nora was unnerved, but they weren't in his front yard anymore; they were in hers. Students and parents still filled the sidewalks on both sides of the parking lot, and the Marzen bus rumbled at the curb. She gave Gideon a raking look from head to foot that hearkened back to her days as one of the two undisputed queens of Pershing High School. "What do you want?"

A small muscle in his cheek jumped. It was a flinch, and Nora let him know she saw it. "You told the cops I was at that teacher's house."

Mason had questioned him. Good. Though he hadn't arrested him, apparently, and Nora didn't know what to think about that. "What were you doing there?"

"That's none of your business."

"Adam was my friend. That makes it my business."

Gideon took a step closer and pointed at her. "You stay away from my nephew. He doesn't need any more trouble."

Nora thought about all the trouble Sal already had, much of it this man's fault. She tried to keep her cool, but it was no use: her temper snapped with such force that everyone in the parking lot could probably hear it. "Bullshit. I see that boy every day. He's too thin and his clothes are too small and he lives in a trailer surrounded by trash in the middle of nowhere. Don't tell me you give a damn about him."

Gideon's lips whitened. "Don't tell us how to live. Our people have been on that land for six generations."

"That's no excuse to live like pigs. I don't know how you got custody of him. They must not have bothered to look at that filthy prepper camp you call a ranch. Maybe someone should tell Child Protective Services to pay you a visit."

Nora had never seen someone so angry be so still. She was going to leave him there, but she saw Sal walking toward them, hunched beneath his backpack. Gideon turned to follow her gaze, and the two of them waited as Sal crossed the parking lot. When he reached them Gideon put a hand on his shoulder. Then man and boy turned to Nora, their faces identical and closed. *Is it him?* Nora thought at Sal. *Is Gideon the one whose story you're not telling?* She waited for a nod, a blink, anything, but nothing came. Their conversation hours before, about heaven and watchers and lost stories, might never have happened.

Then Gideon turned around, his hand still on Sal's shoulder, and they walked to his truck. Nora watched them the whole way, waiting for Sal to glance back, but he didn't.

SAL

Sal spent the weekend after the stranger sat on his bench worrying about what the man wanted with Mr. Merkel. He couldn't be Mr. Merkel's friend. A friend would have called Mr. Merkel himself, but the man on the bench had come at him sideways, spying on him and passing messages through Sal. When Sal went to Mr. Merkel's classroom for lunch on Monday he was planning to tell him about the man right away, but Mr. Merkel was standing beside his desk with his black leather briefcase in one hand and a grin on his face.

"I thought we'd have an adventure," he said, with that thin fiber of sound Sal loved pinging in his voice. He led Sal right out the front door without Ms. Pratzer seeing them. As they climbed into Mr. Merkel's car Sal heard the shouts of his classmates on the playground, and despite his unease about the man on the bench his heart fluttered with excitement. This was a much bolder escape than slipping through the fence behind the Dumpster.

They drove a mile out of town, following a rural road until the pavement gave way to dirt and crossed a little dam about two hundred feet wide. Mr. Merkel parked, and he and Sal walked back to look over the low concrete walls that bracketed the road. Twenty feet below the eastern wall was a reservoir, a modest bulb at the end of a narrow ribbon of water that wound through alfalfa fields before disappearing in the sandy distance. Through a gate in the western wall a thin green stream spilled down to where the Humboldt River, strangled now into a creek, meandered away over rounded stones.

"My university office was near the Truckee River," Mr. Merkel said. "Sometimes I ate lunch there with a student of mine. When I heard about this, I knew we had to come."

He hoisted himself onto the eastern wall of the dam and sat with his feet dangling over the reservoir. When Sal climbed up beside him Mr. Merkel handed him a turkey sandwich with a flourish, like a waiter in a fancy restaurant. Sal had never seen him so happy. The stranger paced at the edge of Sal's mind, but he held him off a little longer. It was a beautiful day—the air was cold but the sun was warm—and the bench in the park beside the Lovers Locks seemed very far away.

"This river starts three hundred miles from here, up in the East Humboldt Range," Mr. Merkel said as he unwrapped his sandwich. "Did you know it's the longest river in America that doesn't drain into the ocean?"

Sal had assumed all rivers drained into the ocean. "Where does it go?"

"It dries up in the sand twelve miles west of Lovelock. I must have passed it on the way here." Mr. Merkel sounded regretful, as though the final resting place of America's largest land-bound river deserved more respect than a seventy-mile-per-hour drive-by. Below Sal's filthy sneakers murky green water nudged against the last barrier between it and its doom. Sal felt sorry for it. It might not be much of a river, but nothing deserved the lonely desert death it was headed for.

Mr. Merkel smiled the conspiratorial smile that always heralded one of his math stories. "Let me tell you why this river is going to disappear in twelve miles." He explained how warm air made the river's water molecules so agitated they broke away and floated into the sky. When they reached the cold air high above, they collected around specks of dust to form clouds, and then raindrops. Some of that dust, Mr. Merkel said, came from the thousands of small meteorites from the far reaches of the solar system that burned up in the atmosphere every day.

"Think of that," he said. "Bits of stardust, falling to Earth with the rain."

The awe in his voice made Sal's heart feel slippery. *When he talks about the way math moves the world, he's a poet,* the man on the bench had said. The man might not be Mr. Merkel's friend, but he must know him well, because only someone close to Mr. Merkel could see past the turtle shell to the gentle, wondering soul beneath. Sal took a breath, and when he let it out the words came with it. "I met a guy named Lucas. He said he wants to talk to you."

Mr. Merkel's fizzy delight died. His calm expression, however, did not change. "So Lucas is here. I wondered. How did you meet him?"

"Today when the bus pulled in he came over and asked if anybody knew the math teacher." Sal had come up with this lie over the weekend, but it unnerved him how easily it slid from his tongue.

"Did he say anything else?"

"He said he'll be in the park behind the courthouse at four today, if you want to talk to him." Sal pressed his hands into the chilly concrete of the dam. "Who is he?"

"Lucas Zimmerman." Mr. Merkel's voice thickened around the syllables of the name. "He was one of my students at the university."

"The one you used to have lunch with? The one you ate with by the river?"

"Yes." Mr. Merkel looked straight ahead so that the stem of his glasses hid his eyes. "He was remarkable. His mind was extraordinarily quick and graceful, unlike any I've ever encountered. It was a pleasure to be invited inside it, to watch it work."

Sal felt a sudden tug beneath his ribs. Mr. Merkel had called Sal remarkable, too, but Sal knew his mind wasn't graceful or quick, and it wasn't mathematical, either—he still had trouble with long division, which he was supposed to have mastered in fourth grade. "What does he want?"

"I imagine he wants to talk about how we parted." Mr. Merkel's voice was still measured, but a small tremor shook beneath it.

"Why?"

"Because I betrayed him. And because of that, he lost the only thing that mattered to him."

Below Sal's feet a chill drifted up from the stagnant river, carried from the distant mountains where it was born. The dirty stranger trying to buy OxyContin on the bench hadn't looked like a remarkable math student, but he had looked like someone who'd lost the only thing that mattered to him. "How did you betray him?"

Mr. Merkel didn't answer directly. Instead he said, "Do you have a father, Sal?"

Sal had two fathers. He had the man who'd left before he was born and the father that man would have been if he'd stayed. Both were so fully realized in his head that he would have recognized them on the street. But that wasn't what Mr. Merkel meant, so he said, "No."

Mr. Merkel nodded, as if confirming something he had suspected. "My father built washing machines at a factory in Fresno. When he was a boy he wanted to study aerospace engineering, but he never got to go to college. He hoped I would go to a great university, and build the rocket ships he couldn't."

"Did you?"

"No. As it turned out, I wasn't able to do it, either."

Mr. Merkel spoke as though failing to do this particular thing meant little to him, but the way he talked about the stardust at the center of a raindrop made Sal think he would have loved to build rocket ships, and this made his heart feel slippery again. "Being a math professor sounds cool."

Mr. Merkel smiled. "Thank you. But my father did not agree. The day I graduated from the University of Nevada he gave me a bill. I took out loans to go to school, but I lived with him in the summers. He said he didn't put me up in his house for three months every year so I could go to a second-rate college and be a math teacher."

When Sal was five, he'd told his mother he wanted to be an astronaut. Don't do it, she'd said. Space was too far away, and she'd miss him too much. Sal had promised her he wouldn't, but he knew she wouldn't really have minded if he'd been an astronaut, or anything else. She would have wanted whatever made Sal happy. "That's horrible," he said.

"I used to think so, too," Mr. Merkel said. "But my father was a man who built washing machines for a living. He wanted a son who would build something better. Something he could believe he had also built by raising me. He thought that's what sons were for." He touched the bridge of his glasses. "Lucas was a brilliant mathematician, far more brilliant than I. I wanted to say I'd taught him. That without me, he never would have done the marvelous things I was sure he would do. When I met him, I finally understood my father."

Sal felt another pull inside his ribs, harder this time. He dropped his eyes to the water below. "Are you going to meet him?"

Mr. Merkel let out a long breath that, instead of deflating him, seemed to open him wider. "When I first came here, I didn't think it was possible to balance the ledger of my life. Recently, I've begun to think that perhaps I can lessen the debt I carry after all." He smiled at Sal, and his cheeks were pink. "But I also have to look backward, and make amends where I can. One of those ways is with Lucas. So yes, I'm going to meet him. And I'm going to ask for his forgiveness." He folded his hands on his lap. "The fact that he wants to see me gives me hope that he'll give it."

Sal heard Lucas's voice saying Sal couldn't give Mr. Merkel what he needed. His ribs throbbed now in the talon grip of jealousy, and also a deep, nameless fear. Beneath his feet the water was so dark it was almost black, even in the sunlight.

They finished their sandwiches in silence, listening to the river gurgling through the gate to its doom. Then Mr. Merkel took the wrappers and tucked them in his bag. He climbed off the wall and Sal followed. Back down the quiet country road they drove, through the thin green fields that sucked the river dry, and they did not talk about Lucas any more.

JAKE

Jake stood at the bottom of the fire road, watching the school bus drop off its passengers in front of the general store. The students dispersed down Marzen's narrow streets, but only one headed to the fire road. When Sal reached him Jake said, "Mind if I walk with you a ways?"

"Sure," Sal said, and though Jake could tell he didn't really want the company he fell in beside him. He was pleased to see Sal was wearing the jeans he'd given him.

"Looks like the pants fit."

"Yeah." A sideways glance. "Thanks."

"I can get you more stuff, if you want."

"That's okay. Gideon'll do it."

"Really?"

Sal kicked a rock. "He says he didn't notice my stuff had gotten so small."

Jake thought anyone who bothered to look at Sal would see his clothes were too small, but he didn't say this. The fire road climbed steeply, and after two hundred yards they were already above the roofs of Marzen. Jake remembered watching Grace and her brothers walk up this road from the elementary school, the two boys on either side of their little sister like bodyguards.

"Do you like living up here?" he asked.

"It's okay."

"It's pretty far out of town."

"It's Prentiss land." Sal's chin lifted. "It's been ours for a hundred and seventy years."

Jake looked at him in surprise. The Prentiss place didn't seem like something anyone would be proud of. Grace sure hadn't been. "What do your uncles do up there, anyway?"

"Gideon makes furniture."

There it was again: an undercurrent of pride. Jake didn't understand this, either. The furniture he'd seen in the shed was awful. "What about Ezra?"

Sal hitched his backpack higher on his shoulder. "Ezra doesn't live there anymore."

"Really? When did he leave?"

Sal shrugged. "A few weeks ago."

"Where did he go?"

"Reno, I think."

That was interesting. Before the day Jake brought Sal the Dollar Store clothes and ran into Gideon, he'd never seen either Prentiss brother without the other. In school, in town, at the bar, they were always together, like a pair of dour bookends. Still, he supposed he shouldn't be surprised that Ezra had finally had enough of living in a dump. It was staying that was harder to fathom.

When they came to the low rise that shielded the grove of trees from view, Jake stopped. Reluctantly, Sal stopped, too. He turned his back to the bluff.

"I went up there the other day." Jake nodded his head in the direction of the hill. "Just to see if the police missed anything."

Sal looked up from under his unkempt bangs. "Did they?"

"No. I did find a little trail, though. It goes over the bluff, then down to the Prentiss place. Do you ever use that path to get to the bus?"

Sal shook his head.

"If you thought you could stomach it after everything, it would cut your walk by more than half."

"I'll look for it."

"Did you ever hear of people using drugs up there in that campsite? Shooting up, maybe?" Though the grove was in the middle of nowhere, it did look like the sort of place where junkies would gather, and that would explain the needle. But Sal shook his head again.

"It's on Prentiss land. Nobody else is allowed."

This answer only compounded Jake's unease. Sal started to walk on, but Jake said, "Wait a minute." Sal took two more steps, then turned around. Jake felt like a police officer interrogating a suspect, but he made himself ask the question that had been on his mind since the day Sal found the body. "How come you didn't have your backpack when you came to the station that morning? You said you were on your way to the school bus."

Sal waited a beat too long before answering. "I left it at school. The day before."

Jake didn't believe him, and this scared him, but he wasn't going to push it. Not here, a hundred yards from where the math teacher had died. Instead he said, "Listen, Sal. Your mom was special to me. If you ever need anything, just ask. It doesn't matter what it is."

He'd never told anyone how he'd felt about Grace, but looking at Sal he realized the boy had known it all along. Just by watching Jake in the bar, from his corner table.

"Thanks," Sal said. Then he raised two fingers to his forehead in a small, odd salute and walked away, up the empty road.

That night Jake and his mother ate fried chicken with Mexican rice and roasted peppers in the same kitchen where

Jake had eaten almost every dinner since he'd been born. He ate quietly, replaying his conversation with Sal and how afterward the boy, bowed under the weight of his backpack, had trudged up the hill to the Prentiss place, where only Prentisses were allowed, and only Gideon remained.

It wasn't until he finished eating that the idea struck him. His mother had run Marzen's post office for almost forty years. A plump, warmhearted woman who stood barely five feet tall in her orthopedic shoes, Rosita Sanchez chatted with everyone who wandered in, which was everyone, because everyone in Marzen got their mail delivered to a post office box. She knew more about what went on in this town than anyone else.

"I ran into Gideon Prentiss the other day," Jake said.

"At the Nickel?" Rosita hadn't liked it when her son spent three nights a week there, though Jake suspected she knew why he went.

"I took some things up to the Prentiss place for Sal. I was wondering if it's true, what people say about the Prentisses. That they're criminals."

"They used to be. Rustling, bootlegging, and some Mafia business, too. But Asa wasn't. That's Gideon's father. He made furniture. Lots of folks around here bought from him." Rosita scraped the last of the peppers from her plate. "I don't know about Gideon and Ezra, though. They keep to themselves. Like Prentisses do."

"Why is that?" Jake had always taken the Prentisses' seclusion for granted, but not anymore.

"I imagine it started because they wanted to hide what they were up to. But now I suppose it's become a way of life. The way things do if you do them long enough." Rosita looked around the kitchen, and Jake saw a hint of sorrow in her face. It surprised him. He'd always thought she was happy raising her son in the house where she and her mother and grandfather had been raised.

It was the life she'd expected, and Jake thought living the life you'd expected should make you happy.

"Gideon's the only one left up there now," he said.

Rosita raised her eyebrows. "That's interesting. Though I suppose if any of them was going to stay, it would be Gideon."

"Why?"

"Do you remember what happened to the Simmons boys?"

Jake did, but vaguely. It had been twenty years ago, when he was in high school. "They tried to sneak onto the Prentiss property and got beat up for their trouble."

"Yes, but that's not the whole story." Rosita hesitated. "It was long enough ago that I think I can tell you. But don't go spreading it around."

"I won't."

"They went up there on a dare. I don't know who dared them, or why, but they had cans of spray paint, and they were supposed to spray something on the house."

"What?"

"Something not very nice. About Grace, I think. She had a bit of a reputation, you know. But the Prentisses caught them at it."

The Simmons brothers were older than Jake by about three years, part of a gang of Marzen boys that had caused trouble both here and in Lovelock. Then they'd found Jesus, and now they were married to Marzen girls and working at the mine. Just a couple of solid citizens who'd once thought spray-painting WHORE on a teenaged girl's house was funny.

"So they beat them up."

"Yes. Gideon, Ezra, and Asa. But Gideon was the one who brought them home." Rosita crossed her fork over her knife on the plate. "He had Paul tied to the roof of his truck like a trophy buck. Stuart was tied to the tailgate with about twenty feet of rope, and Gideon made him run barefoot behind the truck all the way down the mountain. Alice Simmons said the bottoms of his feet looked like raw meat."

"I never heard any of that."

"Alice didn't tell anyone but me. Gideon warned her not to. And he said if either of her sons came up there again he'd kill them." She picked up Jake's plate and stacked it on her own. "It stands to reason that someone who's willing to kill people for trespassing on his property isn't going to want to leave it."

"Do you think he really would have killed them?"

Rosita weighed this, plates in hand. "Probably not. The Prentisses might have been up to no good for a long time, but I never heard that they killed anyone." She carried the plates to the chipped blue sink. "Still, it always struck me that it was Gideon, not Asa, who brought them home. It seemed to me that Asa was happy to send the Simmons boys on their way with a beating, but Gideon needed to humiliate them."

Jake didn't think it was the trespassing that had set Gideon off. He thought about Gideon beating up the older boy who'd "messed with" his sister in middle school, and how he'd scowled at everyone in the Nickel who dared to flirt with her. If anything could drive Gideon to murder, it would be someone hurting Grace. But Grace had been dead for almost a year. Jake's shoulders eased a little. Until now he hadn't named the darkest of the fears that had been keeping him up at night, but whatever Sal was hiding, it surely couldn't be that one of his uncles had killed his math teacher.

Rosita started to wash the dishes. Jake got the dish towel from its hook. As she handed him the first plate she said, "I am surprised Ezra left, though."

"Why? I wouldn't want to live there, either."

"Yes, but that's not how the Prentisses work. If you hurt one, you hurt them all, and they'll make you pay. Like the Simmons boys. That sort of family is hard to walk away from."

"Grace left."

"Well, it's different for the girls," Rosita said. "Asa had a sister, and she left, too. Married a man from Imlay, I think. But I don't think there's ever been a Prentiss son who left, until now."

The only women buried in the Prentiss graveyard were wives, Jake remembered. It made sense: the Prentisses wouldn't want a man from outside the family to have a claim on their land. It passed only from father to son. Or uncle to nephew. *It's Prentiss land,* Sal had said. Jake's shoulders tightened again. He wondered what Grace would think about her son spending his life on the isolated property she'd left before she was out of high school. If she was anywhere now, watching what her death had led to, he hoped she felt terrible about it. This was the first critical thought he'd ever had about her, and he rubbed the plate with his towel hard, as if he could scrub the thought from his mind.

Rosita, misunderstanding, put her soapy hand on his and squeezed. "Grace was a good girl. She had a bit of trouble when she was young, as some girls do, but she was doing right by her son in the end."

Except Grace hadn't done right by Sal in the end. She'd given herself over to drugs, and let them destroy her. Now her son was living with her outcast brother in a filthy compound half a mile from a murder scene, and Jake's life was no longer the life he'd expected. He pulled his hand from his mother's and put the plate in the cupboard.

SAL

The Friday before Christmas Sal's customers came and went, all but the old linebacker. They each bought extra bottles of medicine to get them through Sal's Christmas break, which made every transaction more complicated, but still Sal kept an eye out for the man Mr. Merkel loved the way a father loves a son. At last he saw Lucas walking down Western carrying a white plastic bag, his long legs scissoring in his baggy khaki pants. When he sat on the bench Sal tensed, but Lucas made no move to grab his arm. Instead he took a sandwich wrapped in wax paper out of the bag. "You probably don't get to eat, do you?"

He was right—Sal never got to eat lunch on Fridays—but Sal refused to be disarmed by the gesture. He put the sandwich on his lap, pulled a brown bag out of his backpack, and slid it over without a word.

Ezra had been thrilled when Sal told him about Lucas, and he wasn't worried that Lucas had figured out Sal was selling medicine. He'd probably heard it from one of the others, he said, and word of mouth was how they'd grow the business. In fact, Ezra had hoped they'd have a lot more customers by now, but apparently not everybody wanted to buy their medicine on a regular schedule. Some people just wanted it when they wanted it, and when they wanted it they wanted it right away, so they went to the

Colony and bought it from street dealers like his weed guy. Ezra, who bought twenty bottles a month on front, couldn't compete with that sort of operation, at least not yet. Sal secretly hoped he never could. He'd rather sell medicine to people who didn't want it the way the people who bought it in the Colony wanted it.

Lucas tucked the OxyContin into the pocket of his tan windbreaker with fingers that were even quicker than Sal's. A woman walking a corgi passed by, and after a glance at them she looked away. Sal knew what they looked like, two ragged people slouched on a park bench. People who faded. By the time she got to the next corner she would have forgotten all about them.

"Thanks for giving Adam my message," Lucas said. "We had a nice chat."

Sal couldn't tell how that chat had gone. He'd watched Mr. Merkel all week, but for once he hadn't been able to read him, either.

"What did he tell you about me?" Lucas asked.

Sal looked down at his backpack. "He just said you used to be his student."

"Did he tell you I was his favorite?"

Sal busied himself with the backpack's zipper. "No."

"Really? He didn't tell you about the Riemann Hypothesis?" Lucas asked. "I was going to prove it. When I did, he would get the full professorship he'd always wanted, just for being my adviser."

Sal looked up Western for the linebacker and wished he would hurry. He was never this late. It was important to keep to a schedule, he always said, especially when you were retired and lived alone. His wife was dead and his daughter lived in San Francisco and never visited, which Sal thought was terrible. He would have visited, if the linebacker were his father.

"Aren't you going to ask me what the Riemann Hypothesis is?" Lucas asked.

Sal didn't care what the Riemann Hypothesis was, but Lucas didn't wait for an answer. "I'm not sure how to explain it to a kid, actually. It says all the zeroes of the Riemann Zeta Function lie on the same line, reaching out to infinity." He saw Sal's confusion and laughed. "Yeah, you'll never understand it. The point is, I was trying to prove it's true."

Sal didn't care if he understood it or not. He thought this Riemann thing sounded as pointless as the factor trees that covered the whiteboard in Mr. Merkel's classroom. "Why would you want to do that?"

Lucas raised an airy hand. "Mathematicians just like to figure out things like that."

"Does it explain anything? Like, the way stuff works in the real world?"

"Nope. It's entirely theoretical and abstract. That's why it's so great."

That wasn't the kind of math Mr. Merkel liked, Sal thought with a flicker of satisfaction. Mr. Merkel liked math that explained why volcanoes erupted and why there was sand in the desert. No matter how much Mr. Merkel loved Lucas, he couldn't have cared about some formula that told you meaningless information about zeroes and lines. "So it's just a game, then."

"No, it's not just a game." Lucas leaned forward, suddenly serious. "It's a beautiful hypothesis. Pure, wicked math, absolutely elegant. And it's true. Everybody knows it's true. But nobody's been able to *prove* it's true, not even Riemann, even though they've been trying for a hundred and fifty years. How could you not want to prove it, if you could?"

He had that spiky energy about him that Mr. Merkel got when he told his math stories. Sal shifted uneasily on the bench. "So that's it? You just want to do it because nobody else has?"

"That's the whole point of being a mathematician! Ever since

Euclid, people have been coming up with theories about how numbers work and figuring out how to prove them. Brilliant men die before they can prove their theories, leaving the proofs to other men who won't be born for centuries. It's like this incredible conversation that's been going on for five thousand years. All I ever wanted was to be a part of it." Lucas's hands were trembling, and he folded them together to quiet them.

Math is the one true language of humanity, Mr. Merkel had said to a classroom of sixth graders. He'd said it to Lucas, too, and then it became the thing Lucas wanted most. The thing he'd lost, because of Mr. Merkel. "So are you going to do it?" Sal asked. "Prove what that guy said?"

Lucas gave a harsh laugh. "I'd have to start over. The university kept all my work when they kicked me out. Proprietary research, they said, and I wasn't in a position to argue about it." He looked at Sal out of the corners of his eyes. "Do you want to know why I got kicked out?"

Sal did. Even though he wasn't sure he'd like the answer. "Why?"

"I got kicked out for doing what you're doing. Selling prescription painkillers to junkies."

Sal's mouth opened in surprise. Then a loud shriek came from the playground, and a woman ran to pick up a toddler who'd fallen off the slide. It was Sal's customer, the young mother. She cuddled her boy close, and Sal felt a tender surge of protectiveness for her. "They aren't junkies."

"Sure they are. Why do you think they're buying pills from a kid on a park bench?"

Sal knew what junkies were. They were drug addicts. His people weren't drug addicts. They were regular people with jobs and homes and children. They bought OxyContin from a kid on a park bench because they needed medicine for arthritis and football injuries and carpal tunnel syndrome and they couldn't afford doctors, or their doctors wouldn't give it to them. Lucas had no idea what their lives were like. Besides, Lucas was buying it, too, wasn't he? If they were junkies, then so was he.

"How'd you get into this business, anyway?" Lucas asked. "A kid your age, I'd say older brother. But you don't have any brothers, do you? Or parents."

Sal's shoulder blades tightened. "Why do you think that?"

"Your clothes are too small. If you had a younger brother, he'd be wearing them. If you had an older brother, your clothes would be too big. The parent thing was a guess, but not a hard one. It's all over you that you're alone in the world."

Lucas smirked at him, and Sal's scalp prickled. Nobody had watched him the way he watched other people before, and he didn't like it. "I live with my family."

"Maybe you do. But they don't give a shit about you." Lucas ran his hand across his ginger beard. "You don't want to tell me how you got started. That's fine. Because I can guess that, too. You wanted to make a little money. And somebody told you this was easy cash, and wouldn't hurt anybody."

"I'm not doing it for the money."

"Are you getting a cut?" Lucas read his silence. "Then you're doing it for the money."

No, Sal thought, he was doing it because Ezra would send him to foster care if he didn't. Though he had used the money to buy *The Graveyard Book*. And Ezra, after that first day, had treated him like a junior partner instead of a kid he might send back to Mrs. McDonald the social worker. A dead leaf twisted in the sand at Sal's feet, caught by a finger of wind.

"There's no shame in wanting some extra cash," Lucas said. "I sold weed at Chico State because my scholarship didn't cover everything. I should have stuck to that. Nobody cares about a little weed. But when I got to Reno the demand was out of control. Painkillers, Ritalin, coke, dope, grad students will do it all. First they're up, then they need to come down, then they need to focus. Got to get that postdoc, get that internship." Struck by the sun, his eyes were the color of Catellus's, a deep, rich gold. "The problem with a business like that is if one thing goes wrong, it all falls apart. For me, that one thing was Adam Merkel."

The young mother turned her boy loose and walked back to her bench, moving as if in a dream. Sal's thumbs pressed into the soft bread of the sandwich he would throw in the trash as soon as Lucas left. Lucas hadn't just sold medicine. He'd sold a ton of other stuff, too. Bad stuff. Mr. Merkel must have found out, and reported him. That was the betrayal Mr. Merkel felt so guilty about, but he shouldn't, because Lucas was a drug dealer. A criminal.

"That's why you're here," Sal said. "You're mad at him for getting you kicked out of school."

Lucas raised one eyebrow. "You could say that. You could also say I was in the neighborhood. I didn't just get kicked out, I got sent to prison." He saw Sal's shock and laughed. "I spent seventeen months in Lovelock Penitentiary, right up the road. I got out six weeks ago, and a friend told me Adam was here. That's interesting, I thought. He moved to the town closest to where I was locked up. Like he wanted to be near me, even after everything that happened."

That wasn't true, either. Mr. Merkel had come to Lovelock to teach kids at the very beginning of math. He'd said so on the first day of school. Sal dug his toe into the sand.

"But here's the best part," Lucas said. "What does Adam Merkel do when he gets to Lovelock? He finds another dope boy to pal around with. I couldn't believe it when I figured out your setup."

Sal flinched. "He doesn't know about this."

Lucas slapped Sal's back. "I know. That's what makes it so perfect."

NORA

After her encounter with Gideon in the middle school parking lot Nora waited until dinner was done and her father was settled in his recliner, the NCAA men's basketball tournament on the television and his nightly bottle of Michelob in his hand. Then she went to her bedroom.

Her yearbooks were in the back of her closet. She dug them out, sat on her bed, and paged through her freshman book until she found a photo of Grace Prentiss, a dark-haired girl in a peasant blouse who smiled uncertainly despite her obvious beauty. Gideon wasn't with Jeremy and the seniors, but Nora wasn't surprised. Less than half the Marzen kids stuck around to graduate.

She flipped through her other books, looking for more pictures of Grace. Nora and Britta were everywhere, posing in Homecoming tiaras and cheerleading outfits—*Britta Daniels and Nora Wheaton, Cocaptains of the Cheer Squad, show their Mustang Spirit!*—but Grace slipped through almost unseen. She was in no clubs, played no sports, and was in only one candid shot, with a group of football players her sophomore year. She sat on Fen Murphy's knee, and now her smile was wide and electric. There were shades of Sal in her smoky tangle of curls and her wide dark eyes, but not in her smile or her raised, confident chin.

As Nora put the books back in the closet she wondered where Jeremy's yearbooks were.

His door was always closed, but Nora went in once a month to dust, so she knew how to brace herself. While she'd stripped her room of her teenaged self when she moved home, Jeremy hadn't changed his even as he moved into his twenties, so it was a time capsule of him at seventeen, with Michael Jordan posters on the walls and Little League and Pop Warner trophies on every flat surface. The only thing missing was his smell. A week after he died Nora had done the laundry, and the familiar, funky stink of him had driven her to her knees. She'd never smelled it again.

She found Jeremy's yearbooks on his bookshelf and hurried out.

Gideon Prentiss's freshman photo, with its pale eyes and unsmiling face, perfectly foreshadowed the man who'd threatened Nora in the middle school parking lot. In Jeremy's sophomore book she found a third Prentiss: Ezra, a freshman, whose kinship with Grace hovered in his delicate features. In Jeremy's junior book Ezra, a sophomore now, looked sullenly at the camera, while Gideon, in his last year of high school, wore a half smile that was almost a sneer. Nora, well versed in the poses of young boys, saw in that studied smirk something that surprised her: vulnerability. She shut the book with a snap.

When Nora got to the Whiskey an hour later Britta was waiting with two margaritas. "Thank God you called. Jack and Maury have the flu." Britta navigated motherhood with her usual multitasking aplomb, but whenever her kids got sick she handed them off to her husband. Nora laughed and took one of the drinks.

It was Friday, and the bar was filling up. Soon their girls' night out would become a party, so after letting her friend vent about how much better Children's Motrin would be if it had a little Ambien in it, Nora said, "Do you remember the Prentisses from high school? Grace, Ezra, and Gideon. From Marzen."

"I remember Grace." Britta made a tut-tutting sound. "She was a naughty girl."

"That's what I thought. But I can't remember why."

"She dated Fen Murphy, but she dumped him for some Paiute drug dealer in the Colony. She actually moved in with him, even though she was sixteen and he was, like, twenty-four."

Nora didn't remember that, but she wasn't surprised Britta did. Britta had the memory of a natural politician. "She's dead. She had a heart attack last year."

"Really?" It wasn't often Nora knew something Britta didn't. "That's too bad."

"Her son's the one who found Adam Merkel. He lives with Gideon, up near where it happened." Nora dropped her voice. She'd heard Adam's name a half dozen times since she'd arrived, and she didn't want to feed Lovelock's churning gossip mill if she could help it. "I was wondering what kind of support system he has. If Gideon's a decent guy."

Britta mulled this over. "I don't remember him, but I remember Ezra. He was kind of cute. But weird."

"Weird how?"

"Didn't hang out with anybody, lurked in the corners, that sort of thing."

"Do you know where he is now?" Nora couldn't imagine why Sal lived on that godforsaken property if there was another uncle nearby who could take him.

"Marzen, I'd guess." Britta shrugged. Like everyone else in Lovelock, she considered Marzen a black hole from which people emerged for middle school and high school then returned to forever. Though Marzen people shopped in Lovelock's stores and ate in its restaurants all the time, Lovelock people forgot them as soon as they were gone.

"Speaking of the math teacher." Britta's eyes gleamed. "Did you hear about Mary Barnes? I heard she's a suspect!"

"Mary didn't kill Adam," Nora said.

"How do you know? I heard the math teacher and her had a thing, but he dumped her. You know she doesn't take that well."

Nora could imagine the lurid rumors circulating in Britta's coffee shop. For most people in this town, Adam's murder was the most exciting thing that had happened in their entire lives. Still, their willingness to turn on one of their own disgusted her. "Mary and Adam didn't have a thing."

"That's not what Kevin Keegan told me," Britta said. "Remember how she set Mitch's truck on fire when he left her for Susie? She's only gotten more desperate since then. What is she now, fifty? That poor math teacher was probably her last chance."

"Kevin doesn't know shit." Nora's own vehemence surprised her. But Britta had been happily married to her high school boyfriend for fifteen years and sat perched atop Lovelock's social hierarchy like a sleek mother hen; surely she could muster some sympathy for a woman who'd expected the same and been disappointed.

Britta had the grace to back down. "I'm not saying she did it. I'm just telling you what other people are saying."

"Do me a favor," Nora said. "When you hear people say Mary Barnes is some sort of *Firestarter* murderess, shut it down, okay? She's got to live in this place just like the rest of us."

"Okay, fine." Britta raised her glass, and Nora touched it with her own.

Two minutes later Bing Wallerman came over to talk to Britta about a city council special election. Then Mike Conyers had some ideas for a new football scoreboard he wanted to run by her. Soon there were a half dozen people at their table, with Britta at the center, talking up her latest scheme: a Fourth of July hot air balloon festival. It would put Lovelock on the map, she said, and maybe it would, Nora thought, watching her friend with affection. If anyone could put Lovelock on the map, it was Britta.

From time to time Britta looked over at her, and Nora knew she was annoyed by her silence. Britta thought college had made Nora a snob, and she wasn't wrong: right now Jesse Hind was talking about breeding his terrier in grammatically mutilated sentences that made Nora's head pound. But it wasn't really her degree that held Nora apart. Like Mary Barnes, no one in this bar would ever consider leaving this town. They could lose jobs, businesses, and marriages—or be suspected of a brutal murder—and they would get down on their knees and pick up the pieces where they fell. Nora was leaving every piece of her life behind as soon as her father died. That was the chasm she couldn't bridge.

She sipped her margarita, letting her thoughts spin. Gideon Prentiss had been at Adam's house the day after he died, and she could think of no good reason for that. He'd reeked of malevolence, both at the Prentiss place and in the school parking lot. But Sal, who knew a story he wasn't telling, hadn't seemed afraid of him. Mason and Bill hadn't arrested him, either, even after questioning him about why he'd been at Adam's. And as Nora looked around at her neighbors in the bar she remembered what Mason had said about the killer's motive being personal. There were blood feuds in this town that went back generations, yet nobody had killed anybody in half a century. It was hard to imagine what Adam could have done in seven months that would make Gideon—or anyone else here—set him on fire.

But he'd lived in Reno long enough to become a professor, get married, and do something he felt so terrible about that he could only look at pictures of his wife and child in private.

Mason would go to the university, and he'd ask all the right questions. But he'd be as much an outsider there as Adam had been in Lovelock. Nora had spent four years there. It wasn't much, but it might be enough.

She finished her drink and slipped out of the bar. Only Britta saw her go.

SAL

No grass grew on the graves at the Marzen Baptist Church. The church couldn't afford irrigation, and the deacons thought the wild hill grasses too uncouth for reverence, so twice a month Alvira Menendez, the church's groundskeeper, raked the sand and plucked out anything that grew. She did this for Grace Prentiss's grave even after Sal lined it with a neat rectangle of stones that made raking it difficult.

On Christmas, eleven weeks before Mr. Merkel died, Sal stood beside his mother's grave with his uncles. The lines Alvira's rake left in the sand looked like the claw marks of Catellus's demons, and Sal slammed his mind shut against an image of his mother, six feet and six months into the ground. Instead he remembered how pretty she'd been in the metal casket in the church, with her dark hair fanned out on the white pillow. It was easy to remember how she'd looked that day, but it was becoming harder to remember how she'd looked alive.

That morning Sal had walked into the kitchen to find Gideon in suit pants and a white dress shirt, making eggs. When Gideon saw him he banged on Ezra's door until his brother emerged in his boxers and wife beater, blinking and unshaven. The three of them ate in silence, as they always did. The brothers ate quickly, scraping their forks against the Bakelite plates, then drank coffee from chipped ceramic mugs. Sal ate more slowly, savoring. Gideon made eggs the way Sal's mother had, with cheese, onions, and a splash of hot sauce. It was a rare hint of their shared childhood.

When Sal finished, Gideon said, "Today we honor our dead. Go put your dress clothes on."

Ezra saw Sal's confusion. "We always do this on Christmas. Don't ask why."

"We do it because we've always done it," Gideon said.

"That's his answer to everything. If Daddy did it, we've got to do it."

"Daddy did it because his daddy did it. And his daddy before him." Gideon picked up his plate and his mug. "Go get dressed."

"Go fuck yourself," Ezra said, but he went to his room. By now Sal knew that, though Ezra might complain, he always did what Gideon told him to do. Gideon dictated everything, from where Ezra could smoke his pot to when Ezra could borrow the truck to when Ezra got up in the morning and went to bed at night. It was a dominance so ingrained it must stem from when they were boys, and even their division of labor reflected it: Gideon did the more sophisticated chores, like cooking and maintaining the electrical equipment, while Ezra dug the garbage pits and fed the chickens.

The suit Sal had worn to his mother's funeral was still in the bottom of the Samsonite, and it was hopelessly wrinkled. It was also too small: in the pinch of its seams Sal felt every one of the 186 days since her death. When he came out of his room Gideon produced an iron from a narrow pantry, and while Sal sat at the table in his socks and underwear Gideon worked the point of the iron under the shirt collar and knifed creases in the pants. But for all his attention, he didn't notice the suit was too small.

Their first stop wasn't the cemetery in Marzen; it was the Prentiss plot, high on a hill at the end of a thin trail. Sal hadn't seen the small graveyard before, and the small company of stones standing watch over the valley, all bearing the Prentiss name, affected him deeply. They made the land feel ancestral in a way it hadn't when Gideon told him Prentisses had lived there for 170 years. Sal had finished *The Graveyard Book,* where another orphaned boy talked to the dead, and here on this lonely hill the dead seemed just a breath away. He touched the wrought iron fence and felt thousands of cold nights and hot days in the metal and five generations of stories in the earth.

The two oldest stones were side by side at the back: Ezekiel Prentiss and his wife, Wyanet. Ezekiel's stone said GONE ON THE WINGS OF ANGELS WITH THE DEVIL AT HIS HEELS, which made Sal think of Angelus and Catellus. At Ezekiel's and Wyanet's feet lay James and John, born on the same day and buried within five months of one another sixty years later. BELOVED HUSBAND, BROTHER, AND FATHER, said James's headstone. To his left lay Sadie, BELOVED WIFE. John, BELOVED BROTHER, had no one beside him but James. Two more generations followed them: Richard, his wife Mary, their son Saul, and his wife Emmeline.

The newest grave belonged to Sal's grandmother, Elizabeth. Beside her was her husband, Asa, and between them lay Thomas. BELOVED SON, his headstone said. Unlike the others', its lettering was uneven. The grass stirred in a whisper, as if weighted with words just unheard, and Sal looked again at his grandfather's stone. He'd died six days after Thomas.

BELOVED SON. Sal's mother had never mentioned this third brother. Sal marked the years and figured she'd been around sixteen when he died. She'd told Sal she left home at sixteen because she wanted a bigger life. She'd only gone as far as Marzen, but Sal had assumed that was as big a life as she'd wanted. Now he wondered if that was why she left at all.

"These are our people," Gideon said. His eyes found Sal's and held them. "It doesn't do to forget your people." The wind's soft exhalations sounded like voices, as if the dead Prentisses were murmuring their assent.

Now Gideon, Ezra, and Sal stood together in front of Sal's mother's grave, and Sal cried as quietly as he could. He cried because he missed her, and because, as closely as he listened, he couldn't hear her. He cried because he was angry at her, for her carelessness with the needle that had ended her life and ruined his. But he also cried because she was all alone, in this scraped and sandy ground, instead of in the whispering graveyard at the top of the hill, with her brother, in land that belonged to her.

When they got back to the double-wide Ezra invited Sal to come hunting with him. He'd never invited him before, and Sal knew he was only asking because he'd seen him crying in the cemetery. Ordinarily Sal would have said no, but the marks Alvira's rake had left on his mother's grave had left gouges in his mind, and for once he couldn't bear the thought of being alone in his room. So he changed out of his suit and followed Ezra up one of the spidery trails that led out of the valley.

The wide-open sky and the cold, bright air did make Sal feel better. So did the sight of Samson unchained, leaping through the grass. Even Ezra's strides were longer. He hunted almost every day, and watching him now, Sal suspected it wasn't just the birds and the rabbits that drew him into the hills.

"I'm sure this isn't the sort of Christmas you're used to," Ezra said after they'd clambered across a dry wash.

"No." Every year Sal and his mom drove to Lovelock for a tree, and on Christmas Eve they went to church, where she sang "O Holy Night" at the end of the service.

"Your mom loved Christmas when we were kids," Ezra said. "She had a guitar, and she'd sing Christmas carols. She sang real good."

For the first time, Sal wondered what Gideon, Ezra, and his mother had been like as children together. Maybe Ezra and his mother had played with each other more than with bossy, moody Gideon. At the bar, Gideon had watched Sal's mother with intense, protective eyes, but it was Ezra who asked if her back was bothering her, and Ezra's glass, not Gideon's, she refilled when it was empty.

Samson crouched, his tail erect. He was as rigid as a statue, and he pointed his snout at a large clump of sage twenty feet away.

"Quiet," Ezra said. He pulled a whistle from his pocket, put it in his mouth, and lifted his rifle from the crook of his arm to his shoulder. Then he crept through the sage. When he was ten feet from the dog, he blew the whistle, short and sharp.

Samson leaped forward as though released from a spring. A dozen birds erupted from the brush, and a crashing sound made Sal cover his ears—once, twice, three times. In less than five seconds the birds were gone and the gun was silent.

Then Ezra blew the whistle again, and Samson surfed through the sage, nose to the ground. Sal watched, fascinated, as the dog picked something up with his mouth and trotted back to his master.

"Good dog," Ezra said. He showed Sal what he held: a small brown quail, its head limp and its right wing bloody. Sal thought of Ms. Wheaton's spearpoint and the brave young men hunting mastodons ten thousand years ago. That seemed like a fairer fight to him, but in the end the mastodons had lost anyway, and now the brave young men of the Basin had only small birds and rabbits to hunt. Sal felt sorry for all of them: the mastodons, the birds and the rabbits, and the brave young men.

Ezra grinned. "If we get a couple more, we'll have Christmas dinner."

They traced a broad circle. Twice more Samson pointed, and Ezra brought down three more quail that he put in his leather pouch with the first. Finally they crested a hill and came upon the Prentiss graveyard from behind. Ezra rested his rifle against the fence and took out a joint. He lit it with a plastic lighter and drew deeply. Then he jerked his thumb at the graves. "You know anything about them?"

Sal knew what Marzen thought of the Prentiss clan, but his mother hadn't told him anything. "No."

Ezra pointed at each stone. "Ezekiel was a traveling preacher and a cattle rustler. Wyanet was working in a Lovelock whorehouse when he walked in. James and John were rustlers, too. Our great-granddaddy was a bootlegger, running whiskey during Prohibition. Granddaddy was a forger. Drivers' licenses, green cards, birth certificates, shit like that."

From all the talk in Marzen about the Prentisses, Sal had imagined them as a gang of criminals he and his mother had done well to escape. Now Ezra was telling him he'd been right. But standing beside their graves, what struck him most was the word *beloved*. It was on every stone, except the one that was missing.

"Why isn't my mom here?" he asked.

Ezra took another drag on the joint. "Our little brother died."

Sal looked at Thomas Prentiss's stone. He'd been nine. Just two years younger than Sal. "How?"

"He had a bad heart. One day he didn't wake up." Ezra jerked one shoulder. "I guess your mom had a bad heart, too."

When Sal's mom died, Gideon and Ezra had come to the small Lovelock hospital straight backed and gray faced. Jake told them they could have the medical examiner figure out how she died, and when they said no, Sal felt Jake's relief. Now he knew why his uncles had believed Jake when he said she died of heart failure.

Ezra nodded at Thomas's stone. "He was as tough as any of the old Prentisses, Tommy was. He couldn't even go to school, he was so sick. But he never complained."

Sal looked down at his ragged sneakers, surprised by the pity he felt for Ezra. He heard in his uncle's tight voice that he'd loved his little brother as much as he'd loved his sister. Gideon was the only one of his siblings he didn't love, and Gideon was the one he was stuck with. "So that's why my mom left? Because Tommy died?"

"She left because she thought it was our momma and daddy's fault. They never took him to a doctor. Even when he couldn't hardly climb the steps no more." Ezra laughed sourly. "When Momma got cancer and signed up for Medicaid, your mom flipped her shit."

Sal thought about his grandmother with her oxygen tank and her mean, sad eyes. It had lasted less than half an hour, his mother's farewell visit to the woman who'd raised her. Sal and his mother drank Cokes and sat on the couch while brindled cats twined around their legs and the old woman wheezed through the tubes in her nose. Sal couldn't remember a single word being spoken.

"How come they didn't take him to a doctor?"

"That was Daddy's way. We didn't have the money, and he wouldn't take nothing for free. Especially from the government. 'Prentisses don't need handouts,' he said. 'We take care of our own.' All that bullshit Gideon spouts off." Ezra shrugged. "He shot himself a week later, so I guess he reconsidered that line of thinking."

Sal tried to imagine a father who'd let his son die rather than take something he couldn't pay for, but who loved him so much he couldn't live with the guilt afterward. Sal didn't know much about fathers, or families, and as he looked at the headstones he wondered what it would take to make a man think that way. It must have been the way his father raised him, and the way that man's father had raised him, too. Maybe that, more than the cattle rustling and bootlegging, was what made the Prentisses outlaws.

"This place is a fucking prison," Ezra said. "It was a prison for Tommy, it was a prison for your mom, and it's a prison for me."

"But not for Gideon," Sal said.

"Even for him. Though he don't know it yet." Ezra pointed his joint at the hills. "A hundred and seventy years, this has been ours. Because every generation, some poor son of a bitch feels like he's got to go get a wife, bring her back here, and have a son to carry on the line. But Gideon won't do that, because he loved your mom too much."

"Why would loving my mom keep him from marrying somebody?" Sal asked.

Ezra took another hit, and Sal felt him groping for the right words. "Because he thought she was perfect. She couldn't do no wrong, no matter what she did, and believe me, she did a lot, before she had you. No other girl will ever measure up to her, especially now she's dead." He curled his lip. "But what Gideon don't know is he's the last Prentiss that'll ever live up here, because I'm leaving. This business of ours is the ticket I've been waiting for. And when I'm gone he'll be stuck here by himself, knowing that when he dies, I'll sell everything."

Ezra talked about leaving every Friday night when he collected his money, but Sal had never believed he would actually do it. Now he asked, "Where will you go?"

"Reno. That's where the real players are."

That was where Ezra went every few weeks, to buy the pills Sal delivered on the bench. Sal had never been there. He pictured Ezra driving Gideon's truck between skyscrapers that crowded out the sky and walking down sidewalks filled with people in business suits, a foreigner in his jeans and worn cowboy boots. "When are you going?"

"As soon as I have enough money. I gotta get a place and a car, buy a supply outright, set up business. Ten grand should do it, I figure."

Sal had brought so many thousands of dollars home he'd lost count. "Don't you have that already?"

"I got to give my Reno guy too much. 'Cause of the fronting. By summer, though, I'll have enough, and that's the last Gideon will see of me."

Sal thought about how, on some nights, Gideon sought Ezra out and, with a cold beer, invited him to sit on the cinder block steps after dinner. They never said much, but they'd sit for an hour or more, drinking and looking at the stars. As hard as it was to imagine Ezra leaving, Sal had a harder time picturing Gideon without his brother. "You'd really leave Gideon here alone?"

"He won't give a shit," Ezra said. "He don't care about nothing but this land and his furniture. And he won't be alone, will he? He'll have you."

Sal gripped the fence as the enormity of this sunk in. He didn't like Ezra, but Ezra was the only one of his uncles who talked to him, and the only one who treated him, in his grimy way, like one of his people. If Ezra left, Sal would be stuck with a man who spent all his time making furniture in his shed and only seemed to remember Sal when it was time to eat. Eventually Sal would be like Ezra was now: feeding the chickens, digging the garbage pits, and begging Gideon to let him borrow the truck. Except Gideon would never invite Sal to drink beer on the steps.

"Unless you come with me," Ezra said, and once again Sal's mother came alive in his wide, easy grin. "Wouldn't that be something, little brother? You and me, taking our operation to the big leagues. Doing the Prentisses proud." He flicked what was left of the joint onto his father's grave. "The old Prentisses, anyway."

He whistled at Samson, then winked at Sal. "Come on, let's go eat Christmas dinner."

The dog got up from where he'd been lying in the grass and followed his master down the hill. Sal hung back for a moment. From up here the farmhouse and the buildings around it looked small and vulnerable, the way Catellus would see them, but the land around them was solid and immutable. Six generations. Now seven. As Sal cast his eyes over the Prentiss graveyard he saw his own headstone there, shimmering and gone. ABSALOM PRENTISS, it said. It did not say BELOVED.

He didn't want to move to Reno with Ezra. He didn't want to take Ezra's operation to the big leagues, whatever that meant. But as he watched Ezra's thin frame lope through the sage that small, dangerous word sent slender roots deep inside his ribs.

Brother.

The next week Sal went to the Family Dollar with five twenties in his pocket. They didn't have Nikes like Kip's, but they had a pair that looked almost like Adidas, and were just as white.

NORA

There is no rise, no dip, and barely a curve in Interstate 80 as it pummels through a hundred miles of sage and saltbush between Lovelock and Reno. In the middle distance, salt flats shimmer as white as snow. Beyond them the land folds into hills, row upon row of mounds cloaked in sameness and wheat-colored grass, their backs as soft as sleeping cats in the sun.

If you lived in Lovelock, you'd know those hills by name. Your family would picnic at Rabbit Hole Springs. You'd ride your dirt bike down the Winnemucca Wash and hunt quail with your father in Seven Troughs. You'd remember summer nights drinking Colt 45s on Chocolate Butte, surrounded by stars. To you, those hills wouldn't be guardrails along a road you couldn't travel fast enough. They'd be Sundays after church, Saturday mornings at dawn, and Fridays at sunset. They'd be why you loved it here. When you loved it here.

Nora loved the hills because they quieted her mind. On bad days, when her father dipped into his liquor or his pain flared up, she could be a thousand feet above the Basin before the school was empty and have an hour of windswept vacancy before going home. She'd sit on the hood of her car and conjure the vanished Lake Lahontan, drawing it from the sand to drown Lovelock beneath five hundred feet of water, and she wouldn't think about whether her father's cough was getting worse, or how she'd pay for the physical therapy the doctor said he needed, or whether he'd be well, and Jeremy alive, if she hadn't broken her promise to her mother. Up here, she was the woman she'd wanted to be when she was seventeen: far away, on an adventure through time.

On the first day of the school district's spring break, eleven days after Adam Merkel died, Nora was parked below the Lovelock Indian Cave, where a nameless tribe who'd lived in the Basin two thousand years before the Paiute came had stored duck decoys made of woven tule and buried eight of their loved ones. The sky was streaked with clouds as frail as lace and the wind teased her hair. Far below, Interstate 80 was a silver thread in the sand.

An hour before, she'd reheated last night's meat loaf and had lunch with her father in the camper.

"No hike today?" he'd asked. Usually she spent spring break hiking alone in the hills. His happiness at her unexpected company made her look away.

"Not today."

He dipped a piece of meat loaf in ketchup. "I liked that boy you brought by."

Of course he did. Sal had listened to his stories, and Nora's father loved an audience. "Sal's a nice kid," Nora said.

"Isn't he the one who found that teacher's body?"

Nora was surprised he remembered that. "Yes."

"Had to be hard on him."

"I'm sure it was."

He took another bite of meat loaf. "He likes anthropology."

"He liked that spearpoint. Any boy would."

"He liked more than that."

There was no point in arguing. "You're right. He did."

"You could bring him by again." Nora's father looked hopeful. "We could tell him a thing or two, you and me."

Nora pushed her plate away. "I have an appointment." His face fell, and she leaned across the table to kiss his cheek. "I'll be back by dinner."

Nora hadn't been to Reno since she cleared out her dorm after Jeremy died. Other people in Lovelock found reasons to go there, but for thirteen years Nora had found reasons to stay away. She'd stopped at the Indian Cave to collect herself, but now she couldn't put it off any longer: she needed to get to the UNR campus before Dr. Sigurdssen's office hours ended.

She pushed the car ten miles over the speed limit and made the drive in under an hour and a half. She parked behind the dorm where she'd lived her junior and senior years. It looked the same—five stories wrapped in brick—but across from it loomed an enormous new dorm, three times its size. It threw her off-balance. So did the students, who looked impossibly young, even the men with their bushy beards. Two girls walked by, their hair loose over their Free People blouses, and Nora fought the temptation to take out her ponytail.

She crossed Virginia Street to the main campus and lost her bearings again. Her freshman dorm was gone; in its place was a massive, half-finished project that, according to a giant placard, would be GREAT BASIN HALL, A LIVING LEARNING COMMUNITY, whatever the hell that was. The library was gone, too, replaced by a jagged building with the words WILLIAM N. PENNINGTON STUDENT ACHIEVEMENT CENTER stamped on its face in three-foot-tall letters. The trees around it were so new they looked like twigs stuck in the fresh-peated ground.

Nora didn't miss the vanished buildings—they'd been ripe for replacement years ago—but the gaudy new structures with their pretentious names made plain what she'd tried to ignore by avoiding this place for thirteen years: while she'd been stuck in Lovelock, the world had moved on without her.

She refocused on her mission. She'd Googled Adam the night before, and come up nearly empty. He'd been an associate professor specializing in number theory, calculus, and statistics, and he'd been a panelist at a few academic conferences, but he'd disappeared from the university directory—and the internet, so far as she could tell—the year before last. A conference bio said he'd gone to UNR for undergraduate and graduate school, so he'd been in Reno for over thirty years. The only thing that struck Nora as odd was that, despite his age and the decades he'd spent on the faculty, he was only an associate professor. It must have been humiliating for him, getting passed over again and again. Maybe that was one of the reasons he'd left.

Nora's destination wasn't the math department, though; it was the Ansari Building, which was still there, as plain as ever with its alternating horizontal stripes of brick and concrete. Inside she found the same glass railings and recessed lighting that had been state of the art in 1983, and the Anthropology Department offices were still on the fifth floor. Nora pulled at the cuffs of her neat white blouse and walked past doors covered in notices about internships and research opportunities until she reached Dr. Sigurdssen's.

Ingrid Sigurdssen, a specialist in early human anthropology, had rocked the scientific world in 1998 with a blockbuster find in eastern Nairobi: the nearly intact skull of an infant *Homo habilis*. When she'd offered Nora a place on her dig in Kenya after graduation Nora thought the world had thrown its doors wide open. Then came the four A.M. call from Mason. Dr. Sigurdssen never let sentimental obligation get in the way of her work, and her eyes were hawklike behind her round black glasses as Nora thanked her for the offer and waited in vain to hear she would be missed. They hadn't talked since.

Nora knocked, her knuckles firmer than her nerve. "It's open," came the remembered voice, low and gravelly.

The professor sat at her desk behind piles of books and papers. Her hair had gone gray and her face was creased even more deeply by the African sun, but she still wore the black glasses and she still looked wiry and strong. She peered at Nora without recognition, and Nora dug her fingernails into her palms. Then the professor leaned back.

"Nora Wheaton. Good Lord." She waved at a chair. "Come in."

Nora was relieved Dr. Sigurdssen remembered her, but the breezy welcome carried its own sting. Dr. Sigurdssen bore no grudge for the rejected dig offer, and why would she? Thirteen years was more than enough time for other gifted students to come and go. Nora sat stiffly on the edge of the chair. "How have you been, Professor?"

"Busy," Dr. Sigurdssen said. "I've got a dig near Malapa now. It's remarkable, what we're finding there."

Nora was stung by the inference: that she wouldn't know about the recent timeline-altering discoveries in the Malapa region. "*Homo naledi*. I read about it."

The professor tapped her fingertips together. "*Homo naledi* is interesting, yes. But we've found something else."

The gleam in her eye made Nora lean forward. "A transitional species?" Just saying the words sent a thrill down her spine. Ever since the days of the Leakeys, anthropologists had been looking for the hybrid creature that connected the genus *Homo* with its ancestor, *Australopithecus*. The idiomatic missing link. Some researchers initially thought *Homo naledi* had been it, but radiocarbon dating showed it was too recent. Nora felt a sharp stab of grief for the person she'd almost become. She could be there right now, digging the secrets of evolution from a South African cave.

"Let's say we are intrigued," Dr. Sigurdssen said. "You'll read about it in *National Geographic* someday, I'm sure."

Now the patronizing tone was unmistakable, and Nora bristled. "I'll read it where you publish it. If you publish it in *Nature* or *Science*."

She was bluffing—she'd let those subscriptions lapse years ago—but Dr. Sigurdssen laughed, and Nora knew she'd passed some unspoken test. "I'm glad you're keeping up. Though I expected you back for graduate work by now."

"I'm still in Lovelock, taking care of my father."

"Surely that's not all you're doing."

"I'm also teaching history." Social studies, but close enough. Nora left out the middle school part. "I'm finishing up a unit on the Paleoindians, actually."

Dr. Sigurdssen cocked her head. "Is that why you're here? You should speak to Gerald Schmidt. He's heading up the Great Basin Paleoindian Research Unit."

Nora had never heard of the Great Basin Paleoindian Research Unit, but she remembered Professor Schmidt. A young, nebbishy associate professor who specialized in the peopling of the Americas, he'd been gentle when he told her that her spearpoint was useless from an archaeological perspective because they hadn't found it *in situ*. "It would make a good museum piece, though," he'd said, and that was the part Nora had told her father.

"No. I'm here to find out about a professor who left the math department two years ago. I thought you could point me to somebody over there who might have known him."

"Why don't you ask them yourself? You never used to be shy."

The needling tone was back, and though it was warmer this time, Nora's voice sharpened. "Because he was murdered, and I want to know whether it had anything to do with why he left. I need to talk to someone who knew him well. Someone who will gossip."

"One of our math professors was murdered?" Dr. Sigurdssen's eyebrows shot up.

"A former professor. Adam Merkel. He was killed near Lovelock a couple of weeks ago."

Dr. Sigurdssen squinted at Nora over her glasses. "Why are you snooping around about him? Surely the police are investigating."

"They are," Nora said, "but the Lovelock police are small town. They haven't had a murder in fifty years, and they don't know Reno at all. Adam was a friend of mine. I want to make sure they don't miss anything."

Dr. Sigurdssen nodded. She hadn't gotten where she was without taking an extraordinary amount of initiative, Nora knew, and not all of it had been strictly by the books. "I don't know many of the math professors. If you give me your email, I'll ask around."

"Thank you."

A tentative knock came on the door, and the professor sighed. "I don't know why they knock like such mice. These are my office hours, for God's sake."

Nora wrote her email address on a Post-it. "It was good to see you, Professor."

"It was good to see you, too, Nora," Dr. Sigurdssen said, and Nora rode the tailwind of those words past the student achievement center, the living learning community, the new dorm that looked like a Marriott, and all the way back to Lovelock.

SAL

When the Christmas break ended, Sal boarded the school bus with a sense of dislocation. The two weeks he'd spent with his uncles had seemed much longer than that, and the remote, timeless silence of the Prentisses' valley had stretched the distance between the double-wide and the middle school a little farther each day. It had begun to seem as though he would never go back, that his feet might never leave Prentiss land again, and the hills had drawn tighter around him, like a cocoon. Getting on the bus felt both like an escape and a betrayal.

But as the bus turned west on the interstate, Sal's thoughts turned forward, to Mr. Merkel. He wondered how Mr. Merkel had spent the break, and then he imagined him and Lucas having lunches together, talking about the Riemann Hypothesis. Maybe they'd even spent Christmas together. Like family. When Sal got off the bus he hurried to Mr. Merkel's classroom for first period.

Mr. Merkel smiled at him as if he were glad to see him, and this made Sal's heart slow, but he soon saw that something was bothering his teacher. Mr. Merkel was distracted during class, sometimes stopping in the middle of a sentence while Kip and his friends rolled their eyes. During their lunches that week he didn't tell Sal a single math story, and at chess club on Thursday Sal pinned the white king in a corner and said "checkmate" for the first time.

"Well played," Mr. Merkel said.

Sal hadn't played well. Mr. Merkel's moves had been small, and they lacked his usual strategic direction. By this point Sal was wondering if Mr. Merkel was in this strange mood because Lucas hadn't forgiven him after all. This gave him a fluttery surge of hope, but he also resented that Lucas's forgiveness mattered so much to Mr. Merkel that without it he could barely focus on Sal. After a silence like a slow constriction of breath, Sal reached for his backpack. "I drew a new story. Do you want to see it?"

Sal had shown Mr. Merkel many drawings by now. Each time Mr. Merkel was as awed by the artwork and captivated by the stories as he'd been the first time, and now Sal thought of him when he drew, shaping his stories for his audience of one. The drawing he showed him today was of Catellus releasing the demons from Hell. He'd drawn it because Mr. Merkel kept asking why, if Catellus was an archangel, he would do such a terrible thing. Sal still hadn't been able to come up with a satisfactory explanation for this, but he'd wanted to show Mr. Merkel the scene anyway. It was one of the best drawings he'd ever done, with Catellus standing astride a maw in the earth while demons with their beetle-black carapaces poured forth by the thousands, but Mr. Merkel barely glanced at it. "Wonderful," he said, and handed it back without waiting for Sal to explain it. Sal looked down at his new sneakers so Mr. Merkel wouldn't see how hurt he was.

Mr. Merkel didn't set up the board for another game. Sal wondered if chess club was over, but Mr. Merkel didn't stand up to leave, either, so they just sat. Behind Mr. Merkel prime factorization trees rambled across the whiteboard. Sal still didn't understand the point of them, and this made him think of the Riemann Hypothesis, and that made him angry all over again.

He pointed at the board. "I don't get why that stuff matters. It's like a math game somebody made up for no reason."

Mr. Merkel's eyes cleared as he considered this. He looked at the clock on the wall. "Have you ever wondered why hours have sixty minutes instead of one hundred?"

"No."

"Thousands of years ago, the Egyptians invented the sundial, and they divided the day into twelve hours instead of ten. Because they didn't count in groups of ten like we do. They counted like this." With his right thumb Mr. Merkel touched the knuckles of his right index finger. "Three knuckles on each finger. Four fingers on each hand. Twelve. All the Western civilizations that came after them kept the twelve-hour day, even if they used a base-ten counting system. So when Europeans decided to divide hours into minutes, they picked sixty instead of one hundred, because sixty is a multiple of twelve."

It was also a multiple of ten, Sal thought. He'd waited all week for Mr. Merkel to tell him a math story, but this one didn't make any sense. "What does that have to do with factor trees?"

"Sixty is also a good choice if you want to break your hour into smaller parts. You can divide it by every number between one and six, and also twelve, fifteen, and thirty. You can only divide one hundred by five, ten, twenty, twenty-five, and fifty."

Sal still wasn't following. He wondered if Lucas would have. He probably would. He had a remarkable mind, after all.

"Think about the numbers you can divide into sixty that you can't divide into one hundred," Mr. Merkel prompted. "Three, six, twelve, fifteen, and thirty. What do they have in common?"

"I don't know." Sal hated how he sounded—like a sulky little kid—but he couldn't help it.

"They're all multiples of three. Three is a prime factor of sixty, but it isn't a prime factor of one hundred."

Then, in a flash of understanding, Sal got it. One hundred was two times two times five times five. Sixty was two times two times *three* times five, and that made all the difference. He thought of how time was measured, in all its subparts—five minutes or six, ten minutes or twelve, fifteen or twenty or thirty—and how much more fluid it became when the denominator was sixty instead of one hundred. Prime factorization wasn't just a math game like the Riemann Hypothesis after all. It mattered, in real and important ways, like how to keep time. When Mr. Merkel saw that Sal understood, he smiled, and relief warmed Sal's face.

"But." Mr. Merkel held up one finger. "Just because a mathematical exercise doesn't have a real-world application, that doesn't mean it's not worth doing. For some people, solving problems is its own joy, no matter what the solution might mean to anyone else. These men and women are often our greatest thinkers."

He said this with awe and pride, and Sal knew he'd been wrong about why Mr. Merkel had been so distant all week. Lucas had forgiven him, and Mr. Merkel was distracted because, now that his remarkable student was back, he didn't care about teaching math to sixth graders, or telling math stories to Sal. Not when he could talk to Lucas about zeroes and lines and infinity in a language the Egyptians knew but Sal would never understand. The second hand of the clock spun around its face, sweeping through the prime factors of sixty like a wing carving through sky, and Sal shook with jealousy and frustration.

Then an idea stirred in the back of his mind. Half-formed, it groped its way forward. Sal sat on the edge of his chair.

"I read *The Graveyard Book*."

Mr. Merkel lit up with pleasure. "What did you think?"

"I loved it."

Mr. Merkel said, "It's about bravery, isn't it? About being willing to sacrifice everything to save the people you love. That's why Benjamin liked it so much."

Sal didn't think *The Graveyard Book* was about bravery. He

thought it was about how growing up meant losing everything that mattered. Bod, the graveyard boy, had the magic powers of the graveyard and the love of its inhabitants, but when he grew up he lost his powers and was cast out, never to see the ghosts who'd raised him until he became one himself. Sal had closed the book to the sound of his own heart breaking, but here in Mr. Merkel's classroom he said, "That's what I thought, too."

"Who was your favorite character?" Mr. Merkel was looking directly at Sal for the first time in days. "Besides Bod, of course."

That was easy. Sal's favorite character was Silas, the black-winged guardian of the graveyard, who long ago had done terrible things but now stood tall on the book's cover, his arm outstretched, as though pointing the way to victory. He reminded Sal of Catellus, who once had been good and now served Hell. But Benjamin had been only ten, and no one he loved had died, so Sal said, "Miss Lupescu."

"She was Benjamin's favorite, too." Mr. Merkel beamed at him, and a flicker of triumph raced up Sal's spine. Lucas might be one of humanity's greatest thinkers, but there were other stories besides math stories. Deep in Sal's mind Angelus unfurled his wings.

"Which of the graveyard powers would you want most?" Sal asked.

Mr. Merkel's eyes fell on the little rook on his desk. "Benjamin liked the fading power," he said. "But I loved that Bod could talk to ghosts. What a remarkable gift that would be."

"Do you think it's possible?" Sal had wanted to ask Mr. Merkel this ever since he'd visited the Prentiss graveyard on Christmas Day. Surely there was a math equation that could be bent around the possibility of life after death, and the dead moving among the living.

"I'm afraid not." Mr. Merkel picked up the rook. "Even if the people we love do live on as spirits, they seem unable to speak to us."

Sal remembered how the grass on the Prentiss graves had seemed to whisper. "I don't know," he said. "Sometimes I feel like I can almost hear them."

Mr. Merkel looked up. His pupils were tiny black dots behind his glasses. "There's no known science that would allow it," he said, but he stared at Sal for a long time, turning the rook over in his fingers.

The next day, on the bench, Sal took the sandwich Lucas offered and bit into it with relish. Again Lucas had waited until Sal's other customers had gone, and again he took his OxyContin and settled in for a chat.

"You're down one," he said. "The old guy."

The linebacker hadn't come this week either, but now Sal knew why. The night before, Ezra had told him he didn't want the medicine anymore. Ezra was annoyed, because losing a customer meant losing money, but Sal was glad. He would miss the linebacker's gentle face and his football stories, but it was good his knee wasn't bothering him as much.

"He doesn't need it anymore," he told Lucas.

"Really?" Lucas said.

"That's what he told my—" Sal caught himself.

Lucas didn't press. Instead he asked, "Do you know his name?"

"No." Sal didn't know any of his people's names. He knew their pains and their troubles, but he didn't know what their friends called them. It had never occurred to him before how odd this was.

"He liked to chat, though," Lucas said. "Even more than the others."

"He hurt his knee playing football. He liked to tell me about the games."

The weather was unseasonably warm for January, and Sal's

people had come early, as though they wanted to get their business done and enjoy the day. The blond girl was sitting on the grass at the far end of the park, her eyes closed and her face turned to the sun. She had yet to say a single word to Sal, and the only thing Sal knew about her was what her tee shirts told him: she liked classic rock bands. He wondered where she went when she left the park. She looked too old to live with her parents, but too young to live anywhere else.

"Tell me something," Lucas said. "How well do you know Adam?"

"Really well." Sal couldn't keep himself from gloating. "We eat lunch together every day, and he's teaching me chess." He looked at Lucas, hoping to see jealousy, but instead Lucas turned to him with what seemed like concern.

"I like you, Sal. I didn't plan on liking you, but I do. So I'm going to give you some advice."

Sal didn't want Lucas's advice, but he shrugged. "Okay."

"When I was in high school and college, my teachers thought I was just another kid who was good at math. But I knew I was much more than that. It was like I saw colors on the spectrum they didn't even know were there." He said this matter-of-factly, but Sal saw pride in the lift of his chin. "When I got to graduate school I was sure everyone would see how special I was, but nobody did. I got B's from professors who looked right through me while other students, who were nothing but human calculators, got A's. I started to think I'd been wrong. Maybe I wasn't special after all.

"Then I took a class with Adam. One week into number theory, he said the way I looked at numbers was unlike anything he'd ever seen. He told me I had a once-in-a-generation gift. It was what I'd been waiting to hear my whole life. You can't imagine what that felt like."

But Sal could imagine it. He'd felt it when Mr. Merkel told

him the way he could read people's feelings made him special, and again when Mr. Merkel praised the stories he drew. Sal looked away, to the blond girl lying on the grass.

"He told me about the great conversation," Lucas said, "and it blew my mind. I knew number theory, but I'd never thought about its history. How everything we know about numbers comes from just a few people, talking across the centuries about colors nobody else can see."

Sal kept his eyes on the blond girl. Lucas the graduate student sounded too much like the way Sal the sixth grader felt when he listened to Mr. Merkel tell his math stories.

"Naturally I wanted to be a part of it," Lucas went on. "Adam pushed me to take on the Riemann Hypothesis, and he became my adviser. He could never prove the Hypothesis himself. He didn't have that sort of mind. But he had a way of clarifying things. With a word or two, he could help me see a problem from a new angle. I'd never had a teacher who could do that. It's a gift in its own right."

Then Lucas's voice darkened. "But as I got closer to proving the Hypothesis something changed. Adam stopped being my teacher, the guy who believed in me and inspired me to do this impossible thing, and became something else. He started showing up at my apartment at weird hours, wanting to see what I'd done, demanding copies of everything, making me explain every nuance of every move. He wanted a share of the credit, of course, but it was more than that. It was like he was a parasite, crawling into my brain, sucking up every drop of brilliance he could find, and using it to fill some bottomless need I hadn't known was there." He shuddered. "Math was the thing I loved more than anything else. It was how I defined who I was. Now I can't even think about numbers without feeling that desperate little mind inside my head, creeping around and putting its greedy tentacles everywhere."

He was staring, unseeing, into the middle distance. Sal didn't bother to hide his disgust. Lucas might be a genius, but it was Mr. Merkel who'd shown him how to prove the Hypothesis; Lucas had said so himself. Now Lucas was twisting Mr. Merkel's gift into something evil so he could blame his teacher for his own failure, when the truth was he'd ruined his life on his own.

Lucas clenched his fists. "I loved that man. He supported me when nobody else would, and he's the closest thing I've ever had to a father. He wants me to forgive him for turning me in, but he'll never understand that that was the least of what he did to me. He drained the joy out of the one thing that made me special. I don't know if I'll ever get it back, and I can't forgive him for that. I *can't*."

His voice shook with something that might have been fury, or regret, or even love, but Sal didn't care. He was consumed by a rush of triumph. Mr. Merkel thought Lucas had forgiven him, but he hadn't, not really. Eventually Mr. Merkel would see that, and then he would look at Sal with clear eyes again, the way he had before Lucas came. All Sal had to do was wait.

Across the park, the blond girl got to her feet. The back of her denim jacket was flecked with dead grass, brown against the blue. She raised her hand in a small wave, then walked away. Sal barely heard what Lucas said next.

"So go ahead and have your lunches with him, Sal. Play chess with him if you want. But if there's anything special about you, don't let him near it. Because he'll poison it. That's what he does."

NORA

Ivan Kazlov was an assistant professor specializing in "Operator Algebras, a branch of Functional Analysis closely connected with Topology," according to the UNR faculty website. Dr. Sigurdssen's email said he was "inappropriately flirty with female colleagues," so Nora wore her hair down and did not ask Wikipedia about Operator Algebras. She felt like her sixteen-year-old self, scoring cigarettes off Sully, but she pushed that thought aside.

Professor Kazlov's office door was open, and Nora saw him in his chair, a stocky man in his forties with a receding hairline and a neat goatee. He was boasting about a round of golf to someone Nora couldn't see. When he saw her he clocked her from head to toe and his smile landed just on the far side of friendly.

Nora leaned against the doorjamb. "Professor Kazlov?"

"At your service," he said, and Nora stepped inside. When she saw his companion, an Asian man with rectangular-framed hipster glasses and muscular shoulders, Ivan added, "This is Ty Huang."

"Professor Huang," the other man said. "If you get to be a professor, so do I." He looked amused and sounded laconic, and Nora immediately liked him better than Ivan, despite the glasses.

"I'm Nora Wheaton. I'm a former student of Dr. Sigurdssen's in the Anthropology Department. I wonder if I could take ten minutes of your time?"

Ivan folded his hands behind his head. "Have a seat, sweetheart. What can we humble math nerds do for the Anthropology Department?"

Nora sat in the empty chair beside Ty and crossed her legs. She'd worn a denim skirt that rode above her knees. "It's not about anthropology, actually. I'm a friend of Adam Merkel's. I'm sorry if this is news to you, but he died two weeks ago, near Lovelock."

Both men shared a look. "We heard," Ty said. "Someone from the Pershing County sheriff's office came around asking questions a few days ago."

"Then you also know he was murdered." The energy in the room darkened, but Nora plunged on. "I'm trying to figure out if there's anything in his past that might explain what happened."

Ivan pulled his hands from behind his head and folded his arms across his chest. "Why? Are you a reporter?"

"No, I'm really a friend of Adam's."

The men looked at each other again. When Ivan looked back at Nora, his face was closed. "We don't know anything."

Nora backed up. "I'm not asking you to tell me anything personal. I'm interested in things that are common knowledge. For example, I understand he never got promoted to full professor."

Ivan said, "That's right."

"Why not?"

"The usual reasons. Not enough innovation. Not enough publications."

"Is that why he left, do you think?"

Another pause. "I don't know why he left," Ivan said.

"What do you know about his wife? I gather they're not together anymore."

"No. They're not together." Ivan's words were clipped. "But you said you weren't interested in anything personal."

Nora looked over at Ty Huang. He sat with one hand on his

chin, giving nothing away. She switched tacks again. "What was he like as a colleague?"

"He was okay," Ivan said. "Never said much."

"Not much of a golfer?" Nora let her hair fall over one shoulder.

Ivan licked his lips, but Nora's hair wasn't making him any more talkative. Either Dr. Sigurdssen had misjudged Ivan's willingness to gossip, or the subject of Adam's departure was a sore one in the math department. "No," he said.

"Isn't there anything else you can tell me?" Nora asked. "I'm the only friend Adam had in Lovelock."

Now Ivan smirked, and Nora saw her mistake: she'd sounded too desperate, and now Ivan was thinking she'd been more than Adam's friend. He sat back in his chair, disdainful and dismissive. "Look, sweetheart, he was a nice guy. Sorry we can't be more helpful."

That was all she was going to get. After an awkward goodbye Nora fled into the hallway, her face hot. So much for the power of shared history and intradepartmental gossip. So much for unbound hair and batted eyelashes. *Sweetheart*. She wanted to take a shower. She punched the elevator button, hard, and tied her hair back in a knot. When the elevator opened she punched the button for the lobby even harder.

Ty Huang stuck his arm between the closing doors and stepped inside. Nora moved to the opposite wall and crossed her arms. When the elevator started down, Ty said, "Is Nora Wheaton really your name?"

"Of course it is."

"And you're really not a reporter?"

"No."

"Well, Nora Wheaton, Adam Merkel was a friend of mine, too, and I'd like to buy you coffee."

Fifteen minutes later they were at the Starbucks in the new Joe Crowley Student Union building, across from the equally new E. L. Wiegand Fitness Center and the almost-completed Mathewson-IGT Knowledge Center. Nora couldn't remember the last time she'd talked to a man her own age she hadn't gone to high school with, but she was done with the flirty routine. "So Adam was a friend of yours?"

"Honestly, friend is probably too strong a word," Ty said. "How well did you know him?"

"We worked together at the middle school in Lovelock," Nora said. "He was hard to get to know, but I liked him."

"He kept to himself here, too," Ty said. "But I did get to know him a little. I took his graduate-level number theory class, and it kicked my ass. I started going to him for help. He was the worst lecturer in the department, but he was different one-on-one. He made the material come alive in a way no other teacher I've had could do."

Nora thought of Adam teaching chess to a boy who didn't like it very much but who showed up every week anyway. "I think I know what you mean."

"The department lost a lot when he left. It's too bad more people don't know that."

"Do you have any idea why somebody would want to hurt him?"

"Maybe." Ty looked around the coffee shop, which was crowded with students. "This isn't going to make Adam look good. The math department, either. In fact, they did everything they could to keep it under wraps, but I'm sure the police know it now."

Nora wasn't so sure. "What was it?"

Ty lowered his voice. "There was this graduate student. Lucas Zimmerman. Adam was his adviser." He looked at Nora, but the name meant nothing to her. "They were really close. It wasn't a typical adviser-advisee relationship, it was more of a father-son thing."

"But?"

"But Lucas was also a drug dealer. Prescription painkillers mostly, but also coke, Ritalin, weed, even a little heroin. He sold to the grad students, mostly, but some undergrads, too."

"And Adam found out?"

"Not exactly." Ty waited until two students pushed past their table. "Did you know Adam's son died in a car accident?"

Benjamin, fourth grade. Nora tightened her grip on her coffee cup. "No."

"It was two years ago. Adam was driving. When they ran his blood work, it came back positive for OxyContin and heroin. He got it from Lucas."

Nora's fingertips went numb. "Oh my God."

"The department wanted to avoid as much scandal as they could, so they let him resign instead of firing him. That's the last we heard of him until this."

Nora stared at the Starbucks insignia on her cup without seeing it. A lot of what she knew about Adam made sense now. The photographs, wept over in private. The self-imposed purgatory in Lovelock. But the drugs? Her father had been a drinker so publicly and for so long it was hardwired into his personality: Morty Wheaton, good-time guy, always closing down the bar. Nothing about Adam Merkel had said drug addict.

"Are you okay?" Ty asked.

"How come Adam's not in prison?" Nora knew why her father hadn't been charged. In a small town, when the first officer on the scene was your daughter's high school boyfriend, the sheriff had been your weak side linebacker, and you'd coached the district attorney in Little League, the death of your only son can be considered punishment enough. It didn't work that way in Reno, she was sure.

"He cut a deal with the D.A. and gave evidence against Lucas. Lucas went to prison, and Adam got probation conditioned on rehab." Ty's eyes were somber behind the statement glasses. "Lucas might still be in prison. But he has a hell of a reason to be angry with Adam."

The coffee shop was loud with laughter and the calls of the baristas—*Flora! Double latte!*—but a dome of silence descended over Nora and Ty's table. Nora's father had asked her to bring Sal around so he could tell him stories, and Nora had thought, bitterly, that he didn't deserve a second chance at mattering to a young boy. But Adam had been doing the same thing, with the lunches and the chess club, hadn't he? And Nora had been glad the two outcasts had found some solace in each other's company.

Ty was waiting for her to say something. She blinked to clear her head. "What about his wife? Is she still around?"

"Renata divorced him right after. I heard she left town, but I don't know where she went." Ty fiddled with his coffee cup. "She was a nice girl. Shy, but sweet. She was a lot younger than Adam, but they seemed like a good match."

The smiling woman in the Christmas photo had looked both shy and sweet. Nora wondered how hard it would be to find her, and whether Mason had tried. "Tell me about Lucas."

Ty's shoulders twitched a little. This was uncomfortable for him, and Nora liked him more for it. "He was a straight-up genius. But he wasn't very popular around here."

"How come?"

"He had this attitude. Defensive and superior at the same time. He grew up in a trailer park with a single mom, and he did his undergrad at Chico State on scholarship." He looked around, taking in the coffee shop and all the desperate new construction outside. "This isn't the Ivy Leagues, not by a long shot. Nobody here cares where you come from. But he thought everyone looked down on him for it. At the same time, he made sure you knew where he came from, as if that proved he was smarter than the rest of us." He paused. "Though he really was smarter than the rest of us, and he made sure we knew that, too. It drove people crazy."

He sounded more insecure than mean-spirited, Nora thought. Then again, he'd sold heroin to a man who treated him like a son. "He was smarter than everyone in the department?"

"Yes. Like I said, I'm not a number theory guy, but Lucas had a brilliant mind for that stuff." Ty was more at ease now that he was saying good things about Lucas. "There's something called the Riemann Hypothesis. It's one of the Millennium Problems in mathematics. Those are unsolved problems that are so important, and so difficult, there's a million-dollar prize for anyone who can solve even one. I heard Lucas was close on Riemann. It would have made his career, and Adam's, too, depending on how much credit Lucas gave him. It definitely would have put the department on the map."

"Seems like they would have wanted to keep him, even with the felony conviction."

"You'd think." Ty was uncomfortable again. "Except they don't need him. They kept all his work. Claimed it was proprietary research. They've got three number guys working on finishing it right now."

Nora thought the Anthropology Department had been cutthroat. "So that's one more reason Lucas Zimmerman has to be pissed off at Adam Merkel."

"Exactly."

On the drive home Nora didn't see the hills or the salt flats; she barely saw the road. Adam Merkel had been a drug addict. A *heroin* addict. She was astounded the district had hired him, but she supposed his résumé was too irresistible, and it wasn't like Lovelock could get judgmental about substance abuse; half the town abused something or other. And he couldn't have been using in Lovelock. Nora didn't think heroin users made it to work at eight every morning to teach middle school math, and Adam hadn't missed a day of work until the day he died.

She'd gone sixty miles before she sidled up to the worst of it: Benjamin, fourth grade. Adam's addiction had cost him his son. Just as her own father's had cost him his. She pictured Adam at his desk, his gray hair and his gray suits and his gray face, a man out of place in a room full of rowdy middle schoolers. Despite what she now knew he'd done, she found an unexpected reserve of respect for him. Her father barely made it from one day to the next, but Adam had managed to go to rehab and return to teaching, even if it was just a $35,000-a-year job explaining fractions to kids like Kip Masters. Somehow, he'd found a way to live the diminished life that remained to him. Until someone—Lucas Zimmerman, maybe?—decided he shouldn't have even that.

When she got home, she was exhausted. She would reheat the tuna casserole for dinner, she decided as she unlocked the front door. She got as far as the living room before she saw Jeremy's bedroom door was open. She walked down the hall and stopped in the doorway. Her father was sitting on Jeremy's bed with his shoulders slumped. As far as Nora knew, he hadn't been in here since Jeremy died.

"What are you doing?" she asked.

He wasn't crying, but his eyes were wet. "I saw you come in here the other night. What were you looking for?"

Why had she disturbed the shrine, he meant. Nora sat beside him on the twin bed, determined to be gentle. "I wanted to see his yearbooks. There's a man up in Marzen who went to school with him, and I wondered what he looked like then."

Nora felt him turning this over. One of his quieter worries was that another man would replace Mason in her heart. He still hoped he'd come back to her, despite Lily and those three kids. She could ease his mind on that score, at least. "That boy I brought home, Sal, lives with his uncle. I was worried the uncle might not be a good guy."

"Not a good guy how?" Nora's father sat up as straight as his broken body would let him. There had been another boy, Nora remembered, long ago; a small, blond boy on Jeremy's Little League team whose mother's boyfriend went to prison for molestation. Nora's father had been the coach, and Nora had heard the talk even in third grade: Coach Wheaton had saved that little boy. She hadn't understood, then, what he'd saved the boy from, but she'd been proud of him.

"Not like that," she said. "I saw him coming out of Adam's house the day after he was killed. I wondered what he was doing there."

Her father made the leap. "Do you think he had something to do with the murder?"

Nora rubbed her forehead. She shouldn't have started this conversation; she was too tired for it. "Dad, it's late. I'm going to heat up dinner."

As she stood he grabbed her hand. It was such an unexpected gesture that she let him pull her back down. He folded her hand in both of his and looked around the room. "I thought I might feel him, in here with all the things he loved. But I don't."

Nora had never felt Jeremy anywhere, and she didn't believe in visitations from the dead. She pulled her hand away. "That's because he's not here, Dad. He's not anywhere."

She regretted it immediately, just like she regretted every passive-aggressive thing she said to make him feel guilty. Though it would be nice if, just once, her father could stop wallowing in his fucking self-pity for half a second and apologize to her for killing her brother. Never, in all these years of moping and missing, had he done that one simple thing: take responsibility, and try to make amends. As Adam had done, with the rehab and the teaching. It wasn't a coincidence, Nora was sure, that Adam had taken a job teaching kids the age his son would have been if he'd lived.

Two tears slid down her father's cheeks. "It's just that the tournament was always our favorite thing."

Oh, for Christ's sake. This was about the NCAA tournament. That was why he'd come in here: to cry about how hard it was to eat chips and watch a bunch of college boys shoot baskets without his dead son. Jeremy's death was always about him—always. *He* didn't have anyone to watch basketball with. *He'd* lost his drinking buddy. It was never about how Nora had lost her brother, and the future she'd planned for herself. Or about how Jeremy had lost his *entire life*. He'd been dating Bonnie Miller; they probably would have gotten married. By now they'd have had a son like Mason's son, Alex, whose Little League team Jeremy would coach. Later there would have been grandchildren, and high blood pressure, and retirement on a pension, and golfing vacations in Sedona, and arthritic knees, and coffee at Comforts on Saturday mornings with his old high school crew. All those things—the love and pain and joy of the sixty years he wouldn't live—he'd lost because of his father. And his father was crying because he had to watch a basketball game alone.

Nora managed not to say any of this. Instead she stood up, her head pounding, and said, "Don't watch it, then."

"I have to watch it." His shoulders shook with a spasm that was half sob, half cough. "Because he can't."

This knocked Nora off balance, but her defenses, honed by thirteen years of bitterness, hardened in a matter of seconds. "Do whatever you want, Dad. I'm going to reheat the casserole."

SAL

Afterward, when Mr. Merkel and Ezra were gone, Sal would wonder what a time traveler could do to keep it all from happening. Keep Lucas away from Lovelock, definitely. Keep Ezra out of Sal's room with his OxyContin, or stop Sal from buying *The Graveyard Book,* probably. But when Sal looked back at those last weeks, the day that made it all seem inevitable was the day, seventeen days before Mr. Merkel died, when Sal explored the old Prentiss farmhouse.

He'd never be able to explain why he did it. It was his birthday, his first without his mother, but after breakfast Ezra went hunting and Gideon vanished into his shed as if it were any other day. So maybe it was this, the loneliness of Sal's twelfth birthday, that drew him to the farmhouse. Or maybe it was the audacity of being twelve, which seemed much older and braver than eleven. Whatever it was, that morning Sal looked at the broken glass snarling in the farmhouse windows and thought, *Why shouldn't I go in there?* It was the Prentiss homestead. It was where Ezekiel and Wyanet and four generations of their descendants had lived and died. It was Sal's by right.

As he picked his way through the trash that surrounded the house Sal caught the echo of a conversation from when he and his mother came to see his dying grandmother. They were leaving, but Sal's mother had stopped to have a cigarette with her brothers before she got in the car.

"You don't have to live here once she's gone," Sal's mother had said. "There's nothing keeping you."

"We're not moving," Gideon said, speaking for both brothers as usual.

Sal's mother put one hand on her hip. "You don't have to sell it. Just move away."

"You expect us to work for somebody else, live in somebody else's house, pay rent on somebody else's land?" Gideon sounded tired, as though this were an old argument.

"At least fix it up, then. Get rid of the trash. Move back into the house. It's not that far gone. Nothing you couldn't fix."

"This place isn't your business. Not anymore." Now Gideon's anger sounded fresh, and Sal knew his mother had never suggested this before.

That night, when she tucked him in, Sal asked her what the farmhouse had been like when she was a girl. She smoothed the Bob the Builder bedspread across his chest. It smelled like wood polish, she said. There were chickens and goats and cows, and they used kerosene to light their lamps. It was like living in olden times. Her voice was soft with the memory of it.

Now Sal wondered why Gideon hadn't cleaned up the trash, at least. Sal had been here long enough to know that everything Gideon touched was fastidiously neat, from the generator and the solar panels to the kitchen. Yet he had allowed the trash to lie and rot, and the farmhouse and outbuildings to continue to decay.

Sal went behind the farmhouse, away from Gideon's shed. The back door was locked. Sal thought about breaking one of the four windowpanes, but he couldn't bring himself to shatter the wavy old glass, still intact 170 years after Ezekiel Prentiss had installed it. He looked up. Above him were three double-hung windows, two above and one below, and most of their panes were already broken.

He dragged a small walnut table from the debris field and set it beneath the lowest window. When he stood on the table he could reach through a broken pane to the lock at the top of the sash. The window stuck after a foot, but a foot was all Sal needed.

The room he slithered into must once have been a parlor. It was empty of furniture, but there was a formality to the faded, flowered wallpaper and the tiled fireplace in its painted wood surround. Otherwise it was in ruins. Mold blackened its upper corners. The wallpaper was peeling away in strips, and ceiling plaster lay on the floorboards in sugary chunks pocked with mouse droppings and sifted with dust. The light that made it through the front window was gray.

Sal tiptoed to the small entryway, careful not to get dust on his new sneakers. From the entryway a narrow staircase climbed to the second floor, and just past it was a smaller room, probably a dining room. This room was empty, too, save for a broken curtain rod that hung from metal brackets above the window. Behind it was the kitchen. A chunk of ceiling the size of a small car had fallen into it, covering the floor and the counters with plaster. Plain wood cabinets gaped open on empty shelves warped from years of summer heat and winter cold. Below the distant whine of Gideon's table saw Sal heard scurrying in the pantry.

He rubbed his arms in his sweatshirt. He hadn't expected the house to be furnished, but the open cabinets and the broken curtain rod hinted at a frenzied emptying that didn't care about the damage done. Then Sal understood: his family hadn't moved their things to the double-wide, as he'd assumed. The shattered dishes, the mildewed linens, the rotting mattresses, the splintered and weathered furniture that made up the ring of trash around the house—they were the things his family had touched and used every day, until someone ripped them out all at once and dumped them on the sand.

Sal could almost hear it—the shouting and the breaking and the crying—and he wanted to run back outside, away from the madness that had undone his family's home. But as he retraced his steps through the entryway, he saw the footprints in the dust. They led from the front door up the stairs, and there were so many that the center of each tread was clean. At least one of his uncles came into this supposedly forbidden house frequently, and Sal's curiosity overcame his horror. He climbed the stairs.

At the top were four bedrooms facing a wood-floored landing. Sal went to the room above the kitchen. Like the rooms below, it was empty. Faded, striped paper covered the walls, and dust and bits of ceiling covered the floor. Next to that room was a girl's bedroom, also empty. Its walls were pink, and the paint had flaked off in chips so fine that the floor seemed to be covered with cotton candy. Sal crept to the window. From her pillow his mother would have seen the moon rise over the brown hills and the stars in the sky.

The third and fourth rooms were at the front of the house. The one on the left was blue, with darker, poster-shaped rectangles on the wall. Sal wondered what the posters had been. Rock bands, or athletes, or favorite movies? Neither of the men who lived in the double-wide seemed like they'd been boys who'd loved these things.

The footprints in the dust led to the last bedroom. Sal put his hand on the knob. The whine of Gideon's saw had stopped, and the silence of the valley filled the house like a held breath. He opened the door.

It was a boy's room, and it brimmed with arrested life. Plastic models of planes and spaceships filled a pine bookcase. On the floor, covered in dust and mouse droppings, were Matchbox cars, an orange Hot Wheels track, and a city built of LEGOs. A pair of sneakers, too small for Sal, sat beneath the window with the laces tucked inside. The twin bed was unmade, and beneath the plaster and paint chips the sheets were printed with Spider-Man images. Except for the dust and debris, it looked as if the boy who'd lived here would be back any minute to play.

Sal looked down at the footprints in the dust, and his mind hummed with shivery excitement. What if the prints weren't left by one of his uncles after all? What if Tommy's ghost rose from his grave on the hill and returned to his bedroom each night to play? Sal imagined him, a near-corporeal shimmer like the ghosts in *The Graveyard Book,* gliding up the stairs. But the footprints bypassed the toys and led to the pine dresser. It must be something else that drew him; something he cared about more than any of his earthly playthings. Something he wanted to make sure was safe.

Sal made a silent apology to the dead boy. *I won't tell anyone.*

He opened the top drawer.

Underwear and socks. Crawling with spiders, coated in webbing. He slammed it shut. Then he studied the knobs. Only the knobs on the bottom drawer were free of dust. He squatted and pulled it open.

Inside was a shoe box full of OxyContin bottles and a metal cash box.

Sal could barely contain his disappointment. It was just Ezra's stash. It was Ezra who came and went, hiding his contraband in his dead brother's room, where Gideon would never think to look.

"What the hell?"

Sal spun around. Gideon was in the doorway. In two long strides he had Sal by the arm. He scowled down at him, his face flushed. Then he flung him into a pile of metal cars as though Sal weighed nothing. Sal cried out as the cars gouged his arms and back.

Gideon stood over the drawer, every muscle tense. "What is this?"

"I don't know." Sal slid away a few inches. "I—I was just exploring."

Gideon yanked out the drawer. The violence Sal had always sensed in him crackled, and Sal threw one arm over his head. But Gideon turned and walked out. Sal, his heart jumping, followed him out the front door, through the sage that covered the porch, to the double-wide. Gideon must have seen the table and the open window in the back. Sal had been stupid to leave it like that. But how could he have known Gideon would come looking for him? He never had before.

Gideon put the drawer on the kitchen table. Then he sat in the recliner, his fingers templed under his jaw. Sal fled to his room, where he sat on his bed with his arms wrapped around his legs, chilled by a mounting dread.

An hour later Ezra came down from the hills. Sal heard him whistling, then the clanking of the chain as he bound Samson to the wheelbarrow, and finally the tread of his boots on the cinder block steps. The screen door creaked open, and Ezra's footsteps stopped.

"Gideon, wait," he said. Then came the crash of bodies backward through the screen door.

Sal ran down the hall. The screen door hung drunkenly on one hinge, and through it he saw Gideon kneeling over Ezra on the hard-packed sand, his fists slamming into his brother's face again and again. Ezra howled and Samson wailed, but Gideon made no sound. Five, six, seven times he hit his brother. His arm moved like a piston. It was clear he had hit men before. He knew just how to do it.

When he stopped Ezra's face was covered in blood. Ezra turned on his side and spat more blood into the sand, and Gideon kicked him in the back. Then Gideon brushed past Sal, grabbed the drawer from the kitchen table, and walked back out.

Through his swelling eyes Ezra saw what he had. "Fuck!" he shouted. Gideon walked to the dry well beside the water tank. Ezra struggled to his feet. "Don't you dare, you motherfucker!"

Gideon stopped beside the well. He waited until Ezra was five feet away, then he threw the drawer into the well and punched Ezra in the face one more time. Ezra sat on the ground, hard. He raised his hands once, then let them fall.

"If you bring that shit onto this property again, I'll call the cops," Gideon said. "And if you go in that house again, I'll kill you." He walked past his brother, past Sal in the doorway, past the dog on his chain, to his shed. He slammed the door behind him.

Everything was quiet for what seemed a long time. Then, slowly, Ezra stood up. He wiped a stream of snot and blood from his nose and stumbled to where his rifle lay on the ground. He picked it up, balanced it in his hands, and squinted at Gideon's shed. He took a step forward. Blood fell from a cut on his forehead in large, slow drops. Sal put one hand on the broken frame of the screen door.

But Ezra didn't take another step. He flung back his head and roared at the sky, a great howl of rage and despair. It shook the air around him and echoed off the hills, back and forth in a pendulum of sound. When it was done he dropped the gun, sank to his knees, and sobbed like a child. Beside the cinder block steps the quail he'd shot lay on the sand, its broken wings splayed open as though it were flying.

NORA

The day after Nora talked to Ty Huang, she went to the police station. She wasn't going to meet Mason at the Whiskey again. This time she wanted fluorescent lights and a conference table, not Coors and memories of sex on Chimney Rock.

She hadn't been to the station since her divorce, but Marian, the clerk, greeted her as though Nora had been there the week before. "Hey, Nora. You looking for Mason?"

"Is he here?"

"He's finishing something up. You want to wait?"

Nora sat on the long wooden bench opposite Marian's window, and after five minutes Mason walked out with a woman in jeans and knockoff UGGs. He told her to have a seat, then looked at Nora.

"I need to talk to you," Nora said. "About the same thing as before."

Mason was wearing his uniform, which looked as good on him as his baseball uniform had. He was made for matching shirts and pants that were a little tighter than fashion allowed. "Give me a minute," he said.

The woman sat next to Nora. She was about Nora's age, sturdy and pretty, with thick brown hair and a creamy, densely freckled complexion. As she tucked a piece of hair behind her ear Nora recognized her: she was the woman in Adam Merkel's Christmas photo. Adam's ex-wife.

The woman saw Nora staring and pulled her woven purse against her stomach. Renata, Ty had said her name was. She'd been relaxed and happy in the photo, but now she seemed like the type of woman who used her purse as a shield.

Nora gave her a sympathetic smile. "Did somebody break into your car? That happens to out-of-town folks a lot, I'm afraid."

"No, nothing like that." Renata's voice was a surprisingly rich alto, fuzzy at the edges. Before Nora could say anything else, Phil walked in, carrying a manila envelope with something chunky inside. MERKEL, ADAM was written on it in black Sharpie.

"Hey, Nora." If Phil was surprised to see her, his round, placid face didn't show it. He handed the envelope to Renata. "Thank you for waiting, Mrs. Merkel. We're sorry for your loss." He went back down the hallway, and Renata started to stuff the envelope in her purse.

"Merkel?" Nora pretended to puzzle it out. "Are you related to Adam Merkel? The math teacher?"

Renata stiffened. "He's—he was—my husband."

"I worked with him over at the school. I'm so sorry."

"We were divorced, if you didn't know." Renata gave up trying to fit the envelope in her purse and stuck it under her arm. "They called his dad to come pick up his stuff, but he's really sick, so he called me. It's not like I could say no, could I?" She simmered with all the bitterness of a woman who had divorced the man responsible for her son's death. Nora was surprised Adam's father had had the gall to ask this favor of her.

Renata stood to go. On impulse, Nora reached out a hand. "Wait. If you're collecting Adam's things, we have a box of his at the middle school. It's not much, but there is a chess set. It looks like it might be valuable."

A spasm of something that might have been grief flickered across Renata's features. "A wooden chess set?"

"Yes." Nora pulled a pen and a crumpled Safeway receipt from her purse and scribbled her cell number. "Call me if you want it. We're closed for spring break this week, but we're open on Monday."

Renata stuck the receipt in her purse, then walked out without saying another word.

The police station's interview room was a windowless box barely big enough for a table, four chairs, and a coffeemaker. Mason sat at the table with a legal pad and a pen. He looked exhausted, but his smile was warm.

Nora took the chair opposite him. "That was Adam's wife."

"Ex-wife. Renata. Merkel's dad sent her to pick up his personal effects." He nodded at the coffeemaker. "Do you want some coffee?"

Nora didn't, but she said yes. The cup guaranteed her as much of Mason's time as it took her to drink it. He filled two Styrofoam cups and handed her one, then sat back in his chair. "So you wanted to talk about the Merkel case. Do you have something new for us?"

"I went to the university. I still know some people there, so I thought I'd ask around about him."

"That was—irregular." A small vertical line appeared between Mason's eyebrows, and Nora wondered if it had been a mistake to meet him here, with all the uniforms and rules.

"I know. But I found out why he left."

"We know why he left. The accident, the graduate student, the rehab, all of it. We ran his prints from his house, and I talked to the Reno police and the math department myself."

"Then you know about the Riemann project."

"The what?"

Nora raised an eyebrow. "So you don't know all of it."

"Jesus, Nora." Mason shook his head, but one corner of his mouth lifted. Nora let her own mouth break into a grin, and he gave a short, surrendering laugh that made the table in this sterile little room feel like the table in the Whiskey. "Okay, tell me."

"Lucas Zimmerman was working on a huge breakthrough when he got kicked out, and Adam was his adviser. He would have gotten a million dollars if he pulled it off, and it would have put the department on the map. They kept all his work, and they're trying to finish it without him."

Mason's eyes widened; he was impressed. "Who told you this?"

"Ty Huang. A math professor. Who did you talk to?"

"The department chair. He told us how they let Merkel resign once he agreed to enter treatment. He left out the part about the million-dollar prize."

"Is Lucas Zimmerman still in prison?"

"He was paroled from Lovelock Penitentiary November first."

The prison was nine miles up the interstate. It had taken Jeremy less than twenty minutes to drive there every day. "Where is he now?"

"Winnemucca. He's a line cook at the Toasted Tavern." Mason raised one hand. "But don't get too excited. Phil and Smitty talked to him. He said he was working the night Merkel was killed, and his manager confirmed he was on the schedule."

"What time does the restaurant close?"

"Ten. And the cooks usually stick around for a while after to clean up."

The medical examiner had estimated the time of death was between nine and eleven. Winnemucca was an hour's drive from Marzen. Nora sank back, deflated. It would have been terrible if

Adam's mentee had killed him, but it had made so much sense. "So what about Gideon? You talked to him, right?"

She half expected Mason not to answer, but he said, "We brought him in last week."

"Did he say why he was at Adam's house?"

"He said he went to pick up Sal's backpack. Sal helped Merkel make the pies we found, and he left it there."

Nora replayed her memory from Adam's house. The backpack Gideon had been carrying was blue, like the one Sal—and half the middle school—carried. "Do you believe him?"

"Sal confirmed it."

"You brought him in, too?"

"We needed to get his statement about finding the body."

"Did you talk to Sal alone?"

"Yes."

That didn't seem like something Gideon would allow. Then Nora thought of something else. "How did Sal get home after he made the pies?"

Mason gave her a level look. "Merkel drove him."

Nora gave the table a light slap with her palm. "So that's why Adam was up there the night he was killed." Her mind clicked rapidly through a half dozen gears. "Gideon didn't want you to know that. That's why he wanted to get Sal's backpack out of Adam's house."

"That's exactly what he told us. He wanted to keep Sal from being mixed up in a murder investigation any more than he already was."

"Or he wanted to keep you from figuring out he killed Adam himself."

"That's possible. Though Gideon and Sal both said Merkel left the Prentiss place at least an hour before he died."

"What, exactly, did Sal say?"

Now she was straying far into territory Mason shouldn't share with her, but still he didn't hesitate. Later—much later—she would remember this wistfully. Despite everything that had happened between them, no one she'd ever meet would trust her as easily as the boy who'd never kissed a girl before he kissed her, behind the Safeway, when they were fifteen. "He said Merkel dropped him off around eight. He didn't see him again until he found his body on the way to school the next day, and he swears Gideon was home all night."

"Gideon can probably make him say anything he wants, you know."

"I know. But we did talk to Sal alone. We told him we'd take care of him if he had anything to tell us. He stuck to his story."

Nora doubted Sal was brave enough to implicate his uncle in a murder while Gideon was sitting right outside the interview room. "I have a feeling he knows something, though. You're going to have to find a way to talk to him without Gideon around."

"What makes you think he knows something?"

Nora didn't know how to explain Sal's imaginary watchers, who were supposed to tell the stories they saw but didn't always. "I've gotten to know him a little, and he just—he seems like he's hiding something."

"Well, we're not crossing Gideon off the list," Mason said. "The backpack, the drop-off, the location of the murder, it's all fishy. But as far as we know, he has no motive. We have no evidence that puts him at the crime scene. The only witness we have says Merkel left the Prentiss place alive at eight o'clock." He sighed. "And in my gut, I don't think he did it."

"You don't?"

"No. I still think the way Merkel was killed is the key to solving this. And if Gideon wanted Merkel dead, I think he'd be more—direct."

Nora tapped her fingernails on the table. She didn't want Gideon to have done it, for Sal's sake, but she wanted the murder solved, also for Sal's sake. "So who else is on your list? And don't tell me Mary Barnes is."

Mason smiled sheepishly. "We called her in, too. She brought Steve Macomb." Steve Macomb ran a small law office by the courthouse that specialized in bail bond hearings. "She said she was home watching Netflix, and she gave us her username and password. Turns out she watched five episodes of *Jane the Virgin* that night."

"So is Bill going to leave her alone?"

"He's convinced there's a way to fake Netflix account information, but even if there is, I doubt Mary knows how to do it. He'll give up eventually."

Good for Mary. "What about Renata?" Renata had perhaps the strongest motive imaginable, but even as Nora thought this she couldn't picture the nervous woman who'd clutched her purse in the lobby of the police station overpowering Adam, tying him up, and setting him on fire.

"She says she was at an accounting class that night," Mason said. "We'll check that, of course."

"Did she have any idea who else might have wanted to hurt Adam?" Nora asked.

"No. She says she didn't know much about his job while they were married, and she didn't know of anything unusual in his past. He grew up in Fresno, had no brothers or sisters, and didn't keep in touch with anyone from there except his father." Mason wasn't drinking his coffee, Nora saw. It must be terrible, because he looked like he needed caffeine on an IV drip.

"Did she know Lucas Zimmerman?"

"She says she didn't know any of his students." Mason turned a faint pink beneath the pallor of exhaustion. "Nora, I have to ask—

why are you so interested in this case? Was there something going on with you and Merkel?"

Nora hadn't dated anyone since the divorce, and it gave her a jolt of satisfaction to see that the prospect rattled him. She made him wait for a beat, then said, "He was just a friend. But I really liked him. I think I was the only teacher on the whole staff who bothered to try to get to know him."

The blush faded, and Mason was a policeman again. "Did he ever say anything that made you think he was afraid of someone?"

"No. He seemed sad. Broken, really. But that makes sense, now that I know what happened with his son." Nora looked down at the tabletop. The night Jeremy died Mason had held her upright in the morgue where Jeremy lay on the cold metal table. He was the only person who'd seen her that way: flayed by grief and shock, utterly undone. He was still the only person to whom she could imagine entrusting such vulnerability. But here in this stuffy interview room, she didn't want to see the memory of it in his eyes.

She took a sip of coffee. It tasted like tar.

"There's something else you might as well know," Mason said. "Bill's already told the *Review-Miner*." The *Review-Miner* was Lovelock's weekly newspaper, and its last front page had been about nothing but Adam's murder. Mason tapped his notepad with his pen. "We got the toxicology back. Merkel had OxyContin and heroin in his system when he died."

Shit. Nora jerked her head up. "Where did he get it? Lucas?"

"Possibly. We checked his phone and there were a half dozen calls between them in the month before Merkel was killed. But Lucas swears he's clean, and he's all the way up in Winnemucca. It'd be much easier for Merkel to get it in the Colony. We're showing his picture around over there. Who knows? Maybe he got on the wrong side of a dealer with a fire fetish."

Suddenly Nora felt as tired as Mason looked. After all the work

Adam had done to recover, over nearly two years, he'd relapsed. She knew—intellectually, at least—that addiction was a disease that could never be cured, only managed. She knew it was pointless to be angry at him, just as she knew it was pointless to be angry at her father when he drank himself into a stupor on the anniversary of Jeremy's death every year, but she was angry at him anyway. At both of them. She remembered how ill Adam had seemed the Monday before he died and wondered if that was when it had happened. She pushed the coffee cup away.

Mason misread the gesture. "That's not all we're doing. We've got Smitty up in Reno, trying to track down Gideon's brother Ezra. Apparently he lived at the Prentiss place until just before the murder, so he might know if there was bad blood between Gideon and Merkel. Gideon doesn't have an address or phone number for him, and he hasn't talked to him since he left, so my guess is they parted on bad terms. Maybe that'll make Ezra talkative."

Nora didn't say anything, and Mason sighed again. "It's not much, I know. But all we've got is a guy with opportunity but no motive, a guy with motive but no opportunity, and an unknown, possibly pissed-off drug dealer. We're grasping at any straws we find."

He had those pouches under his eyes that he'd had for the last year of their marriage, and Nora softened. It couldn't be easy, trying to solve the first murder in Lovelock in over fifty years when all you'd ever investigated were burglaries, car thefts, and drug deals. She reached across the table and pressed his hand.

"If anybody can figure it out, you can," she said. Mason clasped her fingers briefly, and she couldn't keep herself from marking the moment: it was the first time they'd touched in a decade. She stood to go. The air in the hallway felt cool after the warmth of the little room.

SAL

Ezra spent the week after Gideon dumped his stash sitting on the couch in the double-wide, drinking beer while the bruises on his face bloomed into a riot of colors. Gideon fixed the broken screen door, then moved between the double-wide and his workshop as though nothing had happened.

On Friday Sal went to the library instead of the bench. Next week he would tell Mr. Merkel his made-up tutoring sessions had stopped, but today he wanted to be alone. He ate his bologna sandwich at the table where he'd found *The Graveyard Book* and watched through the window as Kip and his friends played basketball, trailing the admiring glances of sixth grade girls behind them like ribbons. He felt like a misfit, the way he had in the beginning of the year, when he'd eaten his lunch here every day, but he also felt—for the first time—like an ordinary sixth grade boy, one who didn't have to sneak out during recess and deliver illegal medicine, and this made him feel lighter than he had since his mother died. For once he didn't fill his solitude with an archangel story. He just basked in the slow, quiet passing of the minutes until the bell rang for fourth period.

When he walked to the bus that afternoon Lucas was leaning against the wall of the school. "Where were you today?" Sal pushed past him, but Lucas grabbed his arm. "Your people need what you're selling. If you don't give it to them, they'll get it somewhere else."

Sal shook him off, but he was so rattled by his being there that the bus was halfway down the interstate before he thought about what he had said. *Your people need what you're selling.* Sal pictured the young mother wheeling her stroller past the empty bench, and the Honda woman waiting in her car. The blond girl with her chapped elbows and the courthouse man, too—all of them looking for a boy who never came. Worry for them made Sal's throat so tight he could barely swallow. Lucas was right; they needed their medicine, and now they would have to get it somewhere else. Ezra had said there were street dealers in the Colony, but that Sal's people didn't want to buy from them. Sal supposed they would have to now.

Sal had been to the Colony once, about a month before his mother died. They had come to Lovelock to run errands, and when they were done she'd gone straight on Cornell instead of turning toward the interstate. "I have to get something from Taegan," she said.

Taegan was her new boyfriend, the first one she'd had since Sal was born. He was a muscle-bound Paiute man with long black hair and tattoos covering his arms and neck, and he'd only been to the little blue house twice. Now Sal and his mother were driving through the worst neighborhood Sal had ever seen to meet him. Half the houses weren't houses at all, or even mobile houses; they were just trailers up on blocks. All had peeling paint, crumbling roofs, broken fences, and sagging porches. Many of the yards were so densely covered in trash Sal couldn't even see the ground. Block after block they passed until they stopped in front of a ranch house surrounded by a chain-link fence. Its yard was bare of trash but also bare of grass or plants or anything living other than two fierce-looking dogs who watched them through the fence. Taegan's black Mustang was parked in the driveway.

"Wait here." Sal's mother got out and let herself into the yard. The dogs followed her, but she ignored them. She knocked on the door, and Taegan let her in.

Five minutes passed, then ten. Across the street two girls, no more than six years old, jumped barefoot through a hopscotch they'd drawn on the sidewalk. The yard of the house behind them was covered in broken glass. When Sal and his mother finally drove away one of the girls stopped jumping and looked after them, her bare legs like sticks beneath her dirty blue dress. Until his mother died, that moment was the saddest Sal had ever felt. It made him as sad, now, to think of the young mother or the blond girl walking down that same sidewalk looking for someone to sell them the pills they needed.

When Sal got back to the Prentiss place Ezra was climbing the hill on the far side of the valley with Samson. Gideon was waiting for Sal in the double-wide.

"I have something for you," Gideon said. His eyes were bloodshot, but Sal couldn't tell if he was angry or tired.

Warily, Sal followed him across the yard to his shed. Gideon opened the door and beckoned him inside. Sal had never been in the workshop before, and it was the smell that struck him first: a familiar tonic of varnish, sawdust, linseed, tack cloth, and solder. It was the smell of Gideon himself; the smell he scrubbed from his hands but never quite purged from his hair or his clothes. In the light of a work lamp Sal saw dozens of tools lined up on shelves and counters. Their arrangement, careful and neat, reminded him of the chalices and candlesticks on the plain wooden altar table in the Marzen Baptist Church.

A chair made of metal and reclaimed wood sat in the middle of the room. Other than his bed, Sal had never seen his uncle's work up close. The chair was contorted like the bed, but it was sturdy and proud, like a twisted throne on the plywood floor. Sal ran a hand along its curved metal back, then, feeling Gideon watching him, yanked it away.

"You can touch it," Gideon said, amused. "It won't break."

It certainly wasn't fragile. Sal would rather have his plain pine bed from the little blue house, which looked like a bed should look, but here in Gideon's shed he sensed for the first time the power an object could wield if it bent expectations. "How did you learn to make it?"

"My father taught me to make furniture. I just make it differently."

Sal wanted to say he liked it, but he couldn't. Gideon watched him. The work light lit the smooth planes of his face.

"Do you like it here?" he asked.

Sal dropped his eyes. The truth was that he'd rather live in the little blue house, but there was another truth, one that had to do with how solidly tethered to the ground his feet felt when he was up here, that complicated the first truth. Gideon waited. Finally Sal said, "It's Prentiss land."

That was the right answer. Gideon gave a short nod. "I made something for your birthday," he said, and Sal knew why he'd come looking for him when he explored the house. It seemed even worse, now, that he hadn't found him where he was supposed to be.

The gift was a small wooden box, exquisitely made, with lighter wood inlaid on the top and perfectly dovetailed corners. The lid lifted with a touch on invisible hinges, and inside was a photograph of a dark-haired girl in a silver frame.

"I saw you didn't have a lot of pictures of her," Gideon said.

The photo was a school portrait taken when Sal's mother was a little older than Sal was now. Her smile was worried, as if she knew she was being watched and didn't know what was expected of her. It wasn't Sal's mother's smile, which held the attention of everyone in a room with an open and easy confidence.

Gideon folded his arms across his chest. "I would have done anything for her. I want you to know that."

Sal did know it. He knew it because Ezra had told him, but he'd already seen it in the bar, when Gideon glared at all the men; he'd seen it at the funeral in Gideon's straight back and shattered eyes; and he saw it now: Gideon had loved Sal's mother without reservation. She might be the only person he'd ever loved, unless you counted the complicated bond he had with Ezra, which Sal didn't. For all his intuitive watchfulness he didn't know yet that love could be transactional; that it could be offered in trade for things like loyalty and obedience and companionship. He'd only loved two people, after all.

"Do you have any more pictures of her?" Sal knew he should thank him, but he couldn't help himself. He wanted to watch the young face in the frame grow older, year by year, until it became the face he remembered.

Gideon shook his head. "Our mother threw them all out. I cut this from a yearbook."

"Why did she throw them out?"

"Because she left," Gideon said, and in the spaces between his words Sal heard all the beats of the story Ezra had told him. A brother's death. A mother's guilt, and a father's regret. Sal closed the box and ran his hand across it. He pictured Gideon dovetailing the corners and sanding the wood smooth, making something ordinary for the nephew who'd blanched when he saw the extraordinary thing he'd made for him to sleep in.

"I'm sorry I went in the house."

"It's okay," Gideon said. "If you hadn't, I wouldn't have known what Ezra was doing."

His words held no heat. To him, the matter was closed. Ezra had stepped outside the lines, Gideon had shoved him back, and back he would stay. But Sal had replayed the scene outside the double-wide a hundred times: the raw crack of fist against bone, Ezra's hands flailing, and the cruelty of that final blow after Gideon threw the drawer in the well. Sal had never witnessed real physical violence before. It stunned him how much more brutal it was than the battles Angelus and Catellus fought in his mind, but what haunted him most was the memory of Ezra sobbing in the sand and the pity Sal had felt for him. Ezra's business might have been illegal, but it was all he'd had in the world. Gideon had tossed it away, and for what? Gideon's "people" in the Prentiss graveyard had been criminals, too, and they'd done far worse than give medicine to people without a prescription.

Gideon leaned back against the counter. "You need to understand something. I've never laid hands on my brother like that. But he broke a promise. Prentisses were criminals for four generations, until our daddy. He earned a living selling the furniture he made, and he was proud of that. He made me and Ezra promise to do the same. He said it was time for Prentisses to live as honest men, and he was right."

Sal understood about promises and how important they were. He understood it was important to follow the law, too. But Gideon could make furniture. Ezra couldn't make anything anyone would buy. He couldn't get a job, either, because Gideon didn't think Prentisses should work for other people. He couldn't even leave the property without Gideon's truck and Gideon's permission. So while Gideon made the honest living he was so proud of, Ezra drank beer in the double-wide and hunted with the dog he kept on a chain as tight as his own. Gideon would never understand this, just like he'd never understand why Ezra wanted to leave. This place wasn't a prison to him, it was a privilege.

The day before, Sal had wandered through the trash heap again, this time examining the messy footprint of a family's tragedy. He found hundreds of faded baseball cards stuck to pieces of furniture like feathers, board games and baseball mitts, plastic hair clips and a fraying jump rope, a shattered guitar and dozens of delicate glass figurines of horses with their legs snapped off. All of the treasures of all of the children but one. He thought of his mother's bedroom with the pink walls and the stars she could see from her pillow. He thought of the dark rectangles in the blue bedroom, and knew the posters had been of baseball players.

"Why did you move out of the house?" he asked. Gideon frowned at the unexpected question, but he answered it.

"Our little brother died in there. After we buried him, our daddy tore everything out. He said no Prentiss would ever live there again."

That was what Sal had imagined—the grieving, mad father ripping his home apart. But it didn't answer his second question. "Why is everything still lying there?"

Gideon tapped his fingers on the wooden counter. "I don't clean up other people's messes," he said, and Sal knew the conversation was over.

"Thank you for my present," he said, and left. As he closed the door behind him he heard the whine of a sander and the ticking of the small generator behind the shed that powered it.

In the middle of that night Sal woke to a bright, round glare. His brain sorted light from dark until he saw Ezra's face, grotesque in the shadows cast by his headlamp.

"Where's the money?" Ezra hissed.

"What money?"

"The money I paid you! Where is it?"

Sal slid away until his back touched the bone and iron of Gideon's headboard. "Why do you want it?"

"Why do you think I want it? Gideon threw four grand in cash and two grand in meds into the fucking well!" Ezra grabbed Sal's upper arms. "I called my Reno guy today. I told him my brother dumped my stash. He doesn't care. He wants his money, and he wants it now. Four grand I owe him, and I ain't got shit."

That was why he'd gone hunting: to make that call where

Gideon couldn't hear. "I only have three hundred and eighty dollars," Sal said.

"What the fuck? What've you been spending it on?"

"Just a book. And a pair of shoes." Sal didn't bother to hide his resentment. If Ezra had paid him the 10 percent he'd promised, he'd have a lot more to steal in the middle of the night.

Ezra wiped his hand across his mouth. Every sinew in his body was taut with need. "Okay, fine. Where is it?"

Sal got out of bed and pulled out the scrapbook. Before he handed the bills to Ezra he ran his thumb along their edges one last time. He hadn't thought of anything else to buy with them, and now it was too late.

Ezra counted the money twice on the faded bedspread. "It'll be good faith money, I'm thinking. I'll tell him we'll give him all the profit on every sale until we're in the clear. We won't make anything for a while, but it'll be an investment, getting the business back on its feet. And I'll pay you back, brother. Every cent, I promise."

Sal's heart clamored in his chest, as loudly as it had when Ezra first came into his room and explained how the deliveries would work. He pulled his knees up to his chin. "Gideon said he'd call the police."

Ezra waved one hand. "Gideon won't call the police, he hates those bastards. Besides, I've got a plan. He'll never even know."

Sal was pretty sure Gideon would find out within a week that Ezra was disobeying him. Ezra was probably right that he wouldn't call the police, but what he would do to Ezra—and Sal, if he found out his part in it—scared Sal more than the police did. "What about your promise? The one you made your dad?"

Ezra gripped Sal's money tight in one hand. "Gideon told you about that bullshit."

"You promised you'd be an honest man."

"I am an honest man. Prentisses have always been honest men.

We keep our word. We pay our debts. We give fair terms. I'm as honest in my business as Gideon is in his."

He sounded like a man of honor falsely accused, but the silky voice in Sal's head reminded him that Ezra had made him do every dangerous thing for only 2 percent of the take. He looked at his savings in Ezra's hand and said, "That's not true. You cheated me."

"The fuck? How did I cheat you?"

"You never paid me the ten percent you promised."

"Sure I did." Ezra looked hurt. "I only got to keep two hundred out of every thousand, you know. That's how it works, with fronting."

Sal hadn't thought of it that way—that it was 10 percent of the profit, not the whole, that Ezra had promised—and that made him feel stupid. Then he thought of all that money spread out on the bedspread week after week, almost all of it going to a supplier in Reno, and for the first time he saw how desperate and small his uncle's enterprise really was. Ezra wanted so badly to be an outlaw, but he couldn't see he was just another dope boy.

Ezra was watching him from beneath the beady light of the headlamp. "How about we double your share, brother? Twenty percent. It'll be like interest on this loan."

Sal's pity dissolved into surprise. He didn't expect generosity from Ezra. But it wasn't really generosity, he knew. Even the 10 percent hadn't been generosity. Ezra had seen Sal hesitate, and he was afraid Sal wouldn't make his deliveries anymore. Sal's breath snagged in his chest, then held.

"What about thirty?" Ezra said. "That's fair, right?"

Sal looked at a spot behind Ezra's left ear. He knew what this moment meant. Ezra couldn't make him deliver his medicine. He'd never been able to make him, and now both of them knew it. All Sal had ever had to do was tell Gideon, and Gideon would beat Ezra half to death. So if Sal agreed to Ezra's terms, he could never again say he'd been forced into it. He would be complicit in Ezra's criminal enterprise from this day forward.

The silky voice tried to tell him how much more money he'd make with a 30 percent cut, but Sal wouldn't let the money matter. The people in the park, with their pain and powerlessness—they mattered. If Sal told Ezra no, they'd have to go to the Colony and buy from someone who would treat them as faceless marks, and they were too fragile for that. Then there was Ezra, who had treated Sal fairly after all. Not just fairly. He'd called him brother and treated him like family, unlike Gideon with his silences and his shed, where he locked himself away for hours. Ezra needed him, too, just like the people in the park did. The money would just be a good thing that came from helping them, that was all, and only once he'd thought about it that way would Sal let himself imagine the pile of bills in the scrapbook growing thicker and thicker.

"Okay," he said. He felt a hot rush in his veins, as though his blood had doubled in volume. For an instant there was also the taste of iron from his first day on the bench and the weight of Jake's hand on his shoulder on the porch of the little blue house, but then they were gone.

After Ezra left, Sal sat with his back against the bones of the headboard. On the windowsill, the two pictures of his mother—the one he'd brought and the one Gideon had given him—were mute black squares. Through the window Angelus straddled the hills, silhouetted against the night sky. Sal knew what the defender of Heaven would think of the bargain Sal had struck in the smallest bedroom of the double-wide, but when the archangel lowered his shield Sal saw it was Catellus. The gold that edged his black wings gleamed in the starlight, and when he spoke it was in the silky voice that lived in Sal's head.

"I have a story for you," he said, and as the stars wheeled behind him he told it.

NORA

Renata Merkel came for Adam's chess set the Monday after spring break. She texted Nora the night before, and Nora told her to come half an hour before school started. When Renata arrived Nora brought her to the staff room, poured her a cup of coffee, then led her to her classroom. She sat at one of the tables and patted the chair beside her. Renata sat, bewildered but as compliant as a middle schooler.

"You look familiar," Nora said once Renata took a sip of her coffee. "Did you go to UNR? I graduated in 2006."

"I was 2004." Renata looked around for the chess set. Nora pretended not to notice. She had nineteen minutes before the bell, and she planned to use them all. This woman had witnessed Adam's spiral from sober math professor to heroin addict; maybe she could help Nora understand how that journey had unfolded.

"I majored in anthropology," Nora said. "Obviously, teaching middle school wasn't the plan." She laughed the sunny, girlfriend-to-girlfriend laugh she'd perfected in high school, and Renata, though she still sat stiffly in her chair, smiled a little.

"I was in the music department. I don't do much singing now either."

Nora could imagine her smoky alto filling a Reno nightclub. What she couldn't imagine was Renata herself there, with her pilled sweater and homespun prettiness. "Is that where you met Adam?"

The tendons in Renata's hands tightened. Nora kept her face guileless and interested, and Renata relaxed a little. "Calculus was one of my interdepartmental requirements. He was my teacher." A blush flooded her freckles. "I know it sounds gross, but it wasn't like that. I went to college late, so I was twenty-three."

Adam must have been around forty then. It was a little gross, but Nora couldn't see Adam, with his timid smile and stooped shoulders, making the first move on a college girl. "What was it about him? If you don't mind my asking."

"That's okay. I ask myself that all the time." Renata colored again. "I'm sorry. I know you were friends."

"Don't worry, I get it. I look at my ex and can't remember why I even went out with him, much less married him. But there had to be something, right? And mine looked damned good in a baseball uniform, I gotta admit."

Renata laughed, and for an instant she went from merely pretty to beautiful. "I can't say that for Adam. I mean, you saw him." She caught herself, then sobered. "I thought he was decent. That he'd take care of me. I hadn't had much of that." She lowered her eyes, and Nora sensed she was thinking about things that long predated Adam. When she looked up the fragile connection Nora had made was gone. "So you have my chess set?"

Nora didn't see how she could put her off any longer. She got Adam's box from behind her desk. Renata pulled out the chess set and caressed the smooth, varnished wood. "He didn't tell me he'd taken this, too," she said under her breath.

"There's also this." Nora handed her the white rook, which was loose at the bottom of the box.

Renata opened the chess set and fit the rook into its green felt slot. There were bright, angry tears in her eyes, and, impulsively,

Nora laid a hand on her arm. As though her touch had snapped a string, Renata sank into her chair, cradled the chess set in her arms, and wept. Nora handed her a tissue from the box on her desk and sat beside her.

After half a minute Renata pulled herself together. She pressed the tissue to her eyes. "I'm sorry."

"It's the little things that get you, I know," Nora said. Like your brother's last load of laundry, or your mother's yellow afghan.

"This was my grandfather's. I gave it to Benjamin. Our son. Adam was teaching him to play."

Gingerly, Nora stepped onto the ice. "You have a son?"

Renata's face slammed shut. "He's dead, too."

"I'm sorry. Adam never said."

"He wouldn't. He killed him."

Nora didn't have to feign shock. Though she'd thought the exact same thing about her father many times, hearing the words out loud was like a slap. "How did he—how did he do that?"

"He took him out of school for some math party at the university. They'd made pies for it. But Adam was high, and flipped the car on the interstate. Benjamin was trapped inside. The car caught fire."

Nora couldn't find a single word. For thirteen years she'd imagined Jeremy's broken body beside Route 95, but what Renata saw when she closed her eyes was far worse. She was looking at Nora with something close to loathing, for the sin of claiming Adam as a friend, but suddenly Nora wasn't sure she did anymore. Before he died, she'd seen Adam as a kindred spirit—another soul stuck in Lovelock by tragedy and guilt. Now she knew that, while they'd each broken promises, their promises weren't the same. She'd broken a promise to make sure two drunks never got behind the wheel of a car. Adam had broken the promise every father makes to keep his son safe. The same promise Nora's own father had broken. Everything Jeremy had missed out on, Benjamin had lost, too, and more besides. He'd never go to high school, never dance at his prom, never fall in love. As it turned out, the tragedy that had brought Adam to Lovelock wasn't really his tragedy at all: it was Benjamin's. And Renata's.

"He didn't seem the type to have a drug problem," Nora managed to say. It was a weak answer, but Renata's anger drained away, leaving her sad and tired.

"No, he didn't. He had back surgery, and they gave him something for the pain. That was the start of it." She wiped her eyes again. "I should have seen it. But I assumed if the doctors were writing prescriptions it must be okay. And he seemed fine, mostly. I thought he had it under control."

Nora had told herself the same thing about Jeremy and her father when she left for college. Now she told Renata what she'd told herself every day since the accident: "It's not your fault."

"I know it's not my fault." Renata's eyes flashed, and the anger was back. "You can talk about addiction all you want, but all I see are choices. It was Adam's choice to ask for another prescription when the first prescription ran out. It was Adam's choice to try heroin when the doctor wouldn't write him any more. And it was Adam's choice to shoot up before he put our son in the back of his car."

Nora didn't think it was as simple as that, though she knew her father didn't have to get in his truck in Imlay, either. And, if she were being honest, Jeremy didn't have to get in it with him. They were two drunks making a fatal decision in the turn of a key, and the only person who could have stopped them was a hundred miles away studying for her Archaeology of Africa final. "I understand a little of what you're going through," she said. "My dad drove drunk, and killed my brother."

Renata jerked her head up in surprise. "Oh, God. I'm sorry."

"My dad survived, like Adam. It's ruined his life, like it ruined Adam's. Honestly, sometimes I wish he'd died in that car, too." Nora heard the wobble in her voice. She'd never said this out loud.

Renata's knuckles tightened around the chess set. "I wished that every day for two years. When I heard Adam burned to death, I was so glad. I hope he screamed and screamed and screamed. Just like Benjamin."

Her eyes were flat and cold, and a shudder played across Nora's shoulders. In this, at least, she and Renata were different. Nora didn't wish her father had died with Jeremy in the name of brutal, karmic justice. After watching him mark thirteen years of anniversaries with tears and liquor, she wished he'd died with his son because it would have spared him from living with the fact that he'd killed him. Maybe that was the difference between losing a son to your husband and losing a brother to your father. Not the possibility of forgiveness—never that—but the capacity for pity.

Renata flushed again. "I didn't mean that the way it sounded."

"I know you didn't," Nora said, though she was sure Renata had meant it exactly the way it sounded.

Renata wound a lock of her thick, brown hair around one finger. The hardness was gone now, and with her face puffy from crying she looked young. "What did people here think of Adam? Did they like him?"

Nora was surprised Renata cared. She couldn't bring herself to tell her that Adam's students had called him Merkel the Turtle. She still had too many memories of his gentle nature, his diffident smile, and the remorse that had saturated his every breath. "Not many university math professors want to teach middle school," she temporized. "We were glad he took the job."

"Who do people think killed him?" Renata asked. "The police told me a boy found him, way up in the hills somewhere."

"Sal Prentiss. He lives up there, in Marzen. It was hard on him. He was one of Adam's students, and they were very close."

Renata's eyes hooded a little. "Adam could have that effect on his students."

That was interesting. Renata had told Mason she didn't know any of Adam's students. "It's funny you should mention that. People around here are saying there was a student of Adam's who was selling drugs, and Adam turned him in. That maybe he held a grudge. Is that right?"

"I heard there was a student who sold him stuff," Renata said, "but that's all."

Her answer sounded oddly careful. Before Nora could probe further the classroom door opened, and Mandy and Mindy Thompson, identical twins with thick glasses and terrible complexions, started in. Seeing Renata, they blinked in identical confusion.

"It's okay," Nora said, cursing them for their promptness. "You can come in."

Renata tucked the chess set under one arm. "Thank you for this."

Only when the shuffling of her knockoff UGGs faded did Nora remember the photographs. She grabbed the manila envelope and caught Renata at the curb. Renata slid the photographs out and looked at them. She handed the Christmas photo back to Nora. "I don't want this one." Then she walked away. Nora stood at the curb, barely registering the chaos of the morning drop-off, looking at the photo in her hand. At the smiling faces of the man, the woman, and the little boy.

SAL

Eleven days before Mr. Merkel died Gideon made a show of searching the old farmhouse, walking in with a crowbar and a flashlight and reemerging two hours later covered in plaster and cobwebs. Ezra watched from the cinder block steps, a beer dangling from his hand. Sal stood behind the screen door.

"I'm going hunting tomorrow," Ezra said without turning around. "Want to come?"

"Yes," Sal said.

They set off late on Sunday afternoon. Ezra had Samson, his leather pouch, and his rifle, but Sal knew they weren't going hunting. They looped around to the east, ignored Samson when he pointed, climbed to the graveyard, then walked thirty more yards to the top of the hill. Sal gaped at the world spread out before him. The sun carpeted the foothills in gold all the way to the Great Basin, where the sand lay like a soft blanket over the world. At Sal's feet the ground fell away in a steep slope that, to his left, became a bluff so sheer it was almost a cliff. To his right a thin trail zigzagged down, ran through a grove of acacias, and ended at the dirt road Sal walked to the bus every morning. It was a shortcut that would save at least thirty minutes, and he resolved to start taking it the next day.

"That's our land, all the way to that second ridge," Ezra said, pointing. "Not that we do anything with it."

Sal looked around at the empty, shrub-crusted hills, impressed by how much land his family owned. It didn't matter if they did anything with it; they owned it. That meant it could never be taken away, and no Prentiss who lived on it would ever have to leave it the way Sal had to leave the little blue house. Sal felt that pull under his feet again, as though they were bound to the earth by something stronger than gravity.

A black Mustang was parked on the fire road, and when Sal saw it his wonder dissolved into dread. Reluctantly, he followed Ezra down the trail to the grove of trees, where Taegan waited beside a small firepit surrounded by stones. Samson bared his teeth at him, but Taegan ignored him.

"You're late, motherfucker." He jerked his head at Sal. "What's he doing here?"

"This is Grace's kid. He's my business partner."

Taegan laughed. "Business partner. I like it." He was holding a plastic Safeway bag in one hand, and with the other he slapped Ezra's. "You got some fucking balls, making me drive all the way up here. I'm charging you twenty bucks for the car wash."

"I told you my situation."

"I know. Gideon's an asshole. But I'm not driving up here again."

"Okay, I'll figure it out." Ezra glanced at Sal, and Sal knew the next time Ezra needed something from Taegan, Sal would meet his mother's last boyfriend on the bench during lunch. A small knot tightened in his belly, but he looked down at his new sneakers and knew he couldn't say no. He was a real partner now. He had to pull his weight.

Ezra took an envelope from his leather pouch. Taegan counted the money, then reached into the Safeway bag and pulled something out. "For the car wash," he said, then handed the bag to Ezra. "You keep this shit out of the Colony."

Ezra raised his hands. "I never go there, man. That's all you." He was acting cool, but Sal could see he was afraid of Taegan. Sal almost felt sorry for him, but his own nerves were too rattled by the big Paiute.

Taegan's eyes glittered at Sal under his Dodgers hat. "Your mom and me, we went back a long time. There was never nobody like her." He dipped his head, touched the bill of his hat with two fingers, then walked away.

As soon as he was gone, Sal turned to Ezra. "What did he mean, he and my mom went back a long time?"

"She had a thing with him in high school. That's how I met him. He's my weed guy, but he's got tons of other shit going on. He's helping us out on account of her." Ezra was proud of himself now that the deal was done. "This business, it's all about connections."

A connection. That's what Sal's mom had said she and Taegan had. The first night Sal saw him, he came home from the Nickel with her. Sal cracked open his bedroom door and saw them on the couch. His mom's long dark hair lay across Taegan's chest, and on the coffee table was a tool kit that Sal didn't recognize but soon would. He got back in bed, put his pillow over his ears, and three months later his mom was dead.

Now he followed Ezra back up the hill, sweating in the late afternoon sun. Two thirds of the way up, Ezra veered off through scree and sage to where the pitch of the hill steepened to meet the bluff. He stepped onto a narrow ledge of red-brown rock, the Safeway bag looped around his elbow, and called for Sal to follow. Tentatively, Sal did, his fingers digging into the rough face of the bluff. Samson paced on the trail, whining, as they sidestepped along the ledge a hundred feet above the ground.

Halfway across, Ezra disappeared into a clump of sagebrush that grew from the bluff like a giant green whisker. When Sal got there Ezra reached his hand through its jumbled branches and pulled him through.

Sal had never been in a cave before, and the first thing that struck him, other than the darkness, was how cold it was. It was the sort of cold that lives in places that have never felt the sun, and within seconds the sweat that glossed his skin became a thin skein of ice water. The ceiling was low, the walls sloped into the darkness, and an even deeper darkness hovered at the back, near the floor. A swelling claustrophobia closed Sal's throat.

"Me and Gideon found this place when we were kids," Ezra said. "It's on our land, so nobody can come here but us."

Sal breathed deeply, and slowly the claustrophobia retreated. He tried to imagine Gideon and Ezra as boys, roaming the hills and playing in caves. Then, as his eyes adjusted to the darkness, he saw the dusty pile of beer bottles. Not playing, then. It was easier to picture the brothers as teens, feral and bitter, sneaking away to their private den to drink and sulk.

Ezra squatted with the Safeway bag. The floor was covered in a fine dust that smelled dank and old, and it was littered with dozens of cigarette butts. "We can't put our stash in the house anymore, but this place is on your way to school." He pulled out a handful of rubber bags the size of thimbles.

"What are those?" Sal asked. The little bags were different colors—red, green, yellow, and blue—like tiny birthday balloons.

"We're changing the business model." Ezra's voice quickened. "My Reno guy won't front us anymore, so Taegan's letting me have this stuff at cost until we're in the clear. It's a lot cheaper, and it has killer markup. If we sell enough, we'll be fine in no time."

Sal remembered the bits of red rubber lying on the coffee table the morning his mother didn't wake up. His chest felt heavy. "What's in them?"

"Never mind what's in them. It's another kind of medicine, is all."

"Can you put it in a needle?"

In the light that filtered through the sagebrush, the whites of Ezra's eyes were as shiny as peeled eggs. "That's one way to do it." He squinted at Sal. "Why?"

The heaviness in Sal's chest made it hard to breathe. "That's what killed my mom."

"What are you talking about? She died of a heart attack."

"No. She had a needle. And some of those. She got them from him. From Taegan."

Ezra dropped the little balloons in the dust and grabbed Sal's shoulders. "Shut the fuck up. The EMT said it was a heart attack."

"Jake was her friend. He covered it up. He didn't want anyone to know." Sal saw Jake as if he were watching a video, wiping away the bloody froth from his mother's lips.

Ezra's fingers dug deep into Sal's skin. "Fuck," he said. And again: "Fuck."

"We can't sell that," Sal said.

"We have to. I told my Reno guy we were doing this. It's the only reason he's giving me time to pay him. And I swear to you, if we don't pay this guy his four grand, he will fuck me up."

Sal's face felt stiff. He'd imagined that Ezra's source was someone like Ezra himself, shifty and sly but not really dangerous. Now he pictured someone thick and murderous like Taegan. Prison or death, Lucas had said, but it hadn't seemed like that when Sal sat on the bench next to the linebacker and the young mother. It hadn't seemed like that when he piled his twenties in the scrapbook, slipped one out to buy *The Graveyard Book*, or bought his sneakers. He wondered if it had seemed like that to Ezra when he bought the pills from the guy in Reno who now held his life in his hands. He remembered Ezra's glee when he counted the first thousand dollars Sal brought home. *I'm going to be rolling in bank.*

"You have to pay him some other way."

Ezra made a harsh sound. "Where am I going to get four thousand dollars?"

"You could ask Gideon." How many times had Gideon driven off with a truckload of furniture? But Sal knew the answer before Ezra said it.

"Fuck no. He'd sooner kill me himself."

"Wait!" Sal couldn't believe he hadn't thought of this before. "I have money! From selling my mom's stuff. You can have that." A tag sale, the church ladies had said. They would put the proceeds in the bank for him. Surely all the things in the little blue house were worth four thousand dollars. But Ezra grimaced.

"Gideon's the executor, or whatever it's called. He'll never let you have it."

Sal's stomach churned the way it had when he'd left the little blue house for the last time. Somebody else made the rules, nothing was fair, and all the things that should be Sal's were beyond his reach. "There's got to be something you can sell," he said, but he knew there wasn't. The truck was Gideon's. The furniture was Gideon's. Everything at the ranch was junk, but it was Gideon's, too.

Ezra still had Sal by the shoulders, but now his grip was kneading, cajoling. "Believe me, I'd rather sell legit stuff like Oxy. We'll just sell this until we pay off what we owe. Then we'll go back to the pills, I promise."

"But what if they die?" Sal saw the young mother on a couch, a shoestring tied around her forearm. How old was her little boy? Was he old enough to get out of bed and find her?

"They won't," Ezra said. "Look, what happened to your mom was terrible. But you got to understand, that's rare. She took too much, is all. People use this stuff for years if they know how, and we'll make sure they know how. They'll be fine, and they'll buy more, and the more they buy the faster we're in the clear." His grip tightened again. "Please, little brother. I wouldn't be in this mess if it weren't for you going in the house, and I can't sell it on my own. Gideon won't give me the truck at all now."

Sal's head was so light that he seemed to be looking at the balloons in the dust from just below the ceiling. "How do you know they want it?"

"Trudy's already in. The rest will be, too. You can talk to your guy, Lucas. Tell him it works way better, and it's cheaper."

Sal could barely see Ezra in front of him, but he felt Ezra's hands, warm and grasping, on his shoulders.

"Please, brother," Ezra said again.

I did it for you, Catellus had told Angelus beside the Lovers Locks. That was the story he'd told Sal the night Ezra had taken his money: that he'd released the demons to save his brother. He'd been an angel, a servant of Heaven, but then his brother's life hung in the balance, and he'd marshaled the armies of Hell to save him. He'd damned the whole world for Angelus, and Angelus couldn't forgive him for it. Angelus didn't consider them brothers anymore, but Catellus did, and that was why, even as he fought Angelus to a draw over and over, he would never strike a killing blow. He'd do it all again, no matter who got hurt on earth and in Heaven; no matter that he'd been cast out of his home for it; and no matter how warped his soul became in exile, because he loved the brother who had sworn an oath to destroy him.

Did Sal love Ezra? He didn't know, but he felt something for him, something large and sticky-strong that was bound up with the graveyard on the hill and the land under his feet and the shades of his mother in his uncle's face. His mother had loved Ezra, this Sal knew. And Ezra had loved Sal's mother so much that his hand shook as he threw his small clutch of sand into her grave. *It doesn't do to forget your people,* Gideon had said, but he'd also said *I don't clean up other people's messes,* and Sal knew Ezra was right: Gideon, like Angelus, would turn his back on his brother the sinner. His brother the damned.

From the darkness at the back of the cave something whispered, like mice skittering across stone.

"Please," Ezra said once more, and Sal's teeth chattered as he nodded.

JAKE

Jake didn't go to the Nickel much, now that Grace was gone, but once in a while he'd still rather have a beer with Medic Gonzalez or Bill Johnson than watch whatever flavor of CSI his mother had on, so he was there when the reporter showed up asking about Sal.

When she walked in just before seven on a Wednesday night everyone stared at her, and she held her purse in front of her as she sat at the bar, leaving an empty stool between herself and Jake. Jake stared at her, too. He couldn't help it. He couldn't remember the last time a strange woman had shown up in the bar, and this one was pretty, with thick brown hair and pale skin dusted with freckles.

She ordered a Michelob and sat there taking tiny sips without talking to anyone. Besides Jake and Medic, Peter Thornton and Mitch Hurst were at the pool table and Heck Watson and his wife Susie sat at a table in the corner. Gene DeLucci, the owner, was tending bar. His presence was grudging, but he poured and got out of the way, which was all the regulars required.

When the woman finally spoke it took a second for Jake to realize she was talking to him. "Excuse me. I wonder if you can help me." Her prettiness was rooted in regular features and clear skin rather than any striking configuration of bones or coloring, but her brown eyes were deep and warm. "I'm a reporter," she said, and Jake couldn't have been more surprised if she'd told him she was a lion tamer.

"You mean, for a newspaper?"

"Ruth Miller. From the *Reno Gazette.*"

"Are you lost?"

She laughed. "No. You had a murder up here a couple of weeks ago. Adam Merkel. He used to be a professor at the University of Nevada. I'm writing a story about it."

Medic was sitting on Jake's other side. He said, "He wasn't from here. You should ask in Lovelock."

"I'm not here to ask about him." The reporter gave Medic a quick smile. She didn't seem like the flirty type, and it wasn't a flirty smile, but it got Medic's complete attention. "There was a boy who found him. Sal Prentiss. I was told he lives in Marzen."

"He doesn't," Jake said.

"Close enough," Medic said. "The Prentisses live up in the hills south of here."

"Do you know how I could get in touch with him?"

"Why?" Jake asked.

"To ask him a few questions. For my story."

"You'd have to go up there," Medic said. "Them Prentisses, they're off the grid."

The reporter picked at the label of her beer with a square, unpolished fingernail. She didn't look like Jake's idea of a reporter, though admittedly that idea was based on the blond talking heads he saw on KTVN Channel 2, and maybe newspaper reporters were different.

"What's he like?" she asked.

"He's a kid," Jake said. "Like any other kid."

"His mom used to tend bar here," Medic offered. He was

leaning so far forward his wattled neck was practically in his beer. “He’d sit in the corner reading comic books. He never made no trouble, but he’s a strange one.”

“Strange?” The reporter tilted her head. She didn’t sound like a reporter, either, Jake thought. She just sounded curious. Maybe that was a trick reporters used to get people to talk to them.

“He keeps to himself, doesn’t hang out with the other kids,” Medic said. “Like I said, he’s a Prentiss.”

“What does that mean?”

Jake tried to shut Medic up with a glare, but Medic talked right past him. “They was a gang of cattle rustlers and thieves a couple generations back. Some say they’re still up to no good. All I know is they been up there for a hundred and fifty years, and they don’t mix with the rest of us.” Now Medic did see Jake’s warning look, but he misread it. “Except for Sal’s mom. She wasn’t like that.”

“So Sal lives up in the hills with this Prentiss gang,” Ruth said.

“Come on, Medic, they’re not a gang.” Jake turned to Ruth. “They’re not doing anything illegal.”

“That we know about,” Medic said.

“Gideon makes furniture. That’s not a crime.”

“What about Ezra?” Medic asked. “I hear he’s selling drugs in Lovelock.”

“Who says that?”

“People.” Medic gave a sly little shrug, and Jake realized how much he disliked him. He was a gossipy old buzzard who cheated at cards, and Jake had only put up with him all these years because Grace had been behind the bar.

Ruth wasn’t writing any of this down, but maybe she had a tape recorder in her purse. She tucked her hair behind one ear. “Have you heard anything about the murder? Like who might have done it?”

“No,” Jake said.

Medic nudged Jake's arm. "You're the one Sal came to, aren't you? At the fire station?"

Jake wanted to punch his narrow face. "I was just the volunteer on duty."

"You're the one he reported the body to?" Ruth asked. "Did he say what happened?"

"How would he know? He just found the body."

"Did you see it? The body?" Her voice quivered, and now she did seem like a reporter, salivating over other people's tragedies and prying into things that were none of her business.

"No," Jake lied. "I just called it in to the police."

Ruth took another sip of beer so tiny Jake wasn't sure she was drinking at all. "Can you tell me how to get to the Prentiss place?"

Jake would have done almost anything to keep her from finding out how to get to the Prentiss place, but he couldn't stop Medic from saying, "There's a fire road that picks up at the end of Main. Take it up for three miles. But if you really want to talk to Sal, your best bet is to catch him at the school bus stop. It's right in front of the general store, around three thirty."

Ruth put a five-dollar bill on the bar for Gene and slid off her stool. "Thanks. I appreciate your help."

Jake waited three minutes, then followed her out. The street was empty, and the town was quiet in the almost-night. The taillights of the reporter's car headed down the hill, toward the interstate. He looked at his watch. It was only seven thirty. Not too late, he thought, to walk home and get Nora Wheaton's cell phone number from the pocket of his fire department jacket.

SAL

Trudy, wispy and blond, hovering between a tenuous childhood and a too-distant adulthood, sat on the bench wearing a Lynyrd Skynyrd tee shirt and a denim jacket. In a brown paper bag inside Sal's backpack were ten tiny balloons. Four red, four blue, two yellow. The colors of a birthday party. When Sal gave them to her she would give him one hundred dollars, but his arms lay like bands of cement on his backpack.

She scratched her elbow. "So can I have it?" It was the first time she'd ever spoken to him. Her voice was high and thin, like a little girl's.

None of the others were coming. "They're freaked by the needles," Ezra had whispered behind the solar panels, where Gideon couldn't overhear them. "But Trudy knows Jim. Jim knows Cathy. Cathy knows Amanda. Word'll get around that it's no big deal, and we'll have more customers than we can handle." He was trying to sound confident, but his whole body fidgeted.

That morning Sal had gone to the cave on his way to the bus. Ezra had left a headlamp at the entrance, and when Sal put it on he saw a plastic mixing bowl and a battered shoe box on the dusty floor. The shoe box was empty. The bowl was half-filled with colored balloons, with a thin stack of brown paper bags on top. Sal put Trudy's balloons in a bag and left as quickly as he could.

He and Trudy were alone in the park. It had rained earlier, a misty, cold, high-desert rain, and the playground was empty. Trudy dug a handful of crumpled, dirty bills out of her pocket and held them out. They were wadded up in her hand like used tissues. Sal knew he needed to take them. Ezra believed his life depended on them, and Sal was his partner. Not just his partner; his brother. Sal had told himself this all the way from the double-wide to the cave to the bus and all the way from the school to the bench, but his arms remained locked around his backpack.

"Have you tried it?" he asked.

"My boyfriend has. He says it's like heaven."

Sal hadn't thought to ask Ezra what it felt like. Maybe Ezra didn't know.

"I'm afraid of the needles," Trudy said. "But my boyfriend says it doesn't hurt. Is that true?" In the cold, misty air she looked almost translucent, and her edges were blurry.

"I don't know."

"My boyfriend says this stuff is pretty much the same thing as the pills. And it's a lot cheaper. So I thought I might try it, just to see." She kneaded her money with her slender, nervous fingers. Sal saw them, purple and still, hanging from a couch, and the bench seemed to slip sideways.

"Don't." The word hovered in the air. It took a moment for Sal to realize he'd spoken it.

Trudy bit her lower lip with tiny teeth. "How come?"

"My mom did it. She died."

"My boyfriend says—"

"Her fingers were purple."

Trudy blinked. She had a small mole on the bridge of her nose, like someone had touched her with the tip of a brown marker. “How come you’re selling it then?”

“I’m not.” Sal looked up at the smoke-colored sky through the bare branches of the cottonwood tree. “Please go away.”

He felt the slow churning of Trudy’s thoughts, like morning fog in the hills. *Go,* he pleaded silently. *Tell your boyfriend you don’t want to try the needles.* Ezra was afraid the Reno guy would kill him. He had called Sal brother. Sal had made him a promise. But right now none of that seemed as important as keeping this pale, dying girl in her faded Lynyrd Skynyrd tee shirt from walking away with ten colored balloons.

“Okay,” she said. She sounded like she’d decided to pass on a slice of birthday cake, but when she left, her steps were quick, as if she were afraid she’d turn around.

Once she disappeared Sal started to shake. It would be all right, he told himself. He would tell Ezra Trudy had changed her mind. Which she had, basically. He didn’t know how Ezra would pay his debt, but it couldn’t be this way; promise or no promise, brother or not, Sal couldn’t do it. Maybe they could trade the balloons back to Taegan for pills. Ezra said it would take too long that way, but it was better than Trudy sticking a needle into her thin wrist. Sal would sell OxyContin on the bench every day, if that’s what it took.

“She didn’t buy anything.” Lucas wiped the bench dry with the sleeve of his windbreaker and sat. Sal saw him sideways, with the edge of his mind. “What’s the matter? You look like you’re going to throw up.”

“I don’t have any pills.” Sal started to stand.

Lucas grabbed the strap of Sal’s backpack. “Hold on. What about the rest of your people?”

“It’s like you said, they went somewhere else.”

“You missed a week. They didn’t all go somewhere else that

fast." Lucas reached into Sal's backpack and pulled out Trudy's brown bag. He looked inside and whistled. He didn't resist when Sal grabbed it back from him. "Do you know what that is? That's heroin, my friend."

Sal knew what it was. He'd heard about it in classrooms and on playgrounds and in his mother's bar for years. It was what had sent Billy Redmond's mom to rehab; it was what had killed Susie Long's older brother, back when Susie was in second grade; it was what had been in his own mother's veins. But he hadn't let himself think the word, as though not thinking it made it not true. Now Lucas had said it out loud, and Sal's mind echoed him: *heroin*. His hand fumbled with the bag as he stuffed it into his backpack.

"That's why your customers aren't coming," Lucas said. "They're still pill junkies. Your boss is a shitty businessman if he thinks he can get them all to jump to dope before they're ready."

They're not junkies, Sal's mind said reflexively. Then something laid a cold finger on the base of his skull. "What do you mean, before they're ready?"

Lucas crossed his arms. "Your customers are nice, law-abiding folks. They have jobs and houses and cars. They're not dope fiends living under the overpass and shoplifting for their fixes, they just take medicine. That's what they tell themselves. But they're addicted to your pills. Every day they need them more, and eventually their habit will get too expensive. Ten bucks a pill is pretty steep when you need a dozen a day to stand up straight. That's when they'll decide heroin is just another kind of medicine."

"That's not true," Sal said, his voice quick. "You take the pills, and you're not addicted. And the old man stopped taking them. He wasn't addicted, either."

Lucas sat very still. He was hesitating on the edge of something irrevocable, and Sal felt it pulling at him like gravity. Then he said, "The old man didn't quit. He died."

The blood in Sal's veins slowed to a crawl. "What?"

"The obituary was in the paper. He died on December twentieth."

"You don't know that. You don't even know his name."

"Robert James McBride. Mick, to his friends. Seventy-eight years old, linebacker on the high school team in the 1960s." There was pity in Lucas's face, but also something much colder. "He overdosed on OxyContin."

The finger on the back of Sal's neck plunged into his skull like an ice pick. Lucas talked on, relentless. "That part was in the police log. A neighbor called. He hadn't seen him in a couple of days."

Sal remembered the burr in the old man's voice as he told his stories about long-ago football games. He'd made them sound as exciting as Sal's stories about angels and demons. Ezra had told Sal six weeks ago that the linebacker didn't want the pills anymore. The linebacker had been dead for more than a month by then. Sal gripped the bench to steady himself.

"It's not your fault," Lucas said. "He made his own choices. You're just the dealer. It's not the liquor store's fault if people drink themselves to death, and it's not the dealer's fault if somebody OD's. If you're going to be in this business, you'd better understand that, or you'll never sleep at night." He tilted his head. "Or maybe you don't want to be in this business anymore. Is that why you didn't make the sale just now?"

Ezra had said once their customers realized they could get the relief they needed for a lot less money, they'd buy the balloons. Trudy had said she wanted to buy the balloons because they were cheaper than OxyContin. She'd started buying more pills before Christmas. The last three times she'd bought fifty. With bills like the ones she'd offered today, crumpled up like the tips Sal's mother brought home from the bar. Or like cash from selling precious things, a few at a time. Five hundred dollars a week. Sal hadn't thought about how much money that was, only how small his share was in comparison.

"I get it," Lucas said. "You liked the money, and you told yourself you were selling medicine, so it was okay. But now you're selling dope, and people are dying. Shit's getting a little too real."

Was that what Sal's mother had done? Had Ezra's pills gotten so expensive that she'd called Taegan, her old "connection," for something cheaper? The blood that had slowed in Sal's veins raced forward.

Lucas leaned in, and his voice was as silky as Catellus's. "Look, I've been where you are. You want to get out, but you don't know how. So I'm going to give you some advice."

Sal looked up at him. "What?"

"Talk to Adam Merkel."

The thought almost made Sal retch. What would his teacher think when he found out the boy who listened to his math stories and read Benjamin's favorite book was a dope boy? "He'll hate me. And he'll turn me in. Like he did you."

"Adam didn't turn me in because he hated me. He turned me in because he loved me. And he only did it after I ignored his advice one too many times. I spent seventeen months in a cell wishing I'd listened to him." Lucas put a hand on Sal's shoulder. "Trust me. He talks about you all the time. I know how much he cares about you. Show him what's in that bag, and tell him how you got into this mess. He'll get you out of it, I promise."

There were ten minutes of recess left when Sal got back to school. He crept past the basketball game where Kip fist-bumped his friends, then through the empty hallways. His backpack pulled on his shoulders, the ten little balloons as heavy as bricks.

When Mr. Merkel saw him the pleasure that lit his face almost made Sal turn and run. "Your tutoring finished early?"

Sal pulled his chair over and sat with his backpack on his lap. If he said nothing, in five minutes the bell would ring and he would go to fourth period. On his way home he wouldn't stop at the cave and put Trudy's hundred dollars in the shoe box. Later Ezra would creep into his room to ask if he was a hundred dollars closer to lifting the noose from his neck, and Sal would tell him Trudy had changed her mind. There he stopped. He couldn't imagine what would happen after that.

He picked at a seam on his backpack. His mom had bought it for him when he started kindergarten. She'd asked if he wanted the Spider-Man pack, but Sal knew money was tight, so he picked the plain blue one because it was cheaper. He was glad now, because he hadn't known he would have to carry that backpack for the next seven years, and nobody in the middle school had a Spider-Man backpack.

"Sal?" Mr. Merkel said. "Is everything okay?"

Sal's vision blurred. Nobody had helped his mom give up her OxyContin before it was too late, and when it was too late she was dead. Mr. Merkel had tried to help Lucas give up his business before it was too late, but Lucas hadn't let him, and when it was too late Lucas had gone to prison. Nobody had tried to help the old linebacker, either, and he'd been dead for two days before his neighbor called the police. Sal didn't want to know what would happen when it was too late for Ezra, or for him.

"I need help." Every word cut like glass.

"Anything," Mr. Merkel said, and Sal knew he meant it. Before he could second-guess himself he took the brown bag out of his backpack. He turned it over and the ten balloons landed on Mr. Merkel's immaculate desk like a Technicolor pile of dog shit.

Mr. Merkel went still. Sal had wondered if he would know

what the little balloons were, but from the horror on his face it was clear he did. Shame, hot and sticky, wrapped Sal in its thick arms.

"Where did you get these?" Mr. Merkel said.

"My uncle." Sal forced the words out. "We've been selling medicine. To people who can't get prescriptions. I go to the park every Friday at lunch to deliver it. Now he wants to sell them this."

Mr. Merkel didn't say anything for a long time. Then he said, "You don't have tutoring on Fridays?"

Somehow, admitting this was even worse than admitting his part in Ezra's business. "No."

Mr. Merkel's arms had remained frozen, his elbows on his desk, his fingers linked above. Now his fingers twitched, and he looked at them as if willing them to remain still. "What kind of medicine did you sell, I wonder?"

"OxyContin." Sal dug his fingers into his palms. "I thought it was okay. I didn't know it could hurt people." *Liar,* Angelus hissed from somewhere deep inside his skull, and Sal jumped. Angelus was right. Sal had seen it hurt his mother; he'd just thought it was different for the people on the bench. Though he hadn't known it could kill them, or that it could lead you to take something that stopped your heart on your couch while your son slept in his bed down the hall.

"OxyContin," Mr. Merkel echoed. "In the park." He laughed an odd laugh, as though someone had told him a joke yesterday that he'd just gotten today. One of his hands found its way to the desk. It crept close to the balloons but didn't touch them. "But now it's this. Why?"

"My other uncle found the medicine. He threw it down our well. Ezra owes somebody money for it, and he thinks if he sells this he can pay him back faster. I went to the park today to do it. But this is what my mom took. And it killed her. So I couldn't."

"That was the right thing to do," Mr. Merkel said.

"But Ezra's going to want the money."

"What will he do to you if you don't have it?"

It hadn't occurred to Sal that Ezra would do anything other than spiral deeper into panic, but he didn't think he had the violence in him that Gideon had. "He won't hurt me. But he says the guy he owes will hurt him."

"How much does he owe?"

"Four thousand dollars." It sounded so huge. So hopeless.

With one finger, Mr. Merkel touched the blue skin of the balloon closest to him. "Maybe this isn't your problem to solve, Sal. We all have to face the consequences of the decisions we make."

The audacity of this stunned Sal into silence. Could he really do that—leave Ezra to the consequences of his deadly business? Ezra had called Sal brother, and Catellus said brothers were more important than the whole world, but now Angelus was reminding him that Ezra had sold his own sister the medicine that made her sleepy and forgetful and drove her to put a needle in her arm. If his Reno guy came after him, maybe it was what he deserved.

What about you? Angelus whispered from deep inside Sal's head. *You gave the linebacker the pills.*

No, Sal protested. *I didn't know.*

Angelus's wings rustled in Sal's mind. Sal pressed his hands to his temples. There were no easy answers anymore. No valiant warriors on the side of right, no traitors from Hell on the side of sin. What would his mother say? She had forsaken her family, but she'd welcomed her brothers into her bar and filled their glasses for free. One of them had given her the pills that ruined her, but would she blame him for that? Would the linebacker blame Sal? Lucas said they'd made their own choices, and maybe that was true, but on the road from the medicine to the colored balloons, where was the line between choosing and needing? Between guilt and blame?

“Can you help us?” he said. “Please?”

Mr. Merkel sighed, and in that sigh Sal heard a deeper echo of his own hopelessness and knew that Lucas had been wrong. Mr. Merkel couldn’t help him. He was a man of dreams and theories, not of action. He hadn’t been able to save Lucas, and he wouldn’t be able to save Sal.

Then Mr. Merkel pulled out his wallet. “What’s he selling them for? Ten dollars?” When Sal nodded, he took out four twenties and two tens. “Tell your uncle you sold them. That will buy me time to think.”

The bell rang. Sal snatched the money and crammed it in his pocket. In a quick, lashing gesture Mr. Merkel scooped up the balloons and shoved them in his desk drawer. The fluorescent lights glared on his glasses, making him look blind. Sal darted from the classroom, dizzy with something that wasn’t quite relief. Within seconds he felt himself fade, a silent shadow among the jostling students who filled the hall.

NORA

The NCAA basketball tournament was over, so tonight Nora's father was watching the San Francisco Giants' baseball game in the living room. Nora graded seventh grade essays at the kitchen table to the muttering of the announcers and the dim commentary of the crowd until her father appeared in the doorway, leaning on his cane. He wore jeans and a faded Giants tee shirt above those suede slippers he'd had since she was a girl.

"What do you need, Dad?" It must be between innings. No way he would leave the television otherwise.

He grimaced as he sat at the table. He'd brought his beer, which was half-empty. "I've been thinking about that boy. Sal."

"What about him?"

"He's scared. I could see it when he was here."

"He found a dead body. He's upset about it."

Nora's father's breathing was phlegmier than usual. He cleared it with a rattle. "You said you thought his uncle might have killed that teacher."

Nora put her pen down with an irritated snap. She didn't want her father butting into this, dragging his tattered savior complex behind him. "No, I said his uncle was at the math teacher's house afterward. I thought it was strange, but it turns out Sal left his backpack there, and Gideon was just picking it up."

"Why's Sal so scared, then?"

"I don't know, Dad. I'm only his teacher."

Nora heard a bat crack from the television. Not between innings then. Her father looked at her with disappointment. "Your mother never thought she was only a teacher. She cared about her kids outside the classroom. She helped them, sometimes through really hard stuff."

Nora's mother used to give Nora a pillowcase and make her fill it with clothes. She'd have a list, and she'd check to make sure Nora wasn't shortchanging some poor girl in the Colony. At dinner she'd talk about Josie, with bruises on her legs, and Bobby, whose mother reeked of alcohol. If Nora brought up an A on a math test, or Jeremy the home run he hit in practice, she'd tell them how grateful they should be. Other kids would love to have families that supported them in school and bought them sports equipment.

"I'm not Mom," Nora said. "Teaching's just a job to me. You should be thankful. At least I'm taking care of you instead of some kid I barely know."

The ceiling light buzzed as they stared at one another, Nora's glare hardening against her father's wounded shock. Finally he tottered back to the living room. The old leather recliner creaked as he sank into it with a sad little phlegmy sigh, and Nora cradled her head in her hands.

Shit.

She was a terrible person. Her mother was a saint; everybody knew that. There were at least a dozen people in Lovelock who lived decent, boring lives because Camille Wheaton had badgered county services to get them out of abusive homes when they were in middle school. A memorial fund, set up by her fellow teachers, still bought school supplies for underprivileged kids, so she was even helping people from beyond the grave. Then there was Nora, who looked at all that and thought, poor me, I had to give away my clothes.

None of these thoughts were new. Even as a girl Nora had known that where her mother's instinct was to give, hers was to keep. This had made her feel small and mean when she was nine, and it made her feel small and mean now. It was one more reason to leave this town, where she would always be Camille Wheaton's unsaintly daughter.

But her father was right about Sal. Nora pictured Sal's narrow, worried face and she heard her father's sad, phlegmy sigh, and she got up and went into the living room.

When her father saw her he muted the television, and she hesitated one last time. She hated to give him what she was about to give him. But Sal had listened to his story with bright, dreaming eyes, and once upon a time he had saved another sixth grade boy who'd trusted him with a terrible secret, so Nora said, "You're right. Sal's scared. It's something to do with Adam's death, but I can't get him to talk about it." She took a deep breath. "Maybe you could help."

His face glowed with pleasure. "How?" As she explained her idea he listened closely, the game on the television forgotten. When they had it all arranged Nora went back to the kitchen and tried to finish the essays, but now her skin felt too tight and she had a hard time concentrating. When her cell phone rang she answered without looking at the number, and an unfamiliar voice spoke in her ear.

"Nora? It's Jake Sanchez."

The Nickel made the Whiskey look like a tricked-out Vegas lounge. Its rough wooden floors were spongy with beer and liquor, and they gave beneath Nora's boots. The walls were made of the same wide planks, and a dozen pairs of black, buttony eyes—deer, elk, mountain lion, even a snarling raccoon—stared from mounted trophy heads. Two men played pool on a table with stained green felt. Two more men sat at opposite ends of the scuffed wooden bar, and an older couple sat in the corner. Every face turned to Nora when she walked in, and every eye—even the dead ones—followed her as she walked to the bar where one of the two men was, thankfully, Jake.

"Why's it called the Nickel?" she asked as she sat next to him.

"They used to sell shots of whiskey for five cents."

"Somehow that doesn't surprise me." Nora tried to ignore the stares that pressed like hands between her shoulder blades, but she couldn't ignore the man at the other end of the bar. He didn't look away even when she frowned at him.

"Don't mind Medic," Jake said. "We don't get a lot of strange women in here, and you're the second one tonight."

A fat bartender with a greasy beard took his time walking over, looking Nora up and down with frank curiosity. Nora ignored the curiosity and ordered a Coors. Jake was drinking a Stella Artois, which surprised her. She'd figured him for an American beer man.

It had been forty-five minutes since Jake had called Nora about the reporter. Nora had left her father in front of the television, promising to be back by ten. She'd welcomed the excuse to get out of the house. On the drive up to Marzen she'd opened the car windows and let the night air fill her lungs.

"So the reporter wanted to talk to Sal?" she asked Jake. "Not Gideon?"

"That's what she said." On the phone Jake had sounded upset. He was worried that the reporter would manipulate Sal, and misquote him somehow, and that this might get the police involved.

Nora didn't want the police talking to Sal again, either, but on the drive up she'd remembered Sal's uncle, and how he'd leaned over the window of her Civic.

"Gideon would never let her within a hundred feet of him," she told Jake.

"She could stop him when the bus drops him off. That's what Medic told her to do."

Nora gave Medic a reproachful glance. He was still watching them shamelessly. "I can't imagine she'd talk to him without his guardian," she told Jake, but then she wondered: Was there a journalistic code of ethics that prevented reporters from talking to minors without their guardians? "Maybe you could keep an eye out when the bus drops off, just in case. It won't be for long. Eventually the story will die down, and the reporter will move on to something else."

The bartender brought Nora her Coors and a glass. The glass was filmy, so she drank the beer from the bottle. From the pool table came the cracking sound of an efficient break. Beside her, Jake sat glum and unconvinced. She tried a change of subject.

"I went up to Reno last week, to see what I could find out about Adam." He perked up at this, so she told him about Adam and Lucas and the accident that killed Benjamin. It felt good to talk about Adam's murder with somebody who didn't remind her, just by the way he held his beer and wore his uniform, of what she'd cast aside when she'd decided she couldn't spend the rest of her life in Lovelock, so she told him about Adam's relapse, too. "He was high on heroin when he died."

Jake looked thoughtful. Then he reached into his jacket pocket and pulled out a dried acacia leaf. He unfolded it carefully, and inside was a hypodermic needle. "I found this the day I went out to the campsite. It was in the firepit."

The sliver of metal gleamed in the light that hung above the bar. Nora said, "But you haven't given it to the police."

Jake folded the needle back into the leaf. "No. I haven't."

"Why not?"

He had very dark eyes, and they met hers steadily. "I was worried Sal knew something about the murder. I didn't want to give it to the police until I knew what that was."

The bar seemed to go quiet, the voices of the other patrons and the clacking of pool balls muted. "And do you?"

Jake turned his bottle and the red-and-gold Stella label disappeared in his big hand. "I've been thinking. About Gideon."

"What about him?"

"You're not from here. You don't understand the Prentisses. They've been holed up in that valley for a century and a half, and they keep to themselves. They aren't exactly law-abiding, either."

Nora had guessed some of this from the state of the Prentiss property and her conversation with Gideon in the parking lot. "That doesn't surprise me. But what does it have to do with Adam?"

Jake stared at his beer as though it could help him find the words he was looking for. "They're really protective. Of their land. And their family. Gideon even more than the rest."

Medic was trying to eavesdrop. Nora turned her shoulder, blocking him out. "But Adam wasn't hurting Sal. He was just teaching him chess."

"It's not just about hurting. Prentisses don't like it when their people leave. Especially their sons." Jake looked at Nora sideways. "You said Sal and the teacher were close. Gideon might not have liked that."

Nora puzzled through what Jake was trying to tell her. "So if Gideon thought Adam was taking Sal away from the Prentisses somehow, he might kill him for it?" It seemed an unlikely motive for murder, but in the school parking lot Gideon had been protective of Sal to a point that did seem unhealthily possessive. Nora tried to imagine it: Gideon and Adam in the grove, Adam shooting up, and Gideon tying the jump rope around his ankles. It didn't feel right. Mason didn't think Gideon would kill someone that way, and Nora found herself agreeing with him. "I don't think that's what happened."

"I hope not." Jake was stiff with misery. He must have loved Grace Prentiss, because the conflicting loyalties he owed her surviving family were turning him inside out. "But I think Sal's protecting somebody. Who could it be but Gideon?"

"I don't know." Wherever the answer lay, Nora suspected it was in ground nobody had yet tilled, and for the first time she wondered if they might never find it. But she put a reassuring hand on Jake's arm and said, "I'm sure we'll find out eventually."

All around her, the bar murmured with the easy talk of people who'd known each other all their lives. Even more than Lovelock, Marzen was a place apart from the world, bound tight with history and allegiances that ran deep, where life felt predetermined, not chosen. Nora thought of Sal growing up here, becoming a man who played pool at the Nickel and volunteered at the fire station, and wondered if Gideon would allow him even that much. She wondered what other pathways Adam might have shown him, had he stayed sober and alive, and sorrow for both of them settled heavily on her shoulders.

The bartender looked at her hand on Jake's arm and gave her a knowing leer. She glared at him until he looked away.

SAL

When Sal told Ezra Trudy had bought the balloons, Ezra's relief made him sick with guilt. On Monday he walked into Mr. Merkel's first-period class, hoping for a sign that his teacher had come up with a plan, but Mr. Merkel looked like someone who'd stayed up all night trying to think of a plan but hadn't been able to. His eyes were unfocused and there was a faint gloss of sweat on his face. His shirt was wrinkled, as though he'd picked yesterday's shirt up off the floor and put it on. He looked so disheveled that even Ms. Wheaton, Sal's social studies teacher, looked alarmed when she stopped by to say good morning. Sal sat at the misfits' table, cold with dread.

When the bell rang Mr. Merkel stood up and ran one hand through his hair. He turned to the whiteboard and said, "Today we will continue with decimals."

Notebooks opened in a grudging rustle of paper. *126.248,* Mr. Merkel wrote on the board. When he was done he stopped, the marker suspended in the air, as though he'd forgotten what to do next. His hand shook slightly, though Sal thought he was the only student who noticed. The others were waiting listlessly, their bodies slumped in their chairs.

Then, in the back of the room, Kip Masters got to his feet.

"In the hundreds place, we have the number one," Mr. Merkel

said to the board. The marker squeaked as he drew a circle around it, but nobody was looking at him. They were looking at Kip, who stood with his hand raised and his back humped. As Mr. Merkel circled the decimal places ("tens," "ones," "tenths"), Kip mimicked the slight bobble of his head, the craning of his neck, the looping motion of his arm, even the way Mr. Merkel blinked and pushed his lips in and out when he spoke. It was a brilliant impression, far crueler and funnier than his usual hunchbacked mockery. The pretty girls with sparkly shoes tittered. Kip winked at Stacy Wells, a blue-eyed princess with hard new breasts beneath her white tank top, and Sal clenched his teeth. To think he'd thought Kip had anything but cruelty in his heart, just because he'd bought *The Graveyard Book*. As laughter, muffled in hands and shirtsleeves, crescendoed around him, he closed his eyes and tried to listen to Sylvana crooning almost below the range of sound.

A loud *crack!* made his eyes fly open. Kip's arm was still raised, but his sharp features were ferret-like with surprise and dawning fear. Mr. Merkel stood beside his desk. A textbook—a three-inch brick with *Number Theory* on the cover—lay on the scuffed linoleum at his feet. Mr. Merkel's eyes were trained on Kip. His hands were balled in soft white fists that would have looked ridiculous but for the reverberating thunder of the textbook.

Kip scrambled onto his chair and gripped the plastic seat. Suddenly he looked like what he was: a twelve-year-old boy who knew he was in big trouble. Every child in the room stared at him except the other boys at his table, who couldn't look at him at all. Mr. Merkel loomed as large as Angelus, spreading righteous wings over the classroom, and Sal's heart danced with wild exhilaration. *Do it!* he thought. *Do it!*

Mr. Merkel took a step toward Kip. The thin wire of steel that sometimes thrummed at the core of his voice took it over entirely. "Apologize."

"I-I'm sorry," Kip stammered.

Another step. "I didn't hear you."

"I'm sorry." Kip had gone as white as the board. Mr. Merkel came closer, one slow step at a time. The stoop that had given him his nickname now made him look predatory, like a leopard crouching to pounce. Stacy Wells had her hand over her mouth.

"Sir. I'm sorry, sir." Kip shriveled in his chair, and now Sal saw in his cringing the long habit of fear, the shadow play of a boy accustomed to cowering before a man with his hands in fists. His stomach turned over. He looked at Mr. Merkel and thought: *Stop.*

"Get up," Mr. Merkel said. "Bring your things. And your chair."

Kip dragged his chair across the room. His shoulders curved forward and his back rounded. He looked like a turtle.

"Move over, Sylvana," Mr. Merkel said. Sylvana slid her chair away from Sal. Mr. Merkel picked up Kip's chair and set it between them. "This is where you will sit for the remainder of the year."

From Kip's old table came a bark of laughter. It was Rudy Marner, Kip's deputy, ruddy and handsome and loyal no longer. An answering smile flashed across Stacy Wells's porcelain face.

Kip dropped his backpack on the floor and sat. Sal had never been this close to him. He could see the golden fuzz on Kip's cheeks and the pink veins that laced the delicate shell of his ear. The other outcasts stared at Kip as though he'd dropped from outer space, but Kip glared straight ahead at no one, his eyes bright with humiliation and fury. Only Sal saw the sheen of tears. Only Sal remembered the boy who'd come to the book fair alone so his friends wouldn't see that he liked to read. And only Sal imagined the father who stood over that boy with his hands in fists.

Mr. Merkel picked up the *Number Theory* textbook. When he stood he was small again, rounded and timid and familiar. He put the book on the shelf beside his desk and returned to the board, where he finished mapping out the decimals in *126.248*.

"You were right," Mr. Merkel said at lunch. "When you told me to make Kip stop. I thought I could win him over, but boys like that won't stop until someone stands up to them." He was more himself now—the distraction and agitation were gone—but he still looked exhausted and disheveled.

"Do you think it worked?" Sal asked.

Mr. Merkel gave a small smile. "I think he will not forget me."

On his way to Mr. Merkel's classroom Sal had seen Kip leaning against the playground fence while his friends played basketball without him. The disturbance Mr. Merkel had created in the social fabric of the sixth grade hummed like an electric net over the blacktop, but for the first time Sal had seen how small the sixth grade boys were. The seventh grade boys sat in the corners of the yard and watched them with disdain. Next year, Sal knew, Kip's gang would sit in those same corners and mock a new group of sixth grade boys with high voices and expensive shoes. Maybe Kip would even sit with them, the humiliation of this day a stain he alone would remember. But Mr. Merkel was right; he would remember. Just as Sal would remember, years from now and with deep anguish, that the greatest shame his teacher could think to inflict was to force Kip to sit beside him.

"I've been thinking about your problem," Mr. Merkel said, and Sal set Kip aside. Mr. Merkel paused, like a sledder at the top of a hill, then rushed ahead. "Tell your uncle I will buy all the heroin he has for four thousand dollars, if he agrees never to sell it again."

A surge of hope nearly lifted Sal out of his chair. "You would do that?"

"I can think of no better use for my money. Can you arrange for us to meet?"

"Ezra doesn't have a car."

"I'll come to him."

"You can't. Gideon will be there." Then Sal remembered Taegan in the grove. "But there's a place nearby. A campsite, just off the road to our place. I can take you."

Mr. Merkel touched his glasses with one finger. "That sounds perfect."

It was perfect. Ezra would get out of debt, none of Sal's people would use the heroin, and Sal could walk away from the business without anybody else getting hurt. Ezra would have to find another way out of the valley, but if he wanted it badly enough, he would. Mr. Merkel had saved everyone. The archangels in Sal's head, the one who wanted to help Ezra and the one who wanted to punish him, murmured in rare agreement.

"I do have a favor to ask in return," Mr. Merkel said. "It's rather a big one."

Sal would do anything this man asked. "What is it?"

"I'm going to have a party for the eighth grade this Thursday. It's Pi Day." He saw Sal's confusion. "I'll explain that later. More important is that I must bake pies for it, and I could use a helper."

"Sure," Sal said. That didn't sound like a big favor at all.

"Come home with me on Wednesday," Mr. Merkel said. "After we bake I will drive you home, and on the way you can take me to this campsite, to meet your uncle."

NORA

Nora's father was wearing his jeans and one of his few sweatshirts that didn't have a sports team logo on it. He'd combed his hair and put on his loafers instead of his slippers, and he looked nice in a way he hadn't in a decade and a half. As they drove to the school they talked it through again. He would spend first period in the staff room. During second and fifth periods—Nora's sixth grade classes—he would make his presentation. In between, Nora would invite Sal to join them for lunch.

"Don't ask him anything about Adam yet," she said. "We're just trying to get him to trust us."

"I know, I know." She'd said the same thing a dozen times already.

When second period came Nora parked her father's wheelchair by her door and helped him to the chair she'd put beside the bulletin board. The sixth graders stared at him as they came in, but the only reaction Nora cared about was Sal's. He was the last to arrive, and when he saw her father it was there: surprise, and a quick smile.

"We have a special guest today," she told the class. "My father, Mr. Wheaton, is an expert on the First People."

Nora's father struggled to his feet and surveyed the students like a coach assessing who would play shortstop and who would ride the bench. He lingered on Kip Masters in the back, and Nora could almost hear him thinking, *pitcher?* But Kip didn't look like a pitcher today, and he hadn't for the last month. Something had robbed him of his power, and though he still sat with the popular boys, they leaned away from him. Nora had seen it before: sixth grade could be brutal, and Kip deserved his fall from grace, but his eyes were hollow in a way that made her feel sorry for him.

"What's the farthest you've ever walked?" her father asked.

Iain McNeil raised his hand. "I hiked eight miles once."

"That's very good," Nora's father said. "Most Americans walk less than a mile a day. In fact, we spend over half our time sitting down. That's not how the first Americans were. If they walked as little as we do, they never would have gotten here at all." He turned to the map of the late Pleistocene world on the bulletin board. "They walked all the way from here"—he pointed to Siberia, then traced his finger across the Beringian land bridge, down the west coast of North America, and inland to Nevada—"to here. Over ten thousand miles. Though they didn't do it all at once, or even in a single lifetime."

He coughed that phlegmy cough. When his chest quieted he lifted his hand to the map again.

"Thirty thousand years ago, a small tribe followed a herd of bison from Siberia across this land bridge until they ran into a wall of ice." He pointed to where Alaska met Canada. "When they turned back, it was too late. Another wall of ice had blocked them in. For ten thousand years they lived up there, trapped between the glaciers. They had no contact with anyone else in the world for all that time. Slowly, generation by generation, they became different from the people they left behind. They developed their own language and their own culture, even their own DNA. By the time the ice melted, their cousins back in Asia wouldn't have recognized them."

Nora watched Sal. He was rapt, his hand fondling the small white amulet around his neck.

"They were nomads," her father said. "They set up camps, then moved on, tracking the bison and mammoth that had gotten trapped up there with them. So when the ice started to melt, some of them found the narrow passage that opened up along the western edge of North America, and followed it down to where the ice stopped. Then they turned inland, into a wide-open country no human had ever set foot in before." He paused, but this time it was for effect. "There were fewer than two hundred of them. Imagine that. One small tribe, giving birth to all the native people from Alaska to South America." He looked around. "How many of you have native blood in you?"

Nora had never asked her students this. She assumed the Paiute kids wouldn't want to be singled out in a school where they already sat apart from their white classmates. But at the table where the Colony kids sat, Janie, Toby, and Marc raised their hands.

"Your ancestors are the greatest explorers in human history," her father told them. "They left Africa seventy thousand years ago, when humans first started to roam. But while my ancestors went to Europe and settled in, yours walked through the Middle East, across Siberia and Beringia, then down through the Americas all the way to Cape Horn. When the Europeans finally got here five hundred years ago, they had it easy. Your people told them where the rivers were, how to grow corn, and where to hunt. When your ancestors got here there was no one to tell them anything. They survived in a strange country against overwhelming odds, and so did their children and grandchildren, all the way down to the three of you sitting in this classroom."

Janie, Toby, and Marc looked at one another, and Nora saw grudging respect on the faces of a few of their classmates. She'd heard her father tell this story before, but he'd never told it as well as he was telling it now. His voice was strong and his hands were steady as he described the country the First People found, teeming with herds of bison and mammoth and flocks of geese so dense they blocked out the sun from horizon to horizon. By the time he passed the spearpoint around, every student in the room was lost in the world he'd conjured, and they held the weapon as though he'd offered them a holy chalice. They never listened to Nora that way. But then she never talked to them like this, as if history were a story that needed telling. There had to be watchers, Sal had said, to record the stories of forgotten people. Anthropologists were watchers, finding and sharing the lost stories of long ago. Teachers could be watchers, too, like Nora's mother had been, and her father was today. She was not. But maybe, if she tried, she could be.

When the bell rang she asked Sal if he wanted to have lunch with them, and this time she didn't have to wonder if he would come. The three of them sat at a table with their sandwiches, and Nora gave Sal her own chips and a banana to supplement his bologna. She let her father do most of the talking. He told Sal the creation myth of the Paiute, where the god Coyote carried the Paiute in a woven bag from a faraway land and dropped them in the Great Basin. In reality, the Paiute had moved into the Basin from the Great Plains around 1000 A.D., but Nora's father liked the legend better. It wasn't so different from the story that ancient bones and firepits and DNA told about the First People, if you thought about it metaphorically, and who was to say that the Paiute's origin myth didn't carry with it the footprints of that long-ago journey from the Asian steppes?

"So you're not Paiute?" Nora's father asked Sal. It was a fair question, given the golden tone of Sal's skin.

"My great-great"—Sal thought—"great-great-grandmother was."

"That's not enough to get you into the local tribe," Nora's father said, "but you can still trace your ancestry back, through her, to those explorers who walked out of Africa seventy thousand years ago, on their way to the great state of Nevada."

Sal's face opened in the first grin Nora had ever seen on him, and her father smiled back in a way Nora hadn't seen him smile in years. "You remind me of my daughter when she was your age," he said, and Nora remembered when she'd last seen that smile. It was the way he'd smiled at her, when she was a girl who loved "old bones."

"You mean Ms. Wheaton?" Sal's surprise would have been funny if it weren't so understandable.

Nora's father coughed again, a shuddering retch that turned his face a deep red. Nora watched him with alarm. She would call his doctor that afternoon. The appointment would be the following week and the diagnosis the week after that, but now he collected himself and went on as if nothing was wrong. "Your teacher was a great explorer herself. We used to explore together, trying to find the story of the First People."

He'd just told a roomful of sixth graders about people who'd walked across continents and died hundreds of miles from where they were born, yet he thought wandering the hills less than twenty miles from your home made you a great explorer. Nora didn't understand how he could imagine a world so much bigger than his own but have no desire to go and see it. Then she remembered the camper and his plans to drive it all over the country.

"I had a son, too, but Jeremy wasn't interested in exploring," he said, and Nora's pity wilted as quickly as it had bloomed.

"What happened to him?" Sal asked, and the directness of the question took Nora aback. She was about to tell him Jeremy died in a car crash, but stopped herself. No one had ever asked her father this question. No one in Lovelock needed to; they all knew. She wanted to see what he would say.

He took his time. In the hallway a group of seventh grade girls passed by, laughing their tinny laughs. When they were gone he said, "I had too much to drink one night, and I crashed my truck. Jeremy died in the accident."

He spoke as if he were telling Sal the score of yesterday's Giants' game, but to Nora every word was as weighted as a stone. She pressed her hands together to keep from betraying any emotion that might distract him.

Sal watched him as though his answers mattered to him as much as they did to Nora. "So it was your fault?"

"It was," her father said, and every color in the room went a shade paler. Then he said, "But it could have just as easily been Jeremy driving, and me the one who died."

"Why?" Sal asked.

"Whenever Jeremy and I went out together, we had a ritual. When it was time to go home, we threw the keys up in the air, and whoever caught them drove. That night, I caught them."

Nora drew a long, quiet breath. So that was how he lived with what he'd done. He'd told Sal the accident was his fault, but he didn't really believe that. He'd convinced himself it was fate, acting in the random toss of a set of keys. It was so cowardly, yet so like him. He always took the path that let him avoid the hardest truths. He'd been like that when her mother was sick, too; he'd pretended she'd get better right up until the day she died.

"Is it hard?" Sal asked. "To be the one that's still alive?"

Nora's father said, "It's very hard."

"How do you—" Sal stopped. He didn't have the words.

"How do I carry on?" Nora's father asked. "Because Jeremy would want me to. Just like I'd want him to carry on if he'd caught the keys and I'd been the one to die. We were a team, Jeremy and me. When your teammate goes down, you don't stop playing the game. You play it for them."

Now he looked at Nora. A fearful hope lit his face, but Nora barely saw it behind the red scrim that dropped across her vision. It was bad enough that her father didn't think the accident was his fault. Now he was reducing Jeremy's death to a fucking sports analogy. As if this were Little League, when Jeremy had broken his leg sliding into second and Nora's father, the coach, told the other nine-year-olds to play the rest of the season for their teammate in the cast.

"It wasn't a game." The words sliced Nora's throat like razors. "And it wasn't an accident. You're blaming it on chance, but you made a choice. You didn't have to put the key in the ignition. You could have asked someone to drive you home. Or called a taxi."

"Nobody in that bar was any more sober than I was." Nora's father smiled with gentle remonstrance. "And don't forget, our taxi driver had gone to college."

All the oxygen left the room, then slammed back in. "Oh, no," Nora said. "You don't get to blame me. I didn't kill him. You killed him." She saw his shock and a wild, vindictive euphoria seized her. "You *killed him,* Dad. You took away all the years he would have lived, all the children he would have had, all the basketball tournaments he would have watched. Then I had to come back here and take care of you, because there was nobody left alive to do it. Jeremy *died,* and I had to give up my *entire life,* all because you couldn't stay off the road when you were drunk." The world had screwed down to a box just big enough for her and her father. "Now you want a pat on the back for getting out of bed every day? No fucking way. Both of us would have been better off if you'd died that night, too, and you know it."

"Stop!" Sal cried. "Stop it!"

Nora reeled back in her chair. She'd forgotten all about him. He was breathing hard, and his pupils had swallowed the deep brown of his irises. She reached her hand across the table. "Sal. I'm so sorry. You shouldn't have had to hear that."

"It's okay for him to live," he said. "It's okay."

"Of course it is. I didn't mean that. I was upset." Like Renata, when she'd sat at this table. Nora had thought she and Renata were different, but they weren't. She'd meant what she'd said to her father just now. She did wish he'd died that night, and not only to spare him the misery of survival. She wished it for herself. Her father was a drunk who'd killed his son and couldn't take responsibility for it, but Nora was a daughter who wished her father had died so she could have gone to Africa and dug up the bones of people who'd been dead for a quarter of a million years. What did that make her?

"She's right to be upset," she heard her father say. "She could have let them put me in the nursing home and lived her life, but she didn't. She came back and took care of me. She still does, even though I know she'd rather be anywhere but here." Nora felt him looking at her, but she wouldn't look at him. "I don't know why I lived and Jeremy didn't. I know I owe it to him to keep living. But the truth is, she's the reason I get out of bed every morning."

The room sparkled behind a veil of tears, but Nora blinked them away. It wasn't enough. It would never be enough; he would never give her the confession and the apology she needed to begin to forgive him. Instead he was giving her the one thing she didn't deserve: gratitude.

But there was a sixth grade boy in the room, one whom death had touched twice. She took a breath, then another, until she could speak normally. To Sal she said, "We all have to keep living, even after we lose people we love. They would want it, because they loved us, too. My father's right about that."

Sal looked as shaken as Nora felt, and she saw, clearer than ever before, how alone in the world he was. In less than a year he'd lost what were probably the only two people he had ever loved. Nora had lost two people, too. But she had loved four.

Now she did look at her father. His face was shining with the gratitude she'd rejected, but she saw a shadow in his eyes, crouched and fearful. Her insides turned cold. She had seen that shadow before. She'd seen it in her mother's eyes, the night of the basketball championship. She knew she would have seen it there long before then, had she bothered to look.

Her hand moved of its own accord to her father's arm, and she left it there.

SAL

Mr. Merkel's house was as neat and spare as his desk at school. The furniture was black leather and chrome, and it smelled new. There were no knickknacks, no pictures on the walls, and no television. The dun-brown carpet was flattened in a path from the front door to the kitchen by countless feet carrying groceries and takeout, and the kitchen, with its white cupboards and white counters, made Sal think of hospitals.

On the counter were six glass pie plates, a set of measuring cups and spoons still in their packaging, and two mixing bowls. He hadn't realized they would be making so many pies. That must be why Mr. Merkel had said it was a big favor.

Mr. Merkel opened the refrigerator and pulled out a pint of milk. He poured them each a glass, and they sat on the living room couch. Mr. Merkel had no dining table, and Sal wondered if he ate his meals on the couch, too.

"I never really settled in," Mr. Merkel said. One of his legs bounced.

"That's okay," Sal said. "I like it."

"In Reno, we had a bigger house. Three bedrooms. Half a mile from the university, in a nice neighborhood. Renata decorated it. I always thought it was a little fussy, but I never said so. Of course that's all gone now. Everything here is new."

The sofa cushion was hard. Sal didn't like milk, and he hoped Mr. Merkel wouldn't notice he wasn't drinking it. Though Mr. Merkel wasn't drinking his either.

"I have something to show you," Mr. Merkel said, abruptly. He walked down the hall and came back with a white cardboard box that he set on the coffee table. It was filled with toys and oddities. He stood over it, fidgeting with his shirt buttons. "This was all I could get. I didn't have much time before she came back."

He took out a snow globe with the Golden Gate Bridge inside and set it beside the box. White flakes floated around the orange bridge like ashes. "We went to San Francisco when he was in kindergarten. He wanted to live there when he grew up." He pulled out a deck of cards and handed them to Sal. "He was starting to teach me this game."

Sal slid the cards out of their cardboard container. They were bigger than normal playing cards, and each had a picture of a different fantastical figure: wizards, trolls, warriors, and sorceresses. In the corners were numbers surrounded by suns, moons, and crystals. The illustrations were fluid and delicate, the colors watery, and they made stories sparkle below the surface of Sal's mind. He put them beside the snow globe and wiped his hands on his jeans.

Mr. Merkel continued to empty the box, and slowly the particular treasures of a particular boy filled the coffee table. A map of the stars, rolled and rubber banded. A lava lamp he'd had on his bedside table because he was afraid of the dark. A book called *Birds of the Great Basin,* studded with Post-its. A collection of polished rocks. A metal bank shaped like a Model T, clanking with coins he'd been saving to buy a spaceship model. A jump rope made of red and white nylon with wooden handles. He'd done tricks with it, Mr. Merkel said. He was very good at them.

When the box was empty Mr. Merkel sat. He opened his mouth,

but then he shut it again. After all the words that had just tumbled out, the thing he most wanted to say was too big to fit through.

Sal looked at the things on the table and tried to picture the boy who'd owned them. Benjamin had been an explorer of worlds real and imaginary, but he'd been afraid of the dark. He'd loved stars and birds, so he might have built the rocket ships his father and grandfather hadn't, or studied things that flew closer to Earth. He'd liked to jump rope. He'd believed in stories. He'd wanted things he didn't have.

"I was driving the car," Mr. Merkel said.

Sal didn't say anything.

"You knew that, too."

Sal nodded. He'd known it from the careful way Mr. Merkel drove, with his hands at ten and two.

Mr. Merkel pressed his hands on his thighs. "You told me once you thought you were like Bod in *The Graveyard Book*. That you might be able to hear the dead if you listened just right. I told you that wasn't possible. But there are things math and science can't explain, aren't there?" His eyes were bright with agitation. Sal didn't know what he wanted him to say, so he nodded again.

"You're special, Sal," Mr. Merkel said. "You see things other people don't. You see the things people need. You understand the struggle between what's right and what's wrong. If anyone could pierce the boundary between the living and dead, it would have to be you." He waved his hand over the jumble of things on the table. "So I thought maybe, if you had some of his favorite things around you, you could try to talk to Benjamin."

Sal dug his fingers into the hard leather of the sofa cushion. He had rarely wanted anything more than he wanted to be able to do what Mr. Merkel was asking him to do. He looked around the room. The light that came through the windows had faded from day-bright to silver. If he could see the ghosts who moved in the places in-between, Sal thought he should be able to see them now, in the translucent veil between day and evening. But the air was empty.

Mr. Merkel's face seemed to cave in upon itself. He looked gray and defeated, and his edges had gone blurry, like Trudy's in the park. "It's ridiculous, I know. But I had to ask."

The daylight in the room faded a little more. In the snow globe, the last flakes drifted past the bridge. Sal watched them spin lightly down. By the time they settled onto the blue plastic ocean he knew what he had to do. Lucas had been wrong, that first day in the park. What Mr. Merkel really needed, Sal could give him after all. He was the only one who could.

He picked up the globe and held it between his palms. "What do you want me to tell him?"

Mr. Merkel shuddered. The globe was cool in Sal's hands. The empty spaces between the leather furniture and the bare walls trembled with warning, but Sal ignored them.

"Tell him I'm sorry," Mr. Merkel said, his voice breaking. "Tell him if I could do it over again, I would be a rook, and not a king."

Sal closed his eyes. He pressed the snow globe against his chest and groped for another consciousness in the barren room. For an instant he imagined he felt something, a faint touch on the inside of his forehead, but then it was gone. It didn't matter. He knew what Benjamin would say if he were here. It was what Sal would say if he were standing in the in-between and his mother, overcome by guilt for putting that needle in her arm and leaving him behind, asked for absolution.

He opened his eyes. "He forgives you."

Mr. Merkel seemed to come untethered for a moment, then he gathered himself back in. He looked around, straining to see the unseen. "Thank you," he whispered, to both the absent Benjamin and Sal, and now Sal felt the terrible weight of what he'd done.

He'd put words in the mouth of a dead boy, and Mr. Merkel had believed them. Sal had wanted to help him, and he had, but the words were a lie, and that lie would always be between them, a burden of deception and betrayal that Sal would carry forever. He lowered the snow globe to the table, as though it might shatter in his hands. Where his palms had cupped it the glass was damp.

"He's gone now," he said.

Mr. Merkel nodded, the muscles of his throat working. He lifted his glasses and wiped his eyes. Then he sat for a long time, watching the snowflakes in the globe trace their circles around the Golden Gate Bridge in the slowly darkening afternoon. Sal didn't move. He wanted to stay in this pocket of time, between his lie and its consequences, for as long as he could.

At last Mr. Merkel looked at Sal with a fragile smile. "Is there anything here you would like? I believe Benjamin would be happy if something of his could find a home with you."

Sal started to shake his head. He didn't want any of it. Every single thing was heavy with death and deceit and a strangled, cloying love. But against his will his eyes dropped to the deck of cards.

"Of course." Mr. Merkel picked up the deck. He flipped through it until he found the card he wanted. He showed it to Sal. On it was a drawing of a man in a billowing cloak, his face shadowed by a dark hood. He floated in the air with a quill in one long-fingered hand and a scroll in the other. A circle of planets, moons, and suns floated around him on a light blue field. Beneath his feet, in Old English script, was written, THE OBSERVER. When Sal saw it his stomach lurched.

"Benjamin told me this is the most powerful card in the deck." Mr. Merkel's eyes held Sal's even though Sal wanted to look away. "That seems right to me."

He began placing Benjamin's things back in the box. Sal went to the kitchen, where his backpack sat on the floor. He slid the cards into the pocket. He would keep them for the rest of his life, but he would never look at them again.

When he returned to the living room the doorbell rang.

"She's early." Mr. Merkel ran a hand over his hair and went to the door. The woman on the other side had shoulder-length brown hair and the kind of face that should be smiling but wasn't. She stood with her purse clutched to her stomach and her mouth set in a bitter line. When she saw Sal her eyes widened; then she pretended he wasn't there.

"Renata." Mr. Merkel was stiff with politeness. "Thank you for coming all this way."

"We aren't going to talk. Just give them to me."

Mr. Merkel indicated the box. The woman crossed to it and looked inside. She didn't touch anything, but her composure faltered. With her back to him she said, "You had no right to take anything of his."

"I couldn't bear not to," he said. "Renata, he was my son."

She pressed her lips together, biting back the words she wanted to say. She hadn't come to talk, and she held her rage and grief so close to her skin Sal could barely see them. But she couldn't help asking one question. "Why these things?"

"I thought they might be the last things he touched."

She lifted her eyes to the ceiling. Then she turned around. "You son of a bitch."

"I know. I'm sorry. I want you to have them back." Mr. Merkel's shoulders were straight, his face composed. He had a dignity in his repentance that Sal had never seen in him before, and it surprised Renata, too. She stood with her purse, staring at him suspiciously. Then she looked at Sal, standing in the kitchen doorway.

"Who's this? What's he doing here?"

"This is my friend. His name is Sal." Mr. Merkel looked at her without blinking. "He is here to help me bake pies."

The air was heavy with a silence so thick even breath could not disturb it. Mr. Merkel looked at her and she looked at him and the things they said in that silence were beyond Sal's powers to hear. Then she gave Sal a long look, picked up the box with her son's things, and walked out.

NORA

The Toasted Tavern was at the western edge of the commercial district that ran for a mile along Winnemucca Boulevard, Winnemucca's own slice of the old Route 40. Nora rarely went to Winnemucca—its slogan was "The City of Paved Streets," and nothing could have described it better—but she knew the Tavern. It was a classic diner with booths against the front windows, a row of tables running down the middle of a brick-tiled floor, and a bar off the dining area.

She got there at nine, an hour before closing, and ordered dinner. The waitress, a woman in her sixties with gray hair in a long braid, smiled with nicotine-stained teeth and pity. "Just you tonight?" On her left hand was a wedding set with a diamond the size of a sesame seed.

"I'm waiting for one of your cooks to get off work," Nora said.

"Want me to tell him you're here?"

"No, please don't. I'd rather surprise him. How long after closing do they finish back there?"

"An hour if it's busy, but it's Wednesday, so maybe half that. Sometimes they even let a couple guys off before closing, if it's slow."

Nora took her time eating, watching the few remaining diners finish and wander out until she was the only one left. The bartender, a burly man in his twenties, started his closing work. The sound system played a country song about drinking beer in the morning and Nora sipped her chardonnay.

Coming here was a terrible idea, of course. Mason would flip his shit if he knew. But ever since she'd gone to Reno, Nora hadn't been able to get Lucas Zimmerman out of her mind. He had an alibi for Adam's murder, but he had played a central role in Adam's story nonetheless. He'd been like a son to him, yet he'd sold him the drugs he took before getting in the car with Benjamin. So Nora wanted to see him. Surely that couldn't hurt. He didn't know her, and despite what she'd said to the waitress she wasn't going to talk to him.

At five to ten Nora settled her check and the waitress left, a fleece jacket over her Toasted Tavern polo shirt. Nora slid to the back of the booth, out of sight of the bartender and the hostess, and waited.

Twenty minutes later the kitchen doors swung open and three men in stained white chef coats headed for the bar. Nora peeked around the bench seat and saw the bartender dig out three bottles of beer, hand them around, and open a fourth for himself.

It was easy to guess which cook was Lucas—one of the men was barely out of his teens, and the other was in his sixties. Lucas was in his late twenties, with a bedraggled, reddish beard and ill-fitting, faded khaki pants. After he took his beer he seemed not to know what to do with himself, first leaning against the bar, then standing, then leaning again. The younger cook was telling a story about a friend who'd gone to Vegas. Lucas obviously didn't know the friend, or the in-jokes that peppered the story, so he took his cues from the other men, laughing when they laughed, groaning when they groaned. He looked like the kids Nora saw on the edges of playground crowds, trying to worm their way in to the larger group, and she almost felt sorry for him. It was a long way from graduate student on the verge of solving one of math's great problems to convicted felon working as a line cook at the Toasted Tavern.

The hostess saw Nora and walked over. She was a tall girl with knees like baseballs, and looked young enough to be out past her curfew. "Um, sorry. We're closed."

Nora had seen enough. "I was just leaving."

She'd almost reached the door when Renata walked in.

Both women stopped. Nora fought the urge to run. Renata's face registered shock, then anger, then fear.

"Hey, Renata, come have a beer," Lucas called.

"What are you doing here?" Renata whispered furiously.

Nora floundered. What was *Renata* doing here? Lucas walked over and handed Renata a beer. He turned to Nora. Unease crept in as he registered Renata's locked-down shoulders and pinched lips. He slid his arm around her, and Nora had to fight not to gasp out loud.

All I see are choices, Renata had said. It wasn't the dealer's fault; it was the addict's. That's exactly what you'd say if you were sleeping with the dealer. Had the affair begun after Benjamin's death, or before? Lucas had gone to prison after, so probably before. While Adam mentored his brilliant prodigy, the prodigy had romanced his pretty young wife. Nora wasn't sure who disgusted her more, Renata or Lucas.

"Who's this?" Lucas asked.

Renata looked panicked. She clearly didn't want Lucas to talk to Nora, and that made Nora decide that talking to him was exactly what she was going to do. Her mind settled into a chilly, focused calm.

"I'm Nora," she said. "You don't know me, but we have a friend in common."

"Who?"

"Adam Merkel. He was your professor at UNR, right?"

Alarm flickered before Lucas could mask it, but he didn't deny it. "How do you know him?"

"I taught with him in Lovelock. I was hoping to talk to you about him."

Lucas thrust out his jaw. "Are you a reporter? Or a cop? Because I already answered all the questions I'm going to answer."

"I'm not with the police, or the press. I'm really just a friend of Adam's." Nora gave him a conciliatory smile. "I'm trying to understand him a little better. That's all."

Lucas looked at Renata, then at the men in the bar. He might be a math genius, but right now he seemed more cunning than intelligent. "Just for a minute."

They took the booth by the front door. Renata sat with every muscle locked. Lucas leaned back, seemingly relaxed, but Nora wasn't fooled. She knew the fear was still there, below the easy surface.

"How do you know Renata?" he asked.

"We met at the police station when she picked up Adam's things. I told her Adam had a chess set at the school, and she came to get it. We had a nice chat." Nora smiled at Renata, who was staring at the table. "Turns out we have a lot in common."

Lucas maintained his pose of nonchalant accommodation. "And how did you know about me? And where to find me?"

"I heard the police had questioned an old student of Adam's. I graduated from UNR, so I asked around the math department and found out what happened. It wasn't hard to find you after that."

Lucas stiffened a little. "I'm not going to talk about what happened between Adam and me in Reno. Like I said, I've been over all that with the police. And I was here the night he was killed."

"I understand," Nora said. "I'm interested in what Adam was

like before that. I only knew him for a few months, but you and he were so close."

Lucas rubbed one hand across his beard, taking Nora's measure. He made an effort to relax again. "What do you want to know about him?"

Nora wasn't sure where she wanted this conversation to go, so she started with an easy question. "What was he like as a teacher?"

"He was an excellent teacher. The best I ever had."

"He was helping you with a big project, right?" Nora asked. "Some hypothesis that needed to be proved?"

"The Riemann Hypothesis. They haven't proved it yet, have they?"

"I don't know."

"I doubt it. They don't have anybody who can think about it the right way." Lucas spoke mildly, but the arrogance was plain.

"It's too bad you weren't able to finish it," Nora said, just as mildly.

"It was just a math problem." He shrugged. "A game, really."

"The prize money would have been nice, though," Nora said. "I can think of a few ways to spend a million dollars."

"That would have been nice, sure. But I've never had money. It's hard to miss what you've never had."

"We don't need money to be happy," Renata said, glaring at Nora.

Lucas draped his arm across her shoulders. "That's right, we don't."

"How did you two connect, anyway?" Nora asked this casually, as if they were at a cocktail party back in Reno. Renata slid her eyes to Lucas.

"We met while Adam and I were working together," Lucas said smoothly. "Adam had me over for dinner sometimes, and there were the usual faculty parties. But nothing happened between us until after the accident, if that's what you're asking."

"That's good. I'd hate to think Adam's wife was cheating on him with his favorite student."

"I would never have done that to him."

Lucas sounded so sincere that Nora might have believed him if Renata's cheeks hadn't turned bright red. "You must have been a great comfort to her." She smiled sweetly. "In her grief."

Renata drew a sharp breath. Lucas gripped her shoulder, but she shook him off. "You don't get to judge us, or what we did. We love each other. That's all that matters."

"Is it?" Nora dropped the pretense of cordiality. "You told me you married Adam because he was decent. Didn't you think he deserved a little decency in return?"

Lucas shoved his beer away. "Okay, that's enough. Let's go, Renata."

But Renata wasn't done. "I married Adam because he made me feel safe. I did love him for that. But then I met Lucas, and he made me feel alive. Young. Like I had my whole life in front of me. We didn't mean to hurt Adam. I was going to ask him for a divorce. But then the accident happened." She jerked one shoulder. "And I stopped giving a shit about Adam's feelings."

"Well, I'm glad you were able to find some happiness, after such a tragedy," Nora said.

Renata frowned, trying to decide if Nora meant this. "I do deserve to be happy, after everything I've been through."

"Even though everything you've been through is your boyfriend's fault?"

Renata and Lucas both sat back in shock. Nora expected them to walk out now, and that was fine. She gave even less of a shit about their feelings than Renata had about Adam's.

Renata started to say something, but Lucas cut her off with a raised finger. Then he turned to Nora. "I'm going to say one more thing to you. My drug business was a mistake. I accept that. I needed money, and I thought I was just selling people stuff they wanted. I didn't know Adam was in so deep. What happened to Benjamin is something I will regret for the rest of my life."

"And he went to prison for it." Renata's voice shook. "He paid the price. But Adam never served a day. Not one day in prison for the life of our son."

"He got his punishment in the end, though, didn't he?" Nora said. "And you were pretty happy about it, as I recall."

Renata pressed her lips into an angry white line. Lucas put his hand over hers, silencing her again. "Look, Nora. I know you're Adam's friend, and you're upset about what happened to him. But nobody's happy he's dead, or about how he died. Least of all Renata or me."

"Maybe the kid did it," Renata blurted out. "Did you ever think of that?"

Lucas snapped around to face her.

Nora said, "Do you mean Sal? Are you suggesting *Sal* killed Adam?"

"Renata." Lucas's voice was dark with warning.

"He lives up there, doesn't he?" Renata said. "Why hasn't anyone asked where he was that night?"

"Renata," Lucas said again. "Shut up."

"No, Lucas, I won't shut up." She was loud enough now that the men at the bar looked over at them. "I know you said he's just a kid, but they're coming after you for this. You have to protect yourself."

"They're not coming after me. I was here. They know that." Lucas glanced at the men at the bar. "Please, calm down." He ran his hand through his thinning hair. For the first time since they'd started talking he looked truly shaken, but Nora didn't bother wondering why. She couldn't stand to be around either of them for one more second. She grabbed her coat and purse and started to walk away. After three steps, she turned back.

"One more question." Lucas and Renata looked like a pair of refugees huddled together, and that icy calm flooded Nora's veins again. "My waitress said on slow nights the kitchen lets some of the cooks off early. Was March thirteenth a slow night?"

Lucas's eyes shot past her to the other two line cooks. Renata went so white that every freckle stood out. Neither of them said a word.

"I suppose that's a question for the police," Nora said. Then she walked out.

SAL

It took four hours to bake the pies. The cherry ones were the easiest, just canned cherries and sugar poured into a store-bought crust. The pumpkins were easy, too: canned pumpkin with whole milk, an egg, and a sprinkling of ginger and cinnamon. The apple pies took the longest, because you had to slice the apples. Sal wasn't very good at that, so Mr. Merkel had him stir the pumpkin and cherry fillings on the stove while he peeled and pared. The pies baked two at a time, one on each rack.

While they measured and sliced and stirred the sun set and the moon rose, and Mr. Merkel talked. He seemed relaxed, as though a burden had been lifted, and Sal felt better, too, the further they got from the moment when he'd pretended to talk to Benjamin. Mr. Merkel told him he and Benjamin had baked pies for the university math department's Pi Day party every year since Benjamin was four. They'd only baked a cherry and an apple, though, because the other professors had also baked pies. For the middle school party Mr. Merkel had to bake them all himself. There were thirty-six eighth graders, so he'd calculated he needed six pies. Each one could be cut into eight slices, so every student could have one slice and there would be twelve left over, which was exactly how many teachers and staff there were, minus Mr. Merkel himself. Mr. Merkel was so delighted by this that Sal wished he could go to the party, too. Not to eat the pies, but to be there when the teacher the eighth graders had belittled all year served them homemade dessert. He hoped they'd think better of him afterward.

"What's Pi Day, anyway?" he asked as Mr. Merkel slid the cherry pies into the oven.

"I forgot you wouldn't know," Mr. Merkel said. "But why would you? My eighth graders are just learning it now." While apple peels fell into the trash can at his feet he told Sal about the number pi. It was the ratio of a circle's circumference to its diameter, and it was always the same, no matter how big or small the circle was. That made it a "constant," which was a special kind of number that helped mathematicians solve equations. Its first three digits were 3.14, which was why Pi Day was March 14.

"Why is it such a big deal?" Sal was pretty sure no other numbers got special holidays.

Mr. Merkel's paring knife stopped. "Pi is defined by the circle, which is the most perfect form in creation," he said. "It's also at the heart of cycles, which are to time as the circle is to space. You can't define any cyclical process without pi. Wherever there are waves, or orbits, or patterns, it's there. It's in the rhythm of the ocean and the pulse of music, the beating of your heart and the movement of the planets around the sun. In that way, it's more than just a number. It's one of the threads that weave together the fabric of the universe."

His voice was shot through with wonder and a profound sadness, and Sal stood with the spoon frozen in his hand. He still didn't understand pi, and he never would, not in the way Mr. Merkel wanted him to, or in the way Lucas surely did. In Mr. Merkel's words he heard a distant country of knowledge he would never reach and a sorrow he could only lie to ease, and in that moment the burden of what he could not do and what he had done was almost too much to bear.

The day before, Sal had taken Ezra out behind the solar panels and told him he hadn't sold the balloons to Trudy. Ezra's mouth opened in confusion and outrage, but before he could say anything Sal said, "I kept thinking about how my mom looked on the couch. She had stuff coming out of her mouth, and her fingers were purple."

Ezra blanched. Sal watched him without sympathy. Ezra hadn't seen Sal's mother on the couch in the little blue house. He needed to know what it looked like, the kind of death she had. Sal waited for Ezra's imagination to paint the picture, then he skipped ahead to the only other thing that mattered. "The new guy, Lucas, saw me with Trudy. He saw the balloons, too, and he understood why I couldn't sell them. He knows my math teacher from Reno, and he told me I should ask him for help. So I did."

It took Ezra five seconds to process this, then he grabbed Sal by the shoulders. "What the fuck? You told your *math teacher*?"

Sal winced as Ezra's fingers dug deep. "I told him about Gideon throwing everything in the well, and how you owe that guy money. He wants to give you the money to pay him. You just have to give him all the stuff in the cave, and promise not to sell it anymore."

"He's just going to hand me four thousand dollars?" Ezra narrowed his eyes. "What is he, some sort of do-gooder? Wants to keep drugs off the street or something?"

"He says he can't think of a better way to spend his money."

It was the first truly warm day of the year, and the sun blazed on the sand behind the solar panels. Ezra didn't seem to feel it. He let go of Sal and rubbed his chin as suspicion warred with hope. "What if it's a setup? He could bring the cops."

"I told him I'd bring him to where we met Taegan. I didn't tell him where it was."

Ezra paced in a circle, and Sal thought of Samson on his chain, tracing his restless loops. Then he whirled back to Sal. "Tell him to bring cash. I'm not giving him anything until I see it, and only if I'm sure there's no cops."

"We can leave the stuff in the cave. I won't get it until you decide it's okay."

Ezra's jeans hung loose around his hips. He was much thinner than he'd been when Sal came to live with his uncles. "Son of a bitch. You might save my ass after all, little brother." He broke into a wide grin that, for the first time, didn't remind Sal of his mother. "After this we'll go back to the medicine, like I promised. It'll take us longer to get to Reno, but by next summer we'll be there, rolling in bank like a couple of outlaws."

A finger of sweat ran down Sal's back inside his shirt. He thought back to crisp autumn days on the bench and the ordinary people who'd told him their pains and their worries. In return he'd given them comfort in small brown bags and sympathy in quick nods, and their gratitude had made him believe he mattered. It all seemed like it had happened to someone else, a long time ago.

"Did you know that guy died?" he asked.

"What guy?"

"The old man. Mick. You said he didn't need the medicine anymore. Did you know he overdosed?"

"What? No way. You're shitting me. Are you sure?"

Ezra's feigned surprise wouldn't have fooled anyone, and Sal let the lie settle deep inside him. Then he said, "I'm not delivering anything anymore. Not even the pills."

Last summer he would have braced himself for anger, but now he steeled himself for wheedling. Sure enough, Ezra raised his hands in supplication. "Come on, little brother, don't say that. Gideon scared you, sure. And that guy dying, that would freak anybody out. But Gideon won't find our stash in the cave. And Trudy and

Jim and the rest, they'll be fine, like they've always been." He wiped the sweat off his face. "Please. I can't do it without you. And I have to get out of this fucking place, you know that."

"It hurts people. You have to get out a different way."

Overhead, an eagle circled, its shadow flitting across the sand. Ezra took a step back. "Look, we don't have to decide anything now, right? You just think about it, and we can talk after we meet your teacher." It was so much like what he'd said on Sal's first day at the double-wide that Sal walked away without another word.

A full moon hung over the Humboldt Range as Sal and Mr. Merkel drove up the fire road. They were alone; the one car that had trailed them onto the Lovelock-Unionville Road had stopped in Marzen. Mr. Merkel's headlights picked out a small rabbit, its startled eyes glowing green. All around them the hills rose like dark shoulders.

"Here it is," Sal said when they were even with the bluff. Mr. Merkel turned off the car, and night fell about them. He pulled a flashlight out of his black leather bag and they followed its beam up the low rise. Mr. Merkel's bag swung heavily in his hand, and Sal, feeling strangely unweighted, realized he'd left his backpack in Mr. Merkel's kitchen.

At the top of the hill they saw Ezra's headlamp winking in the acacia trees. If he was so worried about the police, Sal thought, he should have left it off.

"You must be Ezra," Mr. Merkel said when they reached the campsite. His voice was light and confident, and as it had on the first day of school, it calmed Sal's jittery nerves.

Ezra stood by the firepit with his hunting rifle in the crook of his arm. "You got my money?"

Mr. Merkel put his bag on the ground and pulled out a manila envelope. "Did Sal explain that you need to give me all the heroin you have?"

"Yeah."

"Then we have a deal."

Ezra's feet fidgeted. The circle of trees seemed to lean in, listening, and he scanned them with his light, looking for policemen and DEA agents in their branches. Then he snapped it back to Sal. "Okay. Go get it."

Beyond the reach of the flashlight and the headlamp the moonlight took over, showing Sal the faint trail up the hill. When he reached the ledge in the bluff he looked down. The two lights shone unmoving in the circle of trees, facing one another in the moon-shot dark. He moved carefully along the ledge, pressing his body against the cool rock. He was so intent on keeping his balance that he didn't see the figure beside the cave until he was almost upon it. Then it moved, and Sal was so startled he took a step backward, off the ledge.

The figure grabbed his arm just before he pitched over. "Careful," it said, and it was Gideon. He pulled Sal into the cave, and Sal tripped on the headlamp Ezra had left for him. He put it on, pressed the switch, and saw Gideon standing beside the bowl of balloons. In the wavering shadows he loomed large and menacing, his eyes black holes in his face.

"How did you—" Sal began. His heart raced, both from his near fall and the shock of seeing Gideon.

"I waited up for you. You didn't come. Then Ezra sneaked off. He came up here first." A muscle jumped in his jaw. "What are you doing here?"

"I'm—I'm helping Ezra."

"With this?" Gideon pointed to the balloons.

"Not like that. I'm helping him—"

"You're lying," Gideon said. "You think I don't know why you were in the house that day? Or why you're suddenly so interested in hunting?"

"That wasn't why I was in the house. I was exploring. I didn't know that was where Ezra kept it, I swear."

"But you've been helping him all along, haven't you? Of course you have. He needs somebody to get it down the hill, and who better than a boy who takes the bus to Lovelock every day?" Gideon's fingers flexed by his side. "Who's he meeting down there? Taegan?"

Sal's knees felt as if they'd turned to sand. How long did he have before Ezra came looking for him? If Gideon and Ezra met in this cave, Gideon would beat Ezra up again, and then everything would fall apart. Sal spoke quickly. "You're right, I was helping him, but I told him I wouldn't do it anymore. Now I'm helping him stop. He owes a guy in Reno that money you threw in the well, and if he doesn't pay him the Reno guy will hurt him. Mr. Merkel is going to give him four thousand dollars, and Ezra's going to give him all this." Sal pointed at the balloons. "So he won't have any more to sell, and the business will be over, like you wanted. Please let me take it. They're waiting."

"The chess teacher?" Something unpleasant colored Gideon's voice. "That's who's down there?"

"Yes. He's helping me."

Gideon's face darkened. "Why is he helping you?"

"Because he's my friend." Sal couldn't help raising his chin a little.

Gideon took three steps closer. Sal smelled his acrid scent of metal and sawdust.

"Answer me this, Sal. Why did you help my brother sell his drugs?"

Sal's mouth went dry. There were many things he could say. He could say he cared about Ezra, or that he cared about the people he'd thought he was helping, or that he liked the money he made.

All of these things had been true, and some still were, but he didn't say any of them. Instead he pictured Ezra sliding bottles of pills across the bar to his sister and said, "He told me if I didn't, he'd send me to foster care."

Gideon's pupils were tiny black dots in the glare of the headlamp. "And why did you tell him you wouldn't do it anymore?"

To this there was only one answer, but Sal wavered, caught by a last flicker of mercy. Ezra had wanted to help Sal's mother. He'd thought he was selling her medicine. He hadn't known what it would do to her, or that it could make her turn to something worse. He wouldn't have sold it to her if he had.

Wouldn't he? Angelus asked, and Sal remembered Ezra in this cave ten days ago. *Fuck*, he'd said when Sal told him what heroin did to his mother. Then he'd sent him to sell it to Trudy. He'd sold the medicine to the young mother and the rest even after he knew the linebacker had overdosed. Now he wanted to go to Reno and sell it to even more people. The flicker of mercy winked out.

"Because I found out what it did to my mom," he said.

Gideon spoke so quietly Sal could barely hear him. "What did it do to your mom?"

"Ezra sold her those pills to help with her back, but she got addicted to them. And after a while they weren't enough. So she got heroin from Taegan." It was the first time Sal had said the word *heroin* out loud, and the naming of it shifted the ground beneath his feet. "When I found her, she still had the syringe in her hand."

Gideon stood locked in deadly stillness. "Ezra gave her those pills?"

"Not gave. Sold." In Sal's mind Angelus flared his wings in approval, and a rush of exhilaration made Sal stand up straight. He could imagine no better avenger for his mother than Gideon. Catellus whispered *No*, but Sal ignored him.

Gideon stepped back, into the shadows. He massaged the palm

of one hand with the thumb of the other. There were scabs over the abrasions on his knuckles where he'd hit Ezra the day Sal explored the farmhouse.

"Go do your business with the teacher," he said.

When Sal reached the grove, breathless from racing down the path, Ezra and Mr. Merkel were where he'd left them, facing each other across the firepit.

"What took you so long?" Ezra said.

"It's dark," Sal said, though he was still wearing the headlamp.

Ezra reached out an irritated hand for the bowl. "Give me the money," he said to Mr. Merkel.

Mr. Merkel held out the envelope. Ezra snatched it and dropped to his knees, setting the rifle and the bowl beside him. As he had so many nights in Sal's room, he spread the money out and counted it twice. When he was satisfied, he grabbed the rifle and stood, leaving the bowl of balloons on the ground. Then he hefted the rifle to the crook of his arm. Sal held his breath. Surely Ezra wouldn't take both the money and the balloons. He was an honest businessman, he'd said. But he was clearly thinking about it.

After five excruciating seconds Ezra lowered the rifle, and Sal exhaled. To Mr. Merkel Ezra said, "I don't know why you're doing this, but I appreciate it."

"A life for a life," Mr. Merkel said. If he knew what Ezra had just been thinking of doing, he gave no sign.

Ezra turned to go. "Come on, Sal."

"I'd like Sal to stay," Mr. Merkel said. "Just for a little while. I'll make sure he gets home."

Sal didn't want to stay. He was afraid Mr. Merkel would ask him to talk to Benjamin again, here in the close circle of watching trees. Then he thought of Gideon, who was surely waiting for Ezra at the double-wide. "I'll be okay. I've got the headlamp."

"Suit yourself," Ezra said. "Don't wake up Gideon when you get back."

Sal watched him go, a dark shadow picking through dark sage. Catellus hissed wordlessly in his mind, but Sal thought about his mother and the old linebacker and all the people Catellus had killed in Sal's imaginary world. *He deserves it,* Sal told him. *Just like you.*

Mr. Merkel's face shone in the moonlight, as if it were lit from within by a steady, pale flame. "Let's build a campfire, shall we?"

NORA

Nora called Mason the morning after she talked to Lucas and Renata at the Toasted Tavern. He was still at home; she heard children's voices in the background: a family breakfast. When she told him she'd talked to Lucas he said, "You did *what*?"

"I know. I didn't plan on talking to him, I just wanted to get a better look at him." Before Mason could interrupt Nora said, "Renata Merkel was there, too. They're together, Mace. They've been together since before Benjamin died."

A little girl shrieked in the background. Then Mason must have stepped away, because the breakfast noises faded. "Renata said she lived in Winnemucca," he said. "It didn't even occur to me she'd be there with Lucas."

"There's another thing," Nora said. "Lucas might not have an alibi after all. My waitress told me if it's a slow night they let some of the cooks go early. I asked Lucas if March thirteenth was a slow night. He didn't answer, but from the way he and Renata reacted, I'm betting it was."

"I'll send Smitty and Phil to check that out today." Mason paused, and Nora knew what was coming. "This is really helpful, Nora, but you've got to stop. You need to stay out of the way and let us do our job."

"I will. But let me know what happens, will you?"

Mason wouldn't promise anything, but during Nora's fourth period class he sent a text: *March 13 LZ let off at 8:30. Bringing him in for questioning now.* Nora smiled, both at the fact of the text and what it said. She spent the rest of the school day in a halo of self-congratulation, imagining Lucas in the police station's interview room. It wouldn't be long before everyone in Lovelock knew that Adam Merkel's killer had been arrested, and maybe then the hunted look in Sal Prentiss's eyes would begin to disappear.

She was still at the school when, an hour after the last bell, Jake called on her cell. He sounded out of breath, as though he'd been running. "That reporter just drove off with Sal."

It took Nora a moment to remember who he was talking about. It had been over a week since the reporter showed up at the Nickel, and Nora had forgotten about her. "How did she do that?"

"I was watching the bus drop-off, like you told me to. She pulled up right after the bus came. She went over to Sal, and they talked, and then he got in her car. I couldn't get there in time."

Nora couldn't believe how aggressive this reporter was. Taking a kid without his guardian's permission almost counted as kidnapping, even if Sal had gone with her willingly. "Where did they go?"

"They headed down the hill to the interstate. What should we do?"

Despite the reporter's pushy tactics, Nora was less worried about her interviewing Sal now that Lucas was in custody. If Lucas had killed Adam, she didn't see how Sal could have known anything about it. Her instinct about Sal being a watcher with an untold story must have been wrong. "I don't know that we can do anything at this point. But she's just a reporter. She'll get a few quotes about finding the body, then she'll bring him home."

"But where did she take him?"

This was a fair point—it was odd that the reporter was taking Sal anywhere at all. It would be easier to talk to him in her car, or somewhere in Marzen, instead of taking him on the interstate. Especially since the closest towns were Lovelock, which was thirty minutes away, and Winnemucca, which was an hour.

The fluorescent lights in the classroom dimmed. Lucas had just been picked up by the police in Winnemucca. Renata probably knew this, and if she did, she also knew Lucas's alibi was gone. And Nora herself had told Renata Sal's name and where he lived, just before the reporter first showed up in Marzen. The skin on the backs of her hands prickled. "What did you say the reporter's name was?"

"Ruth Miller."

"What does she look like?"

"About our age. Brown hair. Lots of freckles. Why? Have you seen her?"

Nora put one hand over her eyes. "I don't think she's a reporter. I think she's Renata Merkel. Adam's ex-wife."

Nora drove to the Marzen exit at eighty miles per hour, but she felt as though she were going twenty. The mile markers trudged past, each one like a hard slap to her face. She had done this. She had gone to Winnemucca and all but accused Lucas of murder, and now Renata had taken Sal from the bus stop. Because Sal knew something about the murder after all. Nora couldn't imagine what it was, but it had gotten Renata to Marzen less than two hours after the police had broken her boyfriend's alibi.

Before she left her classroom, Nora had called 911. She told Marian what had happened and gave her a description of Renata and Sal. Then she hung up and called Mason.

"It's my fault, Mason." She paced behind her desk. "You were right. I should have stayed out of it."

"Hold on. Are you sure it was Renata?"

"Jake Sanchez saw her. She was up there last week, too, pretending to be a reporter and trying to find out where Sal lives." Nora stopped pacing. "Mason, what if Renata killed Adam herself? Or she and Lucas did it together? Do you know if she was in that night class where she said she was?"

"The professor doesn't take attendance," Mason said. "We need to ask the other students, but we haven't had the manpower."

Like Nora, he hadn't thought Renata was capable of killing Adam. But he'd also said the killer wanted Adam to burn, and Renata's son had burned to death because of Adam. Nora remembered how cold her eyes had been when she'd talked about Adam's death in Nora's classroom. "I think Sal knows they did it," she said. "And she's trying to keep him quiet."

"Let's not get ahead of ourselves," Mason said. "We'll talk to Jake, and go from there."

"Are you going to the Prentiss place?" Mason would need to tell Gideon, and Gideon was off the grid. "I'll get Jake and meet you there."

Jake was waiting for Nora in front of the Marzen General Store, and they took his truck up the fire road. The wind was blowing hard out of the Humboldt Range, carrying sand across the track in low, horizontal sheets. Jake's truck waded through them as though they were water.

When they got to the Prentiss place, Nora told Jake to park behind Gideon's truck and wait for Mason. But Gideon had heard them. He came out of his shed, and, reluctantly, Nora and Jake climbed out of the truck. The wind tugged at the sleeves of Nora's blouse.

Gideon sparked with annoyance. "What do you want?"

Nora glanced up the road for Mason, but there was no sign of him. "Sal's missing," she said. "The police are on their way."

Gideon looked at his watch. Then he walked slowly over to them. "Missing?"

A yellow dog walked out of the trash heap. Its snout pointed up the road, and to Nora's relief a squad car rounded the bend. When Mason and Phil got out Gideon strode over to them.

"What the fuck is this about Sal?"

Mason spoke in the soothing tones of a police officer used to dealing with worried family members. "We're still gathering information, Mr. Prentiss, but I assure you we will do everything we can to find your nephew." Then he walked over to Nora and Jake, and after half a dozen questions he knew everything they knew about the woman who'd pretended to be a reporter and picked Sal up at the bus stop.

Gideon listened to every word, his skin taut against his skull. "Who is she?" he asked when they were done.

"We're questioning an old student of Adam Merkel's in his murder," Mason said. "Renata is his girlfriend."

Nora expected to see alarm, but instead something calculating shifted in Gideon's eyes. "What makes you think this guy killed him?"

"We can't share that right now," Mason said. "But if you have any reason to believe Sal knows anything about Merkel's death, you should tell us. It may help us find him."

Now Gideon's expression was unreadable. "I don't."

Mason turned to Phil. "Have Smitty check Lucas's place. And tell Marian to put out an APB on the car. Send it to Highway Patrol and the Humboldt, Washoe, and Churchill sheriffs' departments. We'll need to get tracking on her cell phone, too."

"We could try calling her," Phil suggested. "Marian can pull her number from the file."

"I have it," Nora said. "She texted me about Adam's chess set." She went to Jake's truck, fished her phone from her purse, and found Renata's text. To her surprise, there were two bars of service. She handed the phone to Mason.

Mason walked a few paces away before calling. He waited long enough that Nora knew the call was going to voice mail, then said, "Renata, this is Chief Deputy Greer with the Pershing County sheriff's department. We're looking for Sal Prentiss. We understand he may be with you. Please call us as soon as you can." He sounded as though he was trying to solve a mildly worrying mystery about a boy who didn't come home from school on time, but his entire body was tense. He left the police station's phone number and hung up.

To Gideon he said, "You may want to come wait at the station, since we have no way to reach you here."

"I'll get my jacket," Gideon said.

He'd taken two steps toward his shed when Nora's phone buzzed with a text. Mason read it, and his shoulders sagged in relief. "It's her. She says Sal's fine. She's bringing him home now."

Nora's muscles flooded with adrenaline, and she heard Jake's muttered, "Thank God." Gideon's face slackened, and he closed his eyes.

"She says he has something to tell us about Merkel's murder," Mason said, and Gideon's eyes snapped open.

"What the hell? He doesn't know shit about that teacher dying."

He sounded disbelieving and angry, but Nora saw the faint whitening around his mouth and something inside her turned over, like a paving stone dug up from a path. Before she could figure out what was underneath, Mason sent her, Gideon, and Jake into the double-wide. As a precaution, he said.

As soon as they were inside Gideon went to the kitchen and

opened the sliding window over the sink. Nora and Jake stood on either side of him. Through the bug-crusted screen they watched Mason and Phil lean against the squad car. All around them the wind lifted small dervishes from the sand, made them dance, then let them die.

Twenty minutes passed. Nobody in the double-wide spoke. Nora leaned against the chipped but surprisingly immaculate kitchen counter and wondered why Gideon was so afraid of what Sal wanted to tell the police.

At last a blue car rounded the curve and came to a stop behind the squad car. Inside was Renata, both hands clutching the wheel, and, small and featureless beside her, the silhouette of a boy. Gideon walked out of the double-wide and down the cinder block steps. Mason and Phil positioned themselves fifteen feet from Renata's car. They had their hands on their weapons, but didn't draw them.

"It's okay, Renata," Mason called. "Come on out."

The driver's door opened. The wind tossed Renata's hair high behind her as she stood up. Sal got out, too. He was wearing the Denver Broncos sweatshirt he'd worn almost every day for months, and the wind pressed it against his chest. Nora and Jake leaned closer to the kitchen window. From the bottom of the cinder block steps Gideon watched his nephew with a feral stillness.

Sal walked around the car and stood in front of Renata, as if shielding her. The wind flung one last gale at them, then without warning it died, leaving the land in a hushed silence.

"She didn't hurt me," Sal said. "She just wanted to talk to me." His voice carried perfectly in the dry air.

Mason said, "That's great, Sal. Come on over here, and you can tell us what happened."

Sal looked over his shoulder at Renata. She pressed her hands to her mouth. He turned back to Mason. "Lucas didn't kill Mr. Merkel," he said. "But I know who did."

Renata let out a sob. Gideon took three quick steps, but Sal stopped him with a look.

"Be quiet, Sal." Gideon's hands clenched at his sides. "Don't say another word."

"I'm sorry," Sal said. "But I have to tell them what happened." Then, in the stillness that hung in the wake of the wind, he said, "It was Ezra," and Gideon's head jerked backward.

Five minutes later, Mason, Phil, Gideon, and Sal were in the double-wide, sitting around the kitchen table. Mason had gotten his notepad and a small tape recorder from the cruiser. He'd told Nora and Jake to wait outside with Renata, but as soon as Mason closed the door of the double-wide the three of them went to stand below the open kitchen window. Through the screen they could hear every word.

"How do you know it was Ezra Prentiss who killed Adam Merkel?" Mason asked Sal.

Sal told his story in a calm, measured voice. Ezra had sold prescription painkillers he bought from a man in Reno, and made Sal deliver them in the park. Then Gideon threw Ezra's money and supplies in the well, and Ezra decided to sell heroin to pay his debt faster. Sal couldn't do that because of his mom, who'd died of a heroin overdose. He asked Mr. Merkel for help, and Mr. Merkel offered to pay Ezra's debt if Ezra promised not to sell any more.

Nora put a steadying hand on the double-wide's gray vinyl siding. She'd had no idea about any of this. Of course she hadn't. She hadn't thought of Sal beyond writing C's on his homework, while Adam had invited him to share all those lunches and chess matches.

"So you arranged to meet him at the campsite?" Mason asked.

Yes, Sal said. Mr. Merkel gave Ezra the money and took Ezra's heroin, and after Ezra left, Mr. Merkel and Sal made a campfire. But fifteen minutes later, Ezra came back. He'd decided he wanted the drugs and the money both.

"So he set Merkel on fire?" Mason asked, and Nora heard his skepticism. "Why?"

"I don't know," Sal said. "But when he got the heroin out of Mr. Merkel's bag he found the jump rope and the bottle. He told me to go home. The next day, I saw."

"So you didn't see him set the fire."

"No. But there was no one else there. Just the two of them."

"Did you see Mr. Merkel inject himself with the heroin?"

Sal paused. Then: "He did it while we were sitting at the campfire. I tried to stop him, but he—he said he couldn't resist it."

Nora felt Jake look at her. In her mind's eye she saw the silver needle, glinting in the acacia leaf, that he'd pulled from his pocket in the Nickel.

"Do you know why he had the jump rope and the bottle?" Mason asked.

"I don't know why he had the bottle. But I know why he had the jump rope." Sal explained how, when they were baking pies, Adam had shown him some of Benjamin's things. He'd put them in a box for Renata because he felt bad about taking them, and there was a jump rope there. When Renata came she took the box, but Mr. Merkel must have decided he couldn't give up everything after all.

Mason blew out his breath. Nora pictured the tightness he got around his eyes when he was irritated. "Why didn't you tell us this before?"

For the first time, Sal sounded scared. "I didn't want to get in trouble. For selling the pills. And I didn't want to get Ezra in trouble, either. But Renata told me Lucas had been arrested for killing Mr. Merkel. And Mr. Merkel—" Sal's voice broke. He took a moment to collect himself. "Mr. Merkel wouldn't want Lucas to go to jail."

Mason's voice softened. "Ezra won't be going to jail, either, Sal. He's dead."

"How did he die?" Sal sounded as shocked as Nora felt.

"He was shot," Mason said. "In Reno." Later he would tell Nora that Ezra's body had been recovered in an abandoned warehouse the week before. He'd been shot in the chest with a rifle that had been found next to the body. Phil had driven up to the Prentiss place with a Reno deputy just that morning, and Gideon had identified the gun, and the body's clothes and personal effects, as his brother's. He had been dead for about a month, which put his death at around the same time as Adam's. He must have gone straight to Reno to square up with his supplier, Mason said, and something had gone wrong. His was just another death in the shadowy world of Reno's drug cartels, and his killer would never be found.

The interview ended shortly after that. When Nora heard the scrape of chair legs against linoleum, she, Renata, and Jake moved away from the window. Mason led the way down the cinder block steps, followed by Phil, then Gideon and Sal. Gideon's face was set in lines even grimmer than usual. Sal looked dazed, and he tripped slightly on the steps. When he got to the bottom he seemed to see Nora for the first time. Surprise, then gratitude, flickered across his features. Nora wished she could put her arms around him, but he was too far away.

Mason looked at Renata. "You weren't in your accounting class that night." When Renata shook her head, he said, "Did you pick up a box of your son's things from Adam?"

Her eyes flooded with guilty tears. "I'm sorry. I didn't want you to know I'd been there. I didn't know what you'd think." She twined her fingers together. "Are you going to let Lucas go?"

"Sal's got to sign a formal statement first," Mason said. "We'll take him in and do that now."

Then Mason rested one hand on Sal's shoulder. The look he gave him was tender and respectful. It was the look a father gives a son, and the look Mason surely gave Alex when Alex made him proud. Nora felt a pit open up inside her ribs. What's done is done, she told herself. She would tell herself that for the rest of her life.

"I know that was hard," Mason said. "But you did the right thing."

Behind Mason, Gideon watched Sal with eyes as pale as dimes.

"I know," Sal said.

SAL

The fire took a while to catch, but once it did it was a fierce little thing, small and bright in the ring of stones. Sal and Mr. Merkel had gathered the branches of fallen acacias and used sage for kindling, so it smelled of sage singed with the sweet decay of dead wood. Periodically a burst of sparks erupted and floated skyward.

Sal had never seen a campfire before, so he'd never felt the glow of heat on his face while night chilled his back. It was as if he were straddling two worlds, one hot and light and alive, the other cool and dark and breathless. The in-between would have felt like this, he imagined, that place where you could talk to the dead and tell the living what they said, had he been able to go there when Mr. Merkel asked him to. He shivered, and drew closer to the flames.

Mr. Merkel hadn't spoken since the fire caught. He didn't seem frightened of it the way he had of the trash can fire at the school; instead, it seemed to fascinate him. He sat with his legs crossed, and his glasses reflected the fire so his eyes looked like pits of flame. Sal could imagine Catellus having eyes like that, and that made him think of Ezra. He wondered if he'd gotten back to the double-wide yet. In the dark, on the steep, narrow trail, probably not.

At last Mr. Merkel stirred, and the flames that were his eyes winked out. He picked up the bowl of balloons Ezra had left on the ground and put it in his lap. "Do you know what fire is?"

Sal looked at the fire in the ring of stones. It was mysterious and ephemeral, like a ghost flickering in the dark. “No.”

Mr. Merkel passed his hand over the flames. “This wood is made up of molecules, like the water in the Humboldt River. If you get it hot enough, the molecules vibrate and break away, just like water molecules in the sun. That’s what smoke is. Vaporized wood.” The trees leaned in, listening. “When the smoke hits the air, its molecules combine with oxygen to make different molecules. That releases energy. The energy looks like flame and feels like heat. It’s the same with anything that burns. Its molecules float away, collide with the air, and fire is born.” His face lightened with a hint of his old storytelling smile. “It’s a lovely thing, really. Matter at play.”

The fire gave a pop, and another burst of sparks shot into the night. Mr. Merkel watched them go. “The Vikings used to burn the bodies of their dead. They laid them on pyres with their most precious possessions. Warriors with their swords. Tradesmen with their tools. They believed they would need these things in heaven. They thought the smoke would carry them there, treasures and all.” He was still looking up at the sparks. “I’ve always liked that. It’s such a simple faith, yet so comforting.”

Sal thought burning people on a pyre sounded a lot better than burying them in the ground. If his mother had been burned, Sal wouldn’t be tormented by images of what she looked like in her coffin six months or six years or six decades later. His mother would have wanted to be burned with the hymnal from the Baptist Church, he thought, while he would want to be burned with his colored pencils and a sketch pad.

“What would you want to be burned with?” he asked Mr. Merkel.

Mr. Merkel considered this. “I can’t think of anything.”

"What about your chess set?"

"That was never mine."

Mr. Merkel lifted a blue balloon from the bowl, put the tiny knot between his teeth, and ripped it open. He poured the contents onto his palm. It looked like brown sugar. He tilted his hand, and the crystals slid off into the fire. They hissed when they hit the flames. "Have you ever wondered what your mother felt when she died?"

Sal stiffened. He hadn't let himself think about his mother's dying, but now his mind conjured the image: his mother gasping for air, coughing up bloody foam, and clutching at her chest, all while Sal slept down the hall.

"She felt bliss," Mr. Merkel said. "When you take this, all your pain goes away, and every cell in your body is flooded with light and warmth and joy. Your mother was happier with that needle in her vein than she'd ever been in her life."

While Sal didn't want his mother to have suffered, he didn't want her to have found her life's sweetest moments inside a tiny colored balloon, either. "But it killed her."

"Yes. She fell asleep, and her body forgot to breathe," Mr. Merkel said. "It didn't hurt, Sal. She just floated away on a dream. I want you to know that."

Sal didn't like that, either. It sounded too much like giving up. He wanted his fierce, beautiful mother to have died fighting to get back to him. He poked the fire with an acacia twig, turning over orange embers to find the red ones underneath.

Mr. Merkel wiped the last of the brown crystals on his pants. He set the bowl aside, then folded his hands in his lap. "You promised you would do me a favor."

Sal had thought baking pies was the favor. Then he'd thought talking to Benjamin was the favor. One of these had been easy; the other had been terribly hard; but Sal knew he would never say no to the man beside him. He snapped the twig in half. "Okay."

"Don't be so eager," Mr. Merkel said. "It's a very big favor. First I will tell you why I need it, and why only you can do it."

From beyond the grove came a stealthy shuffling. A coyote, perhaps. Mr. Merkel didn't seem to hear it. He reached over to the bowl and picked up another balloon, a yellow one this time. "I know how this made your mother feel because I've used it. It sent me to a place so far beyond happiness there are no words to describe it. Bliss comes the closest."

He was caressing the balloon the way he'd caressed his ivory rook, and the base of Sal's skull hammered an alarm. "You used it?"

"I was careful, at first. I found people online who said it was possible to do it and still live a normal life. I managed to do that for a while. I taught my classes, I came home to my family, and nobody knew. But as time passed I needed it more often, and the pain of needing it got worse."

Sal licked his lips. The heat from the fire had dried them. "But you don't do it anymore. Right?"

Mr. Merkel held the yellow balloon between his thumb and forefinger. "The day I took Benjamin to the Pi Day party, I was shaking. I thought, just one hit. To calm myself, so I could get through the party."

From among the acacias a twig snapped, but Sal heard it only dimly. Mr. Merkel's words were low and insistent, pushing their way into his head. "I don't remember the accident. I only remember the asphalt under my cheek. Interstate Eighty, three lanes across, and I was lying in the middle lane. The asphalt was hot. The car was against the guardrail, and it was on fire. I smelled gas. People were shouting." Mr. Merkel closed the yellow balloon in his fist. "Benjamin was inside. I heard him screaming. But I couldn't get up."

The little fire in the pit gave a sigh, as if in apology. Sal couldn't feel its warmth anymore. The cold had pushed all the way through.

"How do you go on living after you do that to your child?" Mr. Merkel asked the fire. "It takes a special kind of cowardice. The district attorney said he'd recommend probation if I told him who sold me the heroin, so I told him it was Lucas. The university said they'd let me resign if I went to rehab, so I went to rehab. The rehab center said I could make amends by teaching other men's sons, so I came here. But it was all for nothing, in the end."

"It wasn't your fault," Sal said, though he wasn't sure that was true. Mr. Merkel had made choices, like Sal's mother had. Choices that took away later choices, but choices all the same. Still, when Mr. Merkel got in his car with Benjamin, and Sal's mother put that last needle in her vein, they were at the mercy of the drug, and the drug was stronger than their will to resist it, no matter who it hurt. In that way they had been doomed from the start, by their own mistakes and by the people who sold them what they needed. People like Lucas, and Ezra.

And you, Angelus said. A shadow moved in the trees, just outside Sal's vision, but when he looked, it was gone.

"I bought more pills instead of trying to break their hold on me," Mr. Merkel said. "I bought heroin when the pills got too expensive, even though I knew it was poison. I put the needle in my vein and got in the car with Benjamin, even though I knew I was putting him at risk. Even now, after everything that's happened, I took the pills Lucas offered, and I took your uncle's heroin and used it. I did those things, Sal. The drugs didn't make me do them."

Sal's mind snagged on Lucas's name. "Lucas gave you pills?"

"He said he bought them from a boy in the park." Mr. Merkel saw Sal's face and smiled sadly. "When we met that Monday, he forgave me. As I'd hoped he would. Then he asked if I was having nightmares. When he told me he could get me OxyContin, I didn't hesitate. I told myself the pills were okay. They weren't what made me crash the car, and they would stop the visions of Benjamin that wouldn't let me sleep. That's how weak I am."

Sal's jaw locked shut. Mr. Merkel's remarkable student had come to Lovelock to ruin him, not forgive him. And he'd used Sal to do it. What had he said? Mr. Merkel had found a new dope boy to pal around with, and it was *perfect*.

"Still, I didn't know how to do what I needed to do," Mr. Merkel said, "until you said we would meet your uncle at a campsite. I've become quite a believer in fate since I met you, Sal." He reached inside his black bag and pulled out a liquor bottle, Benjamin's jump rope, and a ziplocked baggie. Inside the baggie was a small bottle of water, a metal measuring cup, a cotton ball, and a syringe.

Sal's heart pounded in his chest. "Mr. Merkel, wait. You can do it again. Go back to the rehab place. Get better. Start over."

Mr. Merkel tore open the yellow balloon. He set the measuring cup on the sand and poured the grainy powder into it. "Do you remember when I told you I wanted to balance the ledger of my life?" He dipped the needle of the syringe into the water bottle, drew up the plunger, and squirted the water into the cup. "I thought I could do that by teaching, in Benjamin's memory. I thought I could do it by helping you, a fatherless boy." He held the measuring cup over the fire, moving it in and out of the flames. "But when you came into my classroom with this, and I felt that craving as strong as it had ever been, I knew I would throw all that away to have it. I am a slave to it. I will always be a slave to it."

Sal watched the measuring cup move from side to side. After Sal had sent Trudy away without her balloons, Lucas had told him to ask Mr. Merkel for help. *Show him what's in that bag*, he'd said. The horror of it paralyzed Sal utterly.

Mr. Merkel set the measuring cup back on the sand. The liquid it held looked like tobacco juice. He took a pinch of the cotton, wadded it into a hard little ball, and dropped it in the liquid. The fire crackled and hissed as he touched the tip of the needle to the ball and drew the liquid through it and into the syringe. When the cup was empty the syringe was full. He put it on one of the flat rocks that ringed the fire.

"I'm not strong enough to balance the ledger. The only debt I can settle is the one I owe Benjamin." Mr. Merkel rested his hands on his knees. "And that is the favor I need from you, Sal. I need you to help me die the way I should have, that day on the freeway."

A breeze ruffled the stillness of the grove. Its fingers brushed Sal's face, but he didn't feel it. His mind spun, uncomprehending. Mr. Merkel's eyes held his with somber gravity.

"You've seen my despair," he said. "You know what I did to my son. You've seen, firsthand, what will happen to me if I stay. And, most of all, you've seen where I'll go. I'll go to Benjamin, and he has forgiven me. You, of all the people in the world, know that my death will be a mercy."

Sal thought of the pies, lined up on Mr. Merkel's counter, and the warmth that had filled the kitchen while they baked. Mr. Merkel had been so happy. But it wasn't the pies, or Sal, that had made him happy. He'd been happy because he was planning to die. Because of the lie Sal had told him in the living room.

Sal's mouth was so dry that his tongue barely worked. "Mr. Merkel, I lied about Benjamin. I didn't see him."

The night around Mr. Merkel jumped, black on black, and in it Sal saw everything that made Mr. Merkel's life unendurable: the pain, the ruin, the hopelessness, the guilt. But Mr. Merkel's smile was gentle. "I don't believe that, Sal. Even I felt Benjamin in that room." He wrapped the jump rope around his ankles and placed one end on the sand beside Sal. Then he rested his hands on his knees again. His back was straight, his shoulders square in his white dress shirt.

"Sometimes, if he's lucky, a sick man can choose to die on his own terms, before his disease destroys him," he said. "I am a sick man, Sal. This is my disease. I can die in the manner of my own choosing, or I can die in a spiral of addiction and relapse that will cost me everything I care for and the little that is still worth remembering about me."

"Mr. Merkel," Sal whispered. "Please, stop."

"The problem is, I don't quite have the courage." Mr. Merkel's voice broke a little. "But you're like a son to me, Sal. Benjamin's brother, almost. It feels right that it should be you who reunites us."

The fire sputtered, then settled. Sal didn't understand what Mr. Merkel was asking him to do, not fully, but he knew he couldn't help him to die. "I can't."

"You can. All you need to do is drop the rope in the fire. The fire will do the rest. I won't feel any pain, I promise. The drug will take care of that, like it did on the freeway. I'll only feel relief." He smiled again. "Think of the Vikings, Sal. And the miracle of matter, changing from one form to another. Like water in a river, turning into clouds."

Sal stared at him in horrified comprehension. Mr. Merkel opened the liquor bottle. He poured the clear liquid over the jump rope, then on his legs and arms and abdomen. He cupped it in his hands and ran them around the back of his neck and through his hair. He was careful, as though anointing himself. Sal watched him as though he were on the other side of a thick, wavy piece of glass. Then Mr. Merkel picked up the syringe and slipped the needle into his forearm. When he drew the needle out his face slackened, and he gave a small sigh. He dropped the syringe into the fire, and Sal's vision narrowed until all he could see was the plastic blackening and curling upon itself.

"Now, Sal," Mr. Merkel said, dreamily. "Please."

The fire hunkered low, gathering itself to leap. But Sal couldn't move. The jump rope lay on the sand inches from his legs, and his fingers stayed locked in his lap. For the rest of his life he would be certain he wouldn't have picked it up—not then—but it didn't matter. Something crashed in the grove, and he jerked his head up to see the shadow in the trees erupt from darkness into form. It strode into the ring of light, and Sal shrank back in terror.

"You fucking coward," Lucas said. The fire jumped at the sight of him, and glinted on the tears that streaked his face.

"Lucas." Mr. Merkel's voice was wondering. "Why are you here?"

"Renata said you might do something stupid. I told her I didn't care, but she said Sal was with you." He looked at Sal. "Don't listen to him. Get out of here."

Blood pounded in Sal's head, nearly drowning out Mr. Merkel's words. "I thought you wanted me to do this. Isn't that why you came to find me?"

"I didn't want you to kill yourself!" Lucas said. "I wanted you to suffer!"

Mr. Merkel laughed, a sad, trilling sound. "Oh, but Lucas, I did suffer."

"No. You didn't. You gave up before you could even begin to suffer." Lucas's lips drew back from his narrow teeth. "You ruined everything I cared about. My career, my chance at the conversation, even the way I see the world. My only consolation was knowing you'd lost everything, too. Then I came looking for you, and I found you sober and teaching." He jabbed his finger at Sal. "You'd even found yourself another son. You had a new life, a second chance, and I had nothing. And then you couldn't even fight for it! You said yes the very first time I asked if you wanted the pills. The first time! It was like none of it mattered, what you did to me and Benjamin and everyone who loved you. All that mattered was your fucking fix."

"You're right. About all of it." Mr. Merkel's words were slurry. "I don't deserve a second chance."

"You should have fought for it anyway!" Lucas said. "You should have spent the rest of your life under an overpass, slobbering for your next hit, waking up every day knowing you'd lost everything not once, but twice. That's what I wanted for you. But you'd rather take the easy way out. And you're not even brave enough to do that. You need a boy to do it for you. *A boy*!"

Mr Merkel blanched, then steadied himself. "Sal is not just a boy. Sal is my son." He looked at Sal with bottomless eyes. "And my watcher."

Sal drew a sharp breath. Above him the stars spun on an axis that plunged straight through the little fire to the iron-hard heart of the earth. He picked up the rope handle. It was slick with alcohol, and he could smell it, an acrid tang in his nostrils. Time stopped. The stars watched and the trees listened and Sal nodded, slowly and once.

He would have done it then. In that pregnant moment of love and duty, with the beneficent, deadly power Mr. Merkel had bestowed upon him, he would have done it. This, too, he would always believe. But Lucas strode over to him and yanked him to his feet. He grabbed the jump rope and shoved Sal so hard that Sal staggered backward and fell. Then he held the rope handle over the fire.

"No!" Mr. Merkel's eyes opened wide with terror. "Please! I need it to be Sal!"

Lucas stood with his hand over the flames, and his entire body shook. Mr. Merkel reached for him, slow and imploring, and Lucas stilled. Cloaked in darkness, with his arm held out and his head lifted, he looked like the drawing of Silas on the cover of *The Graveyard Book*.

Then he said, "Too bad, asshole. It's going to be me."

Sal jumped up, but he was too late. Lucas dropped the rope in the fire.

At first nothing happened. All three of them stared at the rope handle lying untouched in the flames. Sal thought: *it won't work, it won't work*. Then a small, blue ball of light raced along the red-and-white twists of nylon and licked at Mr. Merkel's pant leg. Mr. Merkel screamed and beat at it with his hands, but his pants erupted in flame, then his arms, and he rolled from side to side in the sand as the tame little fire purring in the pit became a great, roaring beast that swallowed him whole. Sal ran for him, but Lucas caught him around the waist and lifted him off the ground, where his legs kicked and his mouth opened and seared the night with a scream that joined Mr. Merkel's, both of them wailing to the sky as Mr. Merkel's arms beat against the sand like the wings of a great wounded bird and his glasses dissolved and his mouth became a black, toothless, shrieking maw. Lucas wrestled Sal to the ground and covered his body with his. He grabbed a fistful of Sal's hair and twisted his head away from the fire and pressed his cheek into the cool sand, where it felt each beat of Mr. Merkel's arms like a distant heartbeat.

Matter at play matter at play matter at play, Sal's mind shrilled, *lovely lovely lovely lovely lovely lovely lovely*—

"Don't look, don't look, don't look," Lucas whispered, while the screaming went on and on and the earth pounded against Sal's cheek.

In Lovelock, death sounds like music. It pulses with guitars and drums and makes you want to dance with bodies that press as close as your lover and shout lyrics you know as well as you once knew your prayers. If only the liquid in your veins were blood and your limbs belonged to you, you would jump and spin, your flaxen hair opening like a fan in a fog of smoke and weed and your lover's breath, but your body is tangled and dry in the Little Mermaid sheets you got for your seventh birthday and it has forgotten how to dance. Until the needle finds another vein, and oh, yes, your lover was right. It does feel like heaven. Now your body aches with song, until, without moving in the sheets, it twirls as it did so long ago that it doesn't feel like the yesterday it was. With the needle in your arm you dance. You dance in all the colors you remember, and when your mother comes to wake you, you are gone.

SAL

At last Mr. Merkel's arms fell still. The fire, though, would not be done for hours yet. The grove was hot with it, it cast shadows that danced with it, the night was filled with its greedy licking popping mutter, and the sweet, sizzling smell of it was thicker than the air. The acacias shrank away, drawing their fingered branches into their limbs, and the bats that hung from them like dark fruit fled into the sky.

Lucas's grip on Sal's hair loosened, and Sal bucked up, throwing him off. Lucas reached for him again, but Sal slipped from his grasp and ran without looking back, down the path to the bluff and up the trail, gasping in the cool night air, hearing Lucas's heavy feet behind him. He broke from the trail and headed for the cave with the mindless urgency of the hunted. When he reached it he flung himself upon the dusty ground. For five breaths he lay there, until he heard Lucas scrambling along the ledge. Then he scuttled feet first over the dusty beer bottles and cigarette butts into the crevice at the back of the cave. There he lay, just far enough inside that Lucas couldn't reach him, and darkness settled about him.

Lucas stumbled into the cave, a dark shape against the moonlit night beyond the sage. The flashlight of his cell phone knifed through the dark until it found the crevice. He dropped to his knees and shone the light inside. Sal blinked in the glare. Every sinew in his body tightened. He was trapped by the man in the cave, the weight of the stone above, and the darkness behind his feet. There were sounds just below the level of hearing and giant wings beating inside his skull. There were six pies on a white counter in a dark house. There was a dead boy's deck of cards in his backpack. Down in the acacia grove Mr. Merkel was flying apart, one molecule at a time.

Lucas made a choking sound. "It was what he wanted. You heard him. I just helped him do it."

Sal's tongue was stuck to the top of his mouth. *Lovely lovely lovely,* his mind chattered. *Matter at play.*

Lucas's flashlight pierced Sal's forehead and sent him farther down the tunnel while the wings beat harder in his head. Lucas wasn't supposed to help Mr. Merkel. Sal was supposed to help him. And Sal was supposed to watch. Mr. Merkel had wanted him to do these things, not Lucas, because in the end he knew that Sal was the one who really saw him, and Sal was the only one he could trust with his story. Now that it was done this was all Sal could think: not that he hadn't wanted to do it; not whether he would have done it; but that he should have done it. It was his to do. His duty, his honor, his obligation, his burden.

"I saw you. You were going to do it," Lucas said. "I couldn't let you. He shouldn't have asked you."

Sal wished he could close his ears. All of this was Lucas's fault. If it weren't for Lucas, Mr. Merkel would have taught sixth grade for twenty more years. The toddlers playing in the playground beside the Lovers Locks would have called him Merkel the Turtle without ever knowing that Kip Masters had come up with that name before they could talk. He would have told Sal a thousand more stories about math and Sal would have drawn him a thousand more stories about angels. Benjamin would have waited in the in-between for decades, watching his father slowly balance the ledger of his life, if only Lucas had stayed away from Lovelock.

"Listen to me," Lucas said. "If neither of us says anything, nobody will ever know we were here." The light wobbled in his hand. "Because it's your word against mine, right? And mine against yours. If anyone found out we were here, nobody would know who to believe. You understand?"

He waited for Sal to say something, but a band was clamped around Sal's throat.

Then, from over the hill behind the bluff, came a distant, rolling crack. It sounded like a dead bolt slamming home at the top of a very long staircase.

"Shit," Lucas muttered. "That was a gunshot." The light swung away and he clambered out of the cave as Sal slithered backward, down the tunnel, into a vortex of beating wings and the smell of stone and blood. It was a gunshot. Ezra had the gun. Gideon was waiting at home. Sal had sent Ezra to him. *Ezra had the gun.* Sal slid back and back and back until his legs dropped over an unseen ledge. He teetered there, emptiness tugging at his ankles. Then he gripped the stone with his fingers and inched forward until his feet were back on rock. He lay there for another minute before he turned over and sat up.

It was utterly dark. The dark felt like a physical thing, pressing against his eyes. He remembered the headlamp, which had slipped down around his neck, but before he could find it his eyes were gone and the dark exploded in shards of violent light. He was somewhere else, outside his body, surrounded by comets and planets and suns that floated in an endless black sky. Stories swept by in iridescent ribbons, a babble of voices rising and falling and dying. Time itself raveled back and forth in vast swooping cycles, and in the rhythm of unseen wings someone said *this is the thread that binds the universe* while a hand turned a spoon in a bowl, round and round and round. Fire leaped and fell, and in the distance two beasts with glittering wings battled with blades bigger than galaxies until one flung the other, heart-stabbed, into the dark. Then Sal's fingers found the headlamp and pressed the button that killed the darkness and all the terrible wonders in it.

He was kneeling, gasping and spent, on a tiny ledge inside a vast stone vault whose walls swept up like the buttresses of a Gothic cathedral. They were veined everywhere with purple crystals that refracted the light from his headlamp into a million lavender stars. Sal touched his face with trembling fingers and felt his bones, the bones of a boy, beneath his skin. The visions of a moment before hovered at the edges of his mind. For the rest of his life he would try to draw them, but no matter how many times he tried his hand would trace only circles, over and over.

Then, limbs quaking, he crawled to the edge of the rock, peered into the abyss for the body of an archangel, and saw, covered in silvery dust, the story another boy had left unfinished, long ago.

Sal lay for a long while, looking into the shaft. Then, carefully, he slipped his feet over the ledge and found a foothold. He stepped from rock to rock until he reached the bottom, thirty feet below. The dust on the floor was much finer than the dust in the outer cave. When he lowered himself to his knees it gave beneath him like down.

The boy was nothing but empty bone and the ancient, dried weave of sandals. His jaw had separated from his broken skull in a wide, silent scream. One arm was lost in his ribs, but the other was flung out, its palm up, the finger bones small and delicate and strange. There was nothing to tell Sal these were the bones of a boy, but he knew it all the same, just as he knew that anyone who loved this boy had been dead for a long, long time. He must have died alone and frightened, but despite the gaping jaw he looked peaceful, a lost boy floating in a galaxy of amethysts.

In the dark Sal had seen ribbons of stories unspooling, then dissolving as the voices that told them fell silent. This boy's story was one of those, left to die in a place out of time, far from any eyes that watched or lips that told. No one would know why he'd come or who had waited in vain for him to come back. No one would know what he'd seen, or how he'd fallen. Here, in the cave within the cave, there were no bats or seers or watchers, no guns or fires or jump ropes, and no mothers or fathers or sons. There were no stories at all, and Sal let the silence fill him all the way up.

Hours passed. Not enough to reach morning, but enough for the fire in the grove to die and the chill of the cave to sink deep into Sal's marrow. Then, like the distant call of a bird, he heard his name. His headlamp had dimmed as its battery faded, so he could see the glow of another headlamp shining through the narrow crevice thirty feet above.

"Sal! Are you in there?" The voice echoed through the cavern. Sal couldn't tell whose it was.

He looked at the boy in the dust one last time. He looked as peaceful as before, but now the silence of his resting place was broken, and it was time for Sal to leave. The boy slept on, undisturbed, even when Sal reached out and took his smallest bone.

With muscles cramped by cold Sal labored up the rock wall to the ledge and back through the tunnel. When he got to the end someone grabbed him by the arms and pulled him out. Once they were both sitting on the floor of the outer cave, Sal saw it was Gideon. He ran his hands over Sal's limbs, as if making sure he was whole. The scabs on his knuckles had broken open, and they had blood on them. He was not hurt in any other way, except in his eyes. Something new lived in them, some haunted thing Sal had never seen before, but might have seen in Lucas's, had he looked.

"Are you okay?" Gideon asked.

Sal opened his mouth, but no words came. He arched his neck and made a gagging sound. Gideon shook him. "What's wrong?"

Sal pressed one hand against his throat. He felt his voice inside, trembling like a trapped moth. In his other hand he held the lost boy's tiniest bone. He clenched it tight, and his voice was free.

"Ezra?" he gasped.

Gideon took his headlamp off and set it on the floor, where it threw the elongated shadows of man and boy against the rough stone walls. "He's dead."

Something brushed against Sal's skin. "How?"

"He came with the gun. I tried to take it. It fired."

That was all he would say, then or later. It was left to Sal to imagine it: the desperate fight for the rifle, the brothers staggering across the sand in a brutish, fatal dance. Sometimes in these imaginings there was a moment when Gideon stepped back with the gun—could have put it down, could have let his brother walk out of the valley—and raised the gun to his shoulder instead. Whenever he saw this, Sal would feel electricity lace his spine, and push the image away. He would never see Ezra's body, either. Gideon would take it before the sun came up. To Reno, where men were killed over unpaid debts.

"The teacher," Gideon said, in a whisper edged with horror. "What happened?"

Cold enveloped Sal's body like a sheath, making it hard to think. He should say that Lucas had done it. That was what Angelus wanted him to say. *He deserves to be punished,* he whispered, with the blood of his dead brother still wet on his scythe. But Lucas had done in hatred what Sal should have done in love, and he'd turned what should have been an act of mercy into an act of vengeance. If Sal told that story it would become true, the way all stories do when they're told.

"He wanted to die," he said. "He asked me to do it." The truth. And, smuggled inside, the truth that should have been.

Gideon gripped Sal's arms with his bloody hands. "Why?"

"He killed his son. He didn't mean to, but he did." *Like your father,* Sal didn't say. Like Tommy.

"But how could he ask you to do that?"

Sal's teeth chattered. "I think—I think it was because he loved me."

Gideon looked like he wanted to hit the wall of the cave. "I saw it, that day he brought you home. It was all around him. I should have kept him away from you."

Sal hadn't believed Gideon would ever do anything to protect him. He'd believed Ezra when he said all Gideon cared about was his furniture and the Prentiss land. Now Gideon knelt before him with Ezra's blood on his hands, a murderer like Angelus. But also like Sal, who had sent Ezra over the hill to Gideon's justice; who had handed death to an old man in the park; and who would have sent the fire to Mr. Merkel if Lucas hadn't. Gideon's hands gripped Sal's arms with the desperate urgency of kinship, and Sal started to shake.

Gideon took off his heavy denim jacket and draped it over his shoulders. "You're freezing. We have to get you home." Great violent shudders rocked Sal's teeth in his head and turned Gideon and the shadows on the wall into pulses of shape and light. Gideon pulled him to his chest. He wrapped his arms around him, and they didn't feel soft like Sal's mother's arms; they felt solid and sure, like bands of steel.

"Don't worry," he said. "I'll take care of it. You just do what I say, and everything will be fine."

AFTER

It was late on a summer afternoon, and heat rippled above the sand. Nora had her windows open as she drove up the fire road from Marzen, and the wind tossed her hair around her shoulders. It was the day before Britta's hot air balloons would fill the sky over the Great Basin, and it was the first time Nora had driven this road since she'd brought Sal home on the last day of school.

At the Prentiss place, Sal waited for her on the cinder block steps with his backpack, the yellow dog's head in his lap. The sun was about to dip below the hills and take the heat with it, but the light it cast on the boy and the dog was still thick and golden.

As Nora got out of her car Gideon came out of his shed, wiping his hands on a rag. He wore jeans and a stained gray tee shirt, and the sawdust in his hair looked like the sand in Nora's. The ring of trash that had surrounded the old farmhouse was gone.

"You cleaned up," Nora said.

"It was time," he answered.

Sal hooked his backpack over his shoulder and walked over to them. He wore new basketball shorts and a tee shirt that fit, and his white sneakers had been replaced by plain black ones. "Are you ready?" she asked.

"Yes." His voice was a shade deeper. It had been only three weeks since school ended, and already he was a seventh grader.

Nora, who'd seen this happen to sixth graders for twelve years, was still surprised to see it happen to Sal. He'd seemed immune to the effects of time, somehow.

"Thanks for letting me take him," she said to Gideon. When she'd driven Sal home on the last day of school she'd asked if she could take Sal to see the balloon festival on the Fourth of July. She hadn't expected Gideon to agree, especially since the balloons would fly at dawn, and she would have to pick Sal up the night before, but he'd said it was fine. Now he turned his pale eyes on Sal.

"See you tomorrow," he said, and Sal nodded. They did not embrace or touch in any way, but Nora felt them bend toward one another, almost imperceptibly.

They were halfway down the road when Sal said, "I want to show you something."

"Sure," Nora said, but when Sal told her to park beside the bluff, her curiosity turned to worry. She followed reluctantly as he walked over the low rise, then through the acacia grove. The ashy shadow on the sand was gone, and Nora, trained in the permanence of fossils and sedimentary layers, found this unnerving. It had been less than four months, but the earth had already forgotten Adam Merkel.

She gasped when she entered the cave in the bluff. In college, one of her anthropology professors had taken her class to the Paisley Caves in Oregon, where the First People had left the humblest of traces: fossilized excrement. Nora had been deeply moved to think that, fourteen thousand years before, a small group of people had stopped there to sleep in chilly safety. Now she saw the beer bottles and cigarette butts on the floor of Sal's cave and wondered if, fourteen thousand years from now, they would be studied as thoroughly as the thoughtless shits those earlier people had taken. She thought not. There was too much other garbage in the world.

Sal opened his backpack and pulled out two headlamps. He

handed one to her, put on the other, and walked to a low crevice at the back of the cave. "It's in here." Before she could say anything, he crawled inside.

Nora bent to peer after him. Her headlamp shone on the soles of his sneakers as they retreated down a narrow tunnel. "Damn it," she muttered, then crawled in. It was a very tight fit, so tight she couldn't raise her head to see where she was going. The rock scratched her elbows and knees as she crept forward a few inches at a time, trying to slow her heartbeat.

Thankfully, the tunnel wasn't long. After fifteen feet or so Nora's head broke through into a larger space, and she crawled out onto a small outcropping the size of her family's kitchen table. She pressed back against the wall as vertigo struck her. She and Sal were in an enormous cavern traced with glittering amethyst crystals. It soared at least fifty feet above and disappeared into a narrower shaft below. She gazed around her, marveling.

Sal said, "That's not what I wanted to show you." He beckoned her to the edge of the outcropping. Carefully, she crawled over and looked down. The chasm was about ten feet across and thirty feet deep, with a thick layer of dust at the bottom. The dust had been disturbed, so it took her a moment to realize what she was seeing. A skull. Ribs. The long bones of limbs. A whole body, its outlines softened by a gray pelt that was finer than sand.

"Oh," she said.

Sal swung his legs over the ledge and began to climb down. He shone his headlamp up at her. "It's not hard."

He was right; there were nooks and ledges and handholds. When Nora's sandals sank into the dust at the bottom Sal was on his knees, and she knelt beside him, moved beyond reverence by the pitiful, broken collection of bones. This was no Gold Rush miner, or California Trail pioneer. These were the bones of someone who'd died hundreds of years ago. Maybe thousands. The desiccated tule sandals told her that. So did the thickness of the dust that covered them. The air in the cave was cool and dry, and in conditions like these the sandals, though not flesh, could have been preserved for millennia.

"How did you find this?" she whispered.

"By accident." Sal whispered, too. All around them, purple crystals winked in the light from their headlamps. "You said there were people who could find stories from bones."

"Anthropologists. Yes." Nora bent closer. The skull was fractured. She hoped that meant death had come quickly. "I imagine these bones have a lot of stories to tell."

"I want people to know them." Sal's headlamp bobbed a little. "I think he'd want that, too."

"He might be a she," Nora said.

"No. He's a boy." Sal reached for the talisman around his neck, and the certainty in his voice convinced her.

"I'll call my old professor. She'll know just the person to send." Gerald Schmidt from the Great Basin Paleoindian Research Unit, probably. Nora's pulse fluttered. This could be a remarkable find, as important as the girl in the Mexican cave or the Anzick Boy in Montana. She couldn't wait to tell her father. The excavation would take months, and the findings wouldn't be published for a couple of years. He might not live that long, but Nora was sure she could get the important details sooner, if she needed to.

Sal was still fondling his amulet, and now Nora got a good look at it for the first time. She'd thought it was a chess pawn, but it wasn't. It was a tiny bone, less than an inch long, flat at the bottom, narrow in the middle, with a little knob at the top. Sal saw her looking and tucked it inside his shirt.

The right arm and hand of the body lay outstretched, and Nora was sure that when it was excavated, one of its fingers would be missing its tip. Nora felt the sudden prick of tears. The boy in the dust had died a violent, lonely death, yet he was also very lucky. Not many of the distant dead were able to reach across time to touch the living.

"It's all right," she said. "Something tells me he wouldn't mind."

Sal's chin moved in the smallest of nods.

The air in the chasm was as quiet as a secret. When they left, Nora would take Sal home, where her father was waiting. They would grill hot dogs on his old Weber and sit on the new patio furniture, beside the tomato boxes Nora had repainted and planted with begonias. She and Sal would tell him about the bones, and the evening would be warm and sweet and wonderful, but it wouldn't be private. Not like this narrow hole in the earth, which felt like she imagined confessionals did.

"Sal," she said. "I want to ask you a question."

Sal shifted on his knees. He knew what she was going to ask him.

"What you told the police, that day with Renata." Nora lowered her voice, as though the dead boy might be listening. "It wasn't true, was it?"

Sal didn't say anything.

"Renata wanted you to tell the police Lucas didn't kill Adam," Nora said. "But all anyone had told her was that you'd found Adam's body. The only way she'd know you were there is if she was there, too. Or Lucas was."

Deep in the cavern something rustled, then quieted. Sal traced a circle in the dust beside the bones.

"You told me watchers don't always tell the stories they see," Nora said. "But you also told me they aren't allowed to lie." She laid her hand on Sal's back, and Sal flinched. "I swear to you I won't tell anyone. But Adam was my friend, too. I think he deserves to have his true story told, if only just once. Don't you?"

Sal drew another circle on top of the first one, and Nora thought he wouldn't answer. Then his voice came, so quietly Nora barely heard it: "Lucas was there."

Nora made her voice just as soft. "Why?"

"Renata called him. She knew what Mr. Merkel was going to do. So he followed us."

"She knew he was going to buy Ezra's heroin?"

"No."

"What, then?"

Sal was still drawing circles in the dust. Nora wished he would stop. "He had a son named Benjamin. He died in a car crash. It was Mr. Merkel's fault."

"I know."

"It was the same thing as your dad."

"I know that, too."

"He thought he should have died with him. So he wanted to die like he did." Sal trembled a little beneath Nora's hand. "In fire."

Nora slid her arm around his shoulders. "Oh, Sal."

"He wasn't like your dad. He didn't want to live anymore. He said it was better to die his own way, not—" Sal clenched his jaw, then released it. "He was trying to be brave."

Nora felt the familiar tightening in her mind. Adam hadn't been brave. He'd decided to kill himself, and he'd dragged this fragile boy along so he wouldn't have to die alone. She thought of her father. For years he'd seemed barely alive, but now, with everything he had, he was fighting the cancer that would kill him. Why couldn't Adam have found that sort of courage? Even if he'd had to rewrite the past to do it, as her father had, that would have been better than a meaningless death that destroyed everyone else you loved.

She took a calming breath. Anger wasn't what Sal needed from her. "What did Lucas do?"

"He stopped me."

"Stopped you from what?"

Nora felt his shoulders rise with his quick breath, and she knew. One boy's jump rope, another boy's hand. What had Sal said in her classroom? Fire is just matter at play. The rage she had suppressed exploded in her mind, spraying shards everywhere. How could Adam have asked this boy to do that? Then she made herself remember the gentle, remorseful man she'd known. She imagined the despair he must have felt, despair so black he couldn't see past his own end to the misery he would leave behind. She closed her eyes. All that damage, all that suffering. But the only suffering that mattered anymore was Sal's.

She ran her hand across Sal's narrow back. "Listen to me. He should never have asked that of you. That wasn't love. It was only pain."

Sal stared straight ahead. Nora hoped her words would travel deep inside him. Maybe someday he would even believe them. She saw the circles he'd drawn in the dust and the shattered, ancient skull of the dead boy, and felt the slipperiness of time, sliding backward and forward like a pendulum. It made her dizzy.

She pushed Sal's bangs away from his forehead. "Who did it, then?" she asked, gently.

He drew one last circle, slowly, with his index finger. When he was done he sat still. Then he said, "Mr. Merkel did it himself."

While Sal watched. Nora had to take another steadying breath. "Okay. But Sal, why couldn't you tell the police that?"

"I didn't want anyone to know." Sal stared down at his circles. "Everyone made so much fun of him already."

Nora didn't want suicide to be Adam's legacy in Lovelock, either. "But they might have arrested Ezra. If he'd been alive."

A muscle jumped in Sal's jaw, and he looked like Gideon, closed and wary. "Ezra was gone. And I just—I guess I thought they'd never find him."

They sat in silence after that. There was something Sal still wasn't telling her, Nora thought. But as she looked at the bones in the dust she wondered: What did it really matter? Ezra and Adam were dead. And in the end, Adam's story wasn't Ezra's or Lucas's or hers; it was Sal's. Adam had bequeathed it to him, for better or worse. As long as he didn't hurt anyone living, he could tell it however he wanted.

"I'm glad you told me," she said. "And I won't say anything. I gave you my word."

Sal nodded, and he looked like himself again. A twelve-year-old boy, tripping over the curb of adulthood. Nora, still feeling the slip of time, saw him as an older boy, then as a man. He would be quiet and strong, aloof and watchful. Like Gideon, but hopefully with one foot in the wider world. She saw herself, too, in graduate school with her father in his grave. She didn't know where she would go after that, but for the first time she felt the draw of mysteries close to home. Like the bones that lay before her. And other untold stories, elsewhere in the Basin. Her father would like that. Maybe Sal would, too.

The rustling began again, louder now. It was bats, Nora realized. Deep in the caverns. It must be close to sunset. She started to tell Sal they had to go, but before she could say anything the rustling became a drumbeat.

"What's happening?" Sal looked panicked.

"Bats," Nora said. "They're about to leave the cave."

She felt the air shift as thousands of creatures began to move at once, deep in the heart of the earth. The drumbeat became a roar, and as the air exploded with sound she looked up to see the outcropping at the top of the chasm vanish in a seething froth. In the light from her headlamp the bats looked as mindless as locusts, a vast, brown, burrowing cloud, spinning like a cyclone into the tunnel that led to the outer cave, and the air was filled with keening cries and beating wings. She threw her arms around Sal, but the bats didn't touch them. They didn't come down into the narrow shaft at all. It was as though Nora and Sal were half a step outside the world, huddled together with thudding hearts, watching.

When the bats were gone everything was as it had been. The boy from long ago lay in his bed of dust, and the air was quiet. It was as if the bats had never come, though they would come again tomorrow, as they had come yesterday, and every day for thousands of years before that. Nora looked at the circles Sal had drawn. They, too, were undisturbed.

Shakily Sal and Nora climbed up the shaft to the outcropping, then crawled through the tunnel to the outer cave. They walked down the hill and past the hearth in the acacia grove, where they didn't look at the unmarked sand. With each step forward they grew steadier, more sure. Then they were in Nora's car, driving down the fire road to Lovelock, where Nora's father waited. The windows were still open, and the air teased their faces with the cool breath of coming night. Above them the bats soared in a graceful, swooping river that stretched across the sky. From the bed of the ancient lake they looked like birds.

ACKNOWLEDGMENTS

Books are hard to write, and they don't get easier to write the second time around. I couldn't have written this one without the support of a number of fellow literary strivers, whose advice, support, and humor got me through many valleys of doubt. My writers' group: Elizabeth Clark, Carey Lifschultz, and Arline Klatt, who slogged through my drafts over club salads and Diet Coke every Wednesday. The gang of "Old" Ladies, great friends and writers, who recharge me emotionally and creatively every time we assemble: Ellen Collett, Judith Edelman, Sharon Hazzard, Jeanne la Liberté, Sharon Knapp, Debbie Michel, and Kathy Stevenson. Melissa Cistaro, who makes it look easy even when it's not. And Julia Johnson, for her terrific wit and for always being frank with me. Thank you one and all.

Thank you also to my editor, Kate Nintzel, who makes everything I write much, much better. I honestly don't know how she does it. She's got some kind of superpower. Thank you to my wonderful agent, Michelle Brower, who always knows exactly what to say, and took a chance on an unpublished writer from the slush pile four years ago. I also owe many thanks to Shelly Perron, Vedika Khanna, and the rest of the staff at William Morrow, and Danya Kukafka and the staff at Aevitas Creative.

Acknowledgments

The inspiration for this book came from an excellent documentary film, *Love and Terror on the Howling Plains of Nowhere*, about a man who burned to death outside a small Nebraska town. In addition to the odd circumstances of the death it examines, its themes about small town life and the arrival of a stranger got my creative cells firing. Thank you, Dave Jannetta and Ed Hughes, for your brilliant work.

Lovelock is a real town, and though my characters are fictional, I want to thank Patty Burke, the owner of Temptations, for modeling the passion the character of Britta has for her hometown. Patty is an ardent and effective advocate for the Lovelock community, and her café is as much a gem as she is. Thanks also to Larry Deleeuw and the staff of the Cadillac Inn and everyone at the Cowpoke Café for your excellent hospitality.

Every word I write is made better by the great teachers I've been lucky to have, especially Alice Mattison, whose book *The Kite and the String* is essential reading for any author. Thank you also to Margot Livesey, my teacher at the Sewanee Writers' Conference, for her comments on the first pages, and to Adam Latham and the rest of the Sewanee staff for a wonderful experience "on the mountain."

Last but most: thank you to my husband, Chris Kearney, whose unflagging support keeps me writing, and who makes every day better just by waking up next to me.